LIMERICK CITY LIBRARY

Phone: 407510
Website:
www.limerickcity.ie/library
Email: citylib@limerickcity.ie

The Granary,
Michael Street,
Limerick.

**This book is issued subject to the Rules of the Library.
The Book must be returned not later then the last date
stamped below.**

Class No......**AF**......... Acc. No. **72137**

Date of Return	Date of Return	Date of Return	Date of Return

THE STREET
PHILOSOPHER

MATTHEW PLAMPIN

The Street Philosopher

HarperCollins*Publishers*

HarperCollins*Publishers*
77–85 Fulham Palace Road,
Hammersmith, London W6 8JB

www.harpercollins.co.uk

Published by HarperCollins*Publishers* 2009
1

A catalogue record for this book
is available from the British Library

ISBN: 978 00 0 727243 3

Set in Meridien by Palimpsest Book Production Ltd,
Grangemouth, Stirlingshire

Printed and bound in Great Britain by
Clays Ltd, St Ives plc

FSC **Mixed Sources**
Product group from well-managed
forests and other controlled sources
www.fsc.org   Cert no. SW-COC-1806
© 1996 Forest Stewardship Council

FSC is a non-profit international organisation established
to promote the responsible management of the world's forests.
Products carrying the FSC label are independently certified
to assure consumers that they come from forests that are managed
to meet the social, economic and ecological needs
of present and future generations.

Find out more about HarperCollins and the environment at
www.harpercollins.co.uk/green

For my father, who kept on about it.

It is unspeakable, godless, hopeless. I am no longer an artist interested and curious, I am a messenger who will bring back word from the men who are fighting to those who want the war to go on forever. Feeble, inarticulate will be my message, but it will have a bitter truth, and may it burn their lousy souls.

Paul Nash, Letter from Passchendaele,
October 1917

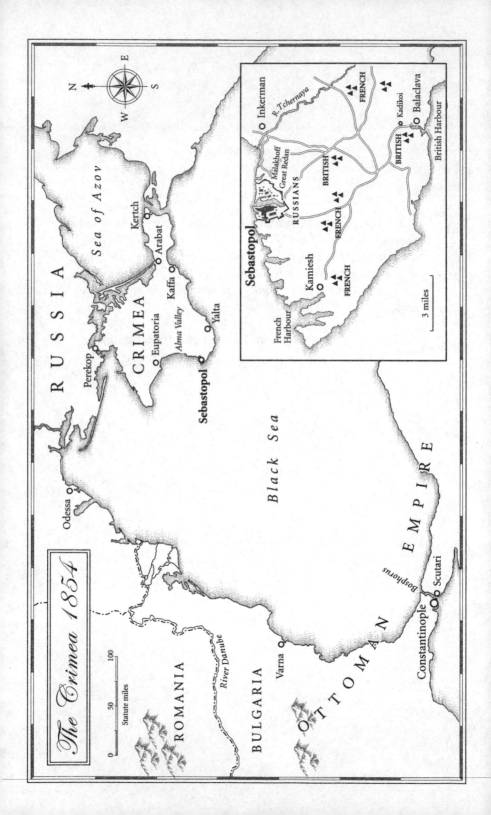

Crimean Peninsula
September 1854

1

Kitson's well-worn boots crunched through the shingle as he walked down towards the shore. It was a cold, unwelcoming afternoon. The sky was low and slate-grey, and the waters of the bay churned with a heavy swell. Sea birds croaked dismally as they hung, wings outstretched, on the brisk wind. Most of the men who filled the landing zone were in uniform, but there were enough ragged-looking civilians among them for Kitson to stride past without remark. Reaching a small rise in the stony beach, he paused to scratch his beard and take stock of the scene around him.

On this, the third day of the invasion, it was the turn of the Earl of Cardigan's Light Brigade to disembark. Kitson pulled a pocketbook and pencil from his shabby, faded frock-coat. Squinting, he peered out at the rows of troop transports and frigates anchored in the deeper waters, and attempted to make out their names, jotting down those he could see. There were so many vessels in the bay that the horizon was obscured by a dense forest of masts, funnels and rigging. The echoing blasts of their steam horns drifted over to where he stood scribbling intently into his book.

Flotillas of long rowing boats were ferrying soldiers from the transport ships. Teams of blue-jacketed sailors, seemingly impervious to the cold, waded out into the surf to drag the boats' prows up onto the beach. Landing planks were thrown down, and hussars poured out, their scabbards held over their heads to avoid any chance of a freak spray or splash rusting the blades within. Against the dull, washed-out tones of the afternoon, their uniforms seemed intensely colourful, a vivid combination of rich blacks, glowing reds and acid yellows. The blue-jackets stared as the cavalrymen calmly returned their sabres to their belts and strolled slowly inland as if the Crimea were already theirs. Kitson scanned the crowds of plush busbies and brocade-encrusted jackets, noting the regiments for his report.

The breeze changed direction, and a faint, inhuman shrieking reached the correspondent's ears. He stopped writing mid sentence. A bone-white horse was dangling over the side of one of the larger iron-screw steamers, suspended from a small crane. Leather straps were fastened around the creature's torso, its legs hanging limply down as it cried out in terror. Beneath it, rocking precariously on the waves, was a crude raft, made from several rowing boats lashed together. The squat black form of an artillery piece already sat awkwardly upon it, tied down with rope; the makeshift platform was unbalanced by its weight, and tipped drunkenly with the rise and fall of the sea.

After a short, tense descent, the horse's hooves touched the raft. Several sailors reached out at once, unfastening the straps and patting the beast's neck and muzzle reassuringly. The horse slipped on the shining planks, but was quickly on its feet again, nostrils flaring as it snorted with distress. Already, the next was on its way down, a chestnut this time, whinnying loudly as it came; and before long, three warhorses stood upon the raft as it floated unsteadily beneath the overcast sky.

Disaster was so inevitable, and so familiar, that the blue-jackets greeted it with weariness rather than alarm. One of the horses became tangled up in the cords holding down the gun and, immediately panicking, started to kick and flounder, screaming as it did so. The others promptly reared up, shaking off the men who tried to settle them, adding their voices to what was soon a piercing chorus. With a sharp whipping sound, straining ropes started to snap. A second later the gun toppled overboard, pulling the horse caught up in the ropes after it. Both vanished instantly into the murky brown-green water. The raft lurched upwards on the side where the lost gun had stood, causing the two remaining horses to fall, and then slide off messily into the sea.

Back on the beach, Kitson winced and made a quick entry in his pocketbook.

A few other rafts, similarly troubled, bobbed and span among the looming iron-clads. Some of the transport captains, seeing the mayhem below, had decided to dispense with any attempt at conveying the horses to shore and were simply having them pushed from the deck, leaving it to the beasts themselves to find their way to the beach. Kitson watched them tumble down the sides of the tall ships into the waves, legs kicking wildly, landing in an explosion of foam. He tried to trace the dots of their heads as they swam for the shore. Some of them he lost; others didn't seem to be moving at all, so slow was their progress. His eyes started to ache with the effort.

Blinking, Kitson remembered the telegram, which he'd tucked inside the pocketbook's front cover. He pulled it out. The crumpled piece of yellowed paper bore terse words from O'Farrell back in London, shouted out in mechanical script: *Illustrator Robert Styles STOP Lands Eupatoria sixteenth September STOP HMS Arthur STOP*. It had arrived about three weeks earlier, at the telegraph office in Varna. Cracknell, predictably enough, hadn't been impressed.

'Men dropping dead from bloody cholera all around us, not a drop of decent brandy for five hundred bloody miles, a bloody great *war* about to commence, and what does our editor send out to his brave correspondents? A bloody *illustrator!*'

Kitson had muttered his concurrence. Inwardly, however, he'd been intrigued, and pleased that the *London Courier*'s reporting team was to be enlarged. After months spent following Richard Cracknell through the brothels and slums of Constantinople, and then trailing behind him across the meadows of Bulgaria, Kitson had come to feel almost as if he were a manservant rather than a junior reporting partner. The thought of a peer, an equal, had a distinct appeal – and what was more, this Mr Styles, as an illustrator, a professional artist, would surely be a man of some culture. He'd know about the successes and failures of the Academy Summer Exhibition, at least. Kitson longed for such conversation in a manner he wouldn't have thought possible half a year earlier.

Before him, the waiting hussars yelled encouragement as horses started to reach the shore. Kitson looked up from the telegram. The blue-jackets in the sea were attempting to get hold of the dazed animals before they could stagger out of the water, but the men were inexperienced, and allowed many to escape. Once on the beach, the horses shook their manes, looked quickly about them, and then bolted. One, a grey, charged by close to where Kitson stood, hooves clattering through the stones, eyes wide with fear, water streaming down its sea-darkened flanks. Several hussars gave chase, raising their arms in the air, whistling shrill signals that, on this occasion, the highly trained horse failed even to notice.

The stiff breeze knocked off one of the cavalrymen's busbies. Cursing, he left the pursuit and strode crossly to where it lay amongst the pebbles.

Seeing his chance, Kitson tucked away the telegram and turned over a fresh page in his pocketbook. 'Excuse me, trooper, but might I enquire as to your orders? D'you know when are we to move upon Sebastopol?'

The hussar was a tall corporal with a thick blond moustache, dressed in the blue overalls of the King's Royal Irish. He snatched up the busby and brushed it roughly with the back of his hand. Then he looked at Kitson, irritation written plainly on his face. 'What?'

'I'm from the *London Courier*,' Kitson explained. 'We are reporting on the campaign.'

'And why the devil would you be doin' that?'

Kitson met the man's hostile stare with a brief, amiable grin. He had been asked similar questions many times before, in the same suspicious tones, and had a standard response. 'Why, so that the British public might read of the heroism of their troops, of course, and the progress of their noble undertaking, thereby easing—'

The hussar was not listening. 'I cannot be seen conversin'

with the likes of you,' he interrupted impatiently, tugging the busby's golden strap under his chin. 'Now get out the damned way.'

His shoulder struck hard against Kitson's as he sprinted off after the errant horse, which was now somewhere amongst the piles of supplies that covered the rear of the landing zone. Kitson staggered, losing his footing for a moment, and dropping his pocketbook as he waved an arm to steady himself. As he stooped to pick it up, the telegram fell from beneath its cover. Caught by the wind, the slip of paper curled away across the stones, rising up into the air. For a moment, Kitson considered giving chase; but then just watched it go.

The *H.M.S. Arthur*, one of the older frigates in the bay, was anchored a good distance from the beach with her sails rolled. As her passengers were non-military, she had been allocated only two longboats, making the disembarkation painfully, tediously slow. In addition, the ship was taking on cholera cases for immediate transport back to Scutari. Every longboat from the *Arthur*, after it had been pulled up on to the stones and disgorged its civilian cargo, then had to be loaded with pale, moaning soldiers, each one bound to a stretcher, before it could sail back. Like every other operation that day, lifting the sick up to the ship once they reached her was made many times more difficult by the swell. At least two had been lost to the waves.

The invalids were receiving a great deal of attention from those leaving the *Arthur*. The majority were soldiers' wives who had been camped out with the army throughout the miserable summer in Varna, but left behind when the invasion force had set sail for the Crimea. Rows of anxious faces, framed by grimy bonnets, poked over the deck rail, both hopeful and fearful that someone familiar might be among those being carried aboard so precariously. They gasped when the sailors stumbled, and they wailed when men went into the sea; but they'd already seen far too much death that year to be badly shocked.

Kitson approached the cholera cases awaiting evacuation.

They were laid out in lines across the shingle like rotten railway sleepers. He looked at the soldiers' stained uniforms, streaked with vomit and faeces, their waxy, agonised faces, their rigid limbs that poked out awkwardly from under their blankets like snapped branches, and felt nothing but relief that he had so far managed to escape infection. This cold-hearted reaction would have shamed him six months earlier. Like the soldiers' wives, however, like everyone on the campaign, he had grown somewhat hardened against the misery of others.

He picked his way around to where the disembarked wives had gathered in a large crowd, huddled against the wind, shawls drawn in close around them. Many were calling out names at the invalids, in the slight hope of eliciting responses from them. The only able-bodied men present were the servants of the few officers' wives who had been obliged to travel aboard the *Arthur*, standing alongside their mistresses, a little apart from the grubby spouses of the common soldiery. There was no one present who might conceivably be Mr Styles. Kitson perched on a coil of thick navy rope and lit a cigar, settling down to wait.

Before long, another longboat scraped up on to the shore. Drab civilians piled over its sides, many not waiting for the landing planks in their eagerness to walk again upon dry land. As they dispersed, drifting off into a maze of crates, sacks and assorted pieces of military machinery, Kitson noticed a man vault athletically out of the boat. He threw a leather folder and a canvas bag to the ground, and turned quickly to offer his arm to a slender young woman who was stepping on to the top of a landing plank, holding up the hem of her skirts before descending with practised grace. The poise and careful courtesy of this interaction appeared entirely out of place in that dreary, chaotic afternoon. As Kitson watched, the man retrieved his belongings and the pair started in his direction, the lady's gloved hand in his elbow, their heads lowered against the breeze. A group of sailors heaved a large mahogany trunk from the longboat, puffing as they rushed it inland, overtaking the strolling couple. After thirty yards or so, they set it down with a groan; the black chest was so heavy that it sank several inches into the pebbles. Rubbing their sore palms together, the blue-jackets promptly returned to their boats.

There were some distant screams as a warhorse leapt from the foam close to the soldiers' wives, trampling several of the cholera cases as it galloped off into the landing zone. The pair, who had by now reached the chest, both looked around to find the source of this sound, giving Kitson his first proper sight of their faces. He caught his breath: the woman was Madeleine Boyce. Grinding out his cigar on the navy rope, he got to his feet and walked towards them.

Mrs Madeleine Boyce was a lady of considerable repu-tation. Although only a shade above twenty, her fame as a beauty was already well established. That afternoon, as ever, her clothes were immaculate; a grey silk dress with a dark blue bonnet and cloak, unostentatious but radiating quiet expensiveness. Her cheeks bore the slightest flush from the sharp sea wind and the cold spray it carried. A few strands of dark hair had escaped from under her bonnet, and trailed across her cheek. Seeing Kitson approach, she smiled warmly.

'Mr Kitson! What a pleasant surprise!' Her voice, even when raised against the bustle of the beach, was soft, with the light accent of a Frenchwoman who had been among the English for many years. She gestured at the activity around them. 'How extraordinary all this is!'

Kitson returned her smile, marvelling at her relaxed demeanour. Does she have the faintest notion, he wondered, of the difficulties her presence here will cause? 'It is remark-able, *Madame*, truly remarkable, what wonders can be achieved by our modern armies. Why, King Agamemnon himself would gape with awe at the sight before us today. That so many thousands of fighting men can be landed, and in so short a time, quite amazes the mind.'

He glanced at her companion. The fellow was young also, a number of years younger than Kitson himself, certainly no more than twenty-two or -three. His wide, guileless face was clean-shaven, his skin tanned and unlined, his posture straight – this was no veteran of the staging post at Varna. He wore a black velvet jacket that was not only unsoiled, but also reasonably new and in good repair; a soft, broad-brimmed felt hat in a deep shade of green sat upon his head, and long, light brown curls were tucked behind his ears. The leather folder, now under his arm, was plainly an album of drawings and sketches. There could be no doubt who he was. Kitson had located Mr Styles.

'Allow me to introduce myself, sir,' the young man said, extending his hand, 'Robert Styles. Pleased to make your acquaintance, Mr Kitson. Mr O'Farrell assured me that you would be here to meet me, even if Mr Cracknell was indisposed.'

Kitson took Styles' hand. The skin was oddly smooth against his own callused palm. Standing there, exchanging pleasantries with a fashionable lady and an artist, he was struck by a strange, momentary sense of familiarity, as if his old life in the salons and picture galleries of the Metropolis had somehow followed him to the shores of the Black Sea. 'Welcome to the Crimea, Mr Styles. May I say how glad I am that you are joining us, sir. Your efforts will doubtless enrich our coverage of the coming conflict enormously.'

Styles smiled nervously. 'I only hope I do not disappoint, Mr Kitson. Much faith has been placed in me, it seems.'

'You are too modest, Mr Styles,' interjected Mrs Boyce gently. She met Kitson's eye. 'He is a man of true talent, Mr Kitson. Whilst we were on board the *Arthur*, he took several studies of me, all quite excellent.'

'Really, *Madame*?' Kitson looked at the illustrator. Styles was blushing fiercely, intensely pleased by Mrs Boyce's praise. It was clear enough what had transpired between them. Madeleine Boyce conquered fellows like this Styles without even properly realising that she was doing it. Kitson almost cursed aloud: here was yet another complication to consider. So much, he thought, for my optimism about the arrival of Mr Styles. 'Is that where you first met one another, may I ask? On the *Arthur*?'

Styles nodded. 'The vessel made a stop at Varna, sir, and Mrs Boyce came aboard. We were introduced soon after.'

'Indeed, Mr Styles. What serendipity.' Kitson turned back to the officer's wife. She had removed one of her gloves and was idly studying the exposed hand. 'Well, I must say that it is good to see you again so soon, *Madame*. We poor *Courier* scribes were resigned to meeting you next upon English soil.' He cleared his throat pointedly. 'Mr Cracknell will be especially gratified, I'm sure.'

Suddenly self-conscious, Mrs Boyce pulled her glove back on. 'And how fares your good senior? He is well, I hope?'

Styles was listening very closely, his brow furrowed. Our young illustrator is no fool, thought Kitson. He saw the change that came over her when I mentioned Cracknell's name. 'He perseveres, Mrs Boyce, in his usual manner. His, ah, inexhaustible passion for our task continues to inspire all in his orbit. Myself in particular.'

She smiled at this reply – not the confident smile that charmed and dazzled so many, but a genuine, involuntary expression of deep delight. Kitson looked away.

A small mule-cart was weaving slowly through some Commissariat tents pitched at the rear of the landing zone, heading in their direction. It was driven by a stout infantry sergeant, with a private sat at his side. The brass regimental number on the front of their shako helmets was just visible: these soldiers were from the 99th Foot.

'I see that your escort approaches, *Madame*,' Kitson observed, unable to keep a note of relief from his voice. 'The Lieutenant-Colonel will be most pleased to learn that you have arrived without mishap.'

The dreamy smile vanished. Mrs Boyce inclined her head stiffly in reluctant acknowledgement of her husband's existence.

'And we must leave you now, I'm afraid,' Kitson added apologetically. 'There are duties we must perform, and certain facts of our present situation with which Mr Styles here must be familiarised. I feel sure, however, that we will encounter one another again in the near future.'

Farewells were exchanged – rather hastily, as Kitson wished to avoid being caught conversing with Mrs Boyce by one of her husband's non-commissioned officers. It would be reported, various assumptions would be made, and trouble would surely follow. He was starting to feel that trouble was something with which the nascent *Courier* team was already too familiar.

Madeleine watched the newspapermen walk away across the stones, taking care to give the cart a wide berth. A minute later, the modest vehicle pulled up close to where she stood. The squat brown mules were shaking their heads and braying, unsettled by the sounds of the teeming landing zone.

'Mrs Boyce?' said the sergeant. 'We're 'ere t'collect you, ma'am.' She nodded absently. The two soldiers climbed down from the cart and started towards the chest.

Turning away, Madeleine gazed inland, past the beach to the farmlands beyond. '*Je suis ici*, Richard,' she whispered, '*je suis ici*.'

2

More cholera cases were being carried down towards the sea from the camps, bound for the *Arthur*. Kitson and Styles pressed themselves against a row of ammunition crates to let them pass. The men already seemed beyond all help, flies clustering around their mouths and eyes in black knots. The illustrator felt a clammy nausea close around him. He was not yet used to such sights.

The new colleagues walked on through a copse of short, small-leafed trees and out into a broad expanse of farmland. An undulating quilt of lavender and wheat stretched away to the horizon, dotted with farmhouses, fruit orchards and wide-bladed windmills. A few rays of sunlight broke through the clouds, dappling the landscape beneath. Soon the diseased soldiers were left behind, and Styles began to recover himself. The Crimean countryside was a welcome change indeed from the open sea, and seemed remarkably peaceful. Even the mass of white military tents pitched off to the east looked like the site of an enormous fair. Red-coated infantry drilled in long lines, the shouts of their sergeants mingling with the jaunty tunes of regimental bands, and the clanking of count-less pans and kettles.

Styles asked whether they might stop for a moment, so that he could take in this sight properly – perhaps even make a quick sketch. Kitson continued to stride on ahead at some speed, however, with no sign of having heard him. Hands in his pockets, he was staring down at the ground, entirely absorbed in private thoughts. The illustrator didn't repeat his request. He was determined not to prove an annoyance. Kitson's heavy beard and dusty, discoloured clothes seemed to rebuke him for his late arrival on the campaign, for the months of hardship he had missed – and to demand that he demonstrate his suitability for the task that lay ahead.

Thomas Kitson, also, was someone with whom he felt he had a deep kinship. During the course of his briefings at the *London Courier*, Styles had heard a good deal about the junior correspondent. More than two months after Kitson's departure, the magazine's offices on the Strand still hummed with talk about the unaccountable fellow who had abandoned a promising career in art criticism to follow Lord Raglan's Army. He was exceedingly knowledgeable, these gossips said, and had been expected to rise to the summit of his profession before long – yet he had decided to risk everything, his very life included, to chase after battles with the notoriously unpredictable Richard Cracknell. The verdicts of his former colleagues were harsh – they theorised that Kitson, in the last years of his youth, had developed a craving for glory, for a reputation that anonymous reviews of picture-shows could never bring him. Either that or he had received some sort of hard, disorientating blow to the head.

But one powerful voice had been raised in Kitson's defence, sending his detractors scuttling for cover: that of old Mr O'Farrell, the *Courier*'s editor-in-chief. 'The man of whom you speak so dismissively can summon forth images with his pen that none of you wretched inkhorns could ever hope to match,' he had snapped. 'He desired a challenge, a subject of import, of *weight*, well away from the vapid commonplaces of Metropolitan conversation – and I was not prepared to deny him it!'

This outburst had heartened Styles enormously. This was his wish as well – to witness something *great*, something that would make him more of a man and more of an artist. He, too, had met with his share of opposition, from fearful relatives and uncomprehending friends, all looking at him in utter mystification when he told them of his contract with the *Courier*. Hearing O'Farrell speak of Kitson in this manner had made him believe that his decision was justified, that he was off to perform a noble task with like-minded souls. Yet here he was, out on the campaign at last, in Mr Kitson's company no less, and they had barely exchanged a word beyond their initial greeting. This was not how he had envisioned his first hour as a member of the *Courier* team.

The two men started along a narrow mud track, and the silence stretched until Styles could bear it no longer. 'May I ask where we are heading, sir?' he said, loudly and a little plaintively. 'I'd assumed we'd be going straight to camp in order to commence our duties, but we seem to be heading in the very opposite direction.'

Kitson pointed towards some nearby chimneys, just visible over a bank of brush to their right. 'Mr Styles,' he began, a touch of amusement in his voice, 'you will soon discover that our foremost duty as Mr Cracknell's juniors is not to draw or write but to secure the *Courier*'s provisions. We will find what we need over there.'

'Does the army not provide for us?'

This prompted a sarcastic laugh. 'The army, my friend, can hardly provide for its own. On the first night here the soldiers had no *tents*, let alone sufficient rations – and this was in heavy rain. Sir George Brown, commander of the Light Division, was obliged to take shelter under a cart. We newspapermen are a long way down the list of priorities.' Kitson waved a thin forefinger in the air. 'The first lesson of life on campaign, sir: make your own arrangements!'

The track wound around a low hill to bring them before a large manor house with a walled yard. It was a smart residence indeed, built from even blocks of pale stone. Heavy shutters, painted dark green, covered every window; the house's owners had clearly left to escape the approaching war. The wide, cobbled yard was fringed with outbuildings and stables, somewhat cruder in style but all coated with a creamy whitewash that made them glow warmly against the surrounding hedgerows.

Kitson headed confidently across the yard. A handful of peasants stood behind carts and barrows that had been arranged to form improvised market-stalls, upon which a small selection of produce from the surrounding fields had been laid out for purchase. These peasants resembled the Arabs Styles had seen at Constantinople, but with a touch of the Orient about their eyes. All were male, and most were bearded; they wore mud-stained smocks made from sackcloth and canvas, and brimless fur caps upon their heads. Every one of them was watching the Englishmen closely. A couple made observations in a guttural language Styles was pretty sure wasn't Russian.

'Crim Tartars,' murmured Kitson. 'The original inhabitants of this peninsula, here long before Catharine the Great took it under her dominion. They are serfs, effectively. They've taken to congregating outside this place – the seat of a squire, I believe, or the Crimean equivalent – with whatever wares they can scrape together. The French Commissariat has been coming over here to purchase food for their senior officers, but these fellows will happily sell to us as well.' He took out some coins and jangled them together in his palm. 'They are careful to keep their distance from the camps, though. The private soldier on campaign is not known for his courteous dealings with locals.'

'Did they not think to flee?'

'It would seem not. Some are no doubt hoping that their Russian masters will be defeated, and they will be able to reclaim a portion of this land for themselves. Others, the more loyal ones, are standing guard.'

The illustrator looked about him at the ramshackle market and the shuttered manor house. 'Guarding *what*, sir? Nothing of any value has been left behind, surely?'

Kitson approached a stall and began inspecting some misshapen loaves. 'You would be surprised, Mr Styles. The rich men of the Crimea left their homes in some haste. Ancient volumes, pictures, objects of *virtu* – all have been ferreted away in the slight hope that the storm of war will leave them unmolested.'

He bought one of the loaves with a large copper coin. As he took the money, the stall-holder nodded to the *Courier* man as if in recognition. 'I have tried to draw attention to this matter, but I'm afraid that Cracknell isn't particularly interested, so nothing will come of it. Our good senior is many things, Mr Styles, but he cannot be called a man of culture.'

Mention of Cracknell's name caused Styles to remember Mrs Boyce's singular, unsettling smile back on the beach. It was unlike any look of hers he had seen before – and he had studied her closely, with a devoted eye. 'What is Mr Cracknell really like, Mr Kitson?' he asked suddenly. 'So much is said of him back in London. The most unsavoury stories . . .'

Kitson chuckled. 'Don't believe all that you hear, Mr Styles. Richard Cracknell can be somewhat . . . provocative, it is true, but he is an accomplished correspondent, and a man possessed of a truly fearsome determination. We are fortunate indeed to be with him. He wishes to take this unprecedented chance to experience war at first-hand, and wring everything out of it that he can.'

'And how did you both come to be acquainted with Mrs Boyce?' Styles tried to keep his voice level. 'Why were you so surprised to see her here?'

The correspondent headed for another stall. Upon it was a wicker basket stuffed with scrawny, clucking chickens. 'Mrs Boyce has a rare beauty, does she not?' Kitson's expression was unreadable.

He has detected my attachment, Styles thought quickly; and despite his casual tone, he disapproves. This is why he was so quiet after our meeting. He has been biding his time before delivering his admonition, trying to catch me off-guard, to chide me as if I were an infatuated schoolboy. Styles felt a defiant anger well up inside him. He would not disavow his feelings, nor would he apologise for them. He loved the divine Mrs Boyce with all his soul. They were fast friends, confidantes even, and he was certain that in time they would become much more – regardless of what Mr Kitson might think about it.

He could not deny, however, that Kitson's familiar conversation with Mrs Boyce back on the beach had disturbed him a little. Kitson was no rival, of that Styles was certain; his manner, coolly polite to the point of irony, had indicated this clearly enough. Something disquieting had been there, though – a sense of shared history between Mrs Boyce and the *Courier* correspondents, an earlier chapter Styles was not party to. He had to know more.

'She does indeed,' Styles replied forcibly. 'Beyond any other I have seen.'

Kitson made no reaction to this bold declaration. He pointed out a bird to the stall-holder. The Tartar plucked it from the basket, wrung its neck with practised efficiency, and then exchanged it for two more of the correspondent's coins.

'She was to be sent home, you know, by her husband.' Kitson's tone was matter-of-fact. 'Due to the danger of disease. God alone knows how she managed to change his mind. I only hope that her presence here doesn't prove too problematic.'

Styles frowned. 'What do you mean?'

Kitson tucked the chicken into a capacious pocket. Its scaly feet stuck out, still twitching spasmodically. 'She told you of her husband, I take it? Of how things stand between them?'

'She did.'

Over the course of the voyage from Varna, Mrs Boyce had spoken of her husband at great length. Styles had heard of every trouble visited upon her by Lieutenant-Colonel Nathaniel Boyce – who, by his wife's account, was a despicable, prideful boor given to all manner of senseless cruelty. Intoxicated by the intimacy that had developed so rapidly between them, Styles had sworn to himself that he would free her, that he would bring this precious lady the happiness she so richly deserved.

Kitson regarded him doubtfully. 'One must be very careful, my friend, in trying to build an acquaintance with Mrs Boyce, no matter how, ah, *innocent* it might be. Countless young gentlemen, you understand, have lost themselves in those ebony eyes, nurtured torturous dreams of lying in the tresses of that luxuriant, perfumed hair, and so forth.' He paused, the slightest suggestion of a smile on his lips. 'The Lieutenant-Colonel is famously zealous in dispatching his rivals. They

18

say that he has even shot several of them, in duels or else-where, to convince them to desist.'

Styles studied Kitson's face again. Was this a warning? Or was it mockery? Either way, he decided that he would hear no more. 'Are you trying to *frighten me*, Mr Kitson? Because if so, I must state that Mrs Boyce and I—'

'Mr Styles,' Kitson interrupted firmly, 'enough games. There are some things you should know about Madeleine Boyce.'

But before he could say any more, a ripple of apprehension ran through the Tartar stall-holders gathered in the yard. They began to talk urgently, gesturing beyond the wall. Styles heard the sound of several score of boots marching in time, approaching the farm at a steady speed. The *Courier* men turned together to face the gate, their conversation forgotten.

'Damn it,' Kitson muttered. 'Soldiers.'

There was a hard bark of martial instruction, and the first line of an infantry company wheeled into sight. Guided by their corporals, the square of redcoats advanced to the centre of the yard and stamped to attention. The faces beneath their shakos were sallow and lean, and menacing in their im-passivity. A sergeant-major appeared behind them, three silver chevrons shining on his arm. Walking slowly towards the manor house, a hand on the hilt of his sword, he made a careful, contemptuous survey of the stalls. Seeing Kitson and Styles, he paused, narrowing his eyes. Kitson touched the brim of his hat with a forefinger. The sergeant-major did not reciprocate.

Styles noticed the soldiers' regimental numeral. 'The 99th. Isn't that Boyce's regiment?'

Kitson nodded. 'And best avoided by us *Courier* men if at all possible. Come, we should buy what else we need and be gone.'

The correspondent made for a hand-cart piled with flaccid wineskins. Its owner managed to pull one out and exchange it for the remaining four of Kitson's coins without once taking his eyes off the redcoats. Slinging this latest purchase over his arm, Kitson indicated that they should make good their escape. Before they had gone more than a few feet, however, two mounted officers entered the yard, riding across the cobblestones at a canter. Cutting in front of the soldiers, they came to a noisy halt at the manor house's door, climbed down from their horses and tethered them to a stone water trough.

Kitson was watching them with great curiosity, no longer in such a hurry to depart. 'Captain Wray and Lieutenant Davy,' he noted wryly. 'Old friends of the *Courier*. I wonder what they could possibly be doing out here?'

The two officers were now conversing intently, consulting a scrap of paper and looking up at the house. Captain Wray was a slight man with a long nose, a sharp, pinched look and a set of whiskers that gave him the unfortunate appearance of a rat wearing a ruff. Lieutenant Davy was taller and somewhat younger, his adolescent countenance all but obscured by a profusion of angry pimples. The sergeant-major marched over to them and made a brief report; the pockmarked Lieutenant glared at Kitson and Styles with open enmity.

'A – a reconnaissance mission, perhaps?' Styles suggested uneasily.

Kitson raised an eyebrow but did not reply.

Wray glanced at them with lordly boredom and then turned back to Davy. 'This is the place, Lieutenant,' he announced loudly in a high, lisping voice. 'I am sure of it.'

The Captain pulled open the manor house's grand double doors and walked inside, with Davy following close behind. At this, the alarm of the Tartars in the yard became more vocal. Several stepped forward, as if to pursue the officers into the building. Seeing this, the sergeant-major faced the company and gave the order to present arms. The soldiers' abrupt movements, and the synchronised raising of their long-barrelled rifles, successfully checked the stall-holders' bravery – for the moment, at least.

Styles was growing nervous. The atmosphere in the yard had become charged with violence; it was like being in a tavern seconds before a brawl. He looked quickly at Kitson, hoping for guidance. The correspondent, entirely calm, was moving the sloshing wineskin from one shoulder to the other so that he could take out his pocketbook. Styles suddenly perceived that this unkempt, sardonic fellow, for all his loaded pronouncements and enigmatic expressions, was the same Thomas Kitson whose laudable example had given him such encouragement. I must not quail, the illustrator thought; I must prove myself equal to that which I have taken on. He took a steadying breath and adjusted his hold on his drawing folder, which was growing slippery in his sweating palm.

Several tense minutes passed. The sergeant-major brought his men back to attention whilst the Tartars grumbled amongst themselves. Affecting a new interest in the produce on the carts, Kitson moved slowly towards the open doors of the house, keeping his distance from the soldiers. Styles was attempting to follow suit when the shutters of one of the upper windows were suddenly thrown open. He caught a glimpse of Lieutenant Davy, looking back triumphantly into the dark room.

'It would seem that they have found what they seek, Mr Styles,' said Kitson quietly.

A moment later, deep inside the manor house, there was a loud crash and the sound of boots rushing down a flight of stone stairs. Wray paced quickly through the double doors and over to his horse. He was holding an object in his arms, something weighty and awkward, half-wrapped in a length of sackcloth.

Davy emerged directly after him; and behind the Lieutenant, attached to him in fact, came an elderly Tartar, who was gripping on to the gold braid on Davy's shoulder and shouting angrily. This sight drew some disrespectful sniggers from the company of soldiers, which provoked the Lieutenant to turn furiously on his aged assailant and give him a hard shove. The Tartar reeled, losing his hold on the officer's uniform, and fell heavily against the stone water trough. Davy then unbuckled his sword and, leaving the blade in the scabbard, he stood over the old peasant and began to beat him with it. The sword cracked against the Tartar's skull and thumped across his back. Davy's blemished face contorted with the effort. He showed no intention of stopping, even as the man at his feet began to bleed.

An impulse to intervene came upon Styles with un-expected force. All but running across the yard, he tried to grasp Davy's arm and restrain his next blow. Without even pausing to see who he was, the Lieutenant struck him full in the face with a balled fist. Styles staggered back and fell onto the cobblestones. The soldiers exploded into laughter.

'Eyes front!' yelled the sergeant-major, his face turning as crimson as his coatee. 'Eyes front, damn you!'

Dazed and acutely embarrassed, Styles propped himself up on an elbow and tenderly touched his face. His mouth was hot, the lip split open; he could taste blood on his teeth, and feel its warmth smeared across his chin. He looked around for his bag and drawing folder. Both were on the ground not far from where he lay. Then he saw Kitson, standing in the middle of the yard, addressing Captain Wray – who was by now mounted on his horse, ready to depart.

'Good afternoon, Captain Wray,' called the correspondent cheerfully. 'A fine day, is it not?'

'Well, if it isn't the blasted bog-trotter's lackey,' drawled Wray, regarding Kitson coldly from up on his saddle. 'What the devil are you doing out here?'

Kitson smiled. 'I might ask you the same question, Captain. I don't recall hearing that the Light Division had been assigned any duties away from the camp. Could you enlighten me on this point? For the readership of the *London Courier*?' He was holding his pocketbook ready, his pencil poised, as if in the very act of reporting.

'None of your business, and none of your bloody readers' business either!' came Wray's curt retort. He looked to his Lieutenant, who was still panting with exertion as he re-fastened his sword to his belt. 'Get to your horse, Davy, we must be off.'

Kitson, however, would not release him so easily. 'And what is that you have there, Captain?' he inquired. 'Forgive me, but it looks rather interesting – valuable, even. Can I ask why you have removed it from this fine house?'

Styles peered again at the object Wray now had balanced before him on his saddle. Some of the sackcloth had slipped away, revealing that it was a statuette of some kind, cast in terracotta, about a foot high. Wray and Davy had stolen it from the farmhouse; the elderly Tartar, its custodian, had been trying to stop them. The soldiers were looting.

Wray stared at the horizon, refusing to answer. His horse paced impatiently beneath him, tossing its head.

'Only,' Kitson continued with fearless breeziness, 'the readership of the *Courier* – for whom you evidently hold such an *immense* regard – would be quite fascinated to hear of any antiquities discovered in the Crimea by Her Majesty's Army – of how they were saved for posterity by the forces of enlightenment, so selflessly snatching them from the darkness of barbarism.'

A grin crept across Styles' bloody face.

Wray sighed irritably, seeing that he had been out-manoeuvred. 'Oh, very well, you damned grubber. Here is your blasted antiquity.'

The Captain unwrapped the statuette fully and held it out at arm's length. It was of Saint Catherine, rendered in the flamboyant style of the Italian Baroque. The saint was posed dramatically atop her broken cartwheel, her russet limbs arranged as if she was about to launch herself heavenward. Even from the ground, Styles could see that it was a piece of some quality.

And then Wray let it drop.

The brittle sound of the Saint Catherine shattering on the cobbles echoed around the yard. It was followed by a string of hoarse exclamations from the elderly Tartar, who was trying unsuccessfully to rise from the ground; whether these strained noises were curses or lamentations Styles could not tell. With a self-satisfied smirk, Wray wheeled his horse around and commanded that the company be taken back out to the road. The sergeant-major snarled an order, turning the soldiers smartly towards the gate.

Kitson put his pocketbook under his arm and clapped a round of slow, derisive applause. 'Oh bravo, Captain Wray, bravo!' he shouted. 'Oh, well done, sir! You have surely triumphed! You bested me there, and no mistake!'

Wray did not even look around. Moving ahead of the company, he spurred his horse and was gone. Davy leant over to spit at the correspondent's feet, hissing a few vicious obscenities before riding after his Captain.

As soon as the soldiers had left, the Tartars rushed to help the old man, sitting him on the side of the trough and mopping at a long cut on his brow. A stout woman, her hair bound under a black headscarf, rushed from the farmhouse and threw her arms around his neck, sobbing loudly. Davy's victim would not be comforted, though; shaking off the woman and rising to his feet, he hobbled over to the remains of the Saint Catherine. Seeing that there was no hope of repair, he gave the shards a despairing kick, scattering them across the yard.

'You see now what I was referring to earlier, Mr Styles.' Kitson was standing over him, writing materials stuffed in one pocket, chicken legs poking out of the other. His precise state of mind, once again, was hard to divine; but he did not seem unamused by their encounter with the officers of the 99th. 'Items like that statuette should rightfully be protected, stored well away from rapacious brutes like our Captain Wray.' He offered the illustrator his hand and pulled him upright. 'How is your lip?'

'Sore enough. But I shall live.' Styles regarded his comrade with intense admiration. 'You – you did a fine thing there, Mr Kitson. You bore witness, sir – you stood in the path of wrongdoing.'

Kitson shook his head. 'You exaggerate, Mr Styles. I failed. The statuette was smashed, and these unfortunate people most foully abused.' He turned towards the elderly Tartar, who was now clutching at his ribs and grimacing in pain. Immediately the weeping woman was beside him, embracing him protectively, her expression indicating that she viewed the *Courier* men as entirely complicit in Wray and Davy's depredations.

'But you at least gave them pause, sir,' Styles insisted, 'whereas I plunged in like a hot-headed booby and caused only laughter.' A little ashamed, he wiped his bloody chin on his sleeve. 'We will be reporting this incident, though, won't we? Telling Mr Cracknell, at least?'

Kitson smiled ruefully. 'Mr Styles, your enthusiasm is

refreshing indeed to a jaded soul such as myself. Questions do occur to me, I must admit. Who, for example, directed them to this house? They were certainly acting under another's instructions.'

'And what do you think, Mr Kitson?'

To Styles' dismay, Kitson simply shrugged. 'What does it matter? No one cares, Mr Styles, as Mr Cracknell would be the first to tell you. There is nothing we can do. Far more is at stake out here than *art*, my friend. Between here and Sebastopol, the Russian Army is preparing to repel our forces with all their might. I think our generals can be forgiven for being rather more interested in that, don't you?'

Styles could hardly disagree. Feeling bruised and thoroughly defeated, he picked up his bag and folder, nodding dumbly when Kitson proposed that they head back to camp. As they walked from the yard, he noticed that his black velvet jacket was covered in pale dust. Its left elbow, also, had been scuffed bald against the cobbles.

Kitson cast a sideways glance at the illustrator and brushed at his shoulder. 'Ha! What a mess! We shall make a war correspondent of you yet, Mr Styles!'

3

The night sentries maintained that the mist out by the northern barricades was so dense that it was as if Almighty God had reached down from Heaven and rubbed out a bit of creation with His divine thumb. It was cold out there too, and quiet; a deathly graveyard hush after the ceaseless bustle of the camp. This was where the Russians would come from, it was reasoned, if they were to come at all. Every man who stood watch there half expected to see the enemy at any moment, arrayed in their thousands, marching towards him from out of that eerie grey void. Like some red-coated vision of the damned, they coughed, cursed, and scratched miserably at persistent rashes acquired in the whorehouses of Constantinople, staring always at the thirty yards of open ground between them and the edges of the mist.

Yet on the third night, when someone did appear, for several long seconds they froze up altogether. This man was running fast, his cheeks flushed and his black hair awry, a cap of some kind clutched in his hand. Greatcoat flapping around his knees, he didn't stop or slow down, or even look in their direction. He kept on going, swerving slightly to run roughly parallel to their line, his arms pumping back and forth, his boots pounding through the wet grass. This had to be a Russian spy, of which the sentries had been promised there was a whole devious legion, making a break for his own territory.

The soldiers' firing, when it began, was erratic at best. The spy was a difficult mark, moving quickly, and they hadn't been ready for him. Every bullet went wide; some swore, as they lowered their miniés, that they could see a grin spreading across the villain's face. Then a burly corporal pulled himself up to his full height and swung his rifle's stock expertly against his shoulder. The end of the barrel fixed on the running man and followed him along for a few yards; then the shot rang out, the man stumbled, and was down. There was a cheer, and laughter, and several hearty slaps to the corporal's broad back. The first kill of the campaign!

The laughter faded abruptly as the man got up, his feet slipping in the dew, and set off again, at much the same pace as before. Some started to reload hurriedly, tearing at the paper cartridge packs with their teeth. Others started clambering over the barricades, attaching their bayonets, intending to give chase. It was suddenly clear that the spy was heading for a large thicket of wiry bushes a short way to the east. The soldiers shouted to each other, trying to head him off; but he was too fast.

'Come on, you idle dogs!' he cried as he went. 'That the best you can do?' And then he dived into the bushes, and was gone.

'Raise the alarm!' ordered an excited major, freshly arrived on the scene. 'Full alert! At once! Back to the pickets!'

The soldiers obeyed, and the alarm was raised; but those who had heard the escaping man's taunt knew that if this really was an enemy spy they pursued, it was one with a distinctly Irish-sounding accent.

After crashing through the undergrowth to the open ground on its other side, Cracknell turned to check that he wasn't being pursued. Past the bushes, all that he saw was the billowing greyness of a thick sea fog, blowing in from the bay. The bastards are quick enough to fire from the safety of their barricades, he thought with a triumphant sneer; but giving chase, well, that is another matter entirely.

Panting from the effort of his dash for safety, Cracknell pushed his cap back on his head, and mopped his brow with a stained twist of handkerchief. Somewhere inside him, he knew that it had been mad folly to try to creep back into camp from the north. But he felt not even the faintest tremor of guilt for the tumult he had caused. The sensation of the bullets slicing through the air so close to him, tugging at his clothes even, had been monstrously exhilarating. And now, off in the distance, the bugles were sounding a piercing reveille across the shadowy fields. Torches were being lit, and a multitude of soldiers were stumbling from the lines of white, conical tents, buttoning up jackets and readying rifles with anxious haste. That it was all in his honour made Cracknell's chest swell with a perverse pride. He drew a battered silver hip-flask from his coat pocket, raising it towards the agitated camp before taking a long swig. Then he carried on his way at a considerably reduced pace, one hand pressed against a stabbing stitch in his side.

The *Courier* tent was pitched at the very edge of the camp, close to a shallow, brackish pond. As he approached it, Cracknell dropped to his haunches, keeping to the shadows. Kitson stood in the light of an oil lamp, the triangles of his shoulder-blades clearly visible through his frock-coat. His junior was talking about the alarm – about how there'd been one the night before that had amounted to nothing, and how such scares were to be expected, given the situation. Cracknell took another gulp from his flask, chuckling softly. Our Mr Kitson's becoming quite the weathered field operative, he thought. What change can be wrought by expert guidance and a few months' privation!

He turned his attention to the focus of Kitson's little lecture – the illustrator. The boy was nodding along, plainly determined to put a brave face on the possibility of an enemy attack. And yes, Cracknell admitted grudgingly, he was handsome, as Maddy had said, in a bland sort of way; but Christ, so callow! Was O'Farrell deliberately trying to make his life as hard as possible? First an art correspondent, of all bloody things, now a youth so fresh-faced he looked as if he'd just been released from double Latin!

A large wineskin was passed between them. Cracknell stayed still for a moment or two, listening. Their conversation suggested that a rapport of sorts had been established. So much the better, reflected their senior. It will ease my burden if they're watching out for one another. Just as long as they don't forget who's in charge.

Then the illustrator happened to glance up – straight into Cracknell's eyes. He began stammering and pointing. Before Kitson could look around, Cracknell propelled himself forward, charging into the lamplight towards his reporting partner. He was the heavier man by some distance. They collided, tumbling together into the dirt.

Kitson fought to disentangle himself. The illustrator stood to one side, fists clenched, petrified by uncertainty and incomprehension. Cracknell, now lying on his back, shook with laughter.

'Mr Cracknell!' Kitson exclaimed breathlessly as he climbed to his feet. 'What in God's name—'

Cracknell lit a cigar, holding a match to its tip and sucking with relish. 'Just testing your reflexes, Thomas!' His accent, usually mild, had been thickened by drink. 'Have to keep you on your toes, my lad! How will you face the Bear if you can't manage the more good-natured assaults of your leader? Eh?' He chortled throatily around his cigar, puffing out small jets of smoke.

Kitson, rubbing at a twisted elbow, did not look convinced. 'I suppose, then, that I am expected to thank you for the service?'

With a final loud laugh, the senior correspondent hauled himself up, removed his cigar and took another healthy swallow from his flask. As he smacked his tingling lips, he realised that the young illustrator was staring at him in a manner he did not wholly appreciate. Cracknell smoothed down his wild black beard and made a brusque introduction. Then he noticed a small, dark discolouration at the side of the boy's mouth.

'Is that a *bruise* I see there, sir?' he asked with gruff, slightly menacing good humour.

The illustrator glanced at Kitson. 'It is, Mr Cracknell. A lieutenant saw fit to strike out at me after –'

'A *lieutenant?*' Cracknell grinned. 'You work damned fast, my friend! Why, it took me *weeks* to be struck in the face by an officer, yet you have achieved it in a matter of hours! A fellow after our own hearts, eh, Thomas?'

Kitson nodded in dry agreement.

'To be perfectly frank with you, though,' Cracknell went

on, inserting the cigar back between his teeth, 'I don't quite see the point of your presence here, myself. The *Courier*'s foreign correspondence is about words, mine and Kitson's – the combined efforts of Britannia's two greatest descriptive minds. We are not the *Illustrated London News*. We do not, in my view at least, need anything as crude as *images* to convey our experiences.' He tapped off an inch of ash. 'But I have been overruled by my editor. Here you are, Smiles, here you bloody well are, and we shall make the best of it, by God!'

The illustrator looked confused, uncertain whether he had just been endorsed or denounced. 'I – I thank you, Mr Cracknell. Excuse me though, sir, the name is *Styles* – S, T, Y—'

Cracknell waved Styles quiet with a meaty, indifferent hand. 'There is much fodder in this place, is there not, for your work? Grand panorama and so forth?' Styles lifted up a leather-bound folder, opening his mouth to speak, but Cracknell did not require an answer. 'You join us late, of course, but that is no loss. The most memorable scenes Varna had to offer were of hundreds of soldiers, felled by cholera long before they could see battle, being buried in ditches – and somehow I don't think this was quite what that hopeless old muff O'Farrell envisaged when he signed you up.'

The senior correspondent retrieved the wineskin, dropped when he had tackled Kitson, and hefted its sloshing weight. He smiled approvingly; they had made a good inroad into its contents. If there was a man of spirit and courage who was impervious to the robust charms of liquor, Richard Cracknell had certainly never met him.

'No, young Smiles, this is where the real drama will be staged,' he went on, 'here in the Crimea. This peninsula, y'see, has a rich strategic value. It is the promontory from which the Russian Bear exerts its baleful influence over the Black Sea. Thirty miles in that direction,' he pointed off into the night, 'lies the mighty fortress-port of Sebastopol; and over yonder,' he swung his arm in an expansive arc, 'across the waves, is poor Turkey, Europe's helpless invalid, ailing and weak – and bound to the British Lion by sacred bonds of honour.' Cracknell's excitement was mounting. 'The Bear has been swiping at this feeble bird of late, snapping at it hungrily – so we will go to

Sebastopol and we will knock it down. We have let this Bear grow too hale and hearty, Mr Smiles, and altogether too large, and must now give it a good whipping to remind it of its place! Isn't that so, Thomas?'

'It is, Mr Cracknell.' Kitson had heard all this before, of course, and there was the usual trace of flippancy in his manner. 'The Lion will, ah, whip the Bear. To rescue the turkey.'

Cracknell's eyes misted over with alcohol-fuelled passion. 'A great adventure awaits us, my friends. We shall see the glories of war up close and true, and we will deliver them to the great British public. A more splendid mission is hard to imagine.' He drew the stopper from the wineskin with a flourish. 'Let us drink to this team of ours! Let us drink to all we three shall achieve!'

After a long pull of the rough rustic wine, Cracknell lobbed the skin to the illustrator. When they had all partaken, the senior correspondent straightened his lapels, suddenly business-like. 'Now, gather yourselves. The camp is abuzz, and we must investigate this alarm on behalf of our readers. There is no time to lose.'

Setting off at a vigorous pace, he led his subordinates back around the pond and into the long, foggy avenues of infantry tents. Everywhere, dark shapes were streaming past stretches of pale canvas, stumbling and jostling as they went. The chilly air hummed with shouts, questions and curses. Torches were evidently in short supply; and when one eventually came into view, weaving through the crowds, it revealed only grim turmoil. Cracknell threw away the butt of his cigar and tried to get his bearings. Over to the right, he spotted a makeshift signpost tacked to a pole beneath a naval lantern. It stood at a rutted, muddy crossroads, with arrows pointing off in every direction. He elbowed his way towards it.

Kitson arrived to his side. Cracknell saw alertness and energy in the junior correspondent that mirrored his own exactly. My protégé is keen for proper experience, he thought. He wishes to demonstrate that he has left his time in the *Courier*'s more effeminate regions utterly behind him – that he is fit for manly duty. And his chance surely approaches.

31

'This is chaos, Mr Cracknell!' said Kitson. 'If the Russians were to attack now, we'd surely be swept back into the sea!'

Cracknell grinned. 'Indeed, Thomas! I'm beginning to think this invasion may have lost the element of bloody surprise, aren't you? Well, all the better – it will be a solid fight, with armies meeting on the open field. Glory, my friend, and a swift resolution.' He clapped his hand on Kitson's bony shoulder. 'Do you have a report for today?'

'I have, sir – the disembarkation of the Light Brigade.' He hesitated. 'Also, I feel I should tell you that Mr Styles and I had the misfortune to encounter the grenadier company from the 99th, commanded by none other than Captain Wray. It was then that his Lieutenant, Davy, struck our illustrator about the face. They were looting, Mr Cracknell. Wray destroyed a valuable statuette in front of me, in fact.'

'Is that so!' Cracknell had returned his attention to the sign-post. 'Hardly surprising. I trust you made no mention of this incident in your report. We don't want to puncture the patriotic spirit at this early stage with tales of how soldiers actually behave, now do we?'

'I had assumed that this would be your view. What about yourself? Did you manage to speak with Lord Raglan?'

Cracknell shook his head. 'No, our esteemed commander-in-chief eluded me once again. But I found ample diversion in another quarter.'

The senior correspondent looked again at the illustrator, who was attempting, rather hilariously, to act like a consummate, focused professional, to whom the seething camp was no great thing. He remembered the expression on Maddy's face a few hours earlier, naïve yet sly both at once, as she'd talked about the boy. Cracknell and Madeleine had been lying in each other's arms in her husband's tent, their clothing in disarray, and suddenly she had been filled with a burning desire to discuss the *Courier*'s latest addition, whom she had apparently befriended on the boat from Varna. 'Oh, he's so talented,' she'd said, 'and so handsome! And Richard, I do believe he's a little in love with me . . .' Cracknell, familiar with her tactics for eliciting the declarations of devotion to which she was quite addicted, had merely reached for his cigar case.

Now the young dolt stood before him, with no idea of what was coming. Cracknell took out his flask and emptied it with a flourish. He always enjoyed moments such as these – the moments directly before the delivery of a felling blow. 'By some odd coincidence, I too had a run-in with the 99th this afternoon. Let me tell you both of it.'

As Cracknell commenced his tale, Kitson remembered with stunning abruptness that he had not imparted his warning to Styles.

Soon after leaving the Tartars' market, they had uncorked the wineskin and started to drink. The confrontation with Wray and Davy had fostered a natural sense of solidarity between them. Styles, plainly unused to alcohol, had begun to talk with great warmth of Kitson's personal importance to him – of how learning of the junior correspondent's principled renunciation of the Metropolitan art world had sealed his own commitment to their current mission. This revelation had made Kitson uneasy. Never entirely comfortable with the regard of others, he'd barely recognised himself in Styles' admiring account. That someone had actually gained inspiration from him, and sought to follow him, seemed nothing short of ridiculous.

In his awkwardness, Kitson had quickly changed the subject, prompting the illustrator to tell him instead about the life he'd left back in England. Predictably enough, Styles was an aspiring painter, trained at the Royal Academy schools; they had in fact skirted around the same social circles, and had a small group of mutual acquaintances. Styles had held forth at some length on the desperate insipidity of these people, and the horrible, complacent myopia of London society in general. Kitson could not help smiling at this tirade. He had said similar things himself no more than a few months earlier.

The illustrator had been quieted only by a row of cholera dead, about a dozen of them, laid out beside a low hedge on the outskirts of the camp. The drone of insects had thickened the air, and as they passed by a large bloody rat ran from beneath what had recently been a lance-corporal. Styles, his face suddenly a flat grey, had handed Kitson the wineskin, insisting that he was perfectly fine but could drink no more at present.

Watching the illustrator trying vainly to dampen his horror, Kitson had felt a sudden sense of responsibility towards him. *I am a significant part of the reason he's here*, he'd thought, *in these extraordinary circumstances; were it not for my apparently shining example, this impressionable young artist might well have lost faith in his plan to follow the army to war.* This realisation had annoyed him. Such a burden was unwelcome – but it could not, in good conscience, be set down or ignored.

Already, however, Styles had been failed by Kitson's inattention. The unpleasant truth about Madeleine Boyce had not been revealed – and Kitson knew that this was a lapse for which the illustrator would now surely suffer. Cracknell rapped one of the arrows on the signpost with his knuckle, upon which '*1st Brig, Lt Div*' was printed in crude black letters, and started to walk in the direction it indicated. His pace was more relaxed than before; he adopted the manner of a strolling raconteur, talking loudly and heedlessly, despite the extremely sensitive nature of what he was revealing.

'Whilst hunting Lord Raglan,' he began, 'I chanced upon Major Maynard. You remember him, Thomas? A veteran of the Sikh Wars, Smiles – an India man only recently transferred to the 99th Foot. Not a great friend of Lieutenant-Colonel Boyce, I think it's fair to say. Theirs is the all-too-common enmity that exists between professional soldiers who've actually worked their way up through the ranks, and those damnable gentlemen-officers who owe their rather more rapid ascendancies to the advantages of privilege and wealth. At any rate, Maynard kindly informed me that Mrs Boyce had landed, quite unheralded, and was on her way over from the beach.'

A few more casual enquiries – made in the interests of the *London Courier*, of course – had revealed that the Lieutenant-Colonel had been summoned to meet with his divisional commander and would not be back for some hours. As a result, when Madeleine Boyce pulled back the flap of her husband's tent, Richard Cracknell was seated within, a bottle of champagne filched from Boyce's own personal supply at the ready.

'Her shriek of joy, my lads, as she rushed into my arms, damn near raised the camp.'

Kitson glanced over at the illustrator. He was walking with his head down, his face lost in shadow.

Cracknell pressed on relentlessly. It was obvious that he had guessed Styles' infatuation, and was acting to stamp it out in his customarily brutal fashion. 'I'm sure that I don't have to tell a pair of young bucks such as yourselves how it can be when lovers are reunited. Suffice to say that we lost track of time *completely*. Next thing I bloody know, Boyce is outside, shouting for a servant to bring his supper. And the bugger's damned close – almost at the tent. So, Maddy pulls on her petticoats, stuffs the empty bottle in a trunk and tries to order her hair. I tug on my boots, gather together my clothing, steal a final, delicious kiss – and then squirm out under the back, like a hound digging its way under a bloody fence!'

Over at the barricades, there was a solitary rifle report, ringing through the darkness and echoing faintly against a distant, unseen cliff-face. Several thousand heads turned, accompanied by a great rush of muttering. Officers and sergeants yelled for information, attempting to ascertain whether anything definite had been seen.

Cracknell, unperturbed by this interruption, continued with his lurid story. 'So there I was, in the middle of the camp – not so very far from here, in fact – all but naked. And quite, *quite* drunk into the bargain. Maddy, bless her, can't take much, so I'd sunk most of the champagne myself. And worst of all, there was a gaggle of junior officers, right there before me, reaching for their swords. Chased me right out into the fields, the blighters did. And then, all of a sudden, they bloody well gave up. A few oaths and they were gone, just like that.'

'You were out in open country, Mr Cracknell?' Kitson asked, unable to restrain his curiosity. 'In which direction?'

'To the north-west,' came the insouciant reply. 'Towards Sebastopol.'

'Did you see any sign of the Russians, sir?'

Cracknell shook his head. 'No, Thomas, I did not. Evening was closing in. My only desire at that point was to return here, to my fellows, and find myself a drink. I ran back to the barricades with all the speed I could muster.' He nodded nonchalantly at the restless camp around them. 'Attracted a fair bit of attention along the way.'

There was a pause. Kitson blinked incredulously. 'You caused the alarm, Mr Cracknell?' The senior correspondent's behaviour, as he had learned through a succession of practical jokes and grandstanding confrontations, could be disruptive indeed; but this was well beyond the scale of his usual japery. 'This little patch of bedlam is all your handiwork?'

Cracknell grinned, rubbing at his bulbous, drink-reddened nose. He shrugged in unrepentant admission. 'The men certainly need the bloody practice, I tell you. Although they managed to snag me, look!' He broke off to fumble with his greatcoat, as if searching for something. After a few seconds, he held up the right side and poked his finger through a neat bullet hole. 'Ruined, and four pounds it cost! I've a good mind to bill the fellow responsible.' He started to laugh again, wiggling the finger from side to side. 'Look at that, Mr Smiles!'

Styles looked up sharply, not at Cracknell's coat but straight into his eyes. 'Styles,' he spat with naked loathing. 'My name is *Styles*, damn you.'

Swiftly interposing himself between them, Kitson put an arm across the illustrator's chest and forced him back a few paces. Styles' face was flushed; he was smarting painfully both from the disappointment itself and the elaborate spite with which it had been conveyed. He strained hard against Kitson's arm, seemingly eager to lunge at Cracknell and do him an injury.

Kitson gripped the black velvet jacket, taking hold of it with both hands. Their boots, pushing in opposite directions, slipped a little on the muddy ground. 'Mr Styles,' he said, his mouth close to the illustrator's ear, 'I must beg your forgiveness. I did mean to tell you earlier, but—'

Styles shook him off with considerable vehemence. 'Don't trouble yourself on my account, Kitson!' he growled, clearly determined to show no weakness. 'Don't suppose that I need your damned *protection*!' He had been halted, though; he took two confused steps that led him in a small semi-circle, so that he faced back the way they had come.

Kitson looked around; Cracknell, well satisfied with how

things had gone, was striding onwards, his mind already on other matters. 'Not my intention,' Kitson replied disarmingly – and somewhat dishonestly. 'Not at all. I swear it.'

Styles gave up on his wrathful display, sighing heavily and shutting his eyes. 'Forgive me,' he mumbled, splaying his fingers against his brow, now more ashamed than angry. 'It is nothing. The error is mine. I – I see now that it was before me all the while.'

'Your attitude does you credit, Mr Styles.' Kitson gave the illustrator's shoulder a companionable pat. 'And you are best out of this business, believe me. It will bring those involved nothing but difficulty.'

Styles responded with a couple of halting nods. He was biting hard on his lower lip. The junior correspondent wished that he knew his new colleague better, so that he could tell whether this display of mature-minded acceptance was genuine.

'I think that we shall go back to our tent and get some rest.' Kitson craned his neck, trying to locate their senior amongst the host of soldiery that trudged around them. 'I'll inform Mr Cracknell and then we'll—'

Up ahead, painted upon a whitewashed board suspended above the shako helmets and undress caps, was a large black '99'. They were entering the camp of the 99th Regiment of Foot, the Paulton Rangers – from which Cracknell had fled semi-clothed only a couple of hours earlier.

'Good Lord,' Kitson exclaimed. 'Surely not.'

He hurried forward to the sign, and caught sight of Cracknell approaching one of the larger tents, of the sort reserved for senior regimental officers, which had been pitched a short distance away from the main avenues. Before it, around a lamp set upon a barrel, were arrayed Lieutenant-Colonel Boyce and his staff. They were conferring urgently, like participants in some dramatic biblical scene from the school of Caravaggio. Their coatees were darkened to the colour of port, and the dense patterns of gold braid on their cuffs and epaulettes glinted in the lamplight as they pointed off into the gloom.

And then, without a moment's hesitation, Cracknell of the *Courier* swaggered before them.

4

'Have them flogged,' Boyce was saying coolly, adjusting his cocked hat. 'If they are so drunk that they cannot rise from their tent, let alone lift a rifle, then they must be flogged. Before the entire regiment, at first light.'

Captain Wray saluted and was about to go back to his company when his eyes flickered to the side, and a look of absolute disgust twisted his previously expressionless features. Boyce followed his gaze. Mr Cracknell, the despicable Irish war correspondent, was sauntering casually into their lamp's nimbus.

The Lieutenant-Colonel drew himself up to his full height, glowering fiercely at his adversary. He was a tall, athletic man of forty-five, his neat oval face adorned with a magnificent moustache that was the pride of his existence. Thick and dark above his narrow mouth, it tapered to two sharp silver points, both of which stuck out from his nose at precisely the same angle. It required a daily half-hour of careful maintenance. But the result was worth it – a moustache so perfect, so forbidding, that it inspired awe and respect in equal measure. Boyce liked to think of it as a symbol of sorts, an example to the men of the importance, and also the possibility, of keeping up appearances in their current trying circumstances.

It was an indication of his wrath that, as he faced the *Courier* man that night, he forgot his moustache completely. The Lieutenant-Colonel was not stupid; he knew that something had begun back in Constantinople. The blasted Irishman had been drawn to his wife like a fat, hairy fly to a piece of perfumed meat. Throughout their stay in that cramped, broken-down, filth-caked city Boyce had been dogged by the feeling that every time he entered Madeleine's private rooms, someone else, someone male, had just left them. In the fields of Varna this feeling had grown stronger; whenever he returned to his tent, there had been the rustling of canvas covering close escapes, guys swinging in the wake of recent passage, and strange, conflicted expressions on the faces of his men. And now, after a few days without this feeling, it had suddenly returned in force when he had greeted his wife that afternoon.

She'd been all innocence and light, of course, claiming that her state of undress was in expectation of his arrival. This had been said so earnestly that Boyce had almost checked his laughter; he honestly couldn't recall the last time they had been intimate with one another. Probably late one night, back in Chelsea, when he'd come home from the barracks full of brandy, shown the little minx the back of his hand, and then exercised his conjugal rights without delay. Hardly roses and poetry, he had to confess; but he was her husband, damn it, and a man of action.

As he searched the tent, throwing furniture this way and that, he heard a scuffling commotion outside. The Lieutenant-Colonel emerged to be told that several of his subalterns had run off in pursuit of an intruder. When they finally returned, they were lined up and ordered to explain themselves. Lieutenant Francis Nunn, the oldest and best-born among them, declared that they had chased what they believed to be a Russian spy out of the camp. Gently stroking his moustache, Boyce looked Nunn in the eye. The boy could only meet his gaze for a second or two, before staring out over his shoulder. It was quite plain that he was lying, both to protect Mrs Boyce and to save his commander from embarrassment, but he wouldn't change or enlarge on his story. Boyce didn't need to hear it, though. He knew that it had been Cracknell.

And now the foul knave stood before him, the horrible,

stout little paddy. It made his dishonour all the more acute to think that this wretched specimen was setting the cuckold's horns upon his head. Boyce was convinced that Madeleine had responded to the fiend's advances in order to cause him the greatest possible humiliation. He felt as if his anger would split him open.

'What the devil is this rogue doing here?' he roared. 'Get rid of him, damn it!'

Gathered around the lamp was Arthurs, the 99th's quartermaster, and Nicholson, its surgeon, both of whom were somewhat the worse for drink; Boyce's adjutant, Lieutenant Freeman, who was beginning to look decidedly unwell; and several field officers, including Captain Wray and the Majors Fairlie and Maynard. Of this group, it was Wray who ordered two private soldiers from the shadows and gestured for them to seize hold of the newspaperman.

'Good evening, gentlemen,' said Cracknell in his snide, insinuating manner, sidestepping the privates with practised expertise. 'My colleagues and I are merely passing by, doing our duty to the British people and investigating the alarm. We happened to find ourselves close to your camp, and wondered if you could perhaps enlighten us. *Are* the Russians attacking? Is battle to be joined this night?'

Another civilian scurried up behind him. Boyce dimly recognised this new arrival from Varna – he was the *Courier*'s other correspondent. Although a thin, shabby figure of a man, he still had significantly less of the clown about him than the Irishman.

'You there,' the Lieutenant-Colonel called imperiously, ignoring Cracknell altogether. 'Be so kind as to keep your blasted mick under control. We allow them in the army on the condition that they don't ever speak. I suggest your paper adopts the same policy.' His officers – all except Maynard, Boyce noticed – guffawed at this cutting remark.

'Do excuse our senior correspondent, sir,' the journalist replied with a reasonable approximation of humility. 'He is merely excited beyond measure by this great and noble enterprise – and is especially eager for sight of the enemy. As are we all.'

The Irishman barely tried to suppress a disrespectful snigger. His junior glanced in his direction; the collusion between them was plain. Boyce realised that this must be the same correspondent Wray had blamed for ruining the mission he had been given that afternoon; and indeed, the Captain was staring daggers at him right then. The fellow was not the gentlemanly face of the *London Courier*, as might have been hoped. There was obviously no such bloody thing.

Boyce felt the last of his patience evaporate. 'You are aware that the Russians read everything you publish, aren't you?' he bellowed. 'That all the sensitive information you so thoughtlessly reveal about this army goes straight to Moscow, and is then wired on to the generals at Sebastopol? That having you two blackguards here compromises us all? Why, if it were my decision, your kind would be sent back to England on the first—'

He was interrupted by the all-clear, the sharp notes cutting through the chatter of the camp. When the torrent of shouted orders began a moment later, there was a palpable relief to them. Quartermaster Arthurs let out a gasping huzzah, so glad was the old sot that they had been spared a night-time attack.

'No Ruskis tonight, then,' Cracknell announced, rubbing his hands together. 'D'you know, I think we'll go and have a jaw with your brigade commander. Sir William is bound to know what's what. You have quite enough on your plate, what with restoring order to your errant regiment.' The vile Irishman paused archly. 'And your lovely young wife having just arrived with us from Varna.'

Do not rise to it, Boyce instructed himself strictly, do not rise to this bald provocation, he is trying to make you seem a weak fool in front of your men – *do not rise to it*. Almost of their own accord, his fingers found the hilt of his sword and wrapped around it as tightly as they could.

'Enough of this idiocy.' He turned away. 'See them off, this instant.'

In the corner of his vision, Boyce noticed the departing correspondents meet with another civilian, a tall man in a black jacket, plainly part of their hateful little band, who had been lurking on the margins. Dear Lord, he thought bitterly, how many of them are there? Cracknell repeated his impudent intention to call on Sir William Codrington, waved a mocking, theatrical salute – and then was gone.

The men of the 99th looked to their commander. 'Any man of this regiment,' he said slowly, 'seen consorting with that rapscallion in any way will face the lash. Regardless of rank. Is that clear?'

Amidst the general affirmation, Major Maynard had a query. 'But surely, Lieutenant-Colonel, it is our responsibility to ensure that the press—'

But Boyce was in no mood for the plebeian Maynard and his caveats. Speaking over the Major in a loud, weary voice, he instructed the field officers to return to their NCOs. Then he retired to his tent.

No candle or lamp burned inside. In the dim blue half-light Boyce could just make out the central pole and the small table set at its base, but nothing else. He stood near the flap, calming himself, checking his moustache. She was awake. He could hear her breathing, and the faint rustle of her clothes; he could sense her alertness, her watchfulness. She had been crouched at the tent's entrance, he guessed, listening to the exchange outside, and had then thrown herself into a shadowy corner when she realised that he was approaching.

Boyce cursed his decision to bring her out to the Crimea. It had been pride, plain and simple. She had been going back to London, her passage booked and paid for. Then, aboard the steamer that had borne him across the Black Sea, he'd fallen into conversation with some old acquaintances of his from the Artillery Division. They'd opined that no married officer of good breeding would even think of leaving his spouse behind at this stage in the campaign. To do so, they had declared contemptuously, was to bow to silly modernising talk – behaviour quite beneath a gentleman. Someone, Boyce couldn't even recall who, had asked after the enchanting Madeleine, wondering whether she was following them to the Crimea. Indignantly, he'd replied that of course she was, in a few days' time when it was safe; and then sent word of this change of plan back to Varna as soon as he was able.

He should have known that the degenerate Irishman would be on her the instant she landed. But he could hardly send her away again now. Such a prompt reversal would be the talk of the camp, and an admission of defeat by a truly unworthy foe. No, she must stay. The campaign would surely be a short one, at least – it could only be weeks before the Russians ceded the peninsula. He would simply have to be vigilant. That such vigilance was at all necessary, however, infuriated him beyond measure.

'You bring me such disgrace, girl, such dishonour, that I would be forgiven almost anything I did to you,' Boyce said quietly, into the darkness. 'Were I to blacken your eye, who could possibly think ill of me? Or perhaps if I loosened a tooth?' He swallowed. 'I could break your damned jaw, you wretched *slattern*, and no one would—'

Boyce thought he heard her whisper his name imploringly; but then, a fraction of a second later, Lieutenant Freeman called for him with uncharacteristic vigour. He swept back outside, ducking under the canvas. Close to the lamp was a horseman in a shell jacket and gold-laced forage cap. It was Captain Markham from the divisional staff.

'Sir George's compliments, Lieutenant-Colonel,' said Markham briskly. 'Lord Raglan has sent down his commands.'

Boyce nodded, straightening the front of his coatee.

'All regiments are to strike tents at daybreak and assume full marching order.' The Captain's horse paced beneath him. 'We are moving on Sebastopol.'

5

'The epithet "unforgettable" is employed all too readily in our excitable times, but the sight of our Allied Army – British to the left, French to the right, Turks to the rear – as it advances across the landscape of the Crimea warrants its use without reservation or fear of hyperbole.'

Kitson tried to clear his throat. It was uncomfortably tight with thirst, and his tongue felt like it had been tacked to the roof of his mouth with viscous glue. Putting this from his mind as best he could, he jotted 'too much?' in the margin of the page before him and continued reading.

'A short distance back from the great cliffs and ravines that distinguish its coastline, this peninsula bears a marked resemblance to the Downs of our own homeland. Grass as smooth and green as that of any racecourse covers softly undulating plains, whose surface is broken only by clusters of pale rocks. The columns – fully four miles long, from tip to tail – flow easily across this terrain, the immense stripes of red and blue glittering with steel as they march gallantly onwards to meet their foe with colours flying. Our Light Brigade has been assigned flanking and reconnaissance duties, and the Earl of Cardigan's men dash back and forth across the fields with a brave, impetuous energy. Spirits among the soldiery are high, as well they should be; sight of any senior officer, British or French, brings forth as mighty a cheer as—'

Someone was shouting his name. Kitson laid his pencil flat against the pocketbook, sat up and looked over the side of the supply cart in which Styles and he had lodged

44

themselves. Directly beside this vehicle tramped the left-most column of British infantry, an amalgamation of the Light, Fourth and First Divisions. This vast formation, so solid and resolute that morning when Kitson had started his account, was growing slack as ever-larger numbers of men slowed and even stopped, overwhelmed by fatigue, disease and the fierce afternoon sun. Across a bloated river of shakos and field packs, he saw Major Maynard, who stood waving atop a gentle rise on its opposite bank.

The Major, accompanied by a corporal, had been helping a pair of his private soldiers leave the line. Both were evidently succumbing fast to cholera. A strange silence had descended upon the army, allowing Kitson to hear Maynard instruct the two invalids to rejoin the regiment at camp that night, once they had recovered themselves sufficiently to walk. The officer then set off down the rise and straight into the column, pushing his way through to Kitson's supply cart. He was a thickset man of about forty with a greying beard and a routinely frank expression. Drawing level to the cart, he placed a gloved hand on to its side.

'Mr Kitson, d'you seek your senior?'

Kitson grinned at the clear suggestion in Maynard's voice that this might well not be the case. After the clash with Boyce, and a subsequent (rather desultory) attempt to speak with some of the more senior officers, Cracknell had vanished. He had not shown himself at the *Courier* tent – even as dawn had arrived and his juniors had set about dismantling it and then dragging it down to the beach to be loaded on to a transport vessel. 'I suppose so.'

Maynard chuckled. 'Then the word is that he's right at the front of the column, harassing the 11th Hussars. They say that Cardigan is ready to run him down.'

'Why am I not surprised, Major?'

'That was quite some performance he gave last night. He's developing a real talent for aggravating my commander, isn't he?' The Major stopped smiling. 'That's maybe something you might wish to discuss with him, Mr Kitson – being the more rational of the *Courier*'s correspondents.'

'Faint praise if ever I heard it. And I'm afraid that he

would heed me less than anyone, Major. All we can do is to endeavour to keep them well apart, and hope this campaign is over as quickly as is being predicted.' Kitson turned over a page in his pocketbook and readied his pencil. 'With that in mind, may I ask your opinion on the rumours that Russian forces have been sighted around the Heights at the mouth of the Alma valley – interposing themselves between us and Sebastopol?'

Maynard eyed him wearily and opened his mouth to reply. A loud smashing sound nearby distracted him; some thirty yards back from the column, a group of lancers, splintered off from the Light Brigade, were kicking in the door of a squat peasant cottage, half-hidden in a thick bramble bush. They pulled at the shards with their white-gloved hands and piled inside. Kitson hoped that its inhabitants had abandoned it and fled to safety, well out of the army's path. Some of the marching infantrymen looked over without much interest.

'The noble 17th,' the Major muttered disapprovingly. 'Such robbery is a shameful part of army life, Mr Kitson, as I'm sure you've discovered by now. A part that I for one hope the scrutiny of the press might help to discourage.'

Kitson remembered the statuette and Cracknell's cursory response to the story of its destruction. 'My hope also, Major, but there is scant interest in such matters, and a delicate balance must be struck between—'

Maynard, glowering at the cottage and the horses tethered outside it, was not listening. 'I shall stop them.' He removed his hand from the cart's side and straightened his cap decisively. 'Whether they'll heed an infantry officer – well, we shall see. Good day to you, Mr Kitson.'

The column swallowed Major Maynard back up again and the supply cart trundled on, leaving the lancers and the cottage behind. Kitson glanced around. Styles was perched on a barrel at the other end of the cart, still sketching absorbedly. Loath to interrupt him, Kitson flicked back the page in his pocketbook and looked again at the paragraphs he had written that morning. Something about their triumphal tone was unsatisfactory. He tapped his pencil against his thumbnail; and then noticed Styles' drawing folder, tucked between two crates not far from where he sat. It occurred to him that neither he nor Cracknell had actually inspected the illustrator's work yet – a lamentable oversight indeed. He reached for the folder and unlaced it.

Top of the pile was a loose, urgent recollection of the exchange that had occurred before Lieutenant-Colonel Boyce's tent the night before. It depicted the moment Cracknell appeared before the officers of the 99th. Styles had captured perfectly the contrast between the senior correspondent's careless pose and the startled rigidity of those he confronted. The drawing was animated yet unmannered; accurate yet unfussy; balanced yet dynamic. Kitson drew in a deep breath. He'd been wondering why exactly O'Farrell had been so keen to hire this Mr Styles, given his evident inexperience – and here was the answer. Robert Styles was a man of true ability, of genius even, far beyond the hack illustrators who were usually employed by the *Courier*. Put an artist of this calibre in front of momentous events such as those unfolding in the Crimea, and something of significance was sure to result.

The correspondent leafed through the pile, his smile broadening; there were studies of the minarets and towers of Constantinople, of groups of people huddled against the rail of the *H.M.S. Arthur*, of the landing zone drawn from the sea. All were similarly expert. Then he came to one that made him stop.

It was a portrait of Madeleine Boyce. She was seated in a deck-chair, one hand raised to shield her eyes from strong sunlight. She appeared pensive, as if contemplating something away in the distance. The scene had been treated informally; it showed a young woman, fashionably dressed, relaxing on the deck of a ship. Yet the image was infused with a beauty that entirely transcended this mundane setting. It was plainly a work born of a lover's ardour. The man who had drawn it, Kitson realised, would not give up on its subject as easily as Styles had seemed to do the evening before. There was more to come regarding the *Courier*'s illustrator and Mrs Boyce.

47

Kitson closed the folder and got to his feet. Arms extended slightly to keep his balance in the rocking cart, he made his way to its rear. 'Mr Styles,' he called, 'ready yourself. We must move to the front to find Cracknell. They say he is up there somewhere, badgering the cavalry.'

He reached Styles' side and saw the vista laid out before him. In the wake of the columns was scattered a multitude of spent and dying soldiers, shed from the advancing army like dusty red petals. This was what the illustrator had been drawing with such furious concentration: not magnificence, not glory, but suffering and ignominious death. The sheet in front of him contained studies of collapsed, cholera-ridden men, doubled up in agony or lying insensibly in pools of smoky shadow. Kitson stared hard at Styles for a moment. Ashamed by the vulnerability he had displayed the previous day, the illustrator was trying to cauterise the tender part of his soul by pressing it against that from which it had so naturally recoiled.

'Come,' Kitson said abruptly, handing over the folder. 'We have to go.'

They jumped from the cart and began to walk quickly up the line, their light packs and relative freshness enabling them easily to outpace the exhausted infantry. Without slowing, Kitson lifted his pocketbook and put several heavy pencil strokes through the morning's paragraphs.

Slowly, as Kitson and Styles worked their way along the column, the landscape around the Allied Army began to change, the wide, smooth plains rumpling up into a series of ridges and hollows. They passed several burning farm-steads, the trails of black smoke mirroring those issuing from the fleet steaming along to their right, out on the shining expanse of the Black Sea. This was not the work of mere looters – its purpose was obliteration, done to deny the invaders shelter and sustenance. The Russians were not far away.

The vanguard of the vast army was marked by a concentration of the richly coloured flags and banners that were dotted throughout the columns, and a large block of mounted officers that included several senior generals from the French and British forces. Kitson's thirst, however, was now so intense as to confine his interest solely to locating Cracknell and obtaining something to drink. All in the British ranks suffered as he did; the correspondent grew increasingly mystified as to why no provision had been made to supply this basic want. The young illustrator, too, started to complain about his parched lips and throat. Kitson, his manner entirely serious, assured him that Cracknell would be waiting for them just past the next ridge, cradling a huge stone jug of water. He warmed to this notion, adding bunches of luscious grapes to the picture, and succulent Crimean melons, and ripe peaches too, all heaped plentifully at their senior's feet. Styles could not help laughing at this unlikely vision.

The real Cracknell, however, continued to elude them. He was not bothering the cavalry, as Maynard had reported; a short distance inland, reconnaissance squadrons of scarlet-trousered hussars were galloping across the ridges entirely unimpeded, whooping and whistling as they went. Nor was he trying to speak to the generals. There was no sign of him anywhere. Their little quest was starting to seem hopelessly misguided.

Suddenly a febrile tremor ran through the mass of infantry. Hundreds of soldiers broke from a fatigued plod into a run. The few who still wore their packs shrugged them off; they surged between two low hills, entirely ignoring the protestations of their officers. The *Courier* men, buffeted by charging bodies, tried vainly to work out what was going on. Had artillery been sighted? Were these men running for cover – were Russian cannon about to be loosed? Unable to resist the human tide, they were carried along for fifty yards or more, past the hills and into a shallow valley, before being shoved to one side. The cause of the disruption was revealed. A small river, little more than a stream, was dissolving the infantry column as if it was made from dry sand.

Styles yelped in panic. 'By Jove, Kitson, they'll drink it all up!'

Kitson gave him a withering look. 'Mr Styles, not even the British Army could drink up an entire river.' He looked at the redcoats fighting to get at the trickle of muddy water – and was sorely tempted, for all his high-minded scorn, to rush down and join them. 'We must bide our time.'

It was then that he noticed a familiar, stocky figure, standing atop a moss-spotted rock – the only person in that valley who seemed indifferent to the river. Cracknell had a telescope up to his eye, and was studying something with keen interest.

Kitson smiled, relieved to have finally tracked down their leader. He nudged Styles with his elbow. 'Look at that, Mr Styles. As cool as if he was at the Epsom Derby.' Cupping his hands around his mouth, he shouted out Cracknell's name.

The senior correspondent lowered the telescope immediately and turned towards them. His face broke into a wide grin, and he yelled something back that could not be heard over the commotion down by the river. He started to point insistently.

This gesture directed his juniors to a company of horsemen, riding along the crest of the valley's opposite side. They wore bearskin caps and embroidered kaftans bound at the waist by thick leather belts. Their long beards were brushed into sharp, two-pronged forks. Each had a barbed lance in his hand and a musket across his back. They were like nothing Kitson had ever seen before – irreducibly alien, like characters from a fantastical novel set in exotic eastern lands – and they were *close*, no more than a hundred yards away. Somewhere behind him, the Allied buglers began to sound. The men in the river looked up, falling quiet; a good number started to hurry back to their regiments.

The horsemen remained in full view for a few more moments, trotting on with deliberate insouciance, returning the scrutiny of the soggy redcoats. Then they spurred their mounts and were gone.

Cracknell's voice thundered throughout the valley. 'Cossacks, Thomas!' he cried excitedly. *'The enemy!'*

Manchester
May 1857

1

The short, guttural howl was alarmingly loud, and seemed to come from directly below Kitson's window. He started, dropping his pen, which then rolled across the threadbare rug and under his desk; he'd been pacing the attic's meagre length in his shirtsleeves, trying to relieve the constricting ache in his chest whilst reading through the afternoon's work. Before he realised fully what he was doing, he'd rushed from his rooms, down three flights of stairs and out through the tenement's peeling doors.

Princess Street was shadowy and quiet, with only a couple of small tradesmen's carts progressing along it. To his right, Kitson could see the brightly illuminated thoroughfares of the warehouse district, still heavily populated by both pedestrians and traffic despite the hour. The faint haze of factory exhalations, ever present in Manchester, hung about the street in silky drifts tinted orange by the distant gaslight.

Kitson listened for the sound again. A large crowd of spinners started up the street, clearly just released from their labours, strands of unwoven cotton still clinging to their rough clothes. He guessed that they were heading across town towards the concert rooms and drinking dens of Deansgate. Several already had bottles in their hands, which were being passed round with aggressive, determined merriment. After a burst of hard laughter, they began to belt out a bawdy song. *'She's a rum-lookin' bitch that I own to,'* they roared, *'an' there is a fierce look in 'er eyes . . .'*

Slipping into a side alley, Kitson walked along the tenement's wide brick flank until he stood under his window. Back on Princess Street, the spinners strode noisily by; and then a gurgling moan came from somewhere up ahead, further down the alley. Kitson went towards it. Away from the neat grid of commercial streets around Piccadilly, of which Princess Street could just be considered a part, Manchester soon crumbled into a ramshackle maze of winding passages, interspersed with foul-smelling doorways and grubby, impassive casements. Where there were lights, the even yellows and oranges of gas were replaced by the glaring white-green of lime, lending a spectral pallor to the few who passed beneath them.

It took Kitson some minutes to locate the source of the moan. A man wrapped in a cloak lay sprawled in the corner of a stinking, unlit yard. It was too dark to see any more than this. He approached the stricken man slowly, crouching down and stating that he was there to help. The man merely whimpered in response. Relying on touch, as he had been taught, Kitson took the man – who was narrow-shouldered and light, and easily moved – in his arms and began to examine him. It had been many months, years in fact, since Kitson had performed such ministrations, yet he found that he had forgotten nothing; the medical procedure was still deeply impressed upon his mind. Feeling the glimmer of a long-lost confidence, he quickly discovered a metal object jutting out of the man's side, something like a long nail with a catch of some sort at its end. There could be no doubt – this man was in serious danger, and had to be taken to a hospital as soon as possible. Kitson rose slightly to lift him, hoping to get the man to an alley where help could be obtained more easily.

This adjustment caused the uncomfortable pain that had been lingering in his chest all day to intensify abruptly. He gasped, his hand going instinctively to the deep scar on his ribcage. Beneath the scored skin, his lungs rattled as they tried haltingly to draw in sufficient air. The man, meanwhile, was reaching for the object in his side. Too late, Kitson went to stop him – just as he succeeded in wrenching it out.

Blood spurted from the wound, splashing hotly on to Kitson's thighs. Its sickening metallic tang filled his nostrils, smothering completely the sense of purpose that had brought him into the yard. As he reeled, gagging helplessly, a half-heard voice spoke his name. It was unnervingly close, almost at his shoulder; he turned, but saw only blackness. Another voice called out, high with fright, from somewhere past the fallen man. Several others joined it a second later. They were talking in Russian.

Kitson tensed. The stones of the yard began to vibrate beneath him, faintly at first, but with a gathering, horrifying rhythm. A ripple ran through the fetid puddle at its centre. There was a dull rumbling, then a thud, and the sound of a shutter smashing; and then he was once more in the ruined suburbs of Sebastopol, a heavy artillery bombardment underway all around him. Others were nearby, his old colleagues – he could hear their boots, scrabbling frantically through the rubble. Several pistol shots were fired in quick succession. Brick dust, thrown up by a collapsing wall, made him cough hard. In the thick, soupy darkness, the body lying before him seemed to blur and shift, becoming someone else altogether. Kitson stared disbelievingly at this dreaded form, tears coursing across his cheeks and chin; and his guilt pressed down on him like a slab of icy granite, crushing him slowly beneath its weight.

With a violent shudder, the stabbed man barked out a single flat syllable, an awful, involuntary sound dredged up from deep within him. Kitson squeezed his eyes shut for a moment, swallowed down the bile that was burning his throat and fought to recover his reason. Variations of this waking nightmare had visited him before, on countless previous occasions, but it had not manifested with such disorientating vividness for some time. He blinked until he was firmly back in the present, wiped his wet face with trembling hands and forced himself to consider the person slumped before him.

Anonymous once more, the poor fellow had fallen silent and was apparently unconscious. Kitson had experience of such wounds; he knew that unless it was staunched right away, the victim would surely bleed to death. Ignoring the cramp that still bit at his chest, he struggled out of his waistcoat, screwed it into a tight ball and, guided by the flow of blood, pushed the wadded material hard against the injury. Then he turned his head and shouted for help with all his strength.

Moments later, to Kitson's enormous relief, a thin shaft of lantern-light fell across the alleyway outside. This lifted the darkness a little and enabled him to make a proper survey of the yard. It was choked with refuse, broken crates and rotting sacks heaped everywhere. Against this drab, mouldy backdrop, two objects stood out. A large parcel, freshly wrapped, had been dropped near the yard's entrance, and a velvet-covered hatbox stood in the puddle. Both bore the mark of one of the city's finest tailors. The story here was plainly a familiar one; a wealthy gentleman, pressed for time, had foolishly decided to chance the back streets.

Footfalls echoed out in the alley. Kitson, still holding his waistcoat against the wound, considered the hatbox again. Dirty water was slowly saturating the fabric, climbing darkly up its sides. It struck him as strange that the man's assailant hadn't bothered to take these new clothes. They would be quite valuable, certainly worth the while of any street criminal.

An elderly woman in clogs and bonnet appeared in the yard. Seeing Kitson and the wounded man, she gaped in horror. 'Goodness, what's 'appened 'ere? Murder?'

Hurriedly, Kitson explained that a serious assault had taken place – that the victim had been stabbed but lived still, and needed to be taken to the Royal Infirmary with all haste. Impressed by the efficiency of his speech, and the education evident in his diction, she bustled to his side. He indicated where the wound was, and asked if she would hold the waistcoat over it whilst he secured some fresh dressings – thinking that he would have to tear off one or both of his sleeves.

The woman consented, then bawled, *'John! Walt! Tamper's Yard!'* at the top of her voice.

Kitson stood, stretching his muscles. It felt as if he'd been hunched on the ground for hours, not minutes. His side remained acutely sore, and his limbs shook; the events of the past quarter-hour had left him exhausted.

Two sturdy workmen arrived, flooding the yard with light and causing shadows to leap and duck across its soot-stained walls. One was the same age as the woman, and held the lantern in his hand. The other was like a younger version of the same man – plainly his son. Seeing Kitson, they took a step back, the lantern-carrier muttering an oath. Kitson glanced down at himself. He was covered in blood. His trousers were black with it, his shirt and hands shockingly bright.

'This 'ere's the doctor,' said the woman authoritatively from the yard's floor. 'We've got to get this poor shaver to Piccadilly. Come on, John, look lively! Bring that light over!'

Then the stabbed man started to speak. 'Do not let me die here,' he whispered. 'Not in the gutter. I – I beg you.'

The voice, lisping its way through clipped Etonian vowels, was jarringly familiar. Kitson froze. 'No,' he said softly. 'Impossible.' How could *he* possibly be here, in Manchester?

'Who did this dreadful thing to you, sir?' the old woman asked. 'Was it robbers?'

'A cripple,' came the weak reply. 'Most horribly disfigured. I thought I – but . . .'

John was moving forward with his lantern. 'We'll tek 'im that way, Rose,' he said gruffly, pointing off into the night. 'T'Mosley Street. Not far.'

'Bless us!' the woman – Rose – exclaimed as she peeled back the man's cloak. ''E's a soldier!'

Compelled to turn around, Kitson caught a flash of a scarlet infantry coatee and an inch of braid; now all but certain, he bent down and turned the man over so that the lantern shone directly on to his face. Sure enough, there was that long fin of a nose, that narrow, protruding chin, those ridiculous whiskers. His patient was Captain Wray of the 99th.

Their eyes met. Even through the stupor induced by his wound, Wray clearly recognised Kitson. His lips, blue through blood loss, twisted into a frail sneer that expressed more fear and mystification than it did contempt.

Kitson stood back up and walked from the yard. He leant heavily against a damp-swollen doorframe and crossed his arms. So this was why he had run from his rooms, from his work, and searched through some of the city's grimmest corners; had knelt in filth, and used his own waistcoat as a dressing; had strained his chest in ways that might take weeks to mend, and stirred up old ordeals which he had toiled so hard to contain. To save Captain Wray. To save that detestable villain – that *killer*. He shook his head incredulously, almost too stunned to be angry.

'We're going to lift 'im, doctor,' Rose called. 'Carry 'im t'Mosley Street. Will ye follow, sir, and bring our lantern?'

More than anything, Kitson wanted to get away from Wray. The thought that he had the man's blood cooling on his hands disgusted him. Yet he found that he couldn't deny this good-hearted woman's request. It was not right that they should lose their lantern as a result of their misguided kindness. He resolved that he would follow them to Mosley Street and then leave, abandoning Wray to his fate – which, as he knew all too well, was still uncertain at best. It was no less than the brute deserved.

Collecting himself, Kitson watched from the alley as John and Walt took hold of the officer and then heaved him up between them.

''Ow about tha',' remarked Walt with some satisfaction. 'Light as a child.'

Rose still pressed Kitson's waistcoat hard against the wound. 'Come, sir,' she prompted as their ungainly group lumbered by. 'Our lantern, if ye please.'

'Very well,' Kitson replied evenly. 'I'll be directly behind you.'

At the sound of his voice, Wray let out a strangled groan. 'Keep him away,' he slurred, waving a finger vaguely in Kitson's direction. 'The damned *Courier* . . .'

Rose quieted him, telling him that the gentleman he pointed at was a doctor, and his saviour no less, not the wicked cripple who had done him such a nuisance. Then she began proclaiming their approach like a particularly stentorian town crier, in an effort to summon others to assist them – making any further discussion quite impossible.

As Kitson went back into the yard, he noticed something lying on the ground close to where the lantern had been set down. It was a thin metal spike, almost like a stiletto, covered in a sheen of blood – the weapon used to fell Wray. He paused to examine it. The catch at its end, he now saw, was a locking ring; and at its point, the triangular spike had been fashioned into the narrowest of blades. Captain Wray had been stabbed with a British infantry bayonet.

2

The lamplighters had just finished their work on Mosley Street, affording Jemima James a clear view of the crowd that burst excitedly from a side alley, quickly flooding the pavement and overflowing into the path of the early evening traffic. It was comprised of working people, in jackets of canvas and fustian; Jemima sat up, imagining at first that a disturbance of some kind was spilling over from a back-street pot-house. But no – she soon saw that this crowd were working together, towards a unified and compassionate purpose. They bore a man between them, lifting him up almost to shoulder height. He was a soldier, and no private of the line; the gold on his uniform suggested a captain at least. His face, beneath some outlandish military whiskers, was all but white, and an elderly woman was pressing a bloody rag against his side.

Jemima rose to her feet. Her face was now so close to the office window that her breath misted on its surface. 'Dear God,' she said. 'Be quiet for a moment, Bill, and come see this.'

Somewhat piqued, her younger brother stopped his story (an inconsequential piece of gossip to which Jemima had hardly been listening), crossed his arms and pointedly did not get up. He sat surrounded by boxes and parcels, the fruits of a long afternoon spent in the city's finest dressmakers, milliners and tailors. Jemima had endured many hours of solemn, tedious debate over the merits of ribboned flounces, pagoda sleeves and the like, longing all the while to be back in her rooms at Norton Hall, out of her corset, deep in a book or periodical. Bill, however, loved these expeditions. That day, he'd even arranged his own appointments so that he could attend hers as well, and had been a terrible pest throughout. She simply could not be trusted, he'd declared, to select something suitably of-the-moment for the Exhibition's opening ceremony, which was sure to be the event of the season – and if she looked dreary and widow-like before Prince Albert, he would never forgive himself. It had been an outright clash of wills, resolved only by uneasy compromise.

Jemima considered Bill. He was sprawled in his chair, glowering back at her. As usual, his clothes were of the very best quality, and included precious dashes of taste and individuality, like his purple silk necktie and the faint navy stripe in the grey of his trousers. Not for the first time, Jemima wondered what their father honestly made of this dapper son of his, who had no profession yet spent so much of his time in town, and who at twenty-six years of age had never once been linked to a member of the fairer sex.

'I am going outside,' she announced, 'to find out what has happened, and who that poor man is.'

This succeeded in prising Bill from his seat. He crossed the office, glancing at the commotion in the street. 'Is that really wise, Jem? It is Saturday evening, y'know. The mills will just have let out, and the liberated operatives will be debauching in their usual boisterous manner.'

'Your intimate familiarity with the habits of the labouring classes never ceases to astonish, William.' Jemima retied her bonnet. 'I'm sure that we will be quite safe on Mosley Street.'

Bill, checked by this oblique reference to his more clandestine pursuits, swiftly changed tack, arguing instead that the carriage would be there for them at any minute. They could hardly afford to be wandering off into the city when Father would surely be expecting them at dinner. Jemima ignored him, knowing he would follow anyway.

Mosley Street, unquestionably one of Manchester's finest, was home to a number of the city's most august businesses and banks, as well as several prominent cultural societies. The facing rows of grand buildings, many fronted with columns and marble, blocked out all sight of factory chimneys. The crowd bearing the injured officer had come to a halt before the shadowy portico of the Royal Institution. Some began calling loudly for the police – rather unnecessarily, as every constable in the vicinity was already converging upon them with all speed. The victim was set down on the pavement; Jemima watched as the constables tried to reach him through the thickening circle of onlookers. There was a ragged clamour of voices as a dozen different accounts of the attack were delivered at once. After a few seconds of this, a short bulldog of a police sergeant shouted sternly for silence, and then began methodically to extract what solid information he could, devoting much of his attention to the old woman who still tended to the officer's wound.

All traffic along the street had come to a halt. Jemima took this opportunity to cross, with her brother a step behind her.

'By Jove,' muttered Bill as they drew near. 'I believe I know that fellow. Saw him in Timothy's only a couple of hours ago, in fact, having a new dress uniform fitted for the Exhibition's opening ceremony. He's from the 25th Manchesters – a major. Name's Raleigh, Raymond, something like that.'

The sergeant conscripted a dray that had stopped close by to convey the injured major up to the Infirmary at Piccadilly. As the driver began shifting aside the crates that were stacked in his vehicle to make room for his passenger, the major was lifted again. Under the sergeant's careful direction, he was moved slowly to the rear of the cart, past where Jemima was standing.

Finding a last reserve of strength, the major made a feeble attempt to squirm free. 'Get that blackguard away from me,' he croaked desperately. 'Keep him away, damn you!'

The sergeant had noticed Jemima; she was conspicuous on the fringes of that humble crowd. He now shot her an apologetic glance. 'Excuse the language, ma'am. He's in a state o' considerable confusion. Sure ye understand.'

Jemima looked around. 'Who could he be referring to, Sergeant?'

The policeman jerked his head towards a jacketless man sitting on the pavement, well apart from the main throng. 'Gent over there – but the poor cove's got it all backwards. That's the doctor what saved him, stopped him breathing his last in Tamper's Yard.' The many hands bearing the major knocked him inadvertently against the side of the cart. He squealed in agony and released a further stream of profanities. The sergeant patted his arm. 'Easy, there, easy!'

Impulsively, Jemima decided that she would meet this heroic doctor. He was propped against a lamppost at the corner of Bond Street, staring down at his hands. They were shining with water; he'd plainly just been washing them at the pump that stood nearby, to clean off the major's blood. A rusty lantern stood at his side. As she approached, she realised that he was talking in a harsh, low voice, as if admonishing himself.

'Excuse me, doctor,' she began, feeling a little awkward. 'Permit me to introduce myself. I am Mrs Jemima James.' She hesitated. 'I am told that your intervention prevented this man's death. A noble act indeed.'

He looked up sharply, his face hard and lean in the gaslight. 'It was not *noble*, madam,' he replied. 'And I am no doctor.'

Immediately, Jemima's interest was roused – this man had just saved a life, and yet seemed not only angry but strangely ashamed. She smiled disbelievingly. 'Surely you have medical experience of some kind, though? How else could you have treated the major over there with such skill and success?'

'He is a *major?*' The man's tone was faintly hostile.

Jemima nodded, studying him. 'So my brother tells me – from the 25th Manchesters. And he is in your debt.'

The man pulled himself upright. Jemima saw that his shirt and trousers were stiff with drying blood. 'I did little enough, in truth. The major may die yet.'

He was silent for a moment, as if contemplating this bleak fact. Jemima noted that he had not denied her conjectures. She glanced at his boots, always the best indicator of wealth; they were inexpensive and a long way past their best. Perhaps he was once a medical student, she thought, obliged to abandon his studies due to lack of funds.

The man moved back from the edge of the pavement, smoothing his hair and straightening his ruined shirt. There was pleasing angularity to his features, interrupted only by deep crescents beneath the eyes, etched into the skin by want of rest. When he spoke again, his initial terseness was gone.

'You must excuse my attire, Mrs James, and my manners. It has been a trying evening.' He looked past her to the cart bearing the wounded officer, which was preparing to start up the street towards Piccadilly.

Jemima perceived that he was considering flight. 'Tell me, sir,' she said quickly, thinking to halt him, 'if you are not a doctor, then what are you?'

'I am a newspaperman.' He made a shallow bow. 'Thomas Kitson, madam. Of the *Manchester Evening Star.*'

Bill appeared breathlessly at Jemima's side. He congratulated Mr Kitson for his efforts, shaking his damp hand before speculating briefly on the identity of the assailant. Then he informed Jemima that he was going up to his club to tell Freddie Keane and the rest of the chaps about the attack. Jemima tried to contain her irritation; this was typical of Bill. He would now stay out all night, roaming the very same streets he had been voicing such caution about ten minutes earlier – leaving her to endure their father alone. It had happened on countless previous occasions.

'Mr Kitson,' she said brightly, 'would you do me the honour of taking some refreshment in my father's office across the street? You must be in need of fortification after your labours, sir, noble or not. There is brandy, isn't there, William?'

The deal had been proposed. Bill furrowed his brow, but he was not about to object. He nodded, mumbling an affirmative. Mr Kitson tried to protest, but was too tired and too courteous to disappoint her. After accepting Jemima's invitation, he went to the cluster of working people close to the cart – not to check on the injured officer but to point out the location of the rusty lamp to a couple of workmen. It was most extraordinary. He seemed to be actively avoiding the man he had saved, as if he had some personal objection to him. Jemima could not account for it.

Bill walked Jemima and Mr Kitson back to the office, leaving them with the desk clerk. They sat before the window, Mr Kitson moving a chair next to the one Jemima had occupied earlier. The clerk, watching their bloodstained guest very closely, poured a tumbler of brandy and brought it over, setting it on the wide sill. Mr Kitson picked up the glass, hesitating when it was close to his lips. It was clear that he still found something about his hand profoundly distasteful. He had washed both quite thoroughly at the pump, but had evidently not managed to clean them to his satisfaction. Swallowing the liquor in one swift gulp, he put the glass back down and muttered an apology for his hastiness.

Jemima knew little of the *Evening Star*, but she felt that this man could not be a representative example of its staff. He had no real accent, for example – one would surely expect a correspondent from so modest a publication to be a Lancashire man from the lower middle classes, with the speech to match. I'd stake my library, she mused, on Mr Kitson being a recent arrival in our city. Adopting a cordial tone, she began to inquire politely about his situation.

He proved an agreeable if somewhat opaque conversationalist. He'd been in Manchester only since the end of the previous year, as she'd guessed. Other things about him, however, were more surprising.

'I am the *Star*'s society writer,' he revealed. 'A street philosopher, I believe it is called in these parts.'

'A *street philosopher*?' Jemima didn't try to hide her amazement. 'A professional gossip, you mean? The spy who lurks on the margins of our parks and theatres, labelling everyone who passes him with some acidic, facetious sobriquet? Surely not! I mean – you must excuse me, Mr Kitson, but you hardly seem the type.' As a rule, Jemima tried to keep well clear of any publication that vaunted such writing as part of its appeal. It tended to be facile in the extreme, tawdry and vacuous, concerned only with fashion, scandal and money. And it was proving increasingly hard to avoid.

He appeared unperturbed by her reaction; there might even have been amusement in his eyes. 'You flatter me with your doubt, Mrs James, but it takes more expertise than you might realise. There are important lessons to be learned, you know, from the living panorama of the modern city – lessons in the ever-shifting chances and changes of life.' He turned his face away from the window as the major's dray rolled past, a chattering crowd trailing behind it. 'Besides, I was in urgent need of a position, and it was the only one available.'

Was this a mordant joke, or in earnest? Jemima found that she could not tell. 'Are you working now, Mr Kitson? Can I expect to feature in the next edition of the *Star*?'

The smile was a brief one, and obviously infrequent. 'No, madam, I'm afraid that I have other responsibilities at present. My paper has no dedicated art correspondent, you see, so they have assigned me to cover the Exhibition.'

This disclosure made Jemima immediately impatient. The Art Treasures Exhibition was widely held to be the finest undertaking ever to be staged in Manchester, the city's answer to the Great Exhibition of 1851. A vast display had been gathered from the private picture collections of the country, and then assembled in a modish iron-and-glass structure at Old Trafford, on the outskirts of town – well away from the grime of the factories. Charles Norton, Jemima's father, was on the ninety-strong committee of local luminaries who had brought this thing into existence, and she had been made to listen to his boasting and self-aggrandising on the subject for the better part of a year. The building was to be opened in three days' time, with all the pomp and splendour that the rich men of the city could procure. The trip to town for new clothes had been Jemima's final trial before the occasion itself.

'The Exhibition,' she intoned heavily, dragging the word out to its constituent syllables. 'Do you concur with the general chorus of opinion, then, Mr Kitson, and believe that it will be a magnificent triumph?'

'I do, Mrs James, very much so.' He paused. 'But you, I think, do not.'

Jemima sat up in her chair. 'I simply look around me, sir,' she responded with some energy, 'at the slums of Salford, and Ancoats, and elsewhere, and then at the glorious Art Treasures Exhibition, and the many thousands of guineas that have vanished into it, and I cannot help but think that if the masters of the Cottonopolis were really interested in the benefit of all, as they so frequently say, they would realise that an art exhibition is a long way down the list of things that our urban poor require.'

'I must say, madam,' Mr Kitson murmured, 'that for the daughter of a labour-lord, you are quite the radical.'

This was the first indication he had given that he knew who she was, and in whose premises he sat. 'So I am told. Often by the labour-lord himself.'

He smiled again. Mr Kitson and I are forming quite an acquaintance, Jemima thought. She willed further delay upon her coach, thinking that she could happily sit exchanging views with this man for the rest of the evening. Something, at least, had been salvaged from a tiresome day. Across the room, the clerk cleared his throat loudly and turned over a page in his ledger.

The *Star*'s street philosopher began to offer his own opinions on the Exhibition. As he spoke, his ironic nuance fell away and was replaced with warm conviction, making Jemima feel frostily cynical by comparison. For him, the Exhibition was the first in a tradition, the harbinger of a new age: a popular art exhibition, staged for the country at large. Gone would be the days of art being solely an attribute of privilege. With this exemplar, he claimed, the exclusive galleries of old would have an egalitarian counterpoint, and the fruits of mankind's finest endeavours would be available to all.

Jemima was familiar with this position, and frankly thought it a little idealistic; but had never heard it outlined with such eloquent sincerity. 'You feel strongly on this subject, Mr Kitson,' she observed. 'One might reasonably infer that you had been forced to spend time in these exclusive galleries you so despise.'

This dispelled Mr Kitson's enthusiasm completely. He stared

down at the office's elaborately tiled floor. 'I was an art correspondent on a London paper before I came to Manchester,' he admitted. 'I attended countless exhibitions – every one closed to the broad mass of society.'

'A London paper? Which one?'

Mr Kitson did not look up. 'The *Courier*.'

Now Jemima was intrigued. This man had left one of Britain's most prestigious journals, famous for the global scope of its correspondence, to write for the *Manchester Evening Star*, which was barely known even in the next county. 'Why, I take the *Courier* myself! I have probably read your work, Mr Kitson. I shall have to search through my old issues as soon as I arrive home. May I ask why you left?'

He became evasive, volunteering only that he had become fatigued with life in the capital and the vagaries of the London art world. There was something in his manner that made Jemima realise that this man had fled to Manchester. But what could be so bad as to make one look for refuge in the nation's workshop, writing street philosophy for a penny paper? There was an explanation here well beyond the fatigue that Mr Kitson claimed – although he was certainly a man on whom fatigue had preyed.

Jemima peered back into the room, at a row of framed prints on its far wall. 'Do you know, I believe there are some illustrations from the *Courier* in this very office. From the Russian War – the opening stages of the campaign, before the paper's coverage became so controversial, and—'

Mr Kitson sprung to his feet, startling Jemima and the desk clerk and almost knocking over his chair. He strode over to the prints and made a rapid survey of them, stopping before one that depicted the battlefield of the Alma.

'Mrs James, why on earth does your father decorate his sales office with such images?' The question was almost accusatory. He did not turn from the picture as he asked it; his earlier curtness had returned with his distraction.

Jemima remained quite calm. She directed a restraining glance at the clerk, who seemed ready to fetch a constable. 'For all your familiarity with Manchester society, Mr Kitson, you street philosophers clearly know little of our city's business affairs. Charles Norton's meteoric rise is one of the great tales of the town. And the late war played a crucial role in it.'

She rose from her seat, arranged her shawl around her shoulders and crossed the office to stand beside him. His eyes shone as if filmed with tears; his face was impassive, though, and he was gripping one hand with the other to stop them from shaking. They looked at the *Courier* print, at the hillside strewn with the dead, and she told him how her father had found his fortune.

Two and a half years ago, at the start of 1855, Charles Norton had been the master of one of Manchester's smallest foundries – the continuing survival of which was a source of some wonderment to the city's community of businessmen. When he had been approached by William Fairbairn of the mighty Fairbairn shipbuilding and engineering company and asked if he would be willing to travel out to the Crimea to conduct a preliminary survey for a personal project of his, Charles had been in no position to refuse. The favour of the Fairbairns meant much in Manchester, and there was a clear implication that further work might result from this expedition. Whilst there, however, in a decidedly uncharacteristic demonstration of charm and initiative, Charles had befriended several remarkably senior figures in the Quartermaster-General's department. The result of this surprising gregariousness was a sudden flow of contracts for the Norton Foundry.

'First there were spikes for the Crimean railway; then heavy buckles for horse artillery; then more buckles, this time for the cavalry, many thousands of them; then, after the war, buckles for the police, for fire engines and coal carts, for cabs and coach-makers and hauliers of all descriptions. The Foundry has enjoyed a late flourishing, expanding to more than ten times its original size. Strong, affordable Norton buckles on every saddle, belt and harness in England – that is my father's stated goal.' Jemima smiled wryly. 'Last year *Punch* christened him the Buckle King.'

Mr Kitson had managed to tear his attention from the print, and was suppressing his agitation by listening to her account with an absolute focus. 'That I saw,' he said.

Jemima's smile faded. 'Of course, a price was exacted for all this good fortune.'

The street philosopher looked at her inquiringly.

'My husband, Mr Kitson – Anthony James. He died of cholera at Balaclava.'

Her companion flinched, the fine web of lines around his eyes tightening. 'I am sorry, madam. I was aware that you had lost your husband, I confess, but I had no idea that . . .' His voice trailed off. 'Please accept my apologies.'

Jemima waved this away. 'You were not to know, Mr Kitson. The circumstances of Anthony's death are hardly common knowledge. And I have received enough apologies, sir, and enough pity, to last me several lifetimes. The truth is that my husband was quite determined to go, and would not hear otherwise. He was my father's immediate subordinate at the Foundry, and considered his presence on the expedition vital to its success.' Her voice quickened slightly. 'There was a great fashion for it, do you not remember, amongst a certain type of gentleman. They rushed out to the Crimea with a boyish zeal, hungry for adventure, as if it was all nothing but larks.'

Mr Kitson said nothing.

Bridles jangled outside, followed by a coachman's cry; a lantern flashed across the office window. The carriage had finally arrived from Norton Hall. The desk clerk, no doubt looking forward to solitude, darted out of the door and began berating the coachman for his tardiness. Their time together was fast expiring.

Jemima sighed, putting a hand to her brow. 'Oh, do forgive me. I sound as if I am still mired in events well over two years past.' She looked at him. 'I have very much enjoyed our conversation this evening, Mr Kitson.'

He inclined his head. 'As have I, Mrs James. My thanks again for the kind invitation.'

The clerk and coachman entered the office; the latter tipped his cap and then they began loading Jemima and Bill's packages onto the carriage. Bill's absence, being far from unusual, was not queried.

'Will you be attending the opening ceremony on Tuesday, sir?'

'I would be there, madam, even if my employer did not require it of me.' His eyebrow raised a fraction. 'I take it you will be going also, despite your reservations?'

'Like yourself, Mr Kitson, I am obliged to attend, but on pain of disinheritance. What of the ball that evening, at the Fairbairn house – the Polygon? Will you be there as well?'

He hesitated, as if unable to remember. Jemima regretted having asked; it did seem improbable that a society writer from the *Evening Star* would be welcome at such a gathering.

'No matter,' she said lightly. 'I shall look out for you in the Art Treasures Exhibition. Farewell, Mr Kitson.'

The carriage pulled away. Jemima settled back into her seat, watching Mr Kitson leave the office and cross Mosley Street. The stains on his shirt had dried to a muddy brown. He stopped on a corner and cast a last look at her carriage; then he stepped away into the shadows, hunching his shoulders against the evening's chill.

Jemima's mind teemed with questions about her enigmatic new acquaintance. What lay behind his attitude towards the man he had saved, his strange reticence about his time at the *London Courier*, and his extraordinary reaction to those prints? That this street philosopher bore a burden was plain to see, for all his sardonic detachment. The carriage left Mosley Street, rocking as it wheeled around across dung-caked cobbles of Piccadilly. Jemima looked out at the winding lines of gaslights and the people milling beneath, her thoughts turning to the bundle of old *Couriers* that she had packed away at the back of her wardrobe. She would find answers.

3

The study door closed with a deep click. Charles Norton, proprietor of the great Norton Foundry and employer of close to a thousand souls, dropped his hand from the moulded brass door-handle to the key that jutted out beneath, and turned it decisively. He then walked along an expansive bookcase to the window. In the darkness, he could just see the two gaslights mounted at the end of his drive. Back in the room, the visitor shifted position, with a slight suggestion of impatience; on the window pane before him, the black silhouette of a shoulder moved before the lambent reflection of the study fire.

'My thanks, Mr Twelves, for coming out to Cheetham Hill at this hour. I would not have summoned you if it was not urgent.'

There was a short silence. Then, slowly, the visitor drew in his breath. 'I'm sure that is the case, Mr Norton.' His voice was low and nasal, with a heavy Mancunian accent. 'And besides, midnight is not so late for one in my trade.'

Norton turned around. Twelves stood before the massy desk that dominated the study. He was tall and powerfully built, clean-shaven with close-cropped hair. Every piece of his clothing bar an over-starched shirt was black, or at least had been when first purchased. He held a battered stew-pan hat in his hands, and was regarding the labour-lord before him as if all his wealth and accomplishment were nothing – as if he were naught but a fat old fool not even worth the kicking.

'You enjoy something of a reputation, Mr Twelves. Men I trust have told me that you handle the matters set before you with both professionalism and discretion. My expectations are high indeed.'

Norton paused, allowing for a polite interjection, for an earnest assurance that he would not be disappointed. Twelves said nothing. He frowned at the man's brazen impudence. The very last thing he needed was yet another truculent employee.

'A business associate of mine was attacked earlier this evening,' he continued, a little briskly, 'in the centre of the city. He—'

'The soldier,' Twelves interrupted flatly. 'Found off Mosley Street just after eight. Major Archibald Wray – one of Colonel Bennett's men. Admitted to the Infirmary.'

Norton paused again, impressed despite himself by this parade of information. 'That is correct, yes.'

Twelves shrugged. 'Even odds on 'im lasting the night is what I hear. They say the attacker was a cripple – a hideous twisted thing, like old King Richard or summat from a fairy tale.'

This is a colourful fellow indeed, Norton thought as he took the note from his desk. It had been written in a strained hand, the pen strokes scratched across the paper, and in one corner there was a smeared, bloody thumbprint. The author had managed only three slanting, wobbling words: *Kitson is here.*

He showed it to his visitor. 'Wray sent me this. From his hospital bed.'

News of the assault, along with the note, had been brought to Norton at around ten o'clock. He had been dining alone, his daughter having retired early with a headache, his son having stayed on in town like the dissolute popinjay he was proving himself to be. After half an hour's anxious deliberation, he had sent for Mr Twelves.

The investigator glanced down but did not take it from him. 'Ye do not know who Kitson is, then, Mr Norton.' This was not a question. 'But the fact that the Major wrote this in what might well be 'is last moments on Earth rightly concerns you. Per'aps Kitson's this cripple, per'aps he's not.

73

But either way, he's important – and you need to discover who he is, what he wants, and most of all how he can be dealt with.' Twelves sounded distinctly bored by his own summary of the situation.

Norton nodded. 'I must stress again the need for discretion, Twelves. Very few people are aware of my connection with Wray, and I would keep it that way. I cannot chance any interruption to my affairs, not now.'

The investigator took out a notebook and began jotting things down in an economical hand. 'Aye, the timing is rather poor, an't it, Mr Norton? The eve of your Exhibition, with the Prince Consort coming to town, God save 'im.' Twelves turned a page. He continued to write for a moment before snapping the book shut and returning it to his pocket. 'We will find this Kitson for ye. I guarantee it. My comrades and I are like the mighty Argus. Once we turn our attention to a subject, nothing whatsoever escapes our gaze.' He spoke matter-of-factly, without pride. 'And once we 'ave 'im, Mr Norton, what then?'

The labour-lord blinked, running a hand through his white whiskers. 'I don't follow you.'

'Our Mr Kitson, I would wager, is bad news for the Norton Foundry. Running up against a man such as yourself, well, that makes 'im like a second Ajax, don't it, defying the lightning. And the end result will surely be the same.'

Norton scowled at his visitor uncomprehendingly. This Twelves, he was fast coming to realise, was something of an autodidact – that insufferable breed of working-class man who insists on flaunting his limited, self-acquired learning at every possible opportunity. Which was all well and good, but Norton could not see exactly how this precious learning had served him. His profession, if it could properly be termed thus, was by any yardstick a shameful way of earning a crust.

'He will be brought down,' Twelves enlarged, 'down low. It could 'appen sooner rather than later, if ye catch my meaning, with nothing about it that'd attract any attention to speak of. Manchester can swallow a man like you wouldn't believe.' He picked at his hat's narrow brim with a fingernail. 'Why postpone the inevitable, Mr Norton?'

Somewhat taken aback by this proposal, Norton sat heavily in the leather-bound chair behind the desk. He reached for a silver paper knife and began pressing its point against the palm of his hand, trying to disguise his alarm at how casually murder had entered their discussion. 'I . . . applaud your enthusiasm, Mr Twelves. For now, though, just discover what you can.'

Twelves, taking this equivocation as weakness, eyed him with cool, contemptuous pity. 'As ye wish, Mr Norton.' He put on his hat. 'Ye will hear from me soon. A good night to ye, sir.'

The investigator left. Charles Norton stared up at a display case of shining buckles mounted on the study wall, seized by a constricting sense of foreboding that threatened to suffocate him where he sat.

The Valley of the Alma,
Crimean Peninsula
September 1854

1

Lieutenant-Colonel Boyce rode the line on a black mare, the points of his moustache jutting out into the clear midday air like a pair of tusks, waiting for the order to advance.

'Look at that cunt,' muttered Private Cregg, scratching at his sweat-darkened armpit. 'Just look at 'im. Thinks 'e's king, gen'ral and pri' minister all rolled up inter one. God on the bleedin' throne.' He paused to spit a sour pellet of well-chewed tobacco through a gap in his blackened teeth. 'The cunt.'

'Aye,' agreed those who crouched or sat around him, 'the cunt.' They were careful to keep their voices down. The officers of the 99th, although deaf to complaints about the lack of decent rations and shelter, had remarkably good hearing whenever anybody had a bad word to say about the Lieutenant-Colonel. Dozens had been flogged raw for such indiscretion. Dan Cregg, however, wasn't bothered by the lash. They'd done him three times already since the day they set sail from Old England, and would do him as many times again, most likely. He'd erred countless times in his life, and considered his stubborn refusal to learn from these experiences to be bold, manly defiance. He would name things as he saw them, by God, and to hell with them all.

Coming to the end of the 99th, Boyce wheeled his mare about and started back again. Cregg squinted, lifting up his gun as if preparing to fire. 'It'd be so bleedin' easy,' he sneered. '*Bam!* And one less toff cunt in the world, drinkin' up all the brandy.'

There was a low, nervous chuckle. Cregg could be trouble, but today his comrades welcomed his disrespectful talk, if only as a distraction from the scene that stretched out before them. A wide, gently sloping plain, dotted with small copses and the occasional vineyard, led down some two miles to a hamlet of crude stone houses and barns. Behind this, fringed with trees, was the narrow, brownish River Alma. Rising up abruptly on its opposite bank were the Heights. To the men of the 99th, who were mostly from the south of England, these heights seemed positively mountainous, a daunting climb indeed; but climb them they must, for up there, like a dark burn across the soft green hillsides, was the enemy. The soldiers found their eyes returning to the massed ranks of Russians time and time again. For nearly two weeks they had been kept in constant expectation of an enemy attack; and yet here the bastards were, dug well into the perfect defensive position, waiting patiently in the warm sunshine. The redcoats swallowed hard, wiping their clammy palms on their trousers.

It was towards his own men, however, and not the Russians, that Lieutenant-Colonel Boyce's gaze repeatedly wandered. Like him, they were in full dress uniform; squirming and complaining, as the common soldier was so wont to do, tugging gracelessly at their tight tunics, and the leather chin-straps of their shakos, but smart and correct. Boyce had the junior officers well trained. Any attempt by a private to undo a button, or take off his helmet, would immediately be halted, and the miscreant's name taken for punishment.

If only the same rules could be applied to the other ranks, he thought angrily, as his eye snagged on the solid figure of Major Maynard, who stood at the edge of the 99th's battalion with a telescope in his hands, scanning the Heights. Boyce had made his desire for dress uniform quite plain at the regimental briefing that morning. And his own costume, from the shining leather of his boots to the plump ostrich feather bobbing on his cocked hat, perfectly demonstrated the sartorial magnificence available to the field officer prepared to invest in his wardrobe.

Yet Maynard's attire was mixed and decidedly well-worn: a shell jacket, dull boots, threadbare trousers, and a plain undress cap. The overall effect left one in no doubt about his plebeian origins. He looks exactly like what he is, the Lieutenant-Colonel thought – the son of a costermonger, who has wormed his way into Her Majesty's Army like a fat maggot into an apple, instead of purchasing his place like a gentleman. Boyce directed his mare towards the unfortunate Major, his fury mounting.

Madeleine watched the heated exchange between the two officers from the side of a low hill, just behind the main body of the Allied Army. Her husband, who was some distance from where she sat, seemed merely a little scarlet-faced doll, gesticulating with his tiny arms. With a sigh, she raised the gold opera glasses that lay in her lap. The cool metal touched briefly against the top of her cheek, just below the eye; and there Nathaniel was, glaring at poor Maynard as if confronting a child-murderer. Their argument was short-lived. Nathaniel rode away suddenly, cutting the Major off in mid-sentence.

A large group of officers' wives were sitting close to Madeleine, their backs straight as plumb lines, their noses lifted high in perpetual disdain. They cast frequent glances at her, their faces showing a mixture of supercilious curiosity and cold dislike. Beyond them, on the top of the hill, were the British generals and their aides, of whom there seemed to be a great many. Madeleine had no idea who any of them were, besides Lord Raglan, and that was only on account of his missing arm. That limb, as she was regularly reminded by Nathaniel, was lost at Waterloo, to a French cannon-ball. He would say this in the most accusatory manner, as if it was somehow her fault; but all she knew about the battle of Waterloo, besides the fact that Wellington's men prevailed and the French were soundly beaten, was that it took place a very long time ago. You could tell this, in fact, from a single look at the British commander-in-chief. Drawn and withered, and clearly exhausted, Raglan was an old man. His voice, which drifted down the hill occasionally, was demure, gentle, frail even. That is not a leader's voice, Madeleine thought.

She did not know what to make of this day. She understood, of course, that there was to be a great battle. All around the hill on which she sat, there were soldiers, many thousands of them, the British in red to the left, the French in blue to the right – allies now, united against a common foe. Beyond the French Army, out to sea, was a flotilla of battleships, ominously still, their cannon trained on the Heights. Heavy guns were being carted up behind the infantry, to pound the distant redoubts and earthworks within which the Russians lurked. Surely, a voice inside her protested, this was to be a terrible thing. Surely very many men would be killed. Surely Richard, who was down there somewhere, doing his duty to the *Courier* and the British public, was in terrible danger.

But spirits on that hillside were high. The other wives were talking amongst themselves with calm assurance, even laughing from time to time in the nasal, strangulated manner of English ladies. They were not behaving at all like women who, in a few short hours, might be widows. They discoursed at length on the Russian Army, how it was nothing but a disorganised rabble, a rag-tag assemblage of half-starved peasants, criminals and savages, marshalled by a degenerate aristocracy, all corrupted by their perverted religion. They confidently anticipated that this miserable band would crumble before the hard steel of British resolve; that victory would be both easy and fast. Madeleine looked out at the vast allied force, and made herself believe it.

The golden opera glasses, to her frustration, offered only a partial view of the battlefield. She could survey the allied armies, and even follow the winding white roads that ran over the plain before them, through the farms, and the pretty little village on the river's edge. But the hills beyond, and the Russians upon them, were only a brown blur. Cursing softly in French, she turned the small focusing wheel as far as it would go in both directions, pressing her forefinger against the tiny teeth that had been cut into it. It moved smoothly, but no image could be found.

Spotting her difficulty, an aide-de-camp from Raglan's staff came down the hill to her side. He was in his early twenties, slightly built, and dressed in a Hussar's uniform, his round, freckled face half hidden by a busby at least a size too large for him. Introducing himself as Captain Lichfield, he insisted that she borrow his army-issue telescope. 'And may I also suggest, ma'am, that you employ it to take a look at the nobles of Sebastopol, up in their pavilion near the tallest peak, having a jolly old picnic?'

Madeleine smiled warmly. She knew Lichfield's type well: the gauche young officer, so eager to please. 'How kind of you, Captain.' She extended the telescope, the sections sliding neatly into place. 'They watch the battle for amusement, do they, these nobles?'

'Oh yes, ma'am. A very popular Russian pastime, I'm told. I daresay they must be expecting to triumph.' Lichfield's uneasy chuckle was cut short by a terse summons from the top of the hill, calling him back to his duties. He bowed, and was gone.

Madeleine lifted the telescope up to her right eye; and there, under a striped canvas awning close to the summit of the Heights, was a gaily costumed group who appeared to be having something of a party. She could even make out the champagne flutes in their hands, and the laughter on their faces. It was a celebration, mounted in clear expectation of victory – a Russian victory.

Fearfully, Madeleine lowered the telescope a couple of inches. She suddenly found herself staring into a battery. The blunt brass snouts of the cannon poked through the earthwork defences. Behind them stood line upon line of grey-coated infantry, their muskets at the ready. They did not look half-starved, or corrupted, or disorganised. Indeed, they seemed to have much the same sense of grim, regimented purpose about them as the Allied soldiers.

Madeleine's vague alarm turned rapidly to tight, hot panic. She had to find Richard. She had to warn him, and convince him to come back with her, back to safety. Searching for civilians among the redcoats, she settled the telescope upon a series of black and brown backs, groaning aloud with each fresh disappointment. It is hopeless, she thought, tears stinging her eyes.

She considered jumping to her feet and running down the hill, but reason held her in place. Such action would give her away completely. It would be obvious that it was not Nathaniel she was looking for. And this, in turn, would give him proof of what he already suspected. Madeleine knew only too well what would happen then. She would be cast aside, reviled by society. That in itself did not frighten her. Life as an outcast with Richard would be better than any kind of life with Nathaniel; but they must be prepared. The war would be a short one, Richard said. They must be patient.

Calming herself, Madeleine wiped her eyes, cleared her throat, and then looked down at her husband through the telescope. He had drawn his sword a few inches from its scabbard, and was twisting the points of that wretched moustache while looking at his reflection in the blade. How she hated him. She still ached dreadfully from the reprisal he had inflicted two days previously, following his humiliation by Richard in front of his men. He had forced himself upon her with terrifying violence, spitting foul words about how he would ruin her for the Irishman, and beat her all out of shape; afterwards, as she lay bleeding and bruised on the floor of their tent, it had felt as if he'd succeeded. As always, Nathaniel had been careful not to mark her face, neck or forearms. Madeleine's appearance, once she was dressed, gave no indication of what had been done to her. This was her marriage – an unspeakably cruel ordeal, to which she had been consigned by a weak father flattered to have been approached by a well-born Englishman.

The notion sprung into Madeleine's mind, seemingly unbidden, that the coming battle might well provide the solution to all her troubles. Nathaniel was a conspicuous figure indeed, sure to attract the attention of those Russian riflemen. She gasped in shock, never having suspected that she was capable of such thrillingly brutal calculation.

Then she spied Richard, sauntering past the base of her hill towards the 99th. He was grinning broadly, a cigar stuck in his mouth, his faded jacket flapping open in the mild autumnal breeze; and she knew at once that it was worth enduring Nathaniel to be near him. Here at last was a man who was not in the least frightened or intimidated by her husband, who could see past the uniform, and the family name, and the legion of menacing lackeys to the worthless wretch cowering beneath. Her Richard was a truly brave soul, a man of robust warmth and plain-speaking passion. He would rescue her.

Madeleine leapt up excitedly, waving and calling out his name, all thoughts of Nathaniel gone, and any sense of discretion momentarily forgotten. But he carried on his way with no sign of having heard.

Kitson and Styles sat together on a low dry-stone wall, the *Courier* team's designated meeting place, a short distance behind the First Division. Both had spent a sleepless night listening to soldiers' songs and the distant barks of hungry dogs; and then a hot, tiresome morning watching the armies perform their countless preparations. The thought of what was to occur that afternoon, however, made any fatigue impossible. Both stared out at the valley before them with raw-eyed attentiveness.

Kitson attempted to keep them calm with light-hearted conversation. Discovering that they shared an interest in the French realist school, he was telling the story of how he had managed to meet Monsieur Courbet in Paris eighteen months before.

'We finished up in a gaming house close to the Sacré Coeur,' he said, 'where the great man proved himself something of a card player. He took all my money, then my hat, and finally my boots. I'm certain that he would have taken more, but I slipped from my chair to the floor, quite drunk, and could not be stirred to play another hand.'

Styles' laugh was a little too loud. His gaze did not stray from the valley for a second; his legs twitched with a surfeit of nervous energy.

As usual, Cracknell managed to catch them entirely by surprise. He threw himself to the ground at the base of the wall, its rocks shifting slightly with the impact. 'I've been over with some French officers,' he declared gleefully, 'talking of this and that. Drinking their coffee. Bloody good it was too – some leagues beyond the muck brewed up by our boys. But then, in my experience, all things French have a certain quality to them. Wouldn't you agree, Styles?'

Kitson checked his pocketbook and writing materials, wishing that Cracknell would refrain from his teasing for that one day at least. Styles looked away, seeming to ignore him; but Kitson could tell that a store of resentment was being built up, one that would eventually lead to retaliation.

But he could not dwell on this now. For all his annoyance at Cracknell's continued harrying of the illustrator, he was relieved to see that the senior correspondent was confident – exuberant, even – at the prospect of the coming battle. As the inevitability of combat had slowly impressed itself upon him, Kitson had felt a keen desire for guidance. After months of delay, he was to see his first major action as a war correspondent for the *London Courier* – yet he found that he had not the least idea how to perform this task.

Cracknell, though, clearly suffered from no such anxieties. Lighting a fresh cigar, he called the *Courier* team to order and adopted an easy, business-like tone. 'Now, my lads, the French are pretty certain that they're taking the right flank. Apparently there's a coastal path that the Russians have neglected to defend. A back door left unlocked, if you like. What of the British plan, Thomas?'

Kitson readied his pocketbook. 'I have a complete list of the divisions, Mr Cracknell, and of the battalions in each, and have made a note of their current positions – but as to the strategy they are to follow, I could discover nothing, nothing at all. It seemed almost as if there isn't one.'

The senior correspondent chuckled. 'This is Raglan we're talking about. Wellington will always be his master in matters of warfare. The Bear up a hill, John Bull lined up in front of it – Kitson, old fellow, I wouldn't be surprised if he just marches the poor bastards straight towards 'em, to weather the fire as best they can.'

Kitson hesitated. 'Surely not.'

Cracknell shrugged, unconcerned. 'We shall see, shan't we?' He got to his feet, tapping off some ash and squeezing himself between his subordinates; Styles promptly moved another six inches along the wall.

'Can I ask how we are to, ah . . .' Kitson took a steadying breath. 'How will we conduct ourselves, sir, once the fighting starts?'

Cracknell grinned mischievously. He turned towards the illustrator. 'Tell me, young Styles, if you were preparing a painting for the Academy, a scene from Shakespeare – from *Hamlet*, say – would you choose to present the protagonists, the Prince and his whole unhappy family, as one might see them from the front row, in all their terrible splendour? Or from the top of the upper circle, as no more than little dots scampering around the stage like trained fleas?'

'From the front row, of course.' There was a hard, competitive edge to Styles' voice. Kitson realised that he was determined to prove himself equal in courage and dedication to Cracknell – equal to the man who had won the heart of Madeleine Boyce. This was a troubling development. Their expedition on to the battlefield was being warped into a contest of daring.

Removing the cigar from his lips, Cracknell pointed at the illustrator in triumph. 'Exactly, lad – *exactly*. And that is how we shall position ourselves in order to depict this battle. In the very front row.' He leant around to deliver a firm pat to Kitson's shoulder. 'We want the truth, my friends, and the truth we shall obtain. Are we agreed?'

'We are,' Kitson replied, trying to suppress his uneasiness. 'Wherever you lead us, sir, we shall endeavour to follow, with our pens at the ready.' Styles nodded in mute agreement.

Cracknell was satisfied by this display of allegiance. 'I'm glad to hear it. And you must not fall prey to fright, d'ye hear me? The British Army, on the field of battle, is highly methodical; Christ, it's almost *mechanical*. These men have their formations and tactics seared on to their brains. They run on rails, and I know what to expect. We'll be quite safe. It's just a matter of staying alert, that's all.'

A bugle sounded, some distance away. The time was upon them. Kitson stood, and looked over at the sea of waiting troops. The officers were gathering together, conferring and pointing. Another bugle echoed the first, and then another; then a host of them, all making the same call. Slowly, the army climbed to its feet, the many thousands of boots rumbling like a great landslide as they stamped in the dust. Sergeants shouted for attention, whilst officers moved to the front of their battalions. Kitson felt a cold shiver of nausea. Inside him, behind the valiant certainties so forcefully elicited by the senior correspondent, lurked something else, something uncomfortably insistent and full of doubt; something that might well be fear.

This would not do – he had to keep hold of himself. He had his responsibilities, and not just to the paper. He looked over at Styles. The illustrator was holding his drawing folder in both hands, looking down at his boots with his felt hat pulled low over his eyes. His bottom lip was protruding slightly, an oddly child-like mannerism.

'This is it, my fine fellows!' cried Cracknell, leaping eagerly from the wall. 'This is it, by George! Think of the glory, of the work we shall produce! The Bear is to be soundly rebuked for his blundering incursions into helpless Turkey – and we will be here to see it! This will be the making of us all, you mark my words! Come, we must get ourselves forward.'

As Styles strode wordlessly towards the soldiers and out of earshot, Kitson signalled to Cracknell that he wished to speak. The senior correspondent paused, listening with a tolerance his junior knew would be but momentary.

'Whilst I don't for an instant question the wisdom of advancing with the attacking divisions, Mr Cracknell,' Kitson began carefully, 'I do find myself wondering what would happen should we be separated from our forces in the thick of the fighting. Do you think there is a significant risk of capture, or of—'

'Is that *fright* I see there, Kitson?' Cracknell broke in, his voice harsh. 'Are you choosing this moment to show a womanish side? You're not going to let us down, I hope – myself, or young Styles there, or Mr O'Farrell back in

London, who trusted you, an *art correspondent*, with this vital task?'

'No, Mr Cracknell,' Kitson replied firmly, 'my will is strong, I assure you. My concern is primarily for Mr Styles. He has only been with us for two days. I am worried that he is not ready, and deserves our protection.'

Cracknell's bright flash of scorn faded quickly to patronising amusement. He wrapped a conciliatory arm around Kitson's shoulders. The junior correspondent could smell the liquor on his breath, and see the shadow of dirt behind his ear. 'Ha! Uncle Thomas wants to look out for his best lad, eh? Well, no harm in that. You're alarmed, man,' he continued soothingly, 'and it's an alarming situation, to be sure. Perilous indeed, as you say – the guns, the Russians, vermin like Nathaniel Boyce leading our own. But you need to have a little faith,' he jabbed Kitson's collarbone with his finger in emphasis, 'in the resourcefulness of your senior.'

He pulled back his jacket to reveal an object within, poking awkwardly from his inside pocket. At first, looking past Cracknell's smirk, and the solid roundness of his belly, Kitson could not identify it. He could see a handle of polished walnut, hard and shiny amidst the grimy folds of Cracknell's clothes, from which stemmed greased metal mouldings, delicate parts carefully fitted together. Was it a tool of some kind? A new model of telescopic device, perhaps, which might enable them to hang back from the worst of the fighting?

But then he saw the chambers, and the long tube of the barrel, jutting down through Cracknell's jacket towards the small of his back. It was a revolving pistol.

2

Ten thousand men, four divisions of line infantry, marched across the plain towards the Russian guns. Music from a dozen regimental bands mingled together to form a dense martial cacophony. The battalion from the 99th was advancing at the centre of the Light Division, arranged into two long rows with its colours raised. Boyce, riding out in front, looked back over his troops with pride. The hours of drilling on the parade ground were showing their worth. Not a single private was out of place – more than could be said for some other parts of their division. He permitted himself a dry smile. Finally, after almost twenty years of service, he was leading men into battle. The Russians must be quaking in their boots, he thought, at the discipline, at the courage on display. What a glorious sight they must be!

The line approached a sturdy fence running across their path. Standing close to it, on the corner of a small cross-roads, was a crude fingerpost. It had been whitewashed all over; even the names on the signs had been obscured.

'Lieutenant-Colonel!' someone shouted. 'A word, sir!'

Boyce sighed. It was Major Maynard. Trust him to spoil the moment. 'What is it, Mr Maynard?' he replied impatiently, urging his mare over the fence. She cleared it effortlessly.

'The signpost, sir! It's been whitewashed!' There was alarm in the Major's voice. The soldiers marching behind Maynard, who were listening intently, all swivelled their eyes towards the white wooden fingers.

'Well of course it has!' snapped Boyce, wheeling around. 'They don't want to offer us directions to Sebastopol, do they? Honestly, man!'

Maynard glanced at the long row of attentive faces behind him, and then rushed forward, ducking through the bars of the fence and running up alongside his commander's horse. 'No, sir, with respect, I really don't think that's it,' he said forcefully.

Boyce felt his earlier fury return. Why his superiors sought to torment him by placing this dullard in his regiment was completely beyond his capacity to understand. And his wretched voice, with those horrible twanging vowels – it was, quite unmistakably, the voice of a commoner. 'Then what, pray, is it, Maynard?'

The line met the fence. It creaked as it went down. Soldiers flowed around the fingerpost.

'Artillery, sir. It's for their artillery,' Maynard answered. 'To indicate the limits of range.'

Boyce scoffed, and started to ride on. 'Oh, what absolute rot! Honestly, Maynard, I sometimes think—'

The report of the cannons rolled around the valley. A dozen white smoke-jets leapt from the midst of the Russian redoubts. The black mare started to rear.

Styles froze. There was a split-second pause, and then a shrill whistle, followed by a heavy thud, and shouts from the ranks before him. These were not shouts of distress, however, but of warning; the cannon-balls were hitting the grass some fifty feet in front of the line, and then bouncing towards it. The soldiers could see the shot coming, and step smartly to one side.

Recovering himself, he watched a ball roll away, smoking, across the plain. Some among the redcoats began to yell abuse at the Heights, mocking their enemy's marksmanship. Cracknell trotted on ahead, waving for his colleagues to follow. Styles was at his side in seconds, determined not to let the senior correspondent get ahead and thus have an edge when the time for valour arrived.

As they fell in a few yards behind the soldiers, he looked

the Irishman over, and wondered for the thousandth time what the divine Madeleine Boyce could see in such an empty cad, such an arrogant, self-aggrandising buffoon. It made no sense at all; and the worst of it, the part that made him truly sick, was the certain knowledge that despite the fact that she was being pawed by this scapegrace, freely consenting to it, *enjoying* it even, he loved her still. He loved her more than ever, in fact, with an aching intensity that felt as if it would send him screaming across the valley, straight towards the Russian guns.

But he was also quite certain that he was worth ten Cracknells. And this battle, he thought, gritting his teeth, is my great chance to prove it to her.

A ball whipped past him, so close that a gust of hot, bitter wind blew across his face. It seemed to be travelling much faster and higher than the two-score shots that had come through the 99th so far, and prompted a fearful spasm; a couple of feet to the left, and his campaign would surely have ended right there.

To his relief, this spasm did not linger. There was, in fact, a bizarrely jocular atmosphere to the advance that made his momentary loss of self-possession seem entirely unwarranted. The soldiers continued to joke and laugh whilst their bands played on gaily. The reports of the enemy cannon were distant and grand, like rolling drums, and their shots, including the one that had come so near to him, were still spinning away harmlessly. It was easy to convince oneself that all was well, that careful plans were being skilfully executed, and would lead to swift victory.

Kitson, who had been lagging, finally caught up with them, a hand on his hat like a man struggling through a gale. He seemed to be experiencing serious disquiet; his eyes were darting around furiously, trying to look in several directions at once. Could it be that the junior correspondent, having come this far, did not have the nerve for the challenge ahead – that he had reached the limits of his endurance?

Cracknell turned to them, beaming. 'You see?' he shouted cheerily over the noise of the marching army. 'What did I tell you? All quite mechanical!'

Kitson, plainly unconvinced, crouched down as low as possible whilst Cracknell did the complete opposite, pulling himself to his full height, and then stretching and craning in order to see as much as he could. Keen to align himself with the brave, Styles did the same. He caught sight of Lieutenant-Colonel Boyce, out in front atop his black horse, surveying his dodging men with distaste, yelling at his sergeants to enforce the regimental line.

Then came the sound – metal striking flesh, tearing through it in an instant, like a butcher cleaving a rack of ribs. All laughter among the soldiers stopped abruptly, as if a door had been suddenly slammed on a room full of merriment, and an astonished scream took its place.

Boyce's voice rose above the cannon-fire, somewhere up ahead. 'Leave the wounded for the bandsmen! Leave them where they fall, I don't care what rank they are! Keep steady! Press the advance!'

Another shot hit the 99th. Styles saw a red spray arc briefly above the soldiers' shakos, and a wet ball slide into the grass behind them. The band stopped playing and left the advance. Their sergeant, a flute in his hands, stared dumbfounded at the smattering of broken bodies that lay in the wake of the line. Some of the injured writhed and wailed, others lay motionless and silent. Several were clearly dead, their skulls caved in or organs horribly exposed. Close to the *Courier* men was a corporal, his left leg sheared off just above the knee, a creamy substance oozing from the white shard of bone, mixing with his blood. He was trying to sit up, puffing frantically.

It was happening too quickly, far too quickly. Thinking to take stock for a moment, Styles came to a halt; and found himself staring dumbly at this corporal's wound, drawn in by the savage colours, the cruelly attenuated form, the hideous, pulsing rawness of it. His stomach cramped painfully, and sweat sprung out across his brow, but he could not look away.

A hand closed on his shoulder. It was Kitson. He was facing the sergeant, who still stood resplendent and useless in his richly embroidered bandsman's uniform. 'Aren't you going to do something?' he demanded angrily.

The sergeant started, as if shaken out of a trance. He rubbed his brow with his sleeve, and hung the flute on his belt. 'Orders are to carry 'em back. Fer – fer transport out.'

'Back where? Out where?'

The sergeant just shook his head. Hesitantly, the band members approached the wounded and began to drag them back towards the Allied camp. The corporal, gripped under each arm and trailing fluids, started to sob piteously, but after a few yards fell into unconsciousness.

'Come, Styles,' muttered Kitson. 'We must stay focused on our task. Mr Cracknell won't wait for us.'

Styles nodded, trying to right his stumbling spirits. Such sights were part of battle. Cracknell was up in front, just behind the army, a dirty black blemish on a row of glowing red, jotting something in his pocketbook. They were a good distance closer to the Russian cannon now, the balls cleaving the air above them with wallowing roars. As they arrived at the senior correspondent's side, a private further down the line was struck full in the chest and flung back violently through his fellows. Immediately, an officer began shouting for his men to fill the hole and keep to their places. The voice, high and lisping, sounded familiar; Styles stole a quick glance above the multitude of shining black shakos to see Captain Wray, waving his sword at his soldiers as if threatening them with it, cursing them vehemently for their cowardice.

A shell cracked overhead, a painfully sharp, ringing noise; and several soldiers below were dashed bloodily to the ground. Styles could see several mounted officers conferring ahead of the advance, displaying themselves to the enemy guns with studied nonchalance. An order was given, bugles calling along the line, and the massive force came to a halt. The redcoats lay down under the Russian fire, trying their best to bury themselves in the coarse Crimean grass. Styles realised that someone was tugging at his sleeve. Kitson was pulling him towards a small copse of silver-barked trees just behind the rows of stationary soldiers, in which Cracknell was already stowing himself. Another shell burst, closer and lower this time, throwing up clods of earth. The illustrator was dimly aware of blood-soaked grass, slippery under his feet; then he was lying on his belly in the heart of the copse. The soil beneath him felt cool through his shirt. He could hear the trills of birdsong in the branches above, even over the barrage. The birds must be trapped, he thought, too frightened to take the risk of flight across the battlefield.

Styles peered out through the undergrowth. Officers continued to ride the line, their heads high as if inviting death; shows of courage that even managed, in places, to coax embattled cheers from their men. Gulping down some smoky air, he took out a sheet of paper and a pencil. But he could not draw. His body, his thoughts and his emotions all seemed to be completely beyond his control. He could feel his limbs beginning to tremble. You can endure battle, he tried to tell himself. You are no coward. What are a few shells, some blood, and a spot of cannon-fire? You have to show Mrs Boyce that you are a better man than Richard Cracknell. You have to *show her*. These thoughts ran through his head over and over again, like an incantation intended to firm up the mind and steady the nerves. Yet still he could not draw. At that moment, his many years of artistic training, of study and tireless application, were utterly lost to him.

Kitson had positioned himself upright, behind the thickest trunk. All signs of his earlier anxiety were gone. He now seemed, to the quailing Styles, an enviable exemplar of composure. Notebook out, he was asking Cracknell the reason for the halt.

The senior correspondent checked something inside his jacket; then he climbed warily to his feet and pointed towards the far side of the valley, in the direction of the sea. 'Over there, look! The French are attacking. I should think that Raglan is waiting for them to take the coastal heights before continuing the British assault. All strictly by the book, my friends!'

Styles peered over at these heights. Above them, shell-fire was creating a constellation of drifting, star-shaped clouds. Tiny blue figures swarmed over the river and up into the foothills, breaking formation as they dashed forwards. Russians had descended to meet them, and Styles could see a vicious tangle of bodies where the two sides clashed. The dead dropped on to the steep hillside and rolled away from the fighting, their limbs flailing as they tumbled towards the river.

A series of shells exploded above the copse, deafeningly loud, shredding the soldiers closest to it and smashing several of the trees to splinters. Kitson and Cracknell were knocked to the earth, winded, landing alongside Styles. All three were splattered with sap and viscera. Looking up at the sky in terror, the illustrator saw dark shapes shooting away in every direction, so fast the eye could barely discern them. He thought at first that this must be the scattering of shrapnel; but then realised that it was the birds, finally forced to take flight into the iron-filled air.

On the low hill two miles back from the river, Madeleine watched as a group of Cossack horsemen rode into the empty village by the Alma. Each one wore a fur hat and a long green kaftan, and was carrying a burning torch. A few moments later, thick smoke began to belch from the quaint thatched cottages, soon engulfing large parts of the British line.

This was a dire development. Even with the help of Captain Lichfield's telescope, her hopes of locating Richard, of assuring herself that he was safe, had now dwindled away to nothing. She realised suddenly that the time had come. She had to act.

Lichfield himself was over at his horse, a large bay tethered thirty yards or so from the summit of the hill. He was stowing some papers in a saddle-bag. Madeleine waved to him, and he hurried over obediently.

'Captain, I must get *closer*,' she said, wrinkling her brow in pretty vexation. 'We are too far away here. It is all too far away.'

This was met immediately by a chorus of disapproving noises from the wives behind them. 'I'm afraid that's impossible, Mrs Boyce,' said Lichfield, mildly surprised. 'Quite out of the question. Surely you can still see well enough from here?' He nodded at his telescope, which lay in her lap.

Madeleine shook her head. 'The smoke.' She gestured with vague impatience. 'It makes it impossible to see.' She rose. 'I must be closer. Here is no good. No good at all.'

Lady Cathcart, senior amongst the wives, spoke up in a hard, pitiless voice. 'Look here, you little fool, don't think we don't know what you're up to. The very last thing your husband requires at this moment is you running out to him on the field of battle like some swooning adolescent. Now, we've endured your simpering nonsense all day. A little decorum may not have a place amongst your people, but you should know that amongst the British it is considered quite paramount.'

The other wives nodded, murmuring their agreement. 'Quite paramount, indeed,' echoed one piously.

Lichfield shrugged, smiling weakly, attempting to appear as one who was entirely sympathetic, but whose hands were very firmly tied. 'You must remain here, Mrs Boyce.'

Madeleine decided promptly on another course of action. She gave a heavy sigh. 'Then I shall return to camp,' she said quietly, lifting a limp hand to her brow. 'I fear it is all too much for me. Do not worry, Captain, an escort from my husband's regiment is nearby.' She handed Lichfield his telescope, bade him a sad farewell and started down the hill.

After proceeding a short distance, Madeleine stopped and turned around. The other wives had forgotten her already, returning their attention to the battle; whilst Captain Lichfield was back at the generals' side, receiving some lengthy instructions. The path to his horse was clear.

Madeleine's crinoline obliged her to adopt an awkward side-saddle. The bay, more accustomed to carrying hussars, shifted beneath this strange rider, snorting in bewilderment. She patted its neck soothingly, and urged the horse around the hill, away from its owner and towards the sound of the guns.

They soon arrived at the post road to Sebastopol, a dirt track that ran behind the advance at a rough diagonal. An artillery officer, seeing a lone woman riding in the direction of the fighting, called out to her in alarm. He rushed over in an attempt to take the bay's bridle, but was easily outrun.

Madeleine didn't know precisely what she would do once she was on the battlefield. She imagined finding Richard, pinned down by enemy fire, and galloping to his rescue. Having escaped the fighting, they would then escape the war, and her husband with it, running away together to somewhere they would never be found. She realised that actually bringing this wonderful flight about would be most difficult. Richard could be anywhere in that vast, chaotic valley. And there were other dangers – if Nathaniel were to see her out there, he would guess her purpose immediately. Yet Madeleine knew with a terrible certainty that if Richard were to die, she would die also. If there was a chance that she could save him, then she must act or be forever damned. She resolved to brush aside all her fearful doubts and simply respond to events as they unfurled, whilst keeping her object always in mind. Trotting towards the battle along the post road, she felt full of strong, clear-headed determination.

Despite the heavy screen of smoke, the cannon-fire up ahead seemed to be growing ever more intense, as if the gunners were attempting to compensate for the fact that they were firing blind by firing twice as often. Units of British horse artillery had joined the fight, rolling up close behind the lines of infantry. Even at a mile and a half's distance, the sound was quite overpowering. Madeleine wondered how anyone could stand it for more than a couple of minutes. And the landscape, so picturesque only two hours before, had been thoroughly despoiled by the passage of the army. Fences, hedges and trees had been blasted away, and soft green fields trampled to mud.

She cleared a low rise in the plain. Before her, at least sixty badly wounded infantrymen had been laid out along the sides of the road, flailing and thrashing in their agony. Bandsmen and a handful of civilian orderlies weaved amongst them, binding wounds as best they could with lengths of lint, and passing around canteens of water.

Too late, Madeleine tried to avert her eyes. The bay grew restless, unnerved by the smell of warm blood, lifting its hooves and shaking its head. Then a private, bleeding heavily from the midriff, began to screech in agony as she passed, a horribly high-pitched sound, his legs pedalling against the mud as if he were working a treadmill. The horse started, tossing its mane; then it stepped around the wounded man, leaving the post road and heading towards open ground. Madeleine pulled at the reins as hard as she could, but the animal ignored her completely.

She considered calling to the orderlies for assistance, but something made her hesitate; and before she could change her mind, the bay had quickened its pace to a canter, and she was forced to devote all of her energy to remaining in the saddle. Madeleine flung her arms around the horse's thick neck, and the bay and its helpless rider charged off into the battlefield.

3

Squinting, Kitson looked out from what remained of the copse. Close by were the soldiers of the 99th, gripping their rifles tightly. They had been lying down under fire now for over an hour. Every one of them was drenched with sweat, and flecked with dirt and blood. Their eyes, milky white in their grimy skin, were staring ahead, alert for incoming fire. The riverside village had all but burned to the ground, and the curtain of smoke was gradually being drawn away by the breeze, revealing their foe. The Russian fortifications, studied close up, seemed virtually impregnable; steep, dark walls of earth behind which bristled a multitude of musket barrels.

A mounted messenger was galloping along the line. He pulled up next to two senior officers; Kitson recognised Sir George Brown, the General in command of the Light Division, and Sir William Codrington, the Major-General who led Brown's first brigade.

'Here we go, my lads,' murmured Cracknell, spitting on the ground. 'This is it.'

The buglers began sounding the order to advance a moment later. Wearily, the soldiers got up once again, the officers taking their places in front of the long ranks. Raising himself on to his elbows, Kitson surveyed the ground before the army, stretching down to the banks of the River Alma. A significant proportion of the 99th, he saw, would be advancing through a vineyard, alongside the smoking ruins of the village.

'Hardly parade ground conditions, are they?' the senior correspondent said, noting the direction of Kitson's gaze. 'Be interesting indeed to see how they manage this one.'

Kitson did not reply. He was finding Cracknell's zeal for war increasingly unsettling. Neither had he fully recovered from his dismay at the sight of that revolver. It seemed to imply the horrible possibility that Cracknell's ambitions were not rooted solely in the journalistic sphere; that he might seek out a confrontation with the enemy, and attempt to win glory for himself through the spilling of blood.

Boyce remained in clear view, Captain Wray by his side, conferring heatedly with Major Maynard. Before long, the sturdy Major was dismissed, and sent back to his position on the line. He drew his sword as he walked back towards the ranks, swinging it from left to right as if attempting to ease stiff shoulders. He did not look pleased.

The Lieutenant-Colonel then turned his horse about, stood in his stirrups and addressed his soldiers. 'You men, you're about to go into action. Do not fire until you are ordered. Do not leave the line, for any reason – if you do, you'll taste the lash. You have taken the Queen's shilling, every last one of you, and you will honour your debt to her. I will make sure of it.' The bugles started to sound once again. Boyce raised his voice higher. 'Now, to battle! Advance!'

Cracknell shook with laughter as the army moved off. 'Good Lord, Boyce really knows how to put some fire in his troops, don't he?'

The enemy barrage picked up, pounding into the advancing redcoats. Kitson clenched his fists as tightly as he could and surveyed the assault. In the centre of the line, an exploding shell cut down five men as if they were made from straw.

'Looks a bit hot down there at the moment,' Cracknell said, lighting a cigar. 'I think we'll make a brief pause – allow them to cover a bit of ground before we pick up the pursuit once again.' He drew out his pocketbook and opened the cover. 'Let's get something down. Observations and the like. While they're still fresh in the mind.'

Kitson nodded and tried to work, but was unable to

compose more than fractured notes. A minute or so passed; Cracknell asked for another word for 'unstoppable'.

'Inexorable,' Kitson yelled back over the guns.

'Aha.' Cracknell made a correction. 'Of course. I knew that you were on this campaign with good reason, Thomas.'

Kitson smiled mirthlessly and carried on writing.

There were shouts, and the blasts of NCOs' whistles. The senior correspondent closed his book, got to his knees and looked down towards the river. 'Come, gentlemen. It is time for us to follow.' He heaved himself up, and started out on to the battlefield, stepping through the ragged, barely recognisable bodies that fringed the copse as if they were nothing more than fish heads in the gutters of a city market.

Kitson edged over to Styles, who had not moved. The illustrator had a piece of paper before him, on which he had succeeded only in making a crude study of a dismembered foot. 'Mr Styles,' he said, 'we are leaving.'

Styles quickly packed away his drawing equipment. He looked profoundly scared. Kitson found that he was strangely reassured by this, and liked the illustrator all the more for it. Fear was the only sane reaction to their current circumstances, and formed a welcome contrast to the unflinching bravado of their senior. Taking Styles' arm, he helped him to his feet. 'This way – towards the vineyard. Be sure to keep your head down.' Together, they ventured from the copse.

A heavier trail of corpses marked the path of the advance, bodies crumpled on the ground as if they had been dropped from a height, cast aside by some enraged giant. The loose stone wall surrounding the vineyards had been knocked down, swept away by the force of the line, its rocks kicked amongst the vines by the soldiers' boots. Clearing the remains of the wall, they ducked under the canopy of leaves. Cracknell was nowhere to be seen. The red tunics of the soldiers could just be glimpsed up ahead, moving through the closely planted vines. These provided little shelter from the Russian bombardment, shrapnel having torn through branches and men alike. The two *Courier* men stumbled across a ghastly slick of disgorged innards; Styles fell dizzily to his knees, retching so hard he lost his balance. Kitson leant over him, placing steadying hands on the illustrator's shoulders.

Cracknell pushed through the vine leaves next to them. 'And what's keeping you two, may I ask?' he demanded. A second later, he noticed the sheet-white Styles. The senior correspondent swore. 'What's the matter with him?' His eyes widened. 'Holy Christ, he hasn't been hit, has he?'

'No, Mr Cracknell, I believe he's—'

Cracknell's interest immediately diminished. 'Then what? A fever?' He turned away, checking the progress of the advancing troops. 'Surely he hasn't been around the miasmas of the camp for long enough to have contracted cholera?'

Kitson shook his head. 'No, sir, it is not that either.' He cleared his throat, bracing himself for a ferocious reaction. 'It is for the best, I think, if we pause again, to recover our bearings.'

The senior correspondent was not listening. His attention was given over entirely to the battle. 'Did you hear that, Thomas?' he asked, raising a forefinger. Kitson looked around vaguely, unable to make out any individual sounds in the hellish clamour that enveloped them. 'Muskets! They're within musket range – they must almost be at the river! Come, we must get closer!'

'A pause, sir, that is all I ask, so we—'

Cracknell stared at his junior in utter astonishment. 'A *pause*? What the devil are you talking about, man? We have to *keep up*! We have to *know*, don't you understand?' His irritation was growing with his impatience.

Kitson's careful detachment, straining throughout this exchange, started to give way. This was the ugly reverse of Cracknell's inspiring idealism and frequent invocation of camaraderie: a savage disdain for those he believed were failing or opposing him. The journey between these two attitudes seemed to be a short one indeed. 'You misunderstand me, Mr Cracknell,' he responded, as calmly as he could. 'I merely wish to do what is in the best interests of the *Courier* and its correspondents.'

The senior correspondent heard none of this. 'Oh, do what

you will!' He got to his feet, and started towards the Alma. 'I, at least, intend to do my duty!'

Boyce cleared the vineyard. A shrapnel gash on the mare's side was bleeding on to his left boot, and quite spoiling its shine. He'd tried wiping it with a rag, but this only served to make the problem worse. None of the annals of war, he reflected bitterly, told one that battle was such a confoundedly *dirty* business.

The musket-fire from the enemy positions started like a summer rainstorm. One, then two, then six shots; and then a downpour, the balls pinging off stones, tearing through vine leaves, and slapping into the mud with hissing plops. Boyce's unlucky mare caught one in her haunch, neighing in distress as she spun around, looking for her assailant. The Lieutenant-Colonel struggled to rein her in, his eyes fixed on the Russian redoubts. What an uncivilised horde, he thought. Their fire is utterly uncoordinated – haphazard, even. They have no conception of the basic codes and systems of combat. As he watched, a loose gang of them appeared above a crude parapet directly in front of him, perhaps a hundred and fifty yards up the hill. He could just make out their spiked helmets, and enormous dark moustaches, which were both untrimmed and unwaxed – could there be any plainer indication of their savagery? They did seem awfully close, though, all of a sudden. For the first time that day, Boyce became worried for his safety, and wished that his miserable troops would get the hell out of that vineyard.

Slowly, they emerged, in a rough semblance of the line, to be raked by the Russian muskets. Lieutenant Davy, who bore the regimental colours, was shot in the eye. His body folded neatly earthwards, the flag fluttering down after him. The men behind raised their miniés, and started to shoot back.

'Hold your fire!' Boyce yelled. 'Hold your fire, damn you! Wait for the order! Sergeant, take the names of those men! Lieutenant Nunn, the colours!'

The other battalions of the Light and Second Divisions were arrayed along the gentle slope of the riverbank on either side of the 99th Foot. Marshalled by their officers, they manoeuvred around each other and then plunged into the Alma. Boyce held back until the crossing was well underway, and then urged the mare forward; she leapt in gladly, as if believing that the waters would offer refuge from the battle. The river was cold, and surprisingly fast-flowing. Bullets, shells and shot from the enemy positions were beating the water to foam, and kicking up brown plumes of silt. Riding out to the middle, Boyce tried his best to enforce the line.

And then he saw him, like a sleek black vole, scurrying along behind the ranks of the 99th, and gingerly stepping out into the Alma. That blasted Irishman, the dishevelled paddy reporter, the one who Madeleine was, was – well, he couldn't even bear to think of it. What the devil was he doing here, Boyce wondered, in the thick of battle, at the moment of glory, soiling it with his despicable presence? He waited until the wretch was out of the shallows, and then spurred his horse towards him.

The mare, her eyes bulging with pain and confusion, almost ran the correspondent down. He was knocked to one side, stumbling headlong into the water. Surfacing, he flailed about in an effort to reclaim his cap, which had fallen off and was now floating away.

'Explain yourself, cur!' snarled Boyce over the thunder of the guns.

Cracknell, having seized the lost cap, pulled it back on. 'Why, Lieutenant-Colonel Boyce,' he grinned, 'fancy us meeting here! D'ye have a word on the battle for the *London Courier*?'

'You will *fall back*!' Boyce cried, pointing furiously in the direction of the vineyard. 'You will remove yourself from the field, this instant!'

Staying mostly submerged, Cracknell's grin grew yet wider. 'I'm a civilian, Boyce,' he replied tauntingly. 'You can't give me orders, y'know!'

'You compromise us *all*, you damnable rogue—'

A shell smacked enormously against the surface of the river, detonating an instant later. Boyce's horse bore the brunt of the blast, a large fragment ripping open her throat.

With a choking, rattling whine, the mare sank down, her blood gushing into the Alma. Boyce, blown from his saddle, found that he was caught up in its tattered remains. Muscles screaming in protest, he fought dazedly to prevent the dying horse from collapsing on top of him and pushing him beneath the surface.

Cracknell leapt backwards through the water, his legs paddling as he tried to propel himself as far away from the explosion as possible. The notion of coming to Boyce's aid did occur to him; he wasn't the sort to let a man die in front of him simply because they weren't the best of friends. But the stricken officer had attracted the attention of the enemy's riflemen, and bullets were flicking at the water all around the carcass of the mare. Sorry, Boyce old fellow, he thought as he lunged away through the bloody current towards the opposite bank, it's just a mite too risky.

The senior correspondent was finding the experience of battle extremely invigorating. He'd seen action before, of course, during his famous tour of the North Americas; he'd witnessed the Texas Rangers exchanging fire with the Mexican Army, and skirmishing with Comanche braves. But that was all as nothing next to this. Being there, in the heart of it, made him feel almost indescribably good, as if the fire of life crackling within him had been pumped up to a roaring inferno by a huge pair of celestial bellows. He could swear that his vision and hearing were sharper. Nothing escaped his notice; he felt powerful, completely in control, ready for whatever lay in store.

The loss of his subordinates did not overly concern him. They would either learn, and harden, or they would be left behind. Seeing them so reduced, bold young Styles especially, had proved to Cracknell that they had no hope of ever matching his mettle and resilience.

At the mercy of a treacherous river bed, many of the soldiers around him had slipped over on to their backs, or fallen forwards down unexpected slopes into deep water. Packs and uniforms, heavy enough on land, became unmanageable when waterlogged, and several privates were being dragged under by the weight of their gear. Others were rendered immobile, cursing breathlessly as they splashed and floundered, left for the Russian snipers to pick off at leisure. Unencumbered, Cracknell was making rather more rapid progress. For a moment, he considered offering assistance to some of the more beleaguered cases; the shout of orders from the shore, however, made him realise that to get thus involved would be to miss the next stage of the attack, and so he left events to take their natural course. One could not, after all, afford to be overly sentimental about the private soldier on the field of battle.

Leaving the water, he staggered up the riverbank through a light fall of musket-fire.

'Over 'ere!' called a voice somewhere ahead. 'Oi, cock, over 'ere!'

Grasping at this sound, Cracknell weaved towards it, flopping down under the lip of a long rocky ledge some ten yards beyond the Alma. Several companies of redcoats were hunched there, awaiting their instructions. They were, he saw, from the 99th; it was one of these men who had called out to him.

It soon became clear which one. 'These bastards can't shoot for bleedin' toffee, can they, cock?' shouted a sallow, sunken-featured fellow who crouched close to where he lay. Incongruously cheerful, he turned to the man next to him, who was praying under his breath, and poked him in the ribs. 'Only time you've got to worry is when they're *not* bleedin' aimin' for you! Eh, pal?' The praying man did not react. His garrulous comrade returned his attention to Cracknell. 'You're one o' those newspaper blokes, ain't you?'

Cracknell, panting hard, looked up at the soldier and gave a quick nod. He took off his cap and flicked it against the pale stones of the bank, darkening them with a heavy spray of river water.

'Well, be sure to mention of Private Dan Cregg in yer tellin' o' the battle, Mister Reporter, as a right bleedin' brave an' upstandin' soldier!' This obvious untruth drew a snicker from the men around them. Cregg leant forward and prodded Cracknell with a dirty forefinger. 'Did I really see the

107

Lieutenant-Colonel take a ball back there in the river with you, cock?'

Cracknell, still too breathless to talk, nodded again.

'Ha!' Cregg slapped his palm against the stock of his minié. 'Serve the bastard right! Serve him bloody well right! Bleedin' Boycie – got what 'e deserved, an' no mistake!'

'Enough of that talk, Cregg! D'ye want yet more punishment, man? D'ye *enjoy* it, perhaps?'

Major Maynard was striding along the row of crouching soldiers. Sight of him brought Cracknell immediate cheer. Maynard was a solid cove, and a soldiering man through and through – the very fellow for this situation. Laudatory phrases began to form in his mind.

'No, sir, Major!' replied Cregg with a crooked smirk.

Maynard squatted down next to Cregg. He was about to speak to the soldiers when he noticed the sopping, panting correspondent stretched out amongst them. 'Mr Cracknell!' he cried out in surprise. 'How the devil did you get so far forward?'

With some effort, Cracknell sat up, spat out some thick mucus and reached inside the wet flap of his jacket for his cigar case. 'Grit and – and determination, Maynard,' he replied haltingly. 'Yourself?' He opened the case, releasing a trickle of water and a handful of mashed tobacco.

There was a crashing salvo of cannon-fire somewhere above them. The Major ducked, a half-smile on his face. 'I've heard you boast long about your commitment to your task, Cracknell, but that, I suspected, was brandy talking. I see now that I misjudged you.'

Cracknell, casting the cigar case away with a frown, felt his strength returning. 'Shame on you, Major, for ever thinking such a thing! Now, do you have a comment about the progress of the battle?'

Before Maynard could answer, something happened further along the line that sent a murmur of animation through the soldiers. Cracknell turned around to look. Major-General Codrington had eased his grey Arab charger up on to the ledge, and now shouted hoarsely, 'Fix bayonets! Get up the bank and advance the attack!'

As the men unhooked the long blades from their belts

and started attaching them to the barrels of their miniés, Maynard began firing out questions. 'The Lieutenant-Colonel is down, yes? Where is Major Fairlie? Captain Pierce? Does Lieutenant Nunn still have the colours?'

'Major! I say, Major!' It was Captain Wray, perhaps the most obnoxious of Boyce's creatures, pushing his way purposefully through the soldiers. Cracknell had crossed paths with him on several memorable occasions in Varna and Constantinople. Seeing the *Courier* man, Wray turned furiously to Maynard. 'What in God's name is that blackguard doing here?'

'You have left your company in the middle of an engagement, Captain,' Maynard said sternly. 'This had better be good.'

Cracknell let out a low snigger. Military authority, for once, was on his side.

Wray's eyes bulged out amusingly from his plum-coloured face. 'I only wished to say, *Major*, that we should dispatch some of our skirmishers to discover the fate of the Lieutenant-Colonel, and lend him whatever assistance they can.'

Maynard's brow darkened. 'A respectful tone is called for, Captain Wray, when addressing a superior officer – you would do well to remember that. And you are fully aware of our orders. We cannot break the battalion at this time. Return to your post – we must press the attack.'

As the chastened Captain retreated, scowling at Cracknell as he went, Maynard rose and looked over the 99th. 'Here we go, my lads,' he said, his voice loud but calm. 'We're to proceed up this here hill. Now these Russians will learn exactly who they've been firing on this day.'

Cracknell was left lying on the stones as the redcoats got numbly to their feet. Some began striking at the ledge above them with their rifle stocks, knocking loose rocks and earth in an attempt to make it more scaleable. He glanced along the line. The 19th and 23rd were already on the bank, advancing up the Heights behind Major-General Codrington in open order, their bugles sounding.

Then Major Maynard appeared atop the ledge, his cheeks flushed. 'Advance, men!' he cried, waving his sword like a

109

semaphore flag. 'Forward the 99th! Forward the Paulton Rangers!'

The *Courier* man reached for his pocketbook, thinking to make a record of this stirring scene. Like the cigars, however, it had been utterly destroyed by the waters of the Alma. Several fine passages, including a masterful account of that morning's preparations that he had penned whilst visiting the French camp, were lost. Cracknell let the book fall to the ground, where it landed wetly, spreading open like the wings of a dead duck. Ye Gods, he thought, I need a bloody drink.

The senior correspondent had been gone only a minute or so when Styles recovered. After wiping his mouth on his sleeve, he pulled his felt hat back decisively on to his head and declared himself ready to continue.

'My apologies, Mr Kitson,' he said, 'it will not happen again, I swear it. We must find Mr Cracknell.'

Getting up, they made their way out on to the shell-blasted riverbank. The Alma was clogged with dead, floating face down, bobbing steadily towards the sea. On the other side of the river, beyond the advancing Light Division, loomed the rough crenellations of the Russians' forward redoubt. Kitson could see that the men inside were working with urgent speed, trying to tilt their cannon so the barrels once again faced the approaching British. Musket-fire continued, somewhat ineffectually – the enemy's accuracy was thankfully poor. Styles, keen to atone for his momentary lapse, had taken the lead; raising his folder of sketches above his head, he plunged into the Alma and started to stride through the waters.

The cannon-fire from the forward redoubt began just as Kitson reached the river. It was immediately clear that it was different somehow. Instead of a string of deep, low bangs, followed by the sonorous howl of the iron balls, there was now a more ragged, loose sound, like something being dynamited, and its pieces being thrown in all directions. Then the shout went up – *'Grape!'*

Kitson suppressed a powerful urge to run for cover. He

fixed his eyes on Styles' black jacket, and was wading up behind him when a second round of grapeshot was fired. Three privates from the leftmost company of the 99th were caught by it; their pulverised bodies were swept back over the ledge, almost into the Alma itself. Fragments of metal and flesh splashed all around. Without thinking, Kitson ducked underwater, his hands scrabbling through a ridge of smooth pebbles as he tried to force himself down as deep as possible. He surfaced a few seconds later to the sound of anguished, rasping shrieks, coming from somewhere up on the hillside.

Styles had vanished. There was no trace of him on the gore-strewn riverbank, or in the Alma itself. Knowing he could not linger, Kitson left the water, stumbling a few steps before falling heavily on the stones. He crawled behind the shattered remains of a waterside willow and checked himself for injury, quickly confirming that, besides a few paltry cuts, he was unscathed. As he recovered his breath, he wondered if by some deadly chance Styles had been struck down by grapeshot and then dragged beneath the water by a hidden current. This would account for his companion's sudden disappearance; it would also mean that he had certainly perished. Kitson wiped the grit from his eyes and gazed back dismally over the ruined valley.

Something pale flashed in the corner of his vision, floating in the shallows. It was a sheet of paper, bearing a loose sketch. Styles' folder had been dropped nearby, in amongst a cluster of large stones at the water's edge. Landing on its spine, the folder had fallen open, and was slowly spilling its contents into the bloody Alma. Cracknell's first Crimean confrontation with Boyce, the collapsed soldiers from the march, Madeleine Boyce on board the *H.M.S Arthur* – all were being carried away on the red river.

4

Despite Madeleine's best efforts, the bay would not be controlled. She believed herself to be a good horsewoman, having ridden regularly throughout her youth. Never before, however, had she attempted to traverse a landscape like the charred and bloody one she found herself in that afternoon; and never before had she been atop such a horse. The bay's hide was very dirty, and as Madeleine stroked his neck, she could see her gloves blackening with grime. She murmured softly in both English and French, but nothing seemed to be working. Indeed, the beast was becoming more agitated by the moment.

After a short distance, the horse had turned towards the coast. It took Madeleine a few minutes even to think of becoming worried. She had brought disobedient horses to heel on plenty of occasions. It gradually became apparent, however, that the bay was not going to stop, or slow, or pay any attention to her whispering and caressing whatsoever. What worked on pampered ponies was proving completely ineffective on this brutish warhorse. She looked down at his flanks. They were scarred and scabbed by frequent spurring. He probably can't even feel my hand, she thought, a bud of fear bursting inside her. The British line, the 99th, Richard, were all being left behind. She was now heading into French territory.

There was only one course open to her. The bay wasn't travelling that fast, having slowed to a brisk trot, and the grass flashing by beneath them looked soft enough. The important thing, she told herself quickly, is to launch yourself away into the air, to ensure that you don't get trampled by the rear hooves. She gathered up the beige folds of her dress as best she could, held on to her bonnet, and jumped.

She landed badly, her left foot at an angle, caught between two clods of earth, the ankle then twisting hard as the weight of her entire body was dumped awkwardly on top of it. Her dress ballooned around her as she put out her arms to prevent herself from pitching face-first into the mud. One elbow gave way; her shoulder hit the ground, and she rolled on to her back, suddenly still, staring up at the sky. She could feel the bay's hooves pounding the earth, a dull rhythm that grew rapidly fainter as it continued on towards the sea.

Barely pausing, Madeleine propped herself up and moved her elbow. It seemed to be fine – unbroken, at least. More hesitantly, she climbed to her feet. The left ankle was already starting to swell inside her boot. She tried to stand on it; the pain was so intense that she cried out. She could feel the different parts of the ankle grinding together horribly, and was tempted to sit straight back down again and wait for assistance.

But then the sound of bugles over on the Heights made her look around. Redcoats could be seen in the forward redoubts, filling the batteries that had so frightened her before the battle began. The British had made contact. She fumbled with the purse that hung on her belt, and took out the opera glasses. A white crack ran across one of the lenses; but from her new position on the plain, the glasses now afforded an excellent view of the fighting. Awful things were happening up there. She saw a rifle pushed straight into a man's face and fired; she saw the blood spurt from a Russian's belly as a redcoat stabbed at him mercilessly with his bayonet. And these were but two incidents in a hundred.

Madeleine forced herself to search for Richard amidst the turmoil. It quickly became clear, however, that this was futile. How could she possibly find him when she didn't even know where to start looking? He might be up there on the Heights, in the worst of the combat, but then he might also be safely back in the camp, or crouched under cover on the banks of the river, or even lying dead in a ditch. She felt an absolute, helpless despair gathering inside her.

'*Non,*' she said out loud, as sternly as she could. '*Non, je n'y renoncerais pas. Je le retrouverais.*' Ignoring the burning friction in her ankle, Madeleine started for the river.

Styles clutched at a handful of grass, pulling himself from the Alma and up on to its opposite bank. He slumped exhaustedly onto his side, feeling the cold water run out from the tops of his boots, murmuring thanks to God for his safe delivery.

An enormous explosion roused him abruptly from this torpid prayer. He sat bolt upright and took a startled glance around him as the booming knell rolled around the valley. Up in the heart of the Russian positions, a gigantic fireball was expanding into the sky, an incandescent orange sphere laced with black soot. The British artillery, he quickly surmised, must have somehow struck a powder magazine. The battle was now surely won.

A thick trunk of smoke sprouted from the main redoubt. Styles could clearly see Russian soldiers fleeing their positions, their will broken by the seemingly divine blow that had been cast down upon them. Pressing the advantage, British infantrymen promptly surged forward into the abandoned fortifications. Rows of miniés were levelled, emptied, reloaded and emptied again. Retreating Russians fell in waves, as if tripped by long cables, their grey coats flapping as they tumbled on to the hillside. Styles, beholding this fearsome carnage from afar, felt a dark, irresistible fascination take hold of him. Unthinkingly, he reached for his drawing materials, and cursed when he realised he'd lost them in the Alma; but he continued to watch nonetheless.

It took a woman's scream, a piercing, incongruous sound, to break the illustrator's morbid gaze and finally make him assess his immediate surroundings. After diving into deeper water to avoid the second round of grapeshot, he had become caught in a fast-flowing channel from which he had only just been able to free himself. It had plainly carried him a good distance downstream, far from his colleagues. There was a low stone bridge a short way to his left – it was from this direction that the scream had come. Scrambling to his knees, he crawled quickly to the top of the bank.

To his astonishment, standing at the mouth of the bridge was none other than Madeleine Boyce, the lady who had so pervaded and tortured his imagination over the past weeks. She was sobbing with terror, trying desperately to reach cover but impeded by a severe limp. A musket fired nearby, the bullet chipping against the stone at Mrs Boyce's feet; shocked, she tripped on her skirts, wailing as she fell. Styles followed the path of the shot with his eyes. He saw a group of bearded Cossack horsemen, presumably part of a raiding party that had been missed somehow by the line of Allied advance. They were firing upon Mrs Boyce from their saddles as they made their escape back up to the Heights, all laughing as if it was great sport.

Without another thought, Styles leapt forward and ran over to the bridge, scooping Mrs Boyce up and then rushing back to the bank. Further shots were aimed at them as they went, but none struck close to their target. Once they were safe, the illustrator attempted to drop to his knees and set Mrs Boyce down; but the combination of his depleted strength and her apparent desire not to let go of him meant that they ended up landing on the grass together, still wrapped tightly in each other's arms.

They stayed in this pose for several minutes. Beyond them, up on the Heights, the battle seemed to be coming to an end, the rifle fire becoming sporadic, and interspersed with occasional cheers. Styles barely noticed. He was absorbed instead by Mrs Boyce's thudding heartbeat and frantic breathing; by her trembling hands, clinging to his sodden jacket; by the hard bands of her crinoline as they rubbed against his shins.

'Oh sir,' she gasped tearfully, her face laid upon his chest, 'you saved me. You saved me from them.'

As they lay there, Styles' happiness was so complete that he did not entirely trust it. The situation was simply too perfect – too much like one of the hundreds of fervid fantasies he had composed whilst huddled sleeplessly in his cot. And sure enough, it soon came to an end. 'I could not do otherwise, *Madame*, believe me. I—'

At the sound of his voice, Mrs Boyce started, as if suddenly waking. She withdrew from his embrace with a promptness that made him ashamed not to have moved himself away from her first; then she stood quickly and began smoothing her damp, rumpled gown.

He rose as well, making himself talk on. 'That – that those beasts, those *demons* would fire on a lady – well, it defies my understanding, to be perfectly frank. Might I ask what you are doing out here, Mrs Boyce?'

She retied her bonnet, which had been knocked loose, and looked him up and down. *'Mon Dieu*, Mr Styles!' she exclaimed in feigned amazement. 'You are soaked through! I fear that your fine velvet jacket is quite ruined. Where is your hat? Have you been in the river?'

Styles almost smiled at this crude, oddly charming piece of evasion. He was about to reply when someone further up the river shouted her name furiously. They both turned, Mrs Boyce covering her mouth in dismay. 'Oh no,' she whispered. 'Not *now*.'

It was her husband, striding rapidly along the bank towards them. The Lieutenant-Colonel was drenched, and his head was bare – like Styles, he had obviously taken an unexpected plunge into the Alma. When he was still about twenty yards away from them, he stopped. His eyes were staring wide, his face purple; he seemed quite apoplectic with rage. 'Come here, you little fool!' he spat.

Mrs Boyce was not in the least cowed by him. Refusing to hurry, she took one of Styles' hands in hers. 'Mr Styles, you have my most sincere thanks for what you did. I shall not forget this, sir.'

The sweet tenderness of her voice was almost painful to hear. Styles looked on helplessly as she went to Boyce's side. He seized hold of her as one would a disobedient dog, and then dragged her back the way he had come.

The illustrator did not attempt to deceive himself. It was all but certain that she was out there searching for Cracknell, for the man she loved. But he felt a measure of triumph nonetheless. After his humiliating failure in the vineyard, he had managed to show true courage. He had saved her. Amongst the horrors of that day, the many nightmares that had been unleashed upon him, this was one shining consolation. Cracknell may have her heart; she may have risked everything just to see him once more; but he, Robert Styles, had saved Madeleine Boyce from death, and held her in his arms as she sobbed with gratitude.

He looked to the Heights, his eyes lingering on the slew of bodies that littered the redoubts. Several union flags and regimental colours now hung above these grim charnel-houses – a British victory had been declared. Thinking to locate his colleagues, Styles began to climb the hill.

5

The pavilion was deserted. Several dozen chairs, all finely carved and polished, stood abandoned inside it. A once-neat crescent arrangement had been knocked to a jumble by the haste with which those who had so recently sat there watching the battle had departed for Sebastopol. A rich oriental rug had been spread out across the grass, and then kicked up by fleeing heels; champagne bottles, still dewy from having been packed in ice, huddled together in its folds like fat black fishes. Cracknell prodded a couple with his boot to discover if they contained anything. He was rewarded only with a hollow clunking sound.

Crunching his way over broken glasses, the senior correspondent noted that the striped canvas of the awning had been torn open by shrapnel. Reaching into the pocket of his jacket, which was now almost dry, Cracknell took out a bundle of small, yellowish cigarettes, purchased from a Guards officer in the greater redoubt. He had done this somewhat reluctantly, having abjured the damned things in the past in favour of God's honest cigar, but these were desperate times. Experimentally, he put one in his mouth and lit it. The Turkish tobacco was a touch rough, but it slid down easily enough, warming the passages and bringing that familiar, tingling sense of quietude. Cracknell sucked deep and took in the Heights of the Alma Valley.

It was a victory. Out on the Black Sea, gunboats were ringing their bells and firing off salutes. A panoply of Allied infantry, from kilted Highlanders to red-trousered French Zoaves, crowded along the hilltops, letting out hearty cheers. Men from the Coldstream Guards had climbed atop the largest Russian fortification to raise the Union Jack, their bearskins lined up against the early evening sky like so many matchheads. The Allied armies had carried the day, and he, Richard Patrick Cracknell of the *London Courier*, had been there to witness it. A multitude of vivid recollections vied for prominence in his mind: the fusillades ripping back and forth through the air, the bestial frenzy of the bayonet fight, the strange, keening cry the Russians made as they swarmed out from their earthworks. He had accomplished his goal. He had seen battle up close – and it was astounding material.

But then he turned north, moving around the spectators' pavilion so that he could see the wide plain beyond. It was strewn with debris jettisoned from the retreating Russian Army, which could still be seen clearly as it marched back towards the Crimean capital in long, ordered columns. Not a hundred yards from where he stood was the Light Brigade – a full thousand troopers bristling with lances and sabres. The cavalrymen had scaled the Heights in the battle's closing stages and were now eager to go after the Russians, to attack whilst the enemy was at a pronounced disadvantage.

The order to do so, however, had not arrived. The glittering ranks of hussars, lancers and light dragoons were straining visibly, desperate to be off, like riders in some Olympian steeplechase; but for them, the starter's gun would not sound. Cracknell blew out a lungful of smoke. He could hear the horses' impatient snorts and the stamping of their hooves, and the angry, uncomprehending exchanges of the officers. These two elements, the jubilation on the Heights, and the immense frustration out on the plain, felt at that moment like the two conflicting sides of his own mind; a decisive victory had been won, yet now, for no possible reason that Cracknell could see other than cautious stupidity, the generals were failing signally to capitalise upon it.

Major Maynard appeared, bearing a bundle of dispatch paper and a couple of well-chewed pencils. 'Here you are, you reprobate. Remind me again why I help you.'

Cracknell rounded on him, flicking away his cigarette. 'What the deuce is going on, Maynard? Why doesn't Raglan give the bloody order to pursue? This ever-so-organised retreat could become a full rout – the war could end today!'

Maynard was stained with blood, mud and gunpowder, and his round face was scored with exhaustion. One of his epaulettes was missing, and his sleeve had taken a slice from a sword. 'I – I really cannot say.'

Cracknell took the pencil and paper, shaking his head. 'This is gross incompetence. There really is no other word. To be unable to keep an army free from disease, or well fed and sheltered is one thing – but to not know how to *fight with it* is quite another! Prince Menshikov and his generals got a damned good look at our army this afternoon, Maynard – they'll be running back to Sebastopol to build up their defences, and most likely wire Moscow for reinforcements!'

'What do you want from me, Cracknell?' There was exasperation in Maynard's voice. 'What do you suggest I do?'

Remembering who he was talking to, Cracknell softened his manner a little. 'Not you, Major, not you. You are a gallant hero, sir, you and all the others who came up that wretched hill.' He looked around for something to lean against so that he could start to write. 'But this cannot be overlooked. How the hell can I report only our triumphs when the old fools in command are committing the fighting men to many more such battles with their inexplicable inaction? I shall do something about this, Maynard – you'll see.'

Major Maynard's sigh became a weary chuckle. Never had he met a man so sure of his own righteousness, so spirited in his self belief – no matter how contradictory or hypocritical his position. He had to admire this, for all the annoyance it caused. Perhaps it was the character necessary in a truly effective war correspondent.

Over Cracknell's shoulder, Maynard noticed a strange group emerging from the valley and making for one of the impromptu command posts that had sprung up along the Heights. It appeared to be a half-baked attempt at a regimental staff. He realised that this group were from the

99th Foot: there was Quartermaster Arthurs, rosy-cheeked and unsteady, and Lieutenant Freeman, Boyce's sickly adjutant.

And there, at its centre, flanked by private soldiers, was Boyce himself. He was wrapped in a blue greatcoat, not his own, which appeared to be covered in gun grease. His hat was gone, and his hair awry; and his moustache, devoid of wax, fell free across his face like the hide of some shaggy wolf-hound, covering his mouth completely. In one of his hands was his sword, which was slightly bent. In the other, quite unaccountably, was his young wife, gripped by the upper arm. She was limping badly, her fine clothes streaked with dirt, and across her grubby face were the pale tracks left by copious quantities of tears. Maynard could only guess as to how she had come to be out there. Her husband was coldly indifferent to her suffering. Boyce's attitude was that of the steely disciplinarian, dragging an incorrigible wrongdoer off to the pillory.

'Boyce,' the Major said simply. 'He survived.'

Cracknell looked around; his glare was immediately displaced by a wicked grin. 'I'll be damned. I thought he was finished for certain. And look, Mrs Boyce as well.' He tucked the pencil behind his ear. 'I must pay my compliments.'

Maynard put a hand flat against the correspondent's chest, halting him. 'You do not seem at all concerned by this. I would have thought that Boyce's death would have solved a significant problem for you.'

Cracknell's grin widened. 'But a problem solved, my dear Major, is a meal finished, a bottle drained, a newspaper read. This little drama plainly has another act left to run.'

The Major frowned. 'Is that all it is to you? A *drama*?'

By way of reply, Cracknell attempted to renew his progress towards the Boyces.

Maynard remained in his path. 'No – no, Cracknell. Not now. Think of the great chance that has just been squandered. Think of your report.'

Realising that he could not force himself past, Cracknell stepped back. He straightened his jacket and then lit another cigarette. 'You are right, Maynard, of course – I should permit no distractions. My thanks for the reminder. I shall return to the pavilion and get to work.'

Maynard watched the correspondent saunter behind the tattered canvas and select a chair. Then he set out to intercept his commanding officer.

Boyce was not pleased to see him. Acutely aware of his ridiculous appearance, he demanded a full account of the battle there and then, and was keen to find fault as a means of salving his own sense of dishonour. He was especially interested in hearing of how, after some confusion over orders, the Light Division had fallen back before the greater redoubt, rejoining the fight only when supported by the Guards.

'The Coldstreamers came to your rescue, Maynard, did they not? Had it not been for their arrival on the field, the Russians would have overcome you completely.'

'An unfair assessment, sir, if I may say so. The men only retreated because they were ordered to, and—'

Boyce wasn't listening. He shook his head with heavy disappointment and launched into a lecture on the vital necessity of keeping one's nerve when under fire. It was too important to his pride – Maynard had failed, and he would hear no other interpretation of the afternoon's events.

Suddenly, Mrs Boyce cried out. She had seen something over by the spectators' pavilion; Cracknell, damn him, sat in plain view, writing intently. Feeling the eyes of Boyce's group on him, he looked up and gave Mrs Boyce a sly wink. Beaming with joy, she took an unthinking step towards her lover – only to have her husband pull her back, tightening his fingers viciously around her arm.

As he watched fresh tears shine on Mrs Boyce's cheeks, Maynard felt compelled to act, to challenge this bullying fool in some small way. He cleared his throat. 'Can I ask you, Lieutenant-Colonel, why we are not pursuing the Russians? The Light Brigade stands ready. Surely our generals are making a great mistake.'

Predictably, Boyce was appalled by this notion, as he was by anything remotely critical of the High Command. 'Military honour decrees that having met and bested the foe, we allow him to withdraw. *Military honour*, Major – have you any conception of such a thing?' His eyes narrowed. 'By God, you've been talking to that *Courier* devil, haven't you – against my express instructions!'

Maynard didn't deny it. Mrs Boyce met his eye in momentary collusion. 'His perspective is certainly refreshing, sir, and unencumbered by the dogma that so often hinders our own thinking on matters of strategy.'

'*How dare he*?' Boyce yelled. 'How dare the ruffian doubt Lord Raglan, a man who served under none other than *Wellington himself*? It is positively treasonous. He must be stopped.' He waved his sword furiously, swiping it so close to Maynard's face that it threatened to clip the brim of his cap. 'I will see him sent home – sent home in utter disgrace!'

There was a rifle report, very close; Quartermaster Arthurs exclaimed and then fell over, clutching at his rump. A wounded Russian infantryman, left for dead on a mound of corpses close to where they stood, had caught sight of the officer's uniform and taken a shot with his musket. The privates in Boyce's detail promptly lumbered over to him. The Russian was young and very thin with a wisp of a moustache, and lowered his weapon as they approached, meeting them with a resigned expression. They poked at him listlessly with their bayonets, as if shifting dung with pitchforks at the end of a long day in the cattle sheds. Boyce looked on, not relaxing his hold on his wife for an instant.

'Damn and blast it!' Arthurs spluttered from the ground, blood bulging up blackly between his fingers. 'Do – do excuse me, Mrs Boyce, I – oh, the wretched, goat-fucking peasant! Again, Mrs Boyce, my apologies – damn it!'

Maynard called out tiredly for a stretcher.

Kitson picked his way through the knotted battlefield as quickly as he could. A sour, fetid smell hung everywhere, and the grass slopes of the Heights were slimy with congealing blood. All around, wounded men wept, prayed and pleaded for assistance that did not come. Many requested water, others liquor, and a few, those with the very worst injuries, only a speedy death to end their suffering. Hands clawed and clutched at Kitson's clothes as he went by. They were desperate but weak, and easily shrugged off. He had given his water canteen to the first man to ask, only to be asked again a minute later – and be showered with savage curses when he declared his inability to help. So he had hardened his heart, lowered his head and pressed on.

There were no surgeons at work on those dreadful slopes. Kitson had realised this early in his ascent and had barely been able to believe it. He'd spotted some donkey-drawn hospital vans over at the coast, but these belonged to the French, whose casualties were relatively light. For the hundreds of redcoats – and thousands of Russians – left broken and helpless in that valley there were only the exhausted regimental bandsmen and a smattering of over-whelmed stretcher-bearers. Officers were being seen to first; it would be many hours – days, even – before some of these men received aid, surely too late for a good number of them.

Cracknell was sat close to the spectators' pavilion, writing with feverish concentration, wringing every last second of light from the fading day. He was even more unkempt than usual, the orange tip of a cigarette glowing in amongst the coarse tresses of his beard. His pencil dashed across the paper; he had covered several pages already with his spidery hand. He didn't notice Kitson's urgent approach.

'Mr Cracknell, have you seen any sign of Styles? We were separated in the confusion on the riverbank, and I fear that he might have . . . have been . . .'

Cracknell, barely looking up, pointed to a rocky escarp-ment that overlooked the length of the Alma valley. Styles was perched upon it, missing his hat but otherwise unharmed. He was immersed in a sketch.

Kitson blinked, the dizziness of his relief making him feel suddenly sick. He exhaled hard. 'Thank God,' he mumbled. 'Thank *God*.'

'A late rally,' Cracknell observed sarcastically, puffing on his cigarette. 'He's in a damned strange temper, I must say. Strode up, took some paper and a pencil from me without a word, then walked straight off again. Honestly, anyone would think that it was *I* who had been transformed into a fear-crazed imbecile as soon as the shot started to fly.'

Taken aback by the unforgiving severity of Cracknell's tone, Kitson tried to speak up in Styles' defence but could not find the words. It was like trying to move a dead limb. The will was there yet nothing happened. Closing his eyes, he saw again the faces of the men back on those slopes; and found himself wondering if he had drawn his last untroubled breath.

'I imagined him to be a kindred spirit, y'know,' the senior correspondent went on. 'A worthwhile addition to our brave reporting team. Yet look at what he has turned out to be – naught but a poltroon, a vomit-flecked booby.'

Cracknell had stopped work. He looked over at the plain beyond the battlefield, where the Allied Army was camping out on its hard-won ground, putting up tents and starting fires with wood gathered from the valley. His harangue became a touch more conciliatory.

'You would have done your duty, Thomas, I know that, had you not been burdened by our young illustrator. This is a problem we will have to address. A unified courage will be needed in the months to come.' He lit a fresh cigarette with the end of its predecessor. 'Grave errors have been made today, errors that dash all hopes of a speedy resolution to this campaign. There will be more battles, and bloody ones too – mark my words.' He tapped the sheets resting on his knee. 'All this is explained here, and will go straight to the *Courier*.'

'*More battles?*' The disbelieving anger Kitson had felt on the battlefield returned abruptly, driving away his confusion. 'How the hell can they hope to fight more battles when the injured are just left on the ground to die? How can such – such *murderous* negligence possibly be sustained?'

Cracknell nodded approvingly. 'You are absolutely right, it is obscene. But we will be here to bear witness. Our mission has undergone a change, Kitson. We are messengers, my friend, and together we will ensure these abuses and failings do not go unreported – or unpunished.'

This sounded very noble, as Cracknell's little speeches

invariably did. For the first time, however, Kitson found that he listened with a degree of mistrust.

'You must tell me of your pistol, Mr Cracknell,' he said, the smallest barb in his voice. 'Did it serve you well?'

Cracknell stared at him in astonishment, the rug pulled from under his grand posturing. He reached into his jacket for the revolver and hefted it in his hand, a look of bewilderment on his face.

'Do you know,' he said slowly, 'I forgot completely that I had it.'

Then he lowered it a fraction, and a long spurt of dirty river water ran out of the barrel, dripping down on to the scorched grass below.

Manchester
May 1857

1

'It has often been said that the crowd is one of the great levellers of mankind; that a lord or bishop, placed in a large, adversarial gathering of his peers, will for all his supposed breeding and education behave no better than a navvy brawling outside a pot-house. Reader, the truth of this axiom was well demonstrated on the steps of the Art Treasures Exhibition on the morning of the fifth of May 1857. As the chapel bells of the nearby Blind Asylum began to strike eleven, the appointed hour of opening, the mass of finely dressed ladies and gentlemen pressed up against the Exhibition doors began to strike the glass and rattle the handles with such impatient force that this correspondent feared that they might succeed in bringing them down.

'Like cattle drivers charged with a particularly skittish, heavily perfumed herd, the stewards within eased open their gates and let this noisy throng jostle through. The city's highest in rank, fashion and beauty all but ran up to the turnstiles, the gentlemen removing their hats, the ladies gathering up their skirts to allow for more rapid locomotion. Imprecations not to push were imperiously ignored, yellow admission tickets waved dismissively at attendants, and the revolving metal barriers wrenched around with the utmost violence. Several, in their urgency to get through and secure their seats, tried to pull these barriers the wrong way, resulting in them becoming stuck; and those caught directly behind could only watch in helpless rage as others flew past them on either side, beating them to the best locations.

'Passing quickly into the grand hall, these worthy notables did

129

not gasp at the magnificence of the nave, sweeping down to the cavernous transept with the great bronze tubes of the organ behind; they did not marvel at the enormous skylights overhead, or the intricate web of girders that support them, with every single rivet picked out in gold leaf; they did not stare at the thick red carpet that runs the length of the structure, flanked by statues of white marble, to a dais at its heart, on which is mounted a golden throne; nor did they pause to admire the hundreds of masterful paintings that adorn the walls, almost obscuring the maroon paper behind. They looked only to the chairs and benches, accumulating around the dais like mud on an axle. The triumph with which places were claimed diminished the further they were from the Royal seat: those who had secured the very closest gloated victoriously, whilst those on the fringes of the transept, and stuck out in the aisles of the nave, frowned with disappointment, and wondered to whom they could address their complaints.

'Gradually, however, this first wave of guests recovered their breath, readjusted their ruffled clothes and started to look around them properly. The Art Treasures Palace was finally allowed to exert its undeniable effect, and its girders echoed with exclamations of a rare, entirely unstudied awe.'

Kitson turned over a page in his pocketbook and was about to commence his next sentence when Edward Thorne, editor of the *Manchester Evening Star*, gestured with his walnut walking stick towards a fashionable group standing near the heart of the Exhibition.

'The Baileys,' he declared. 'I happen to know that their latest carriage cost in excess of a thousand pounds.'

Thorne and Kitson sat together on the northern balcony of the transept, which had been set aside for the men of the Manchester press. The *Star*'s editor was present purely for his own entertainment, however, and wrote nothing. In contrast with many of those around him, whose attempts at morning dress spanned the full spectrum of shabbiness, Thorne's grey suit was immaculate, and his habitually sceptical features clean-shaven. It was as if he was trying to correct the somewhat grubby reputation of his journal with his own spruce appearance.

'And there,' the editor continued pointedly, 'is Colonel

130

Bennett and the officers of the Glorious 25th. Without poor Major Wray, of course . . .'

The hall before them was carpeted with a constantly shifting, murmuring mass of humanity, bathed in slanting shafts of sunlight. Above rose the vast, still space of the iron palace, enclosed by girders and glass, and festooned with dozens of bright flags and banners. And crowning everything, in a golden arch above the spray of organ pipes, ran an inscription in a strong, Latinate script, each letter five feet tall: *To Wake the Soul by Tender Strokes of Art.*

Over on the far side of the nave were the soldiers Thorne had indicated. There were about a dozen of them, in full dress uniform, standing in a loose circle beside a densely patterned suit of Elizabethan armour. The sight of the crimson jackets seemed to make the sunny hall grow uncomfortably hot, its atmosphere suddenly close and stifling. Perspiration broke out across Kitson's brow, beneath the hard brim of his hired top hat, and a dull queasiness welled inside him. He looked away for a moment, down at his boots; then he returned his attention to his pocketbook.

Thorne turned towards him in a conspiratorial manner. 'Tell me again how you did it, Kitson. Exactly how you did it.'

The street philosopher stopped writing. He knew that he bore Thorne a heavy debt. The *Star's* editor had taken him on shortly before the Christmas of 1856 with few questions asked. Considerable tolerance had subsequently been shown regarding Kitson's reclusive tendencies, the rarity of his appearances at the journal's premises on Corporation Street, and his general unwillingness to speak about himself at any length. At times, however, Thorne would adopt a gratingly interrogative manner, no doubt thinking to draw out through some oblique questioning that which Kitson would not openly volunteer.

'What more can I possibly tell you, Thorne? The Colonel sent a letter asking if there was anything he could do to thank me for assisting his officer. It seemed like the obvious request.'

That Saturday night, even with his skin scrubbed raw and

his bloody clothes burned, Kitson had been incapable of rest. The encounter with Wray was so unlikely, such a foul trick of chance, that it had kept him pacing back and forth across his attic until several hours past daybreak. He was sorely tempted to go to the Royal Infirmary, confront Wray in his sick bed and demand to know what he was doing in Manchester.

But wisdom had prevailed; and first thing on Monday, he had gone instead to Wovenden's Coffee House and made his inquiries there. This establishment, located in the dead centre of Market Street, was a favourite with his fellow newspapermen and the prime place to obtain information. Wray, he soon discovered, had transferred to the 25th Manchesters only a couple of months earlier, yet already was widely despised as a martinet. In fact, there were strong suspicions amongst the constabulary that it was one of his own regiment who had attacked him, despite the lurid stories of a mad cripple that were circulating throughout the city.

The note from Colonel Bennett had been waiting for him back at Princess Street. He had penned a reply immediately, biting his lip as he wished Wray a speedy recovery and then wondering whether the Colonel could secure him an invitation to the ball at the Polygon the following evening. Bennett, he knew, was a long-standing fixture in Manchester society, and on good terms with the Fairbairns: this was well within his capabilities.

Only after the reply had been sent did Kitson pause to examine why he had asked for such a thing. This was the sort of event he would normally go out of his way to avoid. Then he had remembered Mrs James, and their disputative, unexpectedly intimate conversation in her father's office. He recalled the frown line etched between the light crescents of her eyebrows, and the way her sharp green eyes had looked so intently into his, as if searching determinedly for something. He wished to see her, to speak with her again. This was the reason he had sought an invitation to the Polygon. Kitson had taken a breath, made a quick calculation of his meagre finances and headed back out into the city to obtain some formal clothes.

Thorne straightened his cuffs. 'Well, I must say that it is a welcome change. We had grown used to you being the *Star*'s very own Saint Jerome, Kitson, cowering away in the shadows – but now, all of a sudden, you seem to be the epitome of the well-connected gentleman. I look forward to it opening up a whole new dimension in your work.' The editor tapped at Kitson's shoulder with his cane. 'Aha, look! The Buckle King is among us! And with both offspring in tow!'

Kitson sat up, leaning a little closer to the balcony rail. She was not hard to locate. Compared with the lace-laden ladies through whom she moved, Mrs James was a model of taste and restraint. Her pale blue dress was worn with only a modest crinoline and a simple flounce, complemented by a dark shawl and bonnet. She drew condescending and occasionally hostile glances from those around her, but ignored them all completely. As she passed into the nave, taking it in, the look on her face suggested a reluctant admiration.

Thorne followed the direction of his gaze. 'The widow Jemima. A soul with a natural bent to controversy, they say; quixotic, rebellious, a constant source of concern to her father.' He studied Kitson more closely. 'Are you two acquainted, Kitson, perchance?'

'We met on the night Major Wray was stabbed. She saw me with him on Mosley Street, and we—'

'So this is the true motivation behind all this initiative, this dextrous ingenuity! Mrs Jemima James!' The *Star*'s editor rapped the end of his cane smartly against the balcony's metal floor. 'And there was I, naïve fool that I am, assuming that you acted out of dedication to me, to my paper!'

Kitson could not help grinning. 'I have not forgotten the *Star*, Thorne. Never fear.'

Thorne sighed, sitting back in his chair. 'Well, I wish you luck, Kitson, honestly I do. The only advice I can offer is of a depressingly traditional nature, I'm afraid: *beware the father*. Like all men who have but recently arrived at their fortunes, Norton seeks to elevate himself, and is unlikely to be pleased by the advances of a lowly newspaperman.'

His face darkened a little. 'Believe me, these self-made men are ruthless fellows – and that one particularly so.'

The street philosopher looked across the hall to Charles Norton, the so-called Buckle King. He was in his mid-fifties, bewhiskered and austere, the classic figure of the Manchester labour-lord. He was conversing solemnly with other grandees, accepting compliments on the Exhibition as if it were all his doing alone – as if there weren't another eighty-nine men on the Exhibition Committee, and an Executive Committee to boot.

His children, meanwhile, were heading off into the crowd without him. William Norton, clad in a ruby-red cravat and yellow waistcoat, had taken his sister's hand; they weaved around a gleaming marble statue of a sinuous classical huntsman and slipped through a gap between two display cases crammed with ornamental silverware. Kitson realised that they were making for a trio of chairs positioned off to one side of the dais, deep in the shadow cast by the southern balcony, which were being held for them by a willowy, long-haired young man. Like William Norton, he was extravagantly dressed, and his face was alive with anticipation. He greeted the siblings effusively, shaking their hands with great warmth. Before the three had time to sit, a ripple of applause started down by the doors, gathering quickly to a rousing ovation. Kitson could see nothing, but word soon travelled along the balcony that Lord Overstone, the Exhibition's president, had just made his entrance, and now stood in place ready to welcome Prince Albert. It would not be long now.

'Alfred Keane,' Thorne informed him, indicating the willowy man. 'One of the most notorious sodomites in Lancashire. And a *close companion* of the young dandy Norton, if you follow my meaning.' He gave a low laugh and nodded at Kitson's pocketbook. 'Probably best if you omit that from your account.'

William Norton and his friend Keane, placing themselves on either side of Mrs James, began to talk over her animatedly, gesturing and pointing as they surveyed the enormous audience gathered in the hall. Trapped between them, she read her programme, entirely disengaged from her surroundings.

Kitson was so absorbed in his contemplation of her that it took him a few seconds to notice that William Norton had spotted him. He nudged his sister with an elbow, clearly amused, and directed her attention to the northern balcony. Mrs James' face lifted upwards, and for an instant their eyes met. Kitson's pulse throbbed against his tight collar. He went to raise his hat. She began to smile.

A deep, rumbling roar started up outside, from the direction of the city, the loose chorus of thousands of voices cheering thunderously along the Prince's route to the Exhibition. Every head in the hall turned towards the main doors; then, as one, the audience leapt to their feet, their conversation suddenly escalating in volume as they strained to catch a glimpse of the Royal carriage pulling up outside. Their grand ceremony was about to begin.

When Kitson looked back across the transept, he could not find Mrs James. She was lost in a chaos of top hats and bonnets, all dipping and craning as they vied for a decent view. As he searched impatiently through the shifting multitude, he experienced a startling, unwelcome jolt of recognition. One of the faces he had passed over was familiar – very familiar.

With mounting unease, he made himself look again. There, under the balcony opposite, off behind where he had seen Jemima, in what was probably the darkest corner of the hall, stood a stocky, bearded, black-haired man. Austere portraits of Cromwell and his generals stared down disapprovingly as he leant against a column, half-facing the wall, a cupped hand raised to his lips. A small spark glowed: Kitson realised that, in defiance of the rules of the Exhibition, the man was surreptitiously puffing on a cigarette. He tilted his head back to exhale, forcing the smoke out of one side of his mouth, a look of calm, slightly mocking confidence on his wide, ruddy face. Although he was over a hundred and fifty feet away, and shrouded in shadow, there could not be any doubt. It was Cracknell.

2

The spinners swayed unsteadily, cheering themselves as they did so, delighting in their drunkenness. They had worked fast. The half-holiday granted by their employers was only an hour old, yet already a good number were well on their way to intoxication, quickly drinking away any trace of sickness left over from the night before. They toasted Albert, they toasted the Queen, they toasted the sun, they toasted the policemen who toiled before them to keep the road clear, they toasted anything they could think of. Cheap boots and clogs clacked against the cobbles as they danced dizzy jigs together, and fell laughing into the dirt.

The steam whistles had blown at midday, the mill-gates opening to release a flood of working people that rushed down from Ancoats, Oldham and Hulme, through the maze of streets and alleys towards the Royal route. Its progress was slowed only by visits to gin palaces and beer shops, which found themselves doing a brisk trade indeed for a Tuesday. In an atmosphere of abandoned celebration, the spinners lined the Stretford New Road, popped the stoppers on their bottles and awaited the Prince.

Some, growing restless, found amusement in taunting the lines of policemen who wrestled to keep the vast bodies of people on either side of the road apart. Any good will on the part of these constables was soon used up, and more than a few blows administered with their polished wooden sticks. The better classes of spectator, who sat on the balconies of houses lining the road, or atop the large wooden platforms that had been erected on the intermittent stretches of open ground, peered down at the drab, swirling mass of the poor and shuddered.

Prince Albert, when he finally appeared, did not disappoint. The Royal procession was composed of a long line of open carriages filled with lords and ladies, clad in all their finery, flanked by a company of golden-helmed dragoons. Albert himself sat in the fourth carriage, in the resplendent uniform of a field marshal. His long, sombre face bore an uncertain smile as he surveyed the vast numbers all around; the countless flags and handkerchiefs frantically waving; the signs and banners that hung from every window; the triumphal arches made from wood, cloth and cardboard that had been erected along the route to the Exhibition, swathed with flowers and bearing declaration after declaration of extravagant, patriotic welcome.

At last, the straight road began to turn and the Art Treasures Palace glided majestically into view. After the modest, scattered dwellings of Old Trafford, the purpose-built edifice seemed truly gigantic, equal almost to the famous Crystal Palace that had housed the Great Exhibition. Part cathedral and part railway terminus, this structure comprised three long iron half-tubes, fringed with decorative castings and set upon a two-storey base of red and yellow brick. As the carriages wheeled up before it, sunlight flashed across the semi-circle of its main façade, catching brilliantly against the many hundreds of glass segments encased within the intricately patterned metalwork. The company of dragoons turned about, formed into tight ranks and fired off a salute to announce the Consort's arrival; and Prince Albert stepped down on to Mancunian soil.

Beyond the open doors was a wall of silks, crinolines and morning-coats, and thousands of pink faces, all turned expectantly towards the Royal guest. Lord Overstone, a slight man in his early sixties, came down the steps. From inside the hall there came the sound of a vast choir, a hundred voices or more, singing the national anthem. Overstone greeted

Prince Albert with a bow and a few formal words; and then the Prince and his entourage swept into the building.

Up in the balcony, Kitson rose clumsily to his feet and stumbled back through the rows of newspapermen, deaf to their exclamations of annoyance. Thorne, still sitting at the balcony's edge, looked around for him briefly, but his attention soon returned to the main aisle below, where Prince Albert was commencing his procession to the dais. The voices of the assembled congregation were joining with those of the choir that had appeared before the organ to create a stirring, mighty refrain. Whilst the metal rafters rang to cries of '*God save the Queen!*', Kitson clattered down the balcony staircase, imagining as he went that Cracknell's black eyes were boring into his back with destructive force. To loud tutting, he shoved his way around the corner of the transept and left by the northern door, heading out into the adjacent botanical gardens.

Panting heavily, he leant against the side of an ivy-clad hothouse, taking off his top hat and running a hand roughly through his hair. His chest began to tighten most painfully, forcing him to snatch shallow, grating coughs between his gasps. He was utterly dumbfounded. How had Cracknell managed to locate him? What could he possibly want, after all that had happened between them? What might he be poised to reveal?

The sun was warm upon his sweating face. He looked over to the pale gothic spires of the Blind Asylum, just visible behind a screen of poplars, and then back to the door of the Exhibition building. No one had followed him outside. This meant that either Cracknell had failed to notice him – or that it had not been his former senior after all. Could he have been mistaken? Was it even possible that the incident with Wray had affected him in some deep and injurious manner – that this apparent sighting of Cracknell was a new variation of delusory attack?

Kitson tried to reason with himself. Cracknell used to make a regular show of his lack of interest in art, and he loathed the northern industrial towns with a passion – a significant factor in Kitson's decision to take up residence in one. Why on earth would he attend the opening of the Manchester Art Treasures Exhibition? It started to seem likely that Kitson's regrettably disruptive exit had been made in error.

But it had looked so much like Cracknell: the bulbous nose, the jutting jaw, the domineering self-assurance. Kitson stood still for some time, recovering his breath and waiting for his coughing fit to subside. More music floated over from inside the Palace as the ceremonials got underway: *The Heavens are Telling*, then *The Hundredth Psalm*. The street philosopher stared hard at the ground, a hand on his aching side, trying to work out if he was losing his mind.

3

The orchestra started a waltz, the first few bars looping gently to a short pause. Jemima looked on listlessly from the side of the ballroom as the couples on the floor made their bows and curtseys, changed their partners and resumed the dance. Bill and Alfred Keane were directly behind her. They were discussing Keane's latest backstreet conquest, a clerk from Watts' warehouse on Fountain Street, in the most lurid language. Jemima, who was both widely read and well past the blushes of youthful innocence, was not shocked or scandalised by what she overheard; and she had long ago accepted that her brother was a committed denizen of this clandestine world. She did wish, however, that they would pay more consideration to their surroundings. They were in the Polygon, seat of the great Fairbairn family, and the sanctimonius were everywhere.

The wide ballroom was illuminated by a low-hanging formation of ornate gas chandeliers, which cast a soft yet pervasive orange light on to the guests gathered below. Over a hundred had already arrived, and those who were not engaged in the waltz stood talking of the glorious successes of the opening ceremony with grave satisfaction. The oak-panelled walls, usually covered with paintings, were all but bare: Thomas Fairbairn was chairman of the Exhibition, and had led by example when loaning the curators artwork from his collection.

According to the monstrous clock on the mantle, Jemima

had been at the ball for less than an hour, yet it felt strangely as if she had always been there, consigned to a particularly tedious level of Purgatory. A bibbed, heavily oiled waiter floated past, bearing a tray of crystal champagne flutes. She plucked one off and drank deeply. Bill and Keane, seeing her do this, left their less than private conversation to claim drinks of their own.

'Dearest Jemima,' drawled Keane as he leant past her to pick up a glass, 'has anyone ever told you of your quite startling resemblance to Mr Millais' *Mariana*? D'you know it? You have the same straight nose, and her pale auburn hair is·yours exactly. Most handsome, I must say.'

Jemima looked into Keane's smooth, equine face and thanked him with faint sarcasm. One would not think that this effete character was the second son of one of Manchester's wealthiest cotton magnates. Like her brother, he lived in fear of the family firm and did all he could to forget its inevitable claim on his future.

'Where's Father got to, I wonder,' mused Bill idly, taking a swig of champagne. 'I don't see him. Off strengthening his business contacts in the smoking room, I expect.'

Jemima turned away from the dancing. 'As long as he is not preparing me another suitor from his inexhaustible supply of whey-faced, chinless millionaires, William, I am content.'

Keane snorted with mirth. 'D'you recall the reception at Waite's, Bill, last October? That poor dunce from Liverpool? Why, I thought our Mrs J. was going to reduce him to tears before the entire company!'

Their laughter was intended to be collusive, to show Jemima how much they admired her strength of will, but it irritated her nonetheless. They could hardly understand what it was like to be hawked around as if you were an aging brood mare or an unwanted piece of furniture. This was the humiliation of her position – as a penniless widow entirely dependent upon her rich father, she was forced to endure his intermittent efforts to rid himself of her.

Jemima took a sip of her champagne and surveyed the room, which was growing fuller by the minute. For a

Manchester assembly, she had to admit, it was a remarkably eclectic one. Amongst the usual industrialists and their families were churchmen, nobles of all stripes and a smattering of rather more singular figures. Some were plainly literary in background, or gentlemen from the national press; others she recognised as notable personalities from the art world, such as Sir Charles Eastlake and his statuesque wife, and the bespectacled Dr Waagen of the Berlin gallery.

A handful, however, stubbornly defied any attempt at classification. She spied an especially conspicuous example leaning in the tall stone doorway that led through to the smoking room. Heftily built with a large black beard, he had a cigarette stuck in his mouth and his shirt was open at the neck – a dishevelled appearance more suited to the end of a night's revelry than the beginning. He was watching the ballroom nonchalantly, but there was a wolfish air to him. Jemima felt sure that he was on the lookout for something. Suddenly, calmly, his eyes flickered on to hers, as if he'd been aware of her scrutiny. Smoke trailed out of his nostrils. He gave her a slow wink.

Embarrassed, Jemima turned back quickly to Keane and Bill, saying the first thing that came into her head. 'A – a shame that Prince Albert could not be with us this evening.'

They fell upon this much-discussed topic with enthusiasm, expressing heartfelt sympathy for the recent Royal bereavement. The previous Sunday, the Duchess of Gloucester, last child of mad King George and Victoria's beloved great-aunt, had died. It was this loss that had kept the Queen from Manchester and prevented Albert from attending the Fairbairns' ball.

'You could see the strain in him, I thought,' opined Bill.

'He is right to hurry back to his family,' Keane said sagaciously. 'They need him. It's said that the Queen positively *wallows* in grief. Gets quite drunk on it, she does.'

Jemima nodded along, not listening; after a couple of minutes, she glanced back furtively at the doorway. The bearded man had gone.

Bill caught sight of something behind her, and his face lit up. 'Why, look who's arrived!' he cried. 'Major Wray's guardian angel! Come over, sir, join us! We noticed you leave the opening ceremony in the most dramatic manner – I trust nothing was amiss?'

Mr Kitson appeared at Jemima's side. He looked somewhat abashed at this mention of his departure from the ceremony, and was clearly uncomfortable in the grand surroundings of the Polygon. His evening suit, she saw, had shiny patches on the shoulders, and his features were a little drawn; but his eyes held the same arch intelligence they had done in her father's office on Mosley Street. Jemima felt her pulse quicken slightly, and a smile pull at the corner of her mouth. She adjusted her shawl and surreptitiously checked the pin that was holding up her hair, no longer so thoroughly bored by the Fairbairns' ball.

Talking loudly over the orchestra, which had just struck up the robust rhythm of the gallop, he bade them all a good evening, then bowed to her. 'Nothing of note, thank you, Mr Norton. I only needed some air.'

'You missed little, sir, in truth,' proclaimed Keane loftily. 'The poor Prince's spirits were so depressed that he spoke in little more than a murmur throughout. And the others – the bishop, the mayor and Mr Fairbairn – all adopted the same tone so as not to seem like they were trying to out-speak him. As a result, almost nothing of the ceremonials could be heard beyond the dais. My feeling was—'

Bill pretended to recognise someone across the room, over the charging heads of the gallopers. He hooked his arm through Keane's and dragged his garrulous friend away.

Jemima and the *Star*'s street philosopher were alone once more. She suggested they move away from the commotion of the gallop to a quieter corner, over by the ballroom's long bank of French windows. Since their first meeting on Saturday, Jemima had managed to learn something about the enigmatic Mr Kitson. Finding his work in her back-issues of the *London Courier* had been easy. Although most of that paper's articles were printed anonymously, enough pieces of art correspondence bore the initials 'TK' for her to be able to build up a clear idea of his style. And it was distinctive indeed, deeply knowledgeable yet brimming with savage wit;

he had been unafraid both to champion unknowns, and to go up against the most established and respected figures. His contributions had ceased abruptly, however, in early 1854. If he had not come to Manchester until the winter of 1856, this left nearly two years unaccounted for. Mr Kitson's story, as she had been told it, lacked a chapter.

She told him that she had not expected to see him there, and asked how he had managed to obtain an invitation. He replied that it had been done through Colonel Bennett, out of gratitude for his having helped Major Wray; but that the Colonel, and indeed everyone else at the ball prior to her brother, now seemed markedly reluctant to have anything whatsoever to do with him.

'They have discovered your occupation, I'll wager,' Jemima said. 'They took you for a medical man, as I first did, but have since uncovered the truth.' She shook her head. 'But it is too late – a street philosopher is present at a society ball, like a serpent that has slithered between the bars of the parrot cage.'

His eyebrow moved by the smallest fraction. 'I think you exaggerate their fear of the *Manchester Evening Star*, Mrs James. Although I must say that my editor is certainly excited by the benefit he believes this experience will offer to my work.'

'And you are not, sir?'

'I did not come here with a complete absence of enthusiasm, I admit.' He paused. 'Knowing as I did who else would be in attendance.'

Jemima met his gaze for a second. They both smiled, a little shyly; and a clear, powerful understanding coursed between them. Unnerved by the strength of this silent connection, Jemima looked away suddenly, out through the French windows, across the Polygon's stone terrace to the moonlit lawns beyond.

'There – there is much inspiration for your pen here tonight, I would imagine,' she managed to say, acutely aware of his grey eyes upon her and the beating of her heart beneath her ballgown.

Mr Kitson was quiet for a few seconds longer. 'Indeed, madam. The cravenness and vanity upon which the street philosopher thrives are here in abundance. Especially amusing is the spectacle of the nobility being forced to ingratiate itself with the same industrialists it has disdained and denigrated for so many generations.'

Her composure recovered, Jemima turned back towards him. One side of his face was tinted silver by the moonlight, emphasising the line of his cheekbone; just beneath his jaw was a shaving cut, plainly inflicted by an unsteady hand. His lip curled slightly. 'Over there, for instance, by the fireplace.'

A tall man with a drawn, haughty face was smiling queasily as he listened to the vigorous extrapolations of Mr Gregory Simcock, owner of a successful small-ware mill and an occasional dinner guest of Jemima's father.

'The Earl of Beeston,' Mr Kitson continued dryly, 'has lent a handful of mouldy Ruiysdaels to the Exhibition, and expects the Committee's boundless gratitude for his generous contribution. Yet it is common knowledge that the good Earl is quite bankrupt, having thrown away the family fortune on the *rouge-et-noirs* of various Metropolitan gaming houses – and that he has only submitted his paintings because he needs to sell them as soon as possible.'

Jemima feigned dismay. 'Surely not! What of the stated goals of the Exhibition, Mr Kitson – what of the art education of the poor?'

The street philosopher grinned. 'For the Earl, Mrs James, these are strictly secondary to drumming up a purchaser. And if that wealthy looking fellow he speaks with so superciliously were to offer a half-decent sum, our noble friend would kiss those plebeian chops in sheer relief.'

Jemima's laugh caught her by surprise, causing her to spill what was left of her champagne on Mr Kitson's shoes. She apologised profusely, and attempted to sweep away the droplets on the shining black leather with the hem of her skirts. Her naked elbow brushed briefly against the sleeve of his evening jacket; he took a polite step backwards, assuring her of his unconcern.

They talked on for another minute or so, sharing acerbic observations about a number of the Fairbairns' guests. Mr Kitson's easy articulacy made Jemima remember the scheme she had devised during the slower passages of the opening ceremony. She revealed in a confidential tone that her father, in order to demonstrate his dedication to the Art Treasures Exhibition as both a Committee member and an employer of labour, had recently announced that he intended to pay for a grand expedition of the entire Norton Foundry to the building at Old Trafford. Jemima had learned that there were to be no lecturers or guides present in the Exhibition; it had been assumed that the paintings on display would somehow explain themselves to their unschooled viewers without the need for intermediaries. Pondering this obvious oversight in relation to the Foundry visit, it had occurred to Jemima that she was acquainted with an authority on matters of art.

'The strong belief in the potential of the Exhibition that you expressed when we last spoke surely makes you the ideal person to address my father's workforce. A short talk in the modern galleries is all that will be required, I should think – merely to cast some basic illumination on their contents.'

Mr Kitson nodded; he had divined her plan. He knew that she was trying to engineer a situation where her father was in his debt, and obliged to overlook his humble, slightly disreputable post at the *Star*. Some form of courtesy would have to be extended – perhaps even an invitation to dine at Norton Hall – which would open the way for the two of them to commence a proper association.

'And will you be in attendance, madam, during this visit?'

'I will,' Jemima answered, her smile broadening.

'Then I would consider it an honour.' He glanced down at her empty glass, and reached forward to take it. 'Allow me to fetch you another, Mrs James. Will you wait for me here?'

The dancers were embarking on the first movement of a quadrille. Their numbers had swelled significantly, and Kitson had to push himself up against the wall to pass by the whirling mass of coat-tails and flounces. He barely noticed them. All he saw was her face as she laughed; the thick, loose coils of her hair; the soft curve of her neck, exposed to the Polygon's orange glow.

Kitson had spent the afternoon locked away in his attic.

Pacing across the rug, aiming the occasional kick at his desk or divan, he had forced himself to relive those few seconds on the balcony a hundred times over, striving to recall exactly what he had seen – and to determine whether Cracknell had been real or the product of his diseased imagination. Black doubt crept insidiously into any solid conclusion he reached, though, rotting it away and leaving him floundering once again in miserable confusion. Gripped by a fierce headache, he had lain down upon the floor; and, curled up by the grate, had finally fallen into an exhausted, dreamless sleep, waking only half an hour before the commencement of the ball.

Yet now, less than two hours later, he could hardly recognise this behaviour as his own. They were the actions of a madman – not of the charming, self-possessed lover of the widow Jemima James. The travails of the past few days now seemed trifling. His run-in with Wray was an unfortunate coincidence, best forgotten. The incident at the opening ceremony was the last delusion of a mind now firmly on the mend. All he wanted on Earth was to find a waiter, obtain two glasses, and get back to her as quickly as possible.

Mrs James' assessment of his status at the Polygon ball, however, was woefully correct. Away from the dancing, the street philosopher found himself caught in a great shoal of disapproving faces. A waiter approached, cruising like a clipper through the assembly, his tray aloft. Kitson's attempt to hail him was utterly ignored; the man simply altered his course, cutting towards the Polygon's main hall. At that moment, Kitson was so full of light-hearted hope that he decided to give chase, repeating his hail as he did so. This attracted further opprobrium, with someone clucking 'disgraceful' as he passed them. Neither did it halt the waiter; indeed, he seemed to pick up speed. He left the ballroom, bending away into a servant's corridor, vanishing from sight.

Kitson took four steps into this corridor and stopped. There was no sign of the man he pursued. Away from the orchestra, the hush was striking; a pungent smell of beeswax had replaced the many mingled perfumes of the ballroom, and the dim lambency of candlelight seemed almost like darkness after the gas chandeliers. He wondered what he was to do now.

A hand clapped on Kitson's shoulder, seizing hold of his collar. His first thought was that he was to be ejected from the Polygon by a footman, and separated from Mrs James; but he was shoved instead into a corner beneath the twist of a back staircase and held hard against the wall. It was far worse than that.

'Well I never,' hissed his assailant, his heavy beard scratching against Kitson's ear, 'if it isn't the fellow who saved Archie bloody Wray. Why would he do such a thing, I wonder, knowing what he does?'

'Cracknell,' Kitson gasped. 'Release me, damn it. What do you –'

'Is he on a divinely ordained mission to heal the afflicted, like Saint Elizabeth of Hungary? Does he hold an honest belief in the ultimate bloody goodness within every man?' The grip on Kitson's collar tightened. 'Or has he perhaps forgotten what exactly our Archie is a party to?'

Despite painful protests from his chest, Kitson managed to turn himself around and push the other man back. And there it was, that same face he had glimpsed from the northern balcony, now only an arm's length away. It had gained a few lines, and the black beard was flecked with grey – but it was indisputably the face of Richard Cracknell. Something was different, though; there was a bitterness beneath the old bombastic swagger that both reduced him and made him seem yet more volatile. He grabbed Kitson's lapel, bunching it up in his hairy, tobacco-stained fist.

As his initial shock receded, Kitson felt a rush of fury. His detestation of this man, he discovered, was quite undiminished by the time that had passed. 'Do you suppose I *knew*?' he spat. 'It was dark. I could see nothing. Do you honestly think I would have helped Wray if—' He tried to free himself, but could not. Cracknell was still the stronger. 'What the devil are you doing here? What do you *want*?'

Cracknell's grin was chillingly familiar. 'Let's begin with Mrs James, shall we?'

Kitson frowned uncomprehendingly. He stopped struggling. A cold, deadening heaviness was gathering in his midriff; his fingers were suddenly numb. 'What – what of her?'

148

Seeing that restraint was no longer necessary, Cracknell released him. 'The hand of fate is at work here, Thomas. Can you not feel it? I arrive in Manchester to hear of a stabbing, and discover first that it's Wray – and second that a fellow named Kitson was responsible for saving him. So I root around, as I am wont to do, and I find out that my dear old comrade Thomas Kitson is on the most favourable terms with none other than Charles Norton's daughter. Is this chance? I think not! A higher agency is at work, my friend!'

'What are you talking about?' Kitson could hear the tense uncertainty in his voice. 'You are drunk.'

With a throaty chuckle, Cracknell took a cigarette from his pocket and lit it on a nearby candle. 'I've been watching you two this evening – all that delightful awkwardness and secretive simpering. For what it's worth, I'd say your feet are well parked under that particular table. The gratitude of widows, eh? Still, a good piece of work – almost a shame to think of what must be done.'

Now Kitson was growing properly afraid. 'What is your meaning?'

Cracknell laughed. '*Charles bloody Norton*, Thomas!' he said, as if this was an explanation in itself; then he looked at his former junior incredulously. 'Christ's balls, d'ye really not know? Is that not why you are here, living in this godforsaken cesspool of a city? And cosying up to his daughter?' He hesitated, taking the cigarette from his lips. 'Haven't you looked around the Exhibition yet?'

This caught Kitson off-guard. 'No one has, bar the Committee. It opens to the public tomorrow. Why do you ask?'

Cracknell put a hand on his shoulder, rather more gently than before. 'Introduce me to Mrs James.'

Jolted to his senses, Kitson knocked away Cracknell's hand. 'I will not. I don't know what your purpose is in Manchester, despite all your insinuations, but I will have nothing to do with it.'

Cracknell smiled indulgently, a clear threat in his eyes. 'Introduce me to her, Thomas,' he murmured, 'or by God I will go over there and introduce myself.'

4

It was immediately clear that something was amiss.

When Mr Kitson eventually reappeared, he brought not flutes of champagne but the black-bearded man who had winked at Jemima earlier. The street philosopher's entire demeanour had altered. All peace and good humour had left him; his expression contained the same mixture of anger and shame that it had done on Mosley Street whilst in the proximity of Major Wray. He was stooping slightly, a hand lingering at the side of his chest – clutching at the ribs, Jemima could not help but think, as if it was holding them together.

The bearded man was the obvious reason for Mr Kitson's discomfort, and Jemima found herself disliking him for this alone, before he had even opened his mouth to speak. As they approached the French windows, she saw that this odd person was not in proper evening dress. His jacket and trousers belonged to two different suits, and his puce waistcoat was stained with a variety of unidentifiable substances. He was attracting a good deal of attention, none of it favourable. Jemima wondered who he must know in order to have been invited.

Then, sustaining a neutral tone with evident effort, Mr Kitson introduced him. Jemima recognised the name at once. 'Were you not the Crimean correspondent for the *London Courier*, Mr Cracknell? "The Tomahawk of the *Courier*", didn't they call you, in the later stages of the campaign?'

Mr Cracknell laughed condescendingly. 'Yes, madam, my editor at the time decided to adorn me with that colourful title.'

A brisk polka began, the dancers greeting it with giddy hurrahs. Jemima looked at the two men. The *London Courier* linked them, but the relationship was palpably not that of correspondents working in different branches of a publication who happened to have become acquainted. Their demeanour spoke of something weightier, darker; something that had gone terribly wrong.

'Much as *Punch* recently saw fit to call your father the Buckle King,' Mr Cracknell continued, his voice becoming more loaded. 'It is a silly habit of the press. I rather prefer mine, I must say.' He lifted up his hand, drawing on the cigarette concealed within, and turned to Mr Kitson, who was staring down impassively at the floor. 'Which is not to belittle Mr Norton's accomplishments – Heaven forbid it! How could I, a lowly grubber scorned by the world, possibly cast aspersion on a man who has risen so high, and in such an astonishingly short space of time?'

'His ascent has indeed been remarkable,' Jemima replied carefully.

Tapping ash on to the Fairbairns' carpet, Cracknell shook his head in sardonic amazement. 'What connections the fellow must have.'

With some irritation, Jemima sensed that she was being used by Mr Cracknell to make a point for Mr Kitson's benefit – not that he seemed any wiser than she about what the Tomahawk of the *Courier* was implying. That her father had somehow attracted Mr Cracknell's disapproval did not surprise her; this jaded eccentric appeared to define himself by being antagonistic. She would not, however, simply stand and listen to him pontificate unchallenged.

'So tell me, sir,' she broke in, 'why is the Tomahawk not in India? I have read that the Sepoys are close to open revolt. Is your rightful place not out there?'

The overbearing smirk that had been playing across Mr Cracknell's florid cheeks since their introduction grew forced and mirthless. He did not wish to discuss the Indian mutiny and his great distance from it, and tried to divert their talk back to Charles Norton.

Jemima persisted. 'The *Courier*, I see, has sent someone else. Could it be that you have lost favour with the magazine's proprietors – that the controversy caused by your behaviour during the Russian War has prevented them from appointing you?'

Mr Kitson shifted his weight from one foot to the other, raising his head to watch Mr Cracknell's reaction to Jemima's question.

'It was a complicated situation, madam.' He sighed, as if summoning his patience. 'The war ended badly, as I'm sure you'll recall, with the enemy undefeated and things generally rather unsatisfactory. None were pleased by that spineless treaty drawn up in Paris. The neutralisation of the Black Sea! What the deuce is that?' There was a quick anger in his voice. He leant in towards her, so close that she could see the broken veins in his cheeks. 'The truth is that we gained next to nothing for our staggering losses. The Russians *laughed at us*, Mrs James – we took their port city from them only to give it back a few months later and sail away.' He dropped the end of his cigarette on the floor, and trod on it emphatically. 'Few reputations escaped from that dreadful mess unscathed – my own included.'

A neat enough piece of evasion, but it did not satisfy Jemima for an instant. More blatant provocation was needed if she was to learn anything worthwhile. 'Forgive me, sir, but I was referring to the specific allegations made against you alone. I greatly admired your work in the first months of the war. I must confess that the invasion seemed gratuitous to me from the start, but I had no idea that it was being done so thoughtlessly, with so little regard on the part of the commanders for the lives of those beneath them. You helped to raise awareness of this.'

Mr Cracknell nodded in wary acknowledgement, knowing that a qualification was coming. Mr Kitson had withdrawn into himself once more. Jemima could not tell if he was even listening.

'It is regrettable, though, that you grew so vindictive. There

152

was that one officer with whom you became quite obsessed, that colonel . . .'

He snorted. 'It was warranted, madam, I assure you.'

'But it enabled your opponents to depict you as a mere provocateur, whose views stemmed only from personal animosity. And then there were those letters in the *Times*, accusing you of opportunism and worse—'

'As I think I said, Mrs James, it was most complicated; and, I might add, entirely beyond female comprehension.' Mr Cracknell's tolerant smile now contained a distinct seam of malice. 'I can assure you, also, that there were far more opportunistic people on that Peninsula than I. Compared with some I could name, I was a beginner, a bumbling amateur! If you do not believe me,' he added casually, narrowing his eyes, 'you can ask Kitson here.'

And suddenly Jemima saw it. Her street philosopher had been in the Crimea with Cracknell of the *Courier*. This was the missing episode from Mr Kitson's life.

The orchestra brought the dancing to a close and stopped playing, setting down their instruments. After a round of applause, the flushed participants dispersed throughout the ballroom, adding appreciably to the hum of conversation. The Fairbairns must have returned from Bank Top station, after escorting the Prince to the Royal train; they would be making their entrance at any moment. Someone cleared their throat close behind her. She turned to see Bill, looking at her apologetically.

'Sorry, Jem,' he mumbled, 'but Father insists that you join us. He wants to offer his congratulations to our hosts with his family around him. Or so he says.'

Jemima acquiesced absently, without a fight, her mind trying to assimilate this discovery into what she already knew. It was about the Crimea. It was about these two newspapermen and what had happened between them there; but it was also somehow about her father and the Norton Foundry, and that expedition to Balaclava where her husband had perished. There could be little doubt that Mr Cracknell had a reason for being in Manchester. What precisely it was, however, and what he planned to do, she could only speculate.

Mr Kitson bade her farewell. She looked up, setting her troubling reflections aside. They shared a despondent glance, realising that they would not see each other again that evening. Both knew that their friendship, which had seemed such a gloriously simple thing not half an hour before, was now beset with difficulty; but neither was deterred.

Mr Cracknell was busy introducing himself to a bemused Bill. Jemima took the street philosopher's hand in hers. 'Do not forget, Mr Kitson,' she said evenly. 'Three weeks' time. The Foundry's visit to the Exhibition.' Their fingers locked; she pressed her gloved thumb hard against the side of his hand.

Mr Cracknell, releasing Bill, moved himself back between them. 'Goodbye, Mrs James,' he said, his tone both jolly and dismissive. 'A real pleasure to talk with you, madam.'

Charles Norton watched his children cross the ballroom, wishing they would move faster and put more distance between themselves and the two miscreants at the French windows.

Mr Twelves had made his first report the previous night. The investigator had revealed that this Kitson was a street philosopher with the *Evening Star*, resident in the city for under a year, his previous whereabouts uncertain. Despite the social character of his work, he had few acquaintances or contacts, preferring to treat his topic in more general terms. He was highly regarded by his peers, though, and appreciated by the *Star*'s readers; circulation had doubled since his addition to its staff.

'I've read 'im myself, from time to time,' Twelves had commented slyly. 'All flash and banter, but a good deal better than the rest o' that miserable organ.'

More pertinently, it transpired that Kitson had not been Wray's attacker on Saturday night, as the Major's note had suggested, but rather the opposite. And afterwards, apparently, the fellow had sat in Norton's own office as Wray was taken up to the Infirmary, drinking his brandy at the invitation of his meddlesome daughter; she had not, of course, thought to mention any of this to him herself. Norton had listened with growing confusion, none the wiser as to what it was about Kitson that had prompted such panic in Wray.

Then, at the opening ceremony, he had been talking with Colonel Bennett – the 25th had just taken a consignment of undress belts made with Norton buckles – and had learned that the Colonel had obtained Kitson an invitation to the Fairbairns' ball. It had brought him no little pleasure to inform Bennett that he had asked a street philosopher from a notorious local rag into the house of the most powerful family in Manchester. The Colonel had turned quite pale.

At the Polygon, he had kept his eyes peeled for this person, confident that so modest a character would be easy to spot. He had cursed when he located the man deep in conversation with his daughter. They were doubtlessly building on the acquaintance they had formed in his Mosley Street office. It was typical of Jemima to form associations that would cause him the utmost inconvenience or embarrassment. Charles remembered her marriage, how she had – on purpose, it seemed to him – selected the most argumentative and bloody minded of his managers to be her husband; and how much more outspoken Anthony James had become after their union. James and his forthright opinions had almost cost Norton the greatest chance of his life, in fact. Fortune, thankfully, had intervened.

This Kitson did not look like much of a menace, though. He had the bearing of an impoverished scholar, or a poet perhaps; Norton had expected someone a little more rascally. It was hard to think of this cerebral sort as one who necessitated the attentions of Mr Twelves.

But then the Irishman had joined them and the true nature of the situation was revealed. Everything suddenly made sense. Despite his innocuous appearance, this Kitson was an accomplice of Richard Cracknell, formerly of the *London Courier*, a disgraced and very dangerous man. Norton knew Cracknell well; earlier in the year, he had made a desperate nuisance of himself at the Foundry's London sales office. It had taken the intervention of the police to deter him from his activities. He was an undoubted enemy of the company, and could only be in Manchester to make further trouble.

Mr Twelves would have to be informed – Norton's visitor was arriving in a matter of weeks, and this disturbance had to be resolved by then.

After dispatching Bill to reclaim Jemima from these undesirables, Norton summoned a pair of footmen from the hall, and voiced a suspicion that the bearded man by the French windows was present without an invitation. They bowed, and went to consult with the butler.

His offspring arrived before him. Bill, as usual, looked ridiculous, his waistcoat patterned with golden oriental dragons, his necktie an ostentatious shade of plum. The lad imagines that he is a new Lord Byron, Norton thought ill-temperedly – a Regency buck in search of profligate adventure. Did he not realise that this was a different age, an age of industry and pious discipline? Well, no matter, the labour-lord told himself; he will be made to see it soon enough.

Jemima's brow was furrowed, as if she was deep in thought of a disquieting nature. Charles felt his responsibility towards his widowed daughter keenly, but she made it impossible for him to behave as a kind father should. She was so fractious and deceptive, concealing so much and doing whatever she could to undermine him; and now she was openly fraternising with his enemies. It would stop. He dreaded to think what that deranged rogue Cracknell might have told her.

'You and I will speak, Jemima,' he said sternly.

Before she could respond, Thomas Fairbairn was announced. Everyone turned towards the main doors that led out into the hall; and the chairman entered in the most lordly manner, graciously accepting the congratulations that erupted all around him. Norton beamed, his fears momentarily forgotten, and raised his applauding hands.

'We are being scrutinised,' Cracknell shouted over the uproar, indicating a huddle of conferring servants. 'I propose we go outside.'

They left through the French windows. The night was cool and quiet after the hot crush of the ballroom. Cracknell strolled towards the balustrade, his shoes clacking on the stone terrace, looking out at the stand of silvery oak trees that bordered the garden.

'Well, that was most amusing, wasn't it?' he declared. 'Did you notice how I guessed that you had not told her about your time in the Crimea, Thomas? Perspicacious, no?'

Kitson strode over to Cracknell and grasped hold of his arm. 'You stabbed Wray, didn't you? Deliberately close to my lodgings, so I would hear?'

Cracknell grinned as he shook Kitson off. 'Is that what you were brooding over in there, whilst your she-lion mauled me so savagely? I salute your courage, my friend; these northern fillies have a flintiness about them that is rather frightening.' He lit a cigarette. 'I think she got a taste though, don't you? Something to chew on, at least. She seems the chewing type, does the widow.'

Kitson glared at him, still barely able to believe that he was being forced to battle against this person once more. 'Where is this leading, Cracknell? What is this all-consuming interest in Charles Norton?'

The cigarette made Cracknell cough hard. 'Ye Gods,' he wheezed, 'all these bloody questions, Thomas. I had no idea that you were so damned ignorant. All will be revealed in time, don't you worry. Just be sure to visit the Exhibition as soon as you are able, and know this.' He wiped his eyes on his sleeve, and then said offhandedly, 'Boyce is coming.'

'*Boyce?* To Manchester?'

'Yes, Thomas, to Manchester – to this thing, this Art Treasures Exhibition.' Cracknell spoke slowly, as if addressing an idiot.

'How – how did you discover this?'

'Simply by using the investigative skills that have made me such an effective newspaperman – skills you would do well to recover.' Cracknell drew again on his cigarette, his broad face puckering with malevolence. 'You and I alone know the full extent of that man's crimes. And we're going to punish him. More than that, we're going to bloody well *destroy him.* You'll see.'

Kitson stared speechlessly at the luminous windows of

the Polygon, a profusion of disturbing scenarios playing out in his mind. Addresses were underway inside, the assembled guests suddenly shaking with laughter. He caught a glimpse of Jemima amidst the admiring crowd, standing behind her chortling father, her slender arms crossed with impatience.

The French windows opened, and a pair of footmen emerged. It was obvious who they sought; Kitson looked around, but saw only the moonlit garden. Cracknell had disappeared.

Before Sebastopol,
Crimean Peninsula
October–November 1854

1

'From the western end of the Causeway Heights, just north of Balaclava, the true scale of the calamity is revealed. A skein of shattered bodies is cast across the floor of the valley beyond, the men and their horses intermingled in death, knocked to pieces by grape, canister and shot. Patches of bright colour, the cherry red of a Hussar's overalls, the golden yellow of a standard, or the blue of a Lancer's tunic, can be made out in amongst the dust and blood; and tiny sparks of light ripple over the surface of the carnage, where bridles, spurs, buttons and blades catch the setting sun.'

Kitson lowered his pocketbook and rubbed his aching eyes. He sat blankly for a few moments, then cleared his throat and tried to begin his next sentence. His mind kept stumbling, however, the words emerging in the wrong order or not at all. After six or seven attempts he gave up, and only just managed to prevent himself hurling his pencil down the hillside.

Cracknell came panting up the path from the low-walled redoubts further along the Heights, around which the earlier stages of the battle had been fought. His brow was shining with sweat. 'Damn this country,' he gasped, spitting out a bead of phlegm. 'How vertiginous it is! Enough to bring a fellow's heart to bursting point.'

He staggered over to where Kitson was sitting, complaining about various aspects of life on the peninsula. The view from the summit, however, was enough to silence even Richard Cracknell.

'So there it is,' he said eventually. 'The Light Brigade is lost.'

Black-winged carrion birds were circling down towards the valley floor with the lazy ease of creatures who knew that a certain feed awaited them. There was a distant dash of musketry from the far side of the valley, on the Fedyukhin Hills, where the Russian Army had managed to gain a lasting foothold after the battle. They seemed to be firing on a British detail sent out to retrieve the last of the wounded, which had accidentally strayed into range.

Cracknell turned away, fumbling with a cigarette. 'Hell's teeth,' he muttered, 'they might as well have sent the poor bastards charging straight at the barricades of Sebastopol.'

He sat down heavily and asked to see what Kitson had. The junior correspondent handed over his pocketbook and lay back on the grass, gazing up at the evening sky, following wisps of cloud as they drifted out to sea. Kitson was immensely tired. It had been many nights since he had rested properly. He had always been a light sleeper, easily disturbed; and the noise of the Allied artillery bombardment, although over two miles distant from the small hut Cracknell had secured for them, was more than he could stand. This dull, constant fatigue was slowly leeching away his vigour, his eloquence, and his enthusiasm for his work.

Cracknell, Kitson realised, was pleased. 'This is good, Thomas,' he said approvingly. 'Good indeed. You have a real feeling for the human tragedy of all this – for the plight of the men who are falling victim to our generals' woeful ineptitude. The political and the strategic elements elude you almost completely, of course, but this is to be expected, given your background. You write through sorrow and sympathy rather than anger, a deficiency well supplied by my own commentaries.' He tossed the pocketbook on to Kitson's chest. 'This, my friend, is why we are such an effective partnership.'

Their account of the battle of the Alma and its aftermath had been published mere days after the event, thanks to the wonder of the electric telegraph. Filled with both copious praise for the fighting men and severe criticism of Lord Raglan and his generals, it had been a major success for the *Courier*, completely selling out the issue that had carried it. Telegrams had arrived from O'Farrell relating its impact, and the fierce debate it had provoked – and urging them to keep up the good work. Already, however, there had been signs of how this prominence might have adverse effects. Shortly after publication, the Captain whose vessel conveyed their reports to the telegraph office at Varna had stated that he was no longer prepared to associate with them. Cracknell had found this encouraging, strangely enough, and a new messenger had been secured that same morning; but for Kitson at least, a worrying precedent had been set.

The senior correspondent now started to read out his own work. It was predictably blunt and confrontational, littered with speculation, fearlessly assigning blame to those in command. There was a delight in Cracknell's voice, a deep pleasure in his own polemical savagery that was utterly incongruous with his subject. Kitson closed his eyes.

'*A crime was done today, dear reader,*' the report concluded stridently, '*a great and terrible crime against all the codes and usages of war. Our foe, the men of Tsar Nicholas, took a great chance, rushing out of Sebastopol in massive numbers, cunningly skirting the Allied camps on the plateau to strike at Balaclava, the port supplying their besiegers. They were thwarted, but only after a great many valiant lives had been squandered due to the wretched stupidity of a villainous, cold-hearted cadre of aristocratic buffoons. Our Light Cavalry, among the finest in the world, was left unused at the Alma, when it could have made a real difference; and has now been destroyed needlessly at Balaclava. This reprehensible waste seems the result of a spat between noblemen, between the famous enemies (and, we might add, brothers-in-law) Lucan and Cardigan. The latter, who supposedly led the charge, was interestingly among the very first back to safety; and whilst so many of his men lay bleeding in the dust, the Earl was enjoying a bath on his yacht in Balaclava harbour, with the prospect of a fine dinner before him. Such is the calibre of leadership in the Crimea!*'

His recitation complete, Cracknell launched directly into a passionate tirade about the wider strategic failings of the campaign – about how Raglan had made yet another error in listening to his engineers rather than his generals and bringing up the artillery for a bombardment instead of mounting an immediate attack.

'Now they pound away at earthworks with cannon, achieving nothing and allowing Russians to come at us as they have done here. And still, *still* they talk so lightly of Sebastopol falling in a matter of weeks!' He got to his feet and gazed out at the gruesome panorama before them. 'Honestly, I cannot believe that I supported this war at its outset. I shiver with embarrassment, Thomas, at the praise I heaped on this wrong-headed enterprise. I honestly thought that they had a proper plan of action – that they *had* to have one.' He shook his head, exhaling cigarette smoke. 'But they do not, my friend; they most definitely do not.'

After a few seconds' further contemplation, the senior correspondent let out an exclamation and pointed down at the redoubts. Kitson sat up. Turkish troops were removing the bodies of their slain comrades from the crude defensive structures, piling them up outside the walls like rolls of tattered, bloody cloth.

'Our Turkish allies,' Kitson said. 'I hear that they suffered heavy casualties resisting the Russian advance, before the British forces had turned out. Their sacrifice is worthy of mention, Mr Cracknell, do you not think?'

'Codswallop,' proclaimed Cracknell forcefully. 'The heathen dogs let two forts fall. Their cowardice damn near cost us the day. But I wasn't looking at them.' He tapped Kitson's arm, and then pointed again. 'Highlanders, man. Sir Colin Campbell and his ADC.'

The two officers from the Highland Brigade, in their kilts of dark green tartan and their black feather bonnets, weren't difficult to locate. They stood to one side of the redoubt, in conversation with an upright, bearded civilian in a long blue frock-coat, a peaked cap and highly polished riding boots.

'Russell of the *Times*,' Cracknell growled. 'My great rival. Ingratiating himself as usual. The slimy toad – I'll bet he saw everything.' The *Courier* team, delayed by the unexplained absence of their senior, had arrived in the valley some time after the final shot had been fired, and had been obliged to rely on eye-witnesses for their information on the battle itself. 'Here's what we'll do. I'll go down there, have a jaw with Billy Russell and those two bonnie Scotsmen, and see what more I can learn about the action. You stay here and brush up what we've got so far.'

Kitson jotted a note in his pocketbook. 'What of Styles?' he asked wearily. 'It has been some time since he left for the valley floor.'

'What? Oh yes – don't want him collapsing again, do we, with neither of us around to prop him up!' Cracknell chuckled wickedly. 'Very well – you find the boy then. I want you to keep up your watch on Mr Styles for me, Thomas. The lad's is a little soft in the head, I think. He'll need some careful supervision during the trials to come, you mark my words.'

Kitson watched as the senior correspondent trotted off towards the redoubt, shouting a robust 'hallo' to Russell and the Highlanders. That he could make such avuncular pronouncements with every appearance of sincerity was remarkable. In the month since the clash at the Alma, his treatment of Styles had been consistently, characteristically merciless, both with regards to the events of that day and the enduring issue of Madeleine Boyce. It was this un-relenting mockery, Kitson suspected, that was driving Styles to seek more and more time alone.

Cracknell reached the *Times'* correspondent and his companions, who greeted him with obvious reluctance. Kitson turned and headed down into the valley. He followed a narrow, winding footpath, cut deep into the grass by centuries of passage by Tartar shepherds. The hills around him were smooth and treeless, and dotted with pale rocks. In the distance, beyond the wide plateau that held the main Allied camps, the location of Sebastopol and its fortifications was marked by a few winding trails of grey smoke. To the left, off between two steep green spurs, was the dark ribbon of the sea.

Slowly, the slope began to level out, and Kitson passed through a large, abandoned vineyard. It was yet another corner of the fecund peninsula rendered barren by the invasion, yellow dust caking the withered, trampled vines.

As he picked his way towards the valley floor, the arid furrows became littered with the detritus of a recent battle. A beaten-in dragoon's helmet told him that this was where Brigadier-General Scarlett's Heavy Brigade had repelled the Russian cavalry, just after the struggle for the redoubts. Scraps of uniform from both armies had been sown into the vineyard by hundreds of stamping hooves, and sabre-shards winked like flints in the crumbling earth. Pushing aside a screen of ragged, browning leaves, Kitson saw a hand, severed just below the wrist, lying on the ground before him. White as soap, it was frozen in a loose pointing gesture, with a silver wedding band on the ring finger. Averting his gaze, he hurried on.

Styles was sitting atop a boulder in plain sight, as close to the battlefield as was safe. He was hunched over his paper, hard at work in the soft evening light, a battered cap of uncertain provenance pushed back on his head. Without speaking, Kitson approached, and peered over to see Styles' subject. The drawing in his lap depicted one of the many dead chargers laid out on the bed of the valley. This horse had been gutted by a cannonball, its entrails entirely gone, the carcass lying darkly hollow like an empty shell.

Kitson sighed, leaning up against the boulder and crossing his arms. This grisly scene was becoming typical of Styles' productions. Only one of his drawings, in fact, depicting the battlefield of the Alma, had so far been engraved for the *Courier*; since that day, the illustrator had been exposing himself to the most distressing sights that the war had to offer, dwelling upon them at unhealthy length. The resulting images were nightmarish, and completely unusable.

'Do you really imagine that the *Courier* will run that?' Kitson asked. Despite his best efforts, he could not keep the impatience from his voice.

Styles stopped drawing. He did not reply.

'I realise what you are attempting,' Kitson went on, 'truly I do. And as ever, your great skill is evident. But you must realise that no magazine in England would print such an image.'

The illustrator turned towards him sharply. 'I am only

doing what we came out here for, Kitson,' he snapped. 'To see war for what it is. Or have you forgotten?'

I have lost his confidence, Kitson thought. For some reason, he considers us to be adversaries. How had this happened? He uncrossed his arms and put his hands in his pockets, feeling suddenly ashamed, wondering how he could repair the damage that had plainly been done.

Styles stared out at the valley. 'Do you know what happened yet?'

Kitson brushed a fat autumnal fly from the shoulder of his jacket, trying as he did so to keep his eyes off the slaughter. The light breeze carried over a revolting, fleshy stench, already tainted with putrefaction. Over at the foot of the Causeway Heights, privates from the Highland Brigade were burying fallen hussars. Still clad in their magnificent uniforms, the bodies were being swung into deep pits, their brocaded sleeves flapping behind them as they plummeted to their graves.

'As far as we can deduce,' he said quietly, 'Cardigan's men were supposed to charge the contested redoubts up on the Heights, but went head-on for the Russian artillery instead. God only knows why.'

'So it was a mistake. Not even an ordinary defeat. All this death for the sake of a – a *blunder*.' Styles' voice grew bitterly angry. 'They will try to disguise what happened here, you know. They will try to dress it up in the garb of heroism – make it acceptable, admirable even. I must stand against this in my work, Kitson, do you not see? I must show the *truth*.'

'I do understand that, Styles, believe me, but—'

'Then keep to your business,' he interrupted, 'and allow me to keep to mine.'

Frowning, Kitson glanced away. How could he challenge this? Revelation of the truth of warfare, as he had declared himself on many previous occasions, was the cornerstone of the *Courier*'s presence in the Crimea. Yet for some reason it made him profoundly uncomfortable to hear this from Styles now. This same commitment fuelled Cracknell's grand-iloquent rage, spurring the senior correspondent on to ever more scathing condemnation of the British commanders; in

167

the young illustrator, however, it seemed to be fostering only a dark and violent melancholy.

'Come, Robert,' Kitson said after a while, adopting a conciliatory tone. 'We must not quarrel. God knows, this land needs no more ill-feeling in it. We are friends, are we not?'

Styles had resumed work on his sketch, the pencil scratching busily as it transcribed the charger's mangled remains. 'Yes,' he said after a pause, his voice low and a little strained, 'we are friends.'

2

The brushwood on Inkerman Ridge was thick and almost waist high. Major Maynard fought his way through, muttering curses as brambles and twigs scratched against his legs. He was holding a tin mug of steaming broth up in the air, in the hope of keeping it stable, but the uneven, slippery mud beneath the tangle of bushes was causing him to stumble frequently. Hot liquid splashed over his hands, making the chilled flesh smart and tingle.

Private Cregg followed about five yards behind him, cheeks ruddy from rum-and-water, with his minié rifle ready in his hands. Maynard knew that this was not necessarily a man to be relied upon. He could tell that Cregg was one of those who had fled to the service to escape the law, joining Her Majesty's Army in order to avoid being dangled from the gallows. The scoundrel was famous for his insubordination, and was regularly flogged for it; but the Major had noticed that Cregg treated him, and him alone, with a certain gruff deference. Above all else, Maynard believed in giving every man under his command the chance to prove his worth. So this was it – he was giving Private Cregg his chance.

Finally, they reached the battery. Maynard set the mug down and caught his breath. Lifting a fist to his mouth, he licked the warm broth off his knuckles and looked about him in the early morning half-light. The battery, built in haste as soon as the Allies had arrived on the Heights around Sebastopol, had since been abandoned as it stood too far forward of the rest of the line. It was large, constructed from sandbags and wire gabions filled with white rocks, and had two gun emplacements, designed for Lancasters from the look of them, both now empty.

The Allied positions were already lost in the fog behind them. All he could make out was the battery itself and a small grey ring of the wasteland around it. It was as if they were enclosed in an opaque, smoky bubble, lost to the rest of the ridge. The gloom was quite overpowering. Everything was thoroughly soaked by the drizzling rain that had been falling now for thirty-six straight hours. Maynard took out his watch. There was just enough light for him to see the hands against the white face; it was shortly before five. He put the watch back in his coat and picked up the mug, pressing his hands around it and inhaling the broth's thin aroma. With some effort, he resisted raising it to his lips, and instead began to walk slowly around the battery's perimeter.

'Hello?' he called, trying to keep his voice clear and confident. 'Hello, are you there?'

There was no reply, but he knew what he'd seen. He'd been standing in the forward pickets of the Second Division, talking to Major Hendricks of the 55th, a fellow India man and an old friend. The wind coming in from the Black Sea had shifted the fog slightly, affording him a brief glimpse of the abandoned battery. There, close to the dark mass of sandbags, had been a solitary figure in a cap and a long coat. It had been exposed for just a second before the fog engulfed it once more. Hendricks had laughingly declined to go with him to investigate, and advised him to ready his revolver. The Russians were getting increasingly cunning, he'd said, and audacious as well; their scouts and spies were often seen nosing around the old Sandbag Battery. Undeterred, Maynard had beckoned Cregg to his side, and then set out.

There was a scuffling sound somewhere to his rear. He turned to see Cregg hauling himself on to the battery wall, his charcoal greatcoat falling open to reveal the red tunic beneath, worn to the colour of cured beef by the months of hard campaigning. Once up there, the private adopted a crouched sharpshooter's pose, looking about him keenly as if searching for targets.

'Major,' he hissed urgently, 'what we after, exactly? This bloke you saw – 'e can't very well be one of our own, can 'e? What would 'e be doin' out 'ere, all by 'isself?'

'I believe that I recognised him, Cregg. A fellow from the *London Courier* magazine.'

Cregg's eyes, glinting beadily under the brim of his shako, stayed on the mists. 'You mean the paddy, Major? Fat cove – big black beard? Likes the sound of 'is own voice? I seen you with 'im at the Alma – chum o' yours, ain't 'e?'

Maynard could not help but smile at this vivid description. 'As much as anyone is,' he replied. 'Mr Cracknell and I are acquainted, but I would hesitate before claiming any more than that. I'm quite sure that he would jettison me in a moment if he believed it to be in his best interests – or should I say in the best interests of his work.' He continued his search, peering into the darkest recesses of the battery. They were quite empty. 'It was not him I saw, though – rather a member of his team. An illustrator.'

Now Cregg looked down at him, his face twisted into an uncomprehending sneer. 'What, like an artist, what draws an' that? Why would 'e be out 'ere?'

This was the nub of it. Maynard was but a humble soldier, a career man, not so very different from the scrawny chap up there on the battery. He stood well apart from the grand lords and refined gentlemen who deigned to wear the uniform, and he could not for a moment claim to understand the niceties of art. But even he could tell that it was not a morning for making illustrations.

'Indeed, Cregg.' Maynard completed his circuit. 'Well, there is certainly no one here now. A little mystery we shall not be able to solve, I fear.' He glanced down at the broth that sloshed blackly within the mug, and thought that he might get to drink it after all.

'Major!' said Cregg sharply, suddenly tensing. 'Major, what's that noise?'

For a second Maynard had no idea what the private was talking about. Thus far, the night had been a deathly quiet

171

one, as if the fog was muffling sound as well as obscuring sight. But then, away down the steep slope in front of the battery, he heard the faint creaking of cartwheels bouncing down an uneven road; the chink of metal, and the clump of boots; and, distant but quite clear, the murmuring of hundreds of voices, speaking in a thick alien tongue.

'That's – that's bleedin' *Russian*, that is! The bastards are gettin' ready to attack us!' The private scrabbled down from the battery.

'Calm yourself, man,' Maynard instructed firmly. 'It is but traffic on the road into Sebastopol. Major Hendricks was telling me of this shortly before we left the pickets. It runs along the base of the Chernaya valley. All quite routine.'

This served to confuse the soldier rather than reassure him. 'Supply road? But 'ow are they ever goin' to give it up, if they're gettin' new supplies?'

Maynard had no answer. Cregg was right: the campaign could not come to any sort of an end at present. The sad, simple truth was that the Allies lacked the troops to encircle the city properly, and their forces dwindled a little further with every passing day. Maynard's fear, shared by a growing number of officers, was that the inexplicable delay in mounting an assault on Sebastopol had cost them a quick victory, and that the already ailing army was now doomed to face a Crimean winter.

'You would be well advised to leave such matters to your superiors, Cregg,' he said. 'Now get yourself back to the line. Mrs Boyce and her friend should still be there with their cauldron of hot broth. I think you've earned yourself a cup.'

Cregg saluted and hurried off, plainly glad to be putting some ground between himself and the Sandbag Battery. Maynard turned back to the slope, lifted the mug and took a sip of broth. It was weak and bitter, and now only luke-warm; but he drank the rest down anyway, murmuring thanks to Mrs Boyce once he had finished. He had been most impressed to see her at the pickets, braving the cold and gloom in order to perform such an honest, valuable service for the sentries. Now there, he'd thought, is a person

172

with a proper sense of duty – more than could be said for her damned husband.

Boyce had been appointed to make the two o'clock tour of the line, a responsibility assigned to a different infantry colonel every night for the past three weeks. He had failed to appear, however, leaving Major Maynard no option but to perform this task for him, instead of retreating to his cot for some much-needed rest. No word had been sent, but Maynard knew that the Colonel (as he now was, having recently received an entirely undeserved promotion) had dined in the hut of some senior artillery officers half a mile back from the line. Obviously the attractions of a well-stocked table, and a sufficiently elevated company, had proved too compelling to leave. The Major had been angry, but not particularly surprised. It was hardly the first time Boyce had behaved in this manner.

Before heading back himself, Maynard decided on another circuit of the battery, to make a final check for any irregularities. As he trudged around its front, the dew from the coarse grass washing the mud from his boots, his brow slowly creased with gathering consternation. He wished that Hendricks, who had more experience of this portion of the line, had agreed to come out to the battery with him. The volume of noise rising up from the Chernaya valley seemed great indeed, and was growing by the second. Surely this could not be normal. Suddenly, there was a fresh clamour of Russian voices, shouting as if for order, mingled with the sound of rapidly turning wheels. These were not now the wheels of the Sebastopol supply train, of lumbering ox-carts loaded with flour, milk, or gunpowder, but something altogether lighter and faster, like small carriages or broughams – or pieces of field artillery.

Maynard swallowed, listening hard. This surely warranted an urgent report to Brigadier-General Pennefather of the Second Division. Pennefather might well laugh at him, and call him a lily-livered poltroon; or he might curse and castigate him for raising an unnecessary alarm, and bid him return post-haste to his own section of the line, where he knew what was what.

So be it. Maynard started to walk back in the direction of the pickets, lifting his boots up high in order to move through the mud and brushwood as quickly as he could. After half a dozen paces, he started to run.

3

The cauldron was heavy, and Annabel was glad indeed to set it down. She straightened up and put her hands on the small of her back, rubbing the aching muscles. Who would have thought that broth could weigh so much? The soldiers in the nearest pickets began to look around, nudging each other. Word started to travel along the positions on Inkerman Ridge.

'Broth, my lads!' she announced, peering through the steam that rose from the cauldron. 'Hot broth, come and get some!'

They shuffled towards her out of the early morning fog, holding out their army-issue tin mugs for a ladleful of the watery brown liquid and then retreating. Some muttered thanks. Most said nothing, and kept their eyes fixed on the ground. One or two looked at her most oddly – and none too pleasantly. She suppressed a shudder, keeping a broad, compassionate smile plastered on her face. These men were *killing*, she reminded herself, killing on an almost daily basis, and they were being killed as well, in their droves, and sleeping in dirt, and living on filth. Do not presume to judge them. Judgement is the Lord's right, and His right alone.

'That's right, my lads, drink up. And remember, the light of Almighty God is upon thee always. Speaketh unto Him and thou will be heard. Today is the Sabbath. Be sure to offer up thy prayers and devotions this day. As the good book tells us: *the eyes of the Lord are on the righteous, and His ears are attentive to their cry.*'

As if to fortify her words, through the oppressive gloom came the sound of distant church bells, tolling within the besieged city, calling the faithful of Sebastopol to the first service of the day. Annabel thought about remarking upon this to the soldiers, but decided against it. It was probably best not to remind them of their Christian kinship with an enemy whom they would soon be ordered to fight to the death once more.

Annabel looked around for her young partner in her labours, and for a few seconds could not locate her. The girl had retreated a few yards after putting down the cauldron, and now stood all but enveloped in fog, the hood of her cloak raised against the drizzling rain. There was still something of the officer's wife about her, Annabel noticed. She remained reluctant to mix with the common soldiery.

'Madeleine, what are you doing back there? Come forward, if you please. There is more to be done.'

As Madeleine returned obediently to her side, Annabel was struck yet again by the girl's beauty. Such a woman must be used to the adoration of all London – of all England. That she had chosen to stay in the camps said much, Annabel thought, for the Christian goodness of the soul beneath. The majority of the wives had headed straight back to Constantinople after the shocking loss of the Light Brigade, and the first frost; but this young woman, scarcely out of childhood, had opted to remain, and furthermore was prepared to assist with the alleviation of the suffering of the fighting men.

The unmarried sister of a chaplain from the 93rd Highlanders, Annabel Wade had travelled from Speyside to the Crimea quite independently of the British Army. Motivated by her stern Evangelical faith and a compassionate desire to lend whatever assistance she could, she was inexhaustible in her efforts to relieve the difficulties of the men on the front lines. She had met Madeleine in the Commissariat storehouse supplying the Light Division, where Annabel had been berating the officer behind the counter for the continued lack of winter clothing. They had conversed, and she had welcomed Madeleine's cautious offer of assistance without hesitation.

Annabel could tell, however, that the situation with Madeleine Boyce was not quite as simple as it seemed. Spousal loyalty had played no part in her determination to stay – she only spoke of her husband with barely contained hatred or dismissive contempt. Neither, despite her efforts, was the plight of the soldiers her true reason. There was another motive at play. Annabel entertained no speculation, but she kept her eyes open. She knew that this girl was going to require her help.

Madeleine smiled at a private with a dirty bandage wrapped around his head, who was approaching the cauldron. He stared at her as if she were some manner of apparition come to taunt him in his misery. She looked away uneasily.

Annabel stepped forward, taking the private's mug, filling it, and then pressing it back firmly into his hands. 'There you go, laddie, a lovely mug of broth to warm the bones against this perishing cold. God go with thee.' The man wandered off without a word, casting a long backward look at Madeleine as he went.

This rescue was typical of Annabel. In the weeks that they had been together, this admirable, fearless lady had taken on the role of Madeleine's protector; and as a genuine affection burgeoned between them, she guarded her friend like a Caledonian mastiff.

Madeleine's standard excuses for absenting herself from her husband's tent had soon lost their credibility once the siege of Sebastopol was underway. The official issue of supplies – of what few supplies there were – was now regulated by a Commissariat store so close to where the 99th were pitched that it took but minutes to visit it. The exodus of the other officers' wives back to Constantinople had robbed her of an infinite source of imaginary social arrangements. She had been left with no good reason to do anything but attend on Nathaniel. He had continued in his usual abuses, insulting her, beating her, subjecting her to intimate assaults; and had soon realised that he had a new weapon to use. The notion of sending her back to England had started to be broached several times a day. He had talked of how a couple of the very best men had already ordered their wives home; no longer, it seemed, did such a course of action carry its previous implications of poverty and dishonour. She knew that she would have to think of something quickly.

Then, as if by the divine providence she so frequently invoked, Annabel Wade had appeared. Nathaniel could hardly object to her undertaking such useful work, which was so beneficial to the army, alongside a lady of eminent respectability. Of course, he was deeply suspicious at first; but no matter how much scrutiny he applied to the proposition, not a trace of Richard Cracknell could be detected about it.

And as he rode out one bright October morning, in the hopeful days before the loss of the Light Brigade, none other than Lord Raglan had noticed Madeleine and Annabel distributing slices of fresh cheese to an artillery company. He had ridden over and accepted some both for himself and his horse. Quite charmed, the elderly commander-in-chief had praised their efforts warmly and asked their names. A couple of days later, Nathaniel had been summoned before him, and congratulated at length for possessing a wife whose beauty and grace was exceeded only by her noble generosity of spirit. Raglan revealed that he had been informed that Nathaniel had yet to be made a full colonel, despite having led his regiment into battle at the Alma. This he had remedied on the spot; and Madeleine, having been so instrumental in drawing the commander-in-chief's attention to her husband, was no longer threatened with a passage back to England. Lord Raglan had admired her, so she would remain in the Crimea. Nathaniel's scrutiny had relaxed.

The resulting freedom was dizzying. She could meet with Richard whenever he requested it. Annabel asked few questions. Everyone else in the camps seemed to have more pressing matters to attend to than the movements of Madeleine Boyce. The cost, however, was mornings like this one. Madeleine did not feel that she was at all suited to the duties Annabel assigned her.

'They do not like me,' she said weakly.

Her companion gave a short, dry laugh. 'No, my dear, I think they like you quite well enough. It is lucky indeed that your husband is not a jealous man.'

Madeleine could not help but smile at this. 'Oh Annabel, you do not know what you are saying,' she murmured.

Someone spoke her name, close by; a man with a polished voice, certainly not a common soldier. Madeleine turned to see Mr Styles, Richard's illustrator, clad in a cap and a long black coat. He was unshaven and dirty, his face gaunt. In his hands was clasped a small notebook, open with its front cover bent back; on the exposed page, she noticed, was a sketch of a large crow, pulling at something with its beak.

'Why, Mr Styles,' she answered lightly. 'It has been some time since last we met, sir. How are you faring?'

'I am alive, *Madame*, and persevering as best I can,' he said with a wan grin, removing his cap and closing the notebook. 'It has been a good few weeks, hasn't it? I had hoped that we would meet around the camp.'

There was something accusatory in his manner; Madeleine realised that Mr Styles believed that he had a grievance against her. 'Well, I have been very busy, sir,' she said apologetically, 'assisting my friend here.' She looked to Annabel, hoping to draw her in to the conversation and break the absolute concentration that Mr Styles had fixed upon her. Annabel, however, was fully occupied with the distribution of the broth.

'I *had* hoped,' the illustrator continued, his tone hardening a little, 'that you might seek me out, Mrs Boyce. After I rescued you, I mean.'

Madeleine glanced into his bloodshot eyes. The strange despair she saw there made every thought leave her mind. She hesitated uncomprehendingly. 'Sir, I do not know to what you are referring, but I—'

Mr Styles flinched as if struck. 'My rescue of you,' he broke in. 'Down by the river, during the battle of the Alma. I saved you from those Cossacks, Mrs Boyce. Do you honestly not remember?'

As he spoke, a distinct recollection returned to Madeleine: of standing with a soaked Mr Styles on the Alma's grassy bank – of holding his wet, long-fingered hand between hers – in the moments before she had been seized by her husband and dragged across the Heights like a disgraced child. 'Of – of course. Do forgive me.' She took a tentative step towards Annabel, who, already alerted by the aggressive volume of the illustrator's voice, was now eyeing him watchfully. 'And I remain very grateful, Mr Styles, for what you did,' she said gently, trying to placate him. 'So much has happened since then, though, so many terrible things, that I find one cannot help –'

Mr Styles was not listening. 'But I *saved you*. You said that you would not forget it. You promised. We—' He stopped abruptly, his distress darkening to a suspicious anger. 'Cracknell has been telling you things, hasn't he? That I quailed before the enemy – that I am a – a worthless coward?'

Madeleine turned from him awkwardly, not knowing what to say. During their first liaison after the battle, Richard had indeed described with some relish how her handsome boy-genius, the would-be lover she admired so much, had come apart at the first sight of blood, shrivelling up like a carnation tossed onto the fire. And although vaguely aware that this was not a fair estimation, she had not challenged it.

Her wordless confusion gave the troubled illustrator his answer. Before he could speak, however, Annabel intervened, introducing herself with loud amiability and asking him if he was the same Mr Styles employed by the *London Courier*.

Mr Styles lifted a hand to his brow, and spoke curtly. 'Madam, I must ask you to leave Mrs Boyce and I alone. There are certain matters that we must discuss in private, without your interference.'

There was a sudden animosity in his voice, and a presumption in his words, that made Madeleine catch her breath.

'And what matters might those be, Mr Styles?' Annabel asked, her expression still cordial but her tone now steely and resolute. She moved slightly to the side, interposing herself between Madeleine and the illustrator.

'As I believe I told you, they are *private*,' he replied with deliberate rudeness. 'I will not tell you any more than that. Now, I must ask again that you leave us.'

Madeleine's surprise quickly turned to indignation. The arrogance of the man, imagining that he had the right to demand access to her, and insult her friend so freely! She pushed past Annabel. 'Really, Mr Styles, you forget yourself! I am quite certain that I cannot think of anything – *anything* – more that you and I might have to discuss. Good morning to you, sir!'

She took hold of one side of the cauldron and began to drag it away from the trenches and into the fog, in the rough direction of the British camps. Both Annabel and Mr Styles started after her, then grabbed for the cauldron, one trying to aid in its carrying, the other to halt Madeleine's progress by holding on to it.

'Please, Mrs Boyce,' Mr Styles began desperately, 'you misunderstand me most sorely. My only wish was to communicate to you how much I—'

A series of rapid notes from a nearby bugle, its precise location lost in the fog, brought them to a halt. This sharp sequence repeated, and then repeated again. Officers began to shout; a thousand men got hurriedly to their feet and reached for their weapons.

Madeleine's gaze met Mr Styles'. 'An attack,' he said. 'They're sounding an attack.'

The cauldron fell to the ground, tepid broth slopping over the side, striking against mud rather than the grass that still covered most of the ridge. Annabel saw that they had arrived at the edge of the road that connected the camps with the eastern pickets. It stretched off into the blank, infinite fog; she could not tell which direction was which. The bugles continued, with more joining the chorus. Somewhere, she could hear rifles crackling, and then the elemental sound of cannon, rolling across the ridges and ravines of the Allied lines.

'Dear God,' she whispered.

With a start, Annabel realised that Madeleine and Mr Styles had moved off into the long grass on the far side of the road. They were already only silhouettes against the fog's obliterating greyness, but she could see that the young man was trying to take Madeleine in his arms, whilst she fought against him with all her strength. Annabel reached swiftly into the cauldron and took hold of the iron ladle.

A column of greatcoated infantry loomed suddenly into view, marching along the road at the double, cutting her off from Madeleine like the carriages of a train. Annabel could not wait for them to pass. Summoning her strength, she shoved into the close ranks and began to squeeze her way through. There was much jostling and cursing, and even some laughter. An NCO shouted for the soldiers to keep up the pace. She could smell gun grease and unwashed men. Her bonnet got caught on a button; she tore it off and ploughed onward with all her might.

And then she tumbled out the other side, immediately launching herself in the direction she had last seen Madeleine and Mr Styles. They were soon revealed, in much the same pose as before. Teeth gritted, Annabel drew back her arm to its full extent and swung the ladle at Mr Styles. There was a flat clang as its scooped end connected with the side of his head, and he released Madeleine with a cry. She struck him again; he slipped and fell to the floor, knocking off his cap as he brought up his arms to protect himself.

Annabel raised her ladle a third time, but a hand locked around her wrist, restraining her. She turned to see a lean civilian with a brown beard, dressed much like every other on the campaign – that is to say, like a vagrant, in a combination of old, mismatched clothes. Annabel Wade was a solidly built woman of forty-eight and no stranger to manual labour; she perceived straight away that she was a match for this person and began to strain hard against his grasp.

'Madam, please,' he said, trying to keep his footing, 'we are his colleagues, from the *London Courier*. Halt your attack and we will remove him.'

The man's voice was calm even in its insistence. Something in it made Annabel comply with his request. She stepped back, lowering the ladle. Mr Styles was still on the ground, dabbing at a cut on his forehead. The lean man asked him kindly if he was all right, and received only a surly grunt in response.

Voices were raised a short distance away; one was Madeleine's. Annabel whirled around to see her in another man's arms, this time a hefty fellow with a large black beard. The situation seemed to have roughly reversed, though; she was trying to cleave herself to him whilst he sought to fend her off. Sobbing, she was imploring him not to go to the front line. He replied that he had to, that it was his duty – but that she should return to the camps with all speed. Annabel realised that these two men had been following the column into battle, to report on it for their magazine.

Then Mr Styles, up on his knees now, started once again to beg Madeleine's forgiveness for his behaviour. The black-bearded man rounded on his young colleague savagely, shrugging Madeleine off and walking towards him.

'You seem truly to imagine yourself my rival,' he was saying in a low voice, 'but I'll tell you this for nothing, my lad – a woman like that won't even look at a man such as you. You think it's all about your pretty face, or your skill with a pen, your *prospects*, but it's about none of these. It's about substance – and you, my lad, are a man of very little substance. Why, think of the Alma, when you cowered like an infant! You are—'

The lean man strode between them, pushing the black-beard back with some difficulty. 'Enough, Cracknell! Leave him be!'

Annabel went to Madeleine; but the girl rushed past her, eyes red and swollen, and threw herself at Cracknell, grabbing on to the cape of his greatcoat and beseeching him to come with her to safety in a manner that was painful to behold. Gathering both her slender wrists into one of his hands, he slapped her hard across the face with the other. This silenced her abruptly.

'*Sir!*' thundered Annabel, starting furiously towards him. 'For *shame*, sir!'

He looked around, bidding her good morning with cool self-assurance. 'You must be Miss Annabel Wade. I have heard much about you. I am Richard Cracknell, the *London Courier*'s chief correspondent. This here's Thomas Kitson, my junior.'

The lean man tipped his cap. 'Miss Wade,' he said apologetically, as if embarrassed on his senior's behalf.

Cracknell sneered at the young man on the ground, who was staring down at the grass in mute humiliation, blood from the cut winding slowly around his eye. 'Mr Styles I think you've already met. Would you be so kind as to take Mrs Boyce back to the camps?' He pushed the stunned Madeleine towards Annabel. 'Come, Thomas, let us go. We have work to do. Get up, Mr Styles, for God's sake.'

Annabel caught hold of Madeleine, who seemed about to fall over, and watched as the three men retreated into the fog. Muttering a quick prayer, she eased Madeleine around and began walking her away from the escalating sounds of battle as fast as she could. If ever there had been doubt in Annabel's mind, it had been dismissed. Her new young friend, such a precious, God-given gift, was caught up in something torrid and sinful, something that would surely lead to calamity unless guidance was given. And now there had been a further revelation. The source of this evil, its originator and its protractor, was Mr Richard Cracknell.

4

The claret was surprisingly fine, given the circumstances. Boyce looked over at Retford and Lloyd-Francis, his friends from the Artillery Division, and declared himself impressed. Both men raised their glasses, offering their congratulations for his promotion to colonel. This led to sarcastic talk about what a charitable angel Mrs Boyce had suddenly become, and some genial mockery over the richly deserved travails of men who were so foolish as to marry Frenchwomen. Boyce wore an uncomfortable grin throughout, wondering how much they really knew.

To his relief, the conversation soon turned to the pursuit of treasure. The three officers shared a strong enthusiasm for gathering up whatever choice trinkets the upheavals of war happened to scatter about them. They had, in fact, formed themselves into something of a collective to this end, in order to take full advantage of the situation. Boyce lamented that chances for acquisition were growing increasingly rare; it was, he proclaimed, as if the peninsula were becoming quite drained of its riches.

'And one has to be so damnably careful, what with these blasted prying civilians wandering about – newspapermen and so forth.'

'The middle classes know nothing of the right to acquire, damn them,' Retford agreed. 'They think it so bloody charming when the common soldiery lift Russian uniforms or horses, or whatever blasted souvenirs they can lay their filthy hands on – but when a gentleman's eye happens upon an antiquity, the blighters call it *theft*. Or they bleat on about museums, about putting the object in some ghastly public gallery to be gawped at by the ignorant million . . .'

'It is not like the tales one hears of the Peninsular War,' Lloyd-Francis added wistfully, 'when chaps were perfectly free to wander into the local churches or mansion-houses and remove whatever they could get out through the doors.'

'My own men,' Boyce snarled, thumping his fist on the table, 'have been interrupted most grievously whilst collecting the spoils of conquest on my behalf. My best fellow was threatened with scandal by one of these wretched journalists. He was forced to abandon a statuette of Saint Catherine from the Bernini school – a fine piece by all accounts.'

'How the devil d'you know where to find that?'

'Simple intuition,' Boyce replied smartly. 'I took pains to procure a detailed map of this peninsula before we set sail – one with all the notable houses and estates marked upon it – and have been sending people out to investigate them as the opportunities arise.'

Retford and Lloyd-Francis exchanged a smirk. 'Well, we happen to know of a collection that won't be found on your map, Nathaniel.'

And then the real business of the evening began. Two nights before, it was revealed, a remarkably senior Russian officer had wandered into Retford's battery and proposed an arrangement. Finding the conditions in Sebastopol not to his liking, he desired safe passage to Paris, privately arranged and undocumented. Realising that this was asking a lot in the midst of a war, he had offered something rather astonishing in return.

This officer claimed he was a nobleman, a distant cousin of the Tsar no less. In peacetime, after committing some unnamed indiscretion in Moscow, he had been charged with the stewardship of Nicholas' Crimean residence, a secluded villa a few miles up the Chernaya valley. This villa had never been used, and had been deliberately kept off all maps. Nicholas maintained it as a refuge, a secret bolt-hole should he ever need to disappear from sight.

Accordingly, it had been furnished to receive Royalty; but this fellow, in the languid manner of Russian aristocrats, had failed to arrange the evacuation of all of its valuables before the defeat at the Alma had driven him into Sebastopol. There was a cache still hidden in the cellars, to which he would take them if they would enable his subsequent escape to France.

'We've got him hidden in a hut round the back,' Lloyd-Francis revealed casually, 'along with the servant he brought with him. Locked in for his own safety, y'understand. He tells us his name is Gorkachov, but I think we can safely assume that it isn't.'

The artillery men went on to explain that they lacked the resources to make the necessary expedition – unlike their dear friend Colonel Boyce, who had an entire regiment of infantry at his disposal.

'This is of a different order of magnitude to your little statuettes, though, Nathaniel,' warned Retford. 'This haul would really get people talking, if what our Gorkachov says about it is true. We'll need to acquire it as cleanly as we can, and then find the quietest possible route back to England.' He paused to recharge their glasses. 'You know the Quartermaster-General, don't you? Old Wyndham? Couldn't our package find its way on to an empty transport ship, returning to Felixtowe?'

'He was at Rugby with Lawrence, my elder brother.' Boyce sipped his wine reflectively. 'But Wyndham isn't at all right for this sort of thing. Asks endless questions of anything that's not completely by the book. No: I will send men to collect this cache, and we will consider our next step when it is securely in our possession.'

'So you are on board?'

'Of course. I will do whatever is required.'

A gentlemen's agreement was thus reached, the resulting sense of mutual understanding and enterprise compelling them to make a toast, and then another, until the three fell asleep at the card-table at which they sat.

The news, brought to Boyce at around half-past five by his adjutant Lieutenant Nunn, that a massive enemy assault was being mounted on Inkerman Ridge, and that the Light Division had been turned out to assist in its repulsion, thus came as a particularly unpleasant shock. Finding him still in his chair, Nunn shook him awake and delivered his message in an urgent whisper. Boyce was not at his best in any sense. Once upright, he insisted upon returning to his own hut to ready himself, ignoring his adjutant's protests. Whilst he slowly waxed his moustache (a difficult task due to his unusually unsteady hand), the increasingly restless young officer was made to root through his trunks and prepare his full dress uniform.

Eventually, they set off towards the front, Boyce atop his latest horse, a grey, with Nunn following on a chestnut mare. The Colonel was pleased with his appearance, despite his aching head and sweaty brow. He was glad, also, to have kept Nunn waiting. It was a good thing to show the boy some nerve under pressure, he thought; a bit of proper gentlemanly behaviour. Boyce had taken some care selecting a new adjutant after Freeman's death from fever. The Nunns were a fine old family, and this son of theirs, a tall, hulking fellow, had the makings of a fine soldier. He'd quite distinguished himself at the Alma, by all accounts, slaying upward of five Russians in the fight for the forward redoubt.

The cannon-fire suggested that a major battle was underway, the largest of the campaign so far. This could work to my advantage, the Colonel thought; a full-scale battle will provide the perfect cover for this special mission into the Chernaya valley with our friend Gorkachov. Any number of excuses could be invented to cover Wray's absence.

His satisfaction at this piece of cunning soon faded, however, as they weaved on through the fog, groping for the correct path to the front. How in God's name could the line of attack be properly maintained, he wondered, when the men wouldn't be able to see more than five yards along it? He looked down at the thick brambles through which his horse was treading with hesitant care. Rain continued to fall steadily; the left point of his moustache, he noted with irritation, was already starting to droop.

It was only when, entirely by chance, they located an

improvised treatment station for the wounded that definite information on the state of the counter-attack could be obtained. A Paulton sergeant, nursing a badly broken arm, managed to relate that Major-General Codrington's brigade of the Light Division had been assigned flanking duties, moving around the Sandbag Battery in an effort to wear down the advancing Russians.

'And the 99th?' Boyce enquired. 'How are we faring, man?'

'Well, sir,' groaned the sergeant, 'very well indeed. Major Maynard 'as taken charge, and is doin' great things.'

These words were purest poison to his commander. The humiliations of the Alma rushed back suddenly with excruciating force. It was half-past six. The engagement was well over an hour old, and the Paulton Rangers had been fighting for all of that time. By any standards, their Colonel was rather late. Barely pausing to ascertain his bearings, Boyce set off into the fog once more.

'Not again, damn him,' he swore, spurring his grey. 'This *will not* happen again.'

They soon came to the lip of a long slope – the top of Inkerman Ridge. Boyce could now see a handful of dead soldiers sprawled out on the ground before him, their torsos split open by shards of shrapnel, the steaming blood and spilling organs luridly colourful in the morning gloom. The acrid smell of gunpowder hung heavy in the air, laced with the sickening stench of disembowelment. Cannon-balls had ploughed deep grooves into the ground, overturning grass and uprooting bushes. Ahead, alarmingly close, there was a dense rattle of musketry, and another, and a horrible scream; artillery boomed away in the distance, followed a second later by the shrieking whistle of shot. These sounds, bad enough on the clear afternoon of the Alma, had an additional, disorientating terror when heard through an obfuscating blanket of fog.

But Boyce was not about to hesitate. 'To battle!' he cried, drawing his sword and riding down the slope. Lieutenant Nunn fell in a few yards behind him.

The sight that met them as they rode down this slope to

the Sandbag Battery, however, smashed this brisk soldierly resolve like a cobblestone thrown through plate glass. Boyce's grey stopped dead, snorted loudly in alarm, and took a couple of steps backwards. Nunn's horse had to swerve to avoid him. The fog had lifted slightly as they descended, revealing numbers of Russians that were beyond all estimation. They stretched away endlessly, their grey coats blending with the sea mist so that after a few yards, only their beards, their muskets and the black bands around their caps were visible. And they were advancing fast through the brushwood, screaming like devils as they swarmed forwards. Most did not stop to fire, but levelled their bayonets and went straight for the charge.

It was immediately clear that the British, as well as attempting the impossible task of defending against a massed assault on open ground, were overwhelmingly outnumbered. The infantrymen clung to improvised positions formed behind bramble thickets and rocks. Men were crashing together with enormous force, grappling and stabbing frantically, squirming as they tumbled down into the mud below.

'Christ above!' shouted Nunn, ''tis far beyond the Alma!'

Boyce, also, was taken aback by the savagery of the fighting. This was not war as he had been taught to understand it. Tightening his grip on the hilt of his sword, he made himself think of the Iron Duke at Waterloo; of Lord Marlborough at Ramillies; of the bold barons at Agincourt; of the mighty burden of tradition, of honour, that weighed down upon the well-born Englishman when he took to the field of battle. He visualised a pantheon of great generals looking upon him from their celestial thrones, gimlet eyes gleaming, waiting for evidence of his military distinction. Pursing his lips, he made himself ride onward.

He could see from shako-badges and facings that men from a number of different regiments, from different divisions even, had become mixed together. There were none from the 99th here. And where were the lines? he wondered crossly, finding a reliable focus for his anger. Where were the formations? And where, most importantly perhaps, were the damned officers? There was just a vast scrum of struggling, yelling bodies. It was difficult to know what to do.

Nunn dismounted and allowed his mare to flee into the fog. He was trembling hard. Boyce watched as he drew his revolver and his sword, and closed his eyes to pray. A moment later he was heading towards the battle.

'Mr Nunn!' Boyce roared. 'Where the devil d'ye think you're off to?'

The Lieutenant stopped. His large, simple face showed complete mystification. 'To fight, sir.'

'To *fight*, sir? What, alongside the common soldiers, and against that rabble? Hardly behaviour befitting a gentleman officer, Mr Nunn!'

'Colonel?' Nunn was confused, and humbled by his confusion.

Boyce lifted up his chin, as if displaying his profile to a suitably expensive portrait-painter. 'A man of breeding will only engage his equal. If you are to progress in the service, you would do well to remember that. We are here to lead, not to fight. Now, follow me!'

The Colonel's grey set off westwards, trotting roughly parallel to the ragged, constantly shifting British positions, with Nunn stumbling behind. The lost Sandbag Battery was just visible through the drifting fog. After fifty yards or so, Boyce heard his adjutant calling his name. He pulled on the grey's reins, turning impatiently.

Nunn was pointing urgently. 'Major Maynard, sir! Over yonder!'

Maynard was surrounded by a sizeable crowd of British soldiers – the larger part of three companies, made up from the 99th and a couple of other regiments. Face and great-coat streaked with mud, he was standing up on a rock, his back quite straight, bellowing orders to the men around him and pointing with his sword. They had just beaten back a Russian charge. The ground immediately before them was covered with the dead and dying from both armies.

'I want two firing lines! Come on, make yourselves busy! Two lines, now!' The soldiers did their best to follow his directions, fanning out across the pocked terrain. 'Don't look for targets, you won't find any. Just shoot into the fog.'

191

Peering ahead, Maynard could just make out the Russians. No individual men could be distinguished, but a barrier of shadow out in the mists told him where they stood. They were rallying for another assault. As if in anticipation, some of them had started up their battle cry, an oddly high-pitched, disturbing noise.

'First line, fire!' he shouted. The row of miniés let off their stuttering discharge, and there were cries out in the fog as the bank of shadows was suddenly rearranged; then the second line, with practised precision, moved through the first, who now scrabbled to reload. 'Second line, fire!'

Where there had been movement a few moments earlier, there was only stillness. Some twenty seconds passed. The charge did not come.

'Hold your fire! Stand down!' Maynard ordered, stepping from his rock. 'Save your bullets, men, they've had enough for now. The Bear will need a tot or two of his vodka before he tries that one again.'

There was some weary laughter. 'Could use a spot of that meself, Major!' piped up Private Cregg, who was in the second line, as he packed a fresh cartridge down into his rifle barrel.

Captain Wray, in place somewhere down to the left, started screeching for quiet, promising the lash to all and sundry. Hardly a potent threat, Maynard thought, to men presently under bombardment by heavy artillery.

The sight of Boyce approaching the lines on his grey actually brought Maynard some relief. Here at last, he thought, is someone with the rank to authorise what so plainly needs to be done. 'Good to have you with us, Colonel,' he said with a salute, nodding at Lieutenant Nunn. 'The situation is growing ever more serious. There is a quite desperate need for—'

'You are not *fighting*, are you, Major?' Boyce interrupted, looking down at the blood on Maynard's sword. Maynard hesitated, unsure how to respond. Boyce sighed long-sufferingly. 'No matter. Make your report, if you please.'

'As I was saying, Colonel, the enemy has been pressing this sector quite relentlessly. This is a terrible position, sir – we're exposed to the Russian cannon here, and—'

192

'Cannon? But how is he aiming them, Mr Maynard?'

By way of reply, Maynard waved over Major Hendricks of the 55th who stood nearby. He introduced him to Boyce.

'I know this country, sir,' Hendricks began. 'The guns are on raised ground over there,' he pointed off into the fog, 'there and there, I believe. All Ivan needs to do is fire roughly in this direction and he can be sure of hitting something. He doesn't seem too concerned about doing in his own men, either.'

Boyce was clearly unimpressed. 'So what do you both propose we do?' he asked with studied hauteur.

'We must fall back, sir, immediately,' said Maynard quickly. 'We must regroup, with artillery support. We must wait for this damned fog to lift. There are enemy troops threatening our flank. Only a staged withdrawal will allow us to confront them properly.'

The Colonel paused for a moment, as if deep in thought, and then shook his head with fierce contempt. 'You are proposing nothing less than a retreat, Mr Maynard! That will not do at all! If this position is too hot for you, then we will advance. How much ground can we afford to give them, man? We must advance, advance to the Sandbag Battery and retake it in the name of the Queen!'

'Colonel, did you not hear me?' Maynard felt a familiar despairing disbelief. 'There are Russians on our flank. If we advance, they could get behind us, and then—'

'Enough of this, Mr Maynard! Prepare the men for an attack!'

As Maynard issued Boyce's orders, he thought of his wife, back home in Ilford; of their last night together, when she had held on to him so tightly, sobbing all the while; of her last letter, full of news of the daughter he'd never seen, and hopes for his speedy return. And then, strangely, he found himself thinking of Richard Cracknell, a grin on that crafty face of his, legs crossed beneath him, a brandy balloon in one hand and a cigarette in the other. 'Your commander is naught but a fool,' he was saying, 'a deceitful, incompetent fool. I'd as soon follow him, my dear Major, as I'd follow Charon into his ferry-boat.'

The sight of Boyce calling Wray from his company dispelled these reflections. Maynard knew that there was a long-standing bond between the two men; something to do with their families, he suspected. It certainly led to all sorts of preferential treatment for the cruel, unpopular Wray. He watched as Boyce issued a sequence of very precise instructions to his nodding Captain, and then handed him a crude iron key.

'This will open the hut where the fellow is currently being held,' he heard Boyce say. 'And no one must know we have it, Archie, d'you hear me? Absolutely *no one.*'

Wray saluted, summoned two corporals to his side and headed off into the mists. Maynard's eyes widened in disbelief. Boyce had just ordered the Captain of his grenadier company from the battlefield in the middle of an engagement. He would have an explanation for this, rank be damned.

Then the Russian cannons fired, the shells detonating somewhere above them. A hand slapped on to the Major's shoulder, a little too hard and loose for comfort. As he turned, Hendricks collapsed forward into his arms. Shrapnel had torn into his back. A sharp point of black metal jutted out from the middle of his abdomen. He whispered something, unintelligibly quiet, a name perhaps, blood welling from his mouth as he spoke, and running across his cheek in a red rivulet. Maynard leant in closer, and asked him tenderly to speak up; but Hendricks could offer no reply.

5

The road from the camps did not end so much as dis-
integrate, the single mud track breaking into a profusion of
smaller paths like the branches of a tree departing from the
trunk. There was no indication as to which might lead to
the pickets. Cracknell selected one and they hurried along
it; but, after leading them several hundred yards up an undulating, rocky hillside, it petered out. They were left at the
mercy of the fog.

The noises of battle were everywhere – the shouts, the
clash of steel, the popping and blasting of gunpowder – but
they came in a riotous clamour, and were effectively useless
for the purposes of guidance. Indeed, they seemed to suggest
a number of different directions; Kitson suspected that many
were echoes, bouncing between rocky ravines and cliff-faces.
The *Courier* team looked at each other. None had spoken
since their melodramatic encounter with Madeleine Boyce
and Annabel Wade. Cracknell was scowling at his juniors
around his cigarette, plainly having decided that both Styles'
intemperate advances to Mrs Boyce and Kitson's interruption of the illustrator's dressing-down were signs of grave
disrespect; and Styles was mired in a baleful, disconsolate
silence, deliberately allowing the cut on his forehead to bleed
unchecked. Kitson turned away, amazed by them both.

He felt something against his face – the faintest hint of a
cold breeze. 'Come,' he said impatiently, heading towards it.
'This way.'

After fifty yards or so, the hillside levelled out into a long, flat-topped ridge. The sea wind struck Kitson full on, grating his throat raw as he breathed it in; and a heavy layer of fog melted away. He saw that they stood close to a rocky outcrop, beyond which was a wide expanse of sloping ground, growing gradually steeper as it ran down into the Chernaya valley. In the centre of this slope, about two hundred yards from their position, was the brown block of the Sandbag Battery. Greatcoated soldiers from the two armies could be seen packed around it, battling hard against each other. More men dropped every second, adding themselves to the mounds of dead; but new troops from both sides were streaming in constantly, directed by their commanders to rush into the abattoir.

'At bloody last.' Cracknell sucked in a last lungful of smoke from his cigarette, flicked the butt away and took out a field telescope. This magnified view of the fighting made even the indomitable senior correspondent falter for a second. 'The – the Guards are down there,' he reported, summoning back his steadiness. 'I can see the bearskins. Coldstreamers, I believe. They seem to be pulling back.'

Kitson took out his pocketbook and started to write. He noticed that Styles had fallen to work also, rapidly delineating the landscape before them on a piece of drawing paper.

'The Russians are different,' Cracknell continued. 'At the Alma they had spiked helmets. These ones are in caps, a sort of brimless cap. Reinforcements, I should think, from the mainland . . . Ye gods, there are thousands of them. A fine spot we'll be in if—' He stopped suddenly. 'The 99th are there. I can see Maynard.' Cracknell was growing excited, his equilibrium vanishing. 'They're in front of the battery. They're . . . damn it all, they're totally over-extended. Why the devil would Maynard do such a bloody foolish thing? He knows better than this!'

Even without the aid of the telescope, Kitson could see all too clearly what was happening. Three fresh regiments of Russians, several thousand men, were moving up the slope from the valley, driving back the main body of the British force; but one group of soldiers, only a few hundred strong, had pressed too far forward, past the Sandbag Battery and a good way down towards the River Chernaya. Soon they would be entirely encircled by the enemy. Kitson stopped writing, all words eluding him. These soldiers were surely doomed.

A nearby blast sent shrapnel clattering among the rocks of the outcrop. As well as affording them a view of the battlefield, Kitson realised, the partial retreat of the fog had exposed the *Courier* men to the sight of a pair of Russian gunboats, which had sailed out to the mouth of Sebastopol harbour. Another shell exploded, slightly closer this time; a shard of flying metal nipped a chunk from Kitson's coat. He looked around. Close to their position was a series of narrow ravines, leading into the Chernaya valley.

'There!' he cried. 'Quickly!'

Cracknell dashed past him, leaping into the first one he came to. Styles hesitated, not through fright but a reluctance to leave their vantage point. Kitson grabbed his sleeve, dragging him to the ravine and all but pushing him in.

Together, they skidded down to its floor in a small landslide of stones and mud. It was dotted with gorse bushes, rocks and spent cannon-balls, which lay clustered and inert like gigantic black marbles. Cracknell was already on his feet, clearly exhilarated by the plunge. He made a few quick observations about the Russian ordnance that had just been directed at them – exploding shells fired from ships were apparently a recent Russian innovation – and then announced that they would follow the ravine out into the valley, circling back around to the left towards Inkerman Ridge.

Kitson got up, rubbing at a bruised elbow. They could not hope to survive in the bloody mayhem they had just seen from that outcrop. To believe otherwise was madness. 'Towards the battlefield, you mean?' he asked tersely.

Cracknell, sensing his objection, rolled his eyes. 'Yes, Thomas, towards the battlefield. To *observe*. That is what we are here to do, you remember! Besides, it behoves me, as a friend, to discover how Maynard is faring.' He began picking his way through the rocks and bushes.

'And what precisely are you intending to do, should you discover the Major to be in dire trouble?' Both knew that the revolving pistol, following its submersion in the River Alma, was locked away in Cracknell's sea-chest, acquiring a light film of rust. 'D'you expect us to leap into the middle of a pitched battle armed only with our *pencils*?'

The senior correspondent continued on his way. 'I'll ignore that,' he said crossly, without looking around. 'Don't make me talk to you about courage, man!'

Cracknell had not taken ten steps out into the valley before bullets started to strike the ground around him. He quickly retreated back into the ravine, pointing towards a low cave, half-hidden behind a large slab of stone. The three men rushed inside. It was surprisingly deep, filled with a rich vegetable smell and the sound of dripping water. Moss coated every surface, a strange, pale phosphorescence glittering within it, making the walls of the cave sparkle and shift as they passed. They did not pause to appreciate this magical effect, however, instead scurrying rapidly behind a pile of rocks close to the cave's end.

Kitson crouched down and attempted to catch his breath. He looked over at Styles. The illustrator was curled up in amongst the rocks; his face was entirely hidden in the shadow thrown by the brim of his cap, nothing but a black profile against the weak glow of the cave wall. Cracknell, who was peering over their cover, prodded Kitson's shoulder. Rising to his knees, the junior correspondent saw a group of Russian infantry out in the ravine, stepping from stone to stone with their muskets ready in their hands. He hunched back down with a shiver. Then, to his horror, he felt a hand close around his boot.

'*Vadaa*,' whispered a voice faintly. '*Vadaa. Pozhalujsta*.'

A young Russian soldier, no more than sixteen, lay hidden in the darkness at the back of the cave. His head was bare, his eyes were sunken, and the lines of his skull were clearly visible beneath his skin. His thin neck was covered with flea bites; his musket, which looked as if it dated from the previous century at the very latest, was propped up against a rock. The body of one of his comrades, clearly dead, lay on the floor beside him.

Outside, the searching Russians called to each other. The soldier forced out a few more words through parched lips. His meaning was clear enough.

'He wants water,' Kitson said quietly. 'I have none. Have you any, Cracknell? Styles, how about you?'

The soldier grew angry as his request was not met. Speaking with more strength, he hauled himself up to a sitting position and looked over them with scorn in his eyes. He had heard the men outside, and realised the power he had over these three lost invaders. He started to raise his voice. Kitson moved forward, making placatory gestures, speaking softly; Cracknell offered the soldier a cigarette. This was knocked aside. The soldier jabbed an accusatory finger into Cracknell's round belly, spat out a few hard-sounding words, and put a hand on the stock of his musket.

In the months that followed, Kitson tried many times to recall exactly when he had realised what was about to happen there in the cave. It was certainly at a point when it was too late to do anything to prevent it. He had watched Styles rise to his haunches, and pick up a stone about the size of a man's fist; he had watched him twist around, leaning back into the cave; and he had watched, his mouth now open, as the illustrator struck the stone against the side of the soldier's head with all the force in his body. Whether or not this had killed the boy soldier outright Kitson would never know, but there had been a dreadful sound, uncannily like the breaking of china, and he had slumped to the ground beside his lifeless companion.

Cracknell leapt to his feet, putting a hand over his mouth to stifle an involuntary exclamation. Styles leant back, letting the stone drop on to the cave's floor, where it clacked down amongst its fellows.

They remained in silence for some minutes. Eventually, Cracknell said, 'Well, that was certainly one way to deal with him.' His voice was hoarse and forced, a ghostly approximation of his usual tone.

Styles stared out of the cave. 'The fog's settling again,' he said impassively. 'Those soldiers will have trouble spotting us now. I think we should leave.'

Kitson knew that he had to collect himself. He clasped his hands together and nodded firmly. 'We – we should go right, though, I feel. Up the valley. Inland.'

Cracknell nodded also, for once too shaken to assert his authority. 'Agreed.'

Without a backward glance, the three men left the glittering cave and headed off into the fog.

6

The Russian lifted up his musket, the tip of the bayonet blade finding purchase in the heavy stitching of Cregg's white cross-belt. Cregg was pressed up hard against a large boulder, his arms pinned underneath him. For approximately the eighth time that morning, he told himself that it was all over – curtains for Dan Cregg. With no last thoughts occurring, he looked into the face of his killer. The man was old, at least fifty, his beard full of grey hairs, his wrinkled skin the colour of walnuts. He had that same sour, leathery smell that all of the Russian infantry seemed to have. With a hollow cry, he drove the bayonet forward.

To the great surprise of both men, instead of sinking into the helpless Cregg, the blade bent crazily, folding almost in two. The Russian overbalanced, falling into Cregg's lap. Freeing his arms, Cregg heaved the man away – this was not difficult, he was light as a bird – and grabbed his minié. His bayonet did not bend.

'Did you see that, Major? Did you?' he shouted as he rose to his feet. 'The bastard's blade buckled up like it was tin!' Maynard, who was busy reloading his revolver, did not answer. Cregg went through the dead soldier's pockets. There was nothing of interest within; the fabled vodka ration, in particular, was nowhere to be found. He swore bitterly and gave the old Russian a kick.

Of the three hundred men who had accompanied Colonel Boyce on his wrong-headed advance to the Sandbag Battery, well over a third had already fallen. Many of Cregg's best pals had been cut down before his eyes. He'd seen young Toby Lott, only seventeen, shot in the hip and then bayoneted as he lay screaming in the mud; Scraper Jones, a filthy fiend if ever there was one, lose his jaw to a six-pound ball, and then put a bullet in his own brain to end the torment; and the Pitt brothers, all three of them, blown into a jumble of parts by the same shell.

The contested battery had been far more heavily defended than Boyce had realised. Somehow, the companies under his command had been forced down into the Chernaya valley, a drift that Major Maynard had tried his hardest to halt and reverse; but their formation was broken. Russian reinforcements came up to meet them, and as they sought to regain their bearings, they were subjected to a brutal attack. The companies were split and scattered, and all sense of ranks, tactics and strategies lost. Men fought where they stood, thinking only of surviving the next few minutes by whatever means possible.

Cregg had found himself pushed back to a loose cluster of rocks by concentrated musket-fire, along with sixty or seventy of his comrades. There was a sizeable area of level ground in the midst of these rocks, about forty feet across – like a sort of natural fort. It was already carpeted with dead Russians, whose bloody bodies squelched underfoot as the British soldiers rushed to find cover. The sight of Major Maynard fighting alongside them had heartened him a good deal; whereas that of Boyce, off his horse by now and huddled in a rocky corner, refusing to lift arms with those he had so royally buggered, had the very opposite effect.

Another dozen Russians appeared over the top of the rocks, bawling at the top of their voices as they leapt down towards the waiting British. One fired off his musket. The ball seemed to snag Cregg's left hand, pulling it back sharply and making him drop his minié. Knowing full well what this meant, he clutched at his wrist and forced himself to look. The hand was a bright, ugly mess, broken and twisted like a crab smashed with a hammer. One finger was gone altogether, another was little more than a shard of white bone. A panicked scream started to gather deep inside him.

It never reached his lips. The Russian who had shot him, a giant of six foot or more, struck him on the side of the head with his rifle-stock, and Cregg went down heavily. The man stepped over him, spinning the musket around expertly to ready his bayonet. Cregg barely had time to register what was happening, his mind still full of that image of his ruined hand, and the hot agony that now burned up his arm.

Then the man stumbled, and was flung violently to the ground. The sounds of Major Maynard's shots were lost in the uproar of battle, but all three had hit home. For good measure, he put another into the Russian's twitching body before turning towards the dazed Cregg.

'Get that hand bound immediately, Private!' he shouted, shaking the flattened percussion caps from his smoking revolver. 'Use one of your comrade's tunics – I'm sure they wouldn't begrudge you the use of it. And be sure to bind it tightly!'

Maynard strode towards the highest of the rocks, his sword at the ready. The enemy had been driven back. They had won themselves a moment's respite. Yet as he stood there, a breeze carried a good deal of the fog away, and he could see the next regiment of Russians starting the ascent to their position. More of the enemy had moved around to their flank, as he had guessed they would, preventing a retreat. Eleven of his men had fallen before this latest wave. They wouldn't last much longer. Maynard didn't feel any fear or anxiety; only an immense fatigue, and annoyance that so many good soldiers had been thrown away like waste paper. Taking off his left glove, he looked at his wedding ring. It would be pillaged from his body, and sold on in some pawn shop in Russia, or Turkey, or England, for gin money or whores. He took it off and, crouching down, dropped it into a narrow crevice in the rock.

There was a theatrical groan behind him. He turned wearily. Boyce had taken a bullet in the shoulder, which had knocked him from his horse. It was a very minor wound, one that needn't have stopped him from fighting by Maynard's estimation, but Boyce had laid himself out like Nelson at Trafalgar.

Lieutenant Nunn had been removed from combat to attend on his stricken Colonel, and crouched uncertainly at his side, unsure of what exactly he should be doing.

Maynard realised that it was time to ask. There might well not be another opportunity. 'Where is Wray, Boyce? Where did you send him?'

'I'll thank you to remember my rank when you address me, Major Maynard!' Boyce barked imperiously.

Maynard ignored him. He stared hard into Nunn's eyes for a second – a look that said, *listen well to this*. 'I saw you give him a key. What was it for?'

Boyce was looking down at his blood-stained jacket with a pained expression. 'Captain Wray was dispatched by me to undertake a vital task on behalf of the regiment, away from the battlefield.'

'*Vital task!*' Maynard didn't bother to conceal his fury. 'What the hell can be more vital than this?' He waved his sword at the dead heaped around them.

Boyce met his eye coldly. 'Again, Mr Maynard, I must ask you to remember to whom you speak. The orders I choose to give are my concern, and none of yours.'

Now Maynard felt positively murderous. He paced back over the corpses to the sheltered nook where his commander had secluded himself from the action. 'What, even when they bring about the destruction of *my* men? You will kill us all, damn it, with your wretched, arrogant idiocy!'

'Major, this is gross insubordination!' Boyce cried in triumphant horror, sitting upright. 'The very minute we return to camp, sir, you shall find yourself before a court-martial!'

The Russians, a hundred yards down the slope, began their battle cry once more. 'Here they come, lads!' said a nearby lance-corporal as he lifted his rifle to fire. 'Give the bleeders what for!'

Nunn shifted apprehensively, checking his revolver.

'And to top it all,' Maynard continued, 'you won't even draw your sword beside them. You won't even fight with your own soldiers! You claim honour, Boyce, but I say you have none! None at all!'

'What, pray, would you know of honour, Maynard?' Boyce

sneered. 'Men like you, crawling from your hovels and cottages, joining Her Majesty's Army as if it were a savings bank, or a warehouse, or a cloth factory! Working your way through the ranks like clerks seeking promotion to management! You have as much understanding of true military honour as has an ape of the Indus!'

Maynard drew breath for his reply.

Cregg had bound what was left of his hand in a long strip torn from the tunic of a dead corporal from the 55th. The pain was unlike anything he had ever known. It sat across his chest like a saddle, churned in his stomach, and blazed behind his eyes. Leaning dizzily against a boulder, he could hear the two officers' vicious argument, and the screaming Russians drawing steadily nearer. The British soldiers were firing, but sparingly; many were down to their last few bullets. He knew that when the enemy arrived, he would not be able to resist, and would be dispatched easily. His only hope was to make a break for the Allied lines – to run away, risking the muskets on their flank and the random fire of the artillery. Dan Cregg wasn't proud. If this was the price of survival, he would pay it gladly.

With difficulty, the injured hand hugged in his armpit, he staggered out on to the plain. The rain was easing off, and he realised that the fog, disturbed by the sea breeze, was gradually lifting. Cregg could now see the full hellishness of the slope around them; and also, up near the British pickets, the several battalions of redcoats that were advancing out in long, loose rows. They were already firing on the flanking Russians, breaking their positions and driving them back.

'Major!' the private yelled joyfully, ducking back amongst the rocks. 'Major, gerrover 'ere!'

Major Maynard appeared at his side a moment later. 'Heaven be praised! Salvation is at hand, Cregg. And about bloody time.'

Cregg looked around at the valley behind them. The enemy continued their slow charge. They were still a good forty yards from the rocks. Then the fog continued to drift away on the shifting wind, exposing thousands more enemy soldiers standing ready in the valley below – literally thousands. It was as if every man and boy in Russia was massed against them.

'Enough of this,' declared Maynard, before raising his voice to a roar. 'Retreat! Retreat, open order! Back to the pickets, men! Back to the reinforcements!' He regarded Boyce coldly for a moment. 'Lieutenant Nunn, assist the Colonel. Ensure that he reaches safety.'

'Damn sight more'n the bastard deserves,' Cregg muttered.

The rising fog had cleared a long ridge of raised ground on the Sebastopol side of the Chernaya valley. Standing along this ridge were the guns that had been pounding away at them so steadily, which were now afforded clear sight of their targets for the first time that morning. Cregg saw their crews taking aim, and the plumes of white smoke as they fired; and a second later, heard the reports roll across the landscape. He opened his mouth for a warning shout, but it was too late.

Several of the shells buried themselves deep in the ground before exploding, throwing up enormous gouts of earth and splintered rock. Cregg was knocked over, falling on his smashed hand. He yelped in agony, doubling up and then kicking his legs out as hard as he could, a heavy shower of mud raining down on him. Forcing himself up on to his knees, he retched and brought up his morning biscuit, gasping in the smoky air and trying to blink the stinging tears out of his eyes. The Russians were almost at the hollow, and would be on him in moments. He looked around quickly, preparing to flee towards the pickets.

Fresh casualties lay all about, torn apart and flung around by the artillery fire, and then half-buried by the tons of flying mud. And there, not five yards from where he crouched, was Major Maynard. He was on his back, staring up at the heavy rain-clouds above, his lips moving soundlessly. His trousers were ripped, the tattered remnants black with blood. One of his legs was covered by the disturbed earth; Cregg could see that the other was attached only by a few fine shreds of flesh. His arms were thrown out, one hand still gripping the hilt of his sword, the other open and gloveless, the fingers curling slowly.

7

The road running along the base of the Chernaya valley was strangely empty, all traffic having halted ahead of the massed Russian attack. Like all of the peninsula's roads, it was little more than a dirt cart-track, its ruts and grooves turned to a treacherous mire by the heavy rains. The *Courier* team soon found that the going was easier on the slippery grass verges than on the road itself. Beside them ran the muddy river, bloated by the constant rainfall. More than this they could not see. The fog had billowed back up the length of the valley, smothering everything in its grey haze.

After about half a mile, they found themselves passing through a village of squat white houses, all of which appeared to be deserted. Looters had been busy. Doors hung splintered in their frames, and windows, empty of their shutters, gaped blackly open like the eye-sockets of skulls. A mill-wheel was turning slowly and haltingly in the lazy waters of the Chernaya, suggesting not life and everyday labour, but rather ghostly absence and incipient decay.

Few words were exchanged as they made their way through this bleak place. Kitson glanced frequently at Styles, but the illustrator remained blank-faced, expressionless. It still seemed impossible. Their young artist had killed – had taken up a stone and knocked a boy's skull in with it. Regardless of the circumstances, a crucial boundary had been crossed. One thing was certain: he now had to be sent back to England with all haste. Away from this blighted land, safely at home, there was a chance that he might recover, and rid himself of the peculiar desolation that ate away at him. But he had to depart the Crimea directly.

Soon after leaving the cave, Cracknell had imparted their course of action. They would follow the river, staying on its south bank, for three hours. This should carry them far enough inland, he said, to get them well behind the Allied lines, and past the steepest of the ravines. They would then turn away from the valley, head in the rough direction of Sebastopol, and thus be back in the besieging camps well before nightfall.

Somewhere, however, in the fog, the mud and the ceaseless, chilling rain, this simple plan went awry. The river seemed to fork, and the valley with it. Cracknell made a choice, striding out in front to lead the way; but the sub-valley he selected, rather than rising up to the plateau, grew increasingly deep and rocky. The tributary of the Chernaya beside which they walked became more fast-flowing, rushing in diagonals between swirling, foaming pools. Trees started to appear, and before long the *Courier* team were walking through a dense, silvery wood. Autumn leaves floated down through the fog, gathering in drifts between the stones.

Seeing his opportunity, Kitson hurried forward to Cracknell's side, leaving Styles some distance behind them. His voice hushed, he spoke of the need to remove the illustrator from the war-zone as soon as possible.

Cracknell turned to him irritably. 'Kitson, what the deuce are you on about?' He pushed aside some low-hanging branches, scattering droplets of dew. 'He did what was necessary. What you or I should have been ready to do. That soldier would have given us away – we'd be prisoners by now, or worse.'

Kitson nodded. He had not been so foolish as to expect an immediate consensus, despite Cracknell's alarm in the cave. 'I understand that, sir, but we need to consider the effect his actions might have on his mind. He is not a soldier.'

'*Effect?*' Cracknell said scornfully, screwing up his face in disbelief. 'What the bloody hell d'ye mean, Thomas? He is a *man*, isn't he?'

'Mr Cracknell, Robert Styles is an artist.' Kitson grew angry at his senior's wilful incomprehension. 'An *artist*. He trained in the Royal Academy drawing schools. And he just killed a boy with a rock. Do you not think this *at all* significant?'

Cracknell paused. His eyes held a trace of amusement. 'Good Lord, Thomas, you are fractious today. Is a mutiny brewing, I wonder?'

Kitson ignored this. 'It will be on our heads, sir, if we do not act.'

Putting up his collar, Cracknell looked to the tree trunks ahead. 'We'll discuss this later, back at the camps,' he said with firm finality. 'Now, we must press on. There is still some distance to go.'

Styles hopped across the stones some yards back, absorbed in his own thoughts. He had found the experience of killing a confusing one. It was Religion's greatest sin, the sin of Cain; yet it had actually been rather easy. No thunderclaps or lightning, no horrible shadow of damnation falling over one's soul – all one had to do was pick up a rock and strike with it, much as one might chop a log, or poke a fire. Although it had been the decision of an instant, Styles found that he was not surprised or dismayed by what he had done. As they crept out of the ravine, and made their way along the valley, he had searched for feelings of remorse inside himself, but as yet had failed to find any. All he could think of was Cracknell, reeling in surprise, hand over his stupid mouth, his greasy skin saved by someone he had maligned so ruthlessly – and falsely – for his cowardice.

In short, he felt as if he had finally managed to prove himself. He had shown quite incontrovertibly that he was as capable, as brave as the wretched senior correspondent. How might Mrs Boyce's views of the pair of them change, he dared to wonder, when she discovered what had happened there in the cave? Cracknell's dastardly slander would surely be exposed for what it was.

But this thought led him to a sharp recollection of their encounter out by the pickets a few hours earlier; of the awful antipathy with which she had attempted to dismiss him from her presence. Grimacing, he tried vainly to clear this annihilating, hopeless memory from his mind.

After another half an hour's trudging through the fog, a break in the trees appeared before them. This clearing contained an expansive lawn, a little overgrown but properly seeded and bordered. He heard Kitson calling to Cracknell, off in the fog somewhere up ahead. Styles knew that Kitson had been disturbed by what had happened in the cave, and wished to have him sent away. This was not surprising. Since the Alma, Styles had nursed growing doubts about Thomas Kitson. The man was not his friend, as he had claimed. A similar impulse may have brought them both to the Crimea, but no true kinship existed between them. How could it? He possessed an absolute dedication to the task before them – whereas Kitson had only his endless caveats, queries and reservations. He had overestimated the junior correspondent. The man lacked spirit, and had no place in a war.

As he wandered across the lawn, a large shape slid slowly from the murk before him. At first, he had thought it to be a rock formation, or a particularly close grouping of trees, but as he reached the rest of the *Courier* team he saw that it was neither.

The villa was low and wide, built from light Crimean stone in a simple approximation of the Palladian style. It was two storeys high, with a pediment before the doors, supported by six thick pillars. Most of its tall windows had been smashed, the jagged holes revealing only darkness within. Even in the fog, it was obvious that the location had been carefully chosen for the concealment provided by the nearby woods.

Cracknell whistled. 'Quite a pile. You'd think it would be on the Allied maps. Come on, let's give ourselves a tour.' He made for the doors.

Kitson did not follow. 'Mr Cracknell, should we not exercise a little caution?'

Cracknell turned back, his plump cheeks creased by a sarcastic grin that made Styles wince with loathing. *'Caution,* Thomas? How unlike you, my friend! Don't you want to take shelter from this accursed rain? Lay a fire, perhaps, and dry out your coat?'

'Of course I do, sir,' Kitson replied, 'but what if anyone should be in there?' He looked briefly at Styles.

The illustrator saw apprehension in his face – not due to the threat of the enemy, of Cossack raiders or Russian infantry, but of him, of Robert Styles, of what further acts of violence he might commit that day. Suddenly, Styles realised that he had, in the space of an hour, become a killer of men, a repugnant brute. He looked down at the grass, a perplexing, powerful shame spreading through him. Lucid memories returned to his mind; the way the Russian's skull had caved in beneath his blow; the tiny glimpse he had caught of the eyeball rolling upwards; the fitful shudder of the dead man's limbs. These images and sensations, he realised with a mounting panic, were now etched on to his very soul.

Cracknell let out an exaggerated sigh. 'Looking on the sunny side of the wall as ever, eh, Kitson? The place is quite deserted, surely you can see that. This is a chance for a bit of exploration, a bit of bloody adventure! Is that not why you left the comfort of your picture salons – of your art criticism?' He laughed harshly. 'And anyway, should we encounter some nasty villain within, young Robert here has shown himself extremely able to deal with such dangers, has he not?'

As ever, the senior correspondent's good humour had an aggressive element to it; and the comradely slap he then delivered to the illustrator's back was a little firmer than it needed to be. Styles, lost in remembrance of the Russian's broken skull, of the brittle cracking of his bone, could only mumble wordlessly in response.

A stone coat of arms above the villa's doors contained the double-headed Imperial eagle. This secluded house, Kitson thought, was the property of an important person indeed. The cavernous hall beyond was dark and smelled strangely sepulchral, the odour of candle-wax hanging heavily in the stale air. A faint glow seemed to emanate from the paler sections of the patterned marble floor. Empty niches lined the walls, a single broken Caesar all that remained of their

211

occupants. Tides of brown silt had accumulated on the sills of the smashed windows. There were no signs of life. As his eyes adjusted to the gloom, Kitson saw that the floor was scuffed and covered with a web of cracks, as if many dirty boots and a number of heavy objects had moved back and forth across it, without the usual protective precautions having been taken.

'A speedy exit,' said Cracknell, his voice loud in the hall's stillness. 'And a careless one.'

Kitson tried to tread softly on the fractured marble slabs, but the senior correspondent was intent on demonstrating his heroic indifference as to what – or who – their intrusion into this place might disturb. His steps echoed around the hall as he marched intrepidly across it.

'Kitchens are what we need,' he pronounced, selecting one of the passageways that led off into the rest of the villa. 'Over here.'

Cracknell led Kitson and Styles along a dingy corridor panelled with black wood. It was covered with relief carvings of the beasts of the Russian forest, represented in an exaggerated, folk-tale style. Most, for some reason, had been left unmolested. Bears and boars wrestled around archways; snarling wolves crouched beside doors; round-faced owls perched above window frames. This corridor took them past a succession of grand saloons, each one thoroughly defaced. Paper peeled from walls in long, sagging strips, and rotting carpets were littered with fragments of broken furniture.

Eventually, in one of the building's most far-flung corners, they found a spiral staircase made from roughly hewn stone. At its bottom was an enormous vaulted kitchen. The room was filled with the lapping sound of rain falling on leaves, its high windows, all shattered, showing only flat greyness outside. Again, destruction was everywhere. It had been completely ransacked; shelves had been torn down, dressers and tables overturned, china ground to chips, copper pots bashed out of shape.

A number of heavy doors were set into the walls. The majority had been staved in or pulled from their hinges, revealing the looted pantries or store-rooms on the other

212

side. Kitson noticed, however, that a couple had been sturdily reinforced, managing to withstand what had clearly been determined attempts to breach them.

As they walked deeper into the ruined kitchen, a small horde of rats wriggled away noisily through the debris; Kitson caught sight of several thick pink tails. The numbness that had carried him through the morning was fading fast, and the touch of his rain-sodden garments against his skin was starting to have an icy bite. He looked towards the large fireplace and suggested they get a fire going.

The *Courier* team were dragging the remains of a bench to the hearth when they heard the unmistakable sound of footsteps somewhere above them.

Cracknell set down his part of the bench. 'We have company,' he said, listening hard. 'There's several of 'em. Four – wait, five.'

The footsteps grew louder. 'Christ,' muttered Kitson, 'they're coming this way.'

All three had frozen, alive with excitement, the sense of crisis prompting them to forget their differences once more. There was no other way out of the kitchen. They had to face these people or hide. The proclivity for violence that Styles had demonstrated in the cave had deserted him; he now looked positively aghast at the prospect of further confrontation. The newspapermen were exhausted, unarmed and outnumbered. Even Cracknell saw at once which choice to make.

'Those barrels,' he said, pointing to a heap of empty wine butts on the far side of the room, next to a long iron oven. They hurried over and ducked behind them.

Soon afterwards, the voices arrived at the kitchen staircase – they were talking in English. Cracknell promptly started to stand. Kitson, recognising one of them, pulled him back down with all his strength.

'Must I hide even from my own people, then?' the senior correspondent asked indignantly.

'*Wray*,' Kitson hissed.

Cracknell fell quiet, and peered out from their hiding place with keen curiosity. Many of the wine butts were falling apart, affording the *Courier* team a good view of the room through their loosened slats. Captain Wray, they saw, was accompanied by two corporals from the 99th and a pair of men in civilian clothes. Both these civilians were grubby and unshaven, but had an odd air of refinement about them. One was telling Wray about the villa's history and the circumstances of its construction. A slight accent in his speech told Kitson that he was Russian, and of the highest social rank; the other man, whose demeanour was subtly deferential, was a servant of some kind. The redcoats were very much on their guard, miniés ready in their hands, scanning the shadows.

'It is a terrible, terrible shame,' the Russian was saying. 'I am taken aback, Captain, really I am. Only two months ago this house was fit for the Tsar – almost too good for him, in fact! I do not blame you British. No, I blame the filthy Turks. The beasts have a natural bent towards wickedness and rapine. The stories told in Sebastopol of how they treat the women of countries they occupy curdle the blood. Quite why the noble forces of Britain and France have taken their side I will never, *never* understand.'

Wray's lack of interest was plain. 'Where is it, Gorkachov?'

'Over here, Captain.' The Russian walked across the room, stepping gingerly through the wreckage towards one of the reinforced doors. 'This is it! One of the first modifications I made when I was appointed steward. The cellar below is impregnable, a place no thief can force his way into, reserved for the storage of the most valuable treasures during difficult times such as these.'

He drew off one of his long cavalry boots and shook three keys from it. The door, once unlocked, opened soundlessly, and all five men went through. Gorkachov's amiable voice could be heard for some time as they descended deeper beneath the building, amplified by the stone walls.

'What is this?' Kitson whispered urgently. 'What is going on?'

'Boyce,' Cracknell replied. 'Has to be.'

There was no question of the *Courier* team taking this chance to depart. Even Styles had shrugged off some of

214

his morbidity and was watching the doorway with close interest. After a minute or so, one of the corporals and the Russian servant emerged, carrying a framed wooden panel between them. It was about four and a half feet by three; they set it down against the wall, facing outwards. The corporal then took his rifle from his shoulder and ushered the Russian back down to the cellar with evident distrust.

As they moved away from in front of the panel, a rectangle of lustrous, dazzling colour was revealed, shining warmly through the dullness of the kitchen. It was a painting, depicting a man standing beside a table. He was dressed in the purple toga of a senior Roman official, and was rubbing his hands over a wooden bowl. Clean-shaven and hard-featured, he had the composed face of a capable administrator. Water could be seen dripping down between his fingers: he was washing. In the background was a palace, rows of mighty Corinthian columns stretching off into the distance. A man clad in a long white robe was being led away through these columns by a squad of armoured soldiers. Holy light was breaking through the palace's ceiling in golden shafts, bathing this prisoner as he was taken away.

Kitson registered the subject and style, and started; then he stared in complete astonishment. He had to get closer. Ignoring the protests of his senior, he left the barrels and crept over the kitchen's dusty flagstones as stealthily as he could.

Despite the composure of the rest of the face, the eyes bore the very faintest suggestion of emotion; of a horrible, overwhelming, haunting guilt. Although so small and subtle, this touch was like a tiny spot of blood on a murderer's shirt, sweeping away in an instant all his efforts to detach himself and claim innocence and, once noticed, transforming the picture completely.

'Pilate washing his hands,' he murmured under his breath, unable to stop a grin from breaking across his face.

There were noises from the cellar. Eyes still on the panel, he returned reluctantly to his comrades. 'Styles,' he asked immediately, 'do you know of this work?'

'I – I recognise the style, I think,' the illustrator replied diffidently. 'Is it not Raphael? His Roman manner?'

Recovering this old knowledge brought Styles a palpable relief, and for that moment the warping woes of the Crimean campaign seemed to fall away from him. All is not lost, Kitson thought; Robert Styles may still be saved.

'Indeed – a Raffaelo Sanzio, here in the Crimea. This work is mentioned by Giorgio Vasari as being owned by Cosimo de Medici in 1568, but nothing has been heard of it since. It was thought to be destroyed. This is an incredible discovery – incredible! God only knows how it came to be in this place. Make a sketch, Robert, quickly.'

The illustrator fumbled with his equipment for a few seconds and then started to draw with eager haste.

'They are stealing it for Boyce,' said Cracknell quietly. 'Just you watch.'

Wray's party emerged from the cellar. This time the other corporal carried a strongbox with the servant. It was heavy; they set it down with a groan. Coin, guessed Cracknell, or gemstones.

'Mallender, Lavery,' said the Captain in his lisping drawl of a voice, addressing the corporals. 'Get the cart into that hall upstairs. The less distance we have to move this lot, the better.' They hesitated. 'You can manage that, can't you?'

'Best I stay with you, Cap'n,' answered one of them. 'Can't trust these Ruski bastards, sir. A month in the pickets 'as taught me that much.'

'I can move the cart alone, Cap'n,' added the other. 'Mall can stay.'

Cracknell bit his knuckle. Such misguided loyalty!

Wray sighed, seemingly unable to summon the energy to shout them down. 'Very well, do what you will.'

So Corporal Lavery went back up, whilst Mallender stood guard at the foot of the staircase, out of Cracknell's sight. The loquacious Russian, although clearly pained by thought of a vehicle being driven into the villa, soon recovered his spirits and began to talk about the painting Kitson was so impressed by. The Tsar's father, it turned out, had bought it at the secret sale of a disgraced Austrian Count. It was said that the panel had been given to his family back in the

216

seventeenth century as payment for a nefarious act – an assassination, it was suspected.

Wray was sneering, his features becoming even more rodent-like as the thin lips drew back. 'And your Tsar doesn't mind you using this masterpiece to pay the Colonel for your escape to Paris?'

Aha, thought Cracknell; that's why this Gorkachov's being so bloody cooperative. There is a deal underway – a deal with Nathaniel Boyce.

The Russian smiled. 'Nicholas and I are good friends. He would not want me to suffer in this war. Besides, he does not care overmuch for the painting. Very few people know he has it – not even his own children. The attitude of an emperor to his possessions—'

'You knew about the attack, didn't you, Gorkachov?' interrupted Wray suddenly. 'The attack, this morning. That's why you made your escape when you did. To avoid a big fight.'

The Russian seemed unperturbed by the hostility in Wray's voice. 'Captain, how can you think such a thing? I merely wished to reach Paris for the winter. It is my favourite season in the city. To see the Tuileries frosted with snow is as enchanting as anything I can imagine. Society is alive as at no other time of year, and the distractions for a gentleman are both choice and illimitable.'

Wray let Gorkachov ramble on about Paris, about the balls, the fine restaurants and the charming ladies, for a short while. Then he took the revolver from his belt and lifted it so that the barrel was almost touching the Russian's chest.

This brought the Parisian monologue to an immediate halt. 'C-captain,' the Russian stammered pleadingly, 'I – I do not know what—'

Wray fired twice, felling Gorkachov so quickly that the eye could barely follow it. Without pause, in a single fluid movement, he turned the pistol on the servant, sending him spinning into a splintered crockery cabinet. The gunshots filled the kitchen completely, hitting the ears with a percussive clap and leaving them ringing shrilly.

A second later Corporal Mallender yelled, 'Cap'n Wray, what are ye doing?'

Swivelling around, Wray closed an eye to aim. He daren't, Cracknell thought disbelievingly; not one of Her Majesty's soldiers. But then the Captain fired, and fired again. There was a clattering thump as a large uniformed body struck against the kitchen's stone stairs.

The servant was still alive. Murmuring weakly in Russian, he was trying to crawl inside the cabinet he had fallen against. Wray fiddled with his pistol, cursing the mechanism; then he walked over to the cabinet and put his last bullet in the back of the man's head.

A soldier's boots sprinted across the room above them. Wray idly studied the painting as Lavery rushed down the kitchen stairs – and stopped abruptly when he saw Mallender's body.

'*Jimmy!*' Lavery's cry was hoarse with disbelief. 'Oh no, pal, no, *no . . .*'

'Turns out Gorkachov here had a pistol,' Wray informed him coolly. 'He got off a few shots, I'm afraid, before I could put him and his man down. Dashed bad luck.'

Cracknell looked at Kitson. His junior's face was set in a hard scowl. The illustrator, however, had crossed his arms over his head as if under bombardment. So collected in the cave when he had silenced that Russian infantryman, he had now reverted to his usual ineffectual self.

Corporal Lavery, still on the stairs, had started to sob. 'Ah, Jimmy . . . I served with 'im these fifteen years, Cap'n. An' a better fellow never stepped.'

'Stop that, Corporal,' ordered Wray. 'We have to get this upstairs, and then back to camp. Quickly.'

Lavery shambled mournfully into view and together the two men hefted the strongbox from the kitchen.

As soon as they were gone, Cracknell was on his feet and pacing around the wine butts. 'Murder!' he spat, his voice straining to express the extent of his outrage. 'This is murder! Two defenceless men – and an *English soldier*!'

Corporal Mallender was laid out awkwardly upon the staircase, an ugly red tear in his shoulder and another at the base of his neck. His rifle was still clenched in his hands, and there was an expression of innocent surprise on his face.

'There, Thomas, *there* is a killing to effect the bloody mind! A killing without sense or the slightest bloody justification!' Cracknell spun about. 'Why the hell did he do it? The Russian was *giving him* the painting. The Corporal, poor bastard, was *watching out for him!*'

His subordinates had stood up, and were looking around the kitchen, at the painting and the fresh bodies, with stunned uncertainty. There were noises upstairs; a shout, then the wooden clank of cartwheels.

'We have to leave,' Cracknell told them, 'this second. If Wray finds us we'll be as dead as Corporal Mallender there. You've seen how much he enjoys that pistol of his.'

'But what of the painting?' Kitson said. 'We cannot just allow Wray to take it!'

'Don't fret, Thomas – we will get them for this,' Cracknell promised. 'They won't succeed, my friend. The painting will incriminate them, don't you see? And there's that soldier, Corporal Lavery – he'll talk. We will damn well get them for this, I swear it. But right now, we have to go.'

Feeling more like a true leader than he had done all day, the senior correspondent hurried his team up into the villa and through the first doorway they came to. It took them into a small, circular antechamber with a single broken window. They knocked through the loose shards of glass and clambered out into the rain.

8

'Are you quite finished?' Major-General Sir William Codrington's white sideburns seemed to glow against the reddening skin beneath them. His narrow, lipless mouth was pressed together into a hard line.

Kitson and Cracknell stood side by side in the hut that served as Codrington's brigade headquarters. It was modestly furnished, with several maps of the region mounted on the walls, and smelled strongly of wood resin and boot polish. The Major-General himself sat behind a long trestle table strewn with papers. The *Courier* men were positioned at one end of this table; Boyce and Wray, in full dress uniform, stewed silently at the other.

Cracknell raised his chin, defiant in the face of Codrington's obvious disbelief. 'I believe that's everything,' he replied calmly. 'Call forth Corporal Lavery and then search Boyce's quarters for the painting. That will corroborate what we've told you.'

Codrington sat back heavily, crossing his arms. There was a long pause. He looked out of a window towards the battle-field, his craggy profile framed against the raw planks behind him. 'You seriously expect me to believe,' he said eventually, his gruff voice slowed by incredulity, 'that a rare painting by some ancient Italian was here, in the Crimea – and that Colonel Boyce of the Paulton Rangers entered into a deal with a Russian nobleman to acquire it, which he then broke by having the man murdered.'

'Yes, in order to cover the theft,' Kitson interjected.

'The painting is immensely rare, Major-General, its value beyond all reckoning. Most connoisseurs think it destroyed. It has no provenance, no history since the sixteenth century. Its only link with the Crimea, with the Tsar, was this Imperial steward. By murdering those who led him to the painting Colonel Boyce is free to make up any story about its acquisition that he likes. It is his word against that of whoever might challenge him.'

'And also,' Cracknell added, 'he wouldn't then have to arrange the Russian fellow's passage out of the Crimea, and risk being caught aiding the enemy.'

A couple of the staff officers standing around the edges of the hut stirred uneasily. Whether their arguments were convincing anyone Kitson could not tell. They certainly weren't making any progress with Major-General Codrington. Indeed, every word they uttered seemed to harden the commander of the Light Division's first brigade yet further against them. It was becoming clear to Kitson that their case was an impossible one to make. Boyce and Wray had committed a crime so brazen and unlikely that it would not even be believed, let alone investigated. The army, also, had suffered a traumatic blow only two days previously. Kitson could well understand Codrington not wishing to probe the black corruption that existed amongst his regimental officers whilst the dead were still being pulled from the caves and crevices of Inkerman Ridge. Cracknell, in requesting this audience, had pushed them into a confrontation too quickly simply because he longed to have it.

The Major-General shook his head. 'All of this is ridiculous, all of it. Your accusation regarding the corporal, though, is positively *despicable*.'

'That is the word,' agreed Cracknell emphatically. 'Despicable it most certainly is. This Colonel sent his men away from a major defensive battle for his own material gain, and ordered them to kill – Russians, yes, but also any Englishman who stood in their path. Corporal Mallender's only crime was to refuse to leave Captain Wray alone so that he could execute the steward and his servant. He saw them die, Sir William, and so had to die himself.'

Codrington glared at him, his round eyes black and furious. 'I am a major-general, and will be addressed as such by you,' he snapped. 'We are in the camp of Her Majesty's Army, not one of your grub-street taverns.'

'My apologies, *Major-General*, but I—'

'And my meaning, which you plainly comprehend but choose to ignore, is that you, sir, *you* are despicable for making such an accusation.'

Turning away from Cracknell in disgust, the Major-General addressed Wray. The Captain came to attention with such force that Codrington's quill bounced in its inkpot. Trussed up in his dress uniform he looked like a little bantam cockerel, not the merciless murderer of the villa. He stated that there was no truth whatsoever to any of the news-papermen's foul allegations. He had been fighting against the Russians that morning, from beginning to bitter end. Confirmation of his continual presence on the front line could have been provided by his immediate superior, Major James Maynard, had he not died in Colonel Boyce's advance past the Sandbag Battery.

'And what of these corporals – Mallender and . . . ?'

'Lavery, sir,' Boyce said. His arm was in a sling, and he had a look of noble endurance on his face. 'Both were killed in the advance.'

'So Lavery was done in too, was he?' sneered Cracknell. 'You again, Wray, I suppose, covering your tracks?'

Kitson stared at the floor, wishing that Cracknell would keep quiet. Such combativeness would not help them; and sure enough, Codrington told him bluntly to hold his tongue or be thrown out into the mud.

'They gave their lives for their Queen in the finest fashion,' Boyce continued with stoic reserve. 'I am appalled by this slander, quite frankly, but not altogether surprised by it. I have crossed swords with this paper's senior correspondent before, and know him to be a liar and a cad of the lowest conceivable sort. The man bears a bitter grudge against the army, as any who have read a *London Courier* recently will know all too well. He seems to hold me in particular disdain – a source of no little pride, I must say.'

Someone to the rear of the hut chuckled. Was Boyce making an oblique allusion to the widespread rumours about Cracknell and his wife, Kitson wondered, and using them to his advantage, suggesting that here lay the motive for these allegations?

'I saw the *Courier*'s coverage of the Alma,' mused Codrington. 'It was tendentious, certainly, and quite reckless in its criticism of Lord Raglan and our generals.'

'I assure you that we hold no grudge against the army, Major-General,' said Cracknell darkly, 'only against those who would lead it to ruin through their incompetence.'

Codrington was not listening. He looked at Boyce. 'You know nothing of this villa, I take it – or this painting?'

Boyce said that he did not.

'Is there even anything there?' Codrington asked his staff. 'I see nothing on the maps.'

'I rode out there at dawn, sir,' said a major. 'Found a burned-out ruin, nothing else.'

'Very well.' Codrington sat forward, resting his elbows on the table. Kitson knew then that it was over; his mind was made up. 'This has gone quite far enough. I think we are seeing the hazards inherent in this recent fashion for letting untrained civilians embed themselves amongst the fighting men. Whether these two are crazed by drink, or their experiences of battle, or something else altogether I cannot say, but I absolutely will not allow them to repay the army's misplaced hospitality with fantastical, abusive accusations against an officer who fought with such courage against the Russian attack.' He pointed at the newspapermen, stressing his pronouncements with aggressive jabs of his finger. 'If I hear that you have written a single word of this sorry business in that Whiggish rag of yours I will see you both expelled from the plateau. I have Lord Raglan's ear, and I promise that you'll be back in Constantinople so fast your heels won't touch the bloody ground. It will go no further than this room. Is that clear?'

Cracknell bowed. 'As glass, Major-General.'

An hour later, Cracknell and Kitson sat on the rocky outcrop from which they had watched the ill-fated advance of the 99th two days before. Cracknell was working, and grumbling constantly as he wrote. 'Like a damned gentleman's club, all bloody watching out for each other like that. Blasted Codrington holds his rank only because of a dearth of other candidates. Old men and stop-gaps, that's what the army's reduced to, old men and bloody stop-gaps. And they dare to speak of Maynard! Poor, upright, honourable Maynard . . .'

Kitson gazed out at the scene below. It was a dull day, but clear; he could see the rocky hollows, steep spurs and thick undergrowth across which the soldiers had been made to fight. More than forty hours after the final repulsion of the attack, bodies were still being found. Parties of orderlies searched through the rocks, brushwood and tattered copses, their calls sounding back and forth across the ridge as if competing with one another. *'Six Ruskis – dead!' 'One of ours, Guardsman – dead!'*

Huge ditches had been dug at the edges of the battlefield, into which the stiff-limbed bodies were being tipped with little ceremony, most meeting this grim, undignified end stripped of everything but their greatcoats. This, they had learned, had been Maynard's probable fate. He had been carried back three hundred yards to an improvised field hospital, where both of his legs had been removed. Kitson had seen this often enough already to know what it must have been like. Maynard hadn't lasted more than a couple of hours after this operation. His mutilated body had lain out on the grass for the rest of the day; and then, as far as anyone seemed to know, had been buried in one of the first mass graves dug that evening.

'A *grudge*!' Cracknell was saying vehemently. 'He'll see what a bloody grudge is, Thomas, oh yes! I promised you that he would not get away with what he did in that villa, and I will bloody keep that promise.' He drew a line under his latest paragraph. 'Listen to this.

'So it was a victory, reader, but like that of King Pyrrhus of old: if we are cursed with another such victory, we will surely be undone. A surprise attack of immense proportions engulfed the ridge. There were rushes back and forth, as strategic points were lost, retaken and lost again; there were terrible knots of hand-to-hand, and blade-to-blade fighting; there was deep confusion as lines of

communication broke down in the dense fog. Yet rather than rely on caution and care in these treacherous conditions, many of our commanders became intoxicated by an almost suicidal pride. Much is being said of their courage; but what use is courage without the good sense to make it count for something?

'Some of these incidents are already famous. Sir George Cathcart, for example, threw his life away for a second of questionable glory, disobeying his orders and being shot from his saddle into the arms of his aide-de-camp. Others survived their folly, managing to transfer the penalty on to those unlucky enough to be under their command. Prominent among such figures is Colonel Nathaniel Boyce of the 99th Foot (Paulton Rangers). Hungry for renown after a disappointing Alma, the good Colonel cast aside all notions of tactics or prudence and plunged ahead in a foolish advance that proved fatal for many dozens of the stout-hearted redcoats who followed him. One man's arrogance led directly to—'

Kitson kicked at a rock as Cracknell talked on. He found that he was no longer engaged by the senior correspondent's denunciations. The *Pilate* was lost; Boyce and Wray had escaped all consequences. It all suddenly seemed rather pointless. 'I cannot find Styles, Cracknell,' he interrupted. 'He has not come to the hut since the day of the battle.'

Cracknell snorted, gesturing towards the Sandbag Battery. 'He'll be out there, won't he, with his bodies. A deluge of inspiration for him, I should think.'

'He needs to leave the Crimea. He has become unbalanced, Cracknell. The boy-soldier in the cave, everything else we witnessed that day – it is too much for him to bear.'

Seeming to appreciate that Kitson would not be deterred this time, Cracknell set down his notebook and lit a cigarette. 'So you've said. Shouldn't think O'Farrell will like it. He had high hopes for the lad, as you well know.'

'Surely it's clear by now that they won't be met.'

The senior correspondent sighed, picking a shred of loose tobacco from his lip. 'Very well. When we've finished our report of this battle, I'll write our editor a letter explaining the situation, which I'll see wired back from Varna at the same time. That's the best I can offer.'

Kitson nodded; taking the hint about the report, he reached

for his pocketbook, and then sat staring uselessly at a blank page. He had not written anything since the battle. There was something in him that prevented it, a profound discontent that utterly paralysed his intellect.

There were some shouts from the slope, near its base. Remarkably, a group of injured infantrymen had been found alive in a remote gully. Kitson lifted Cracknell's field telescope; the white-faced soldiers were being lifted over the rocks with evident difficulty. One of them was howling with astonished agony, waving the blackened remains of his arm around as if the wound had just that moment been inflicted. They had lain undiscovered for all this time, he realised, simply because there weren't enough orderlies to come to their aid any sooner.

'I am going to help,' Kitson stated, rising to his feet.

The senior correspondent nodded absently, blew out some smoke and turned over a page. Kitson started down towards the battlefield, leaving Cracknell of the *Courier* perched alone on the outcrop, absorbed in his work.

Manchester
May 1857

1

The line of soldiers stretched across the parade ground, between the kitchen pump and the burning barrack-house. Dragged from their bunks, most were in a state of some undress, with many sporting bare feet and trailing shirt ends. They were wide awake, though, to a man; the air of emergency, the strong, choking smoke and the sight of rising flames against the night sky had served to banish all bleariness. Large iron pails were travelling along this human chain at some speed, losing a good quantity of their contents to the flagstones of the drill square. A group of sergeants had positioned themselves at the barracks end of the line, rushing in dangerously close to hurl what was left of the water on to the blaze. This was proving desperately ineffectual, the water hissing away to nothing whilst the fire grew in size and ferocity.

The two night sentries came running up from the front gate, and were about to set down their Enfield rifles and join in when they were halted by a wild-eyed lieutenant clad only in a nightshirt. He instructed them to conduct an immediate search of the waste ground to the west of the barracks – the cripple had been sighted. The sentries, Privates Donlan and Vernor, looked at each other before heading back towards the gate.

Like every man in the 25th Manchesters, Donlan and Vernor knew all about the cripple. It was, most agreed, pretty damned amusing. A hunchbacked tramp was stalking their heroic officers like a dog circling a duck-pond, and by Christ did he have them a-quacking! Only last week he had got his fangs into Captain Grier, cutting up his arm something nasty; but after the unholy fuss made in the papers over that bastard Wray, Colonel Bennett had been careful to keep it quiet. He wanted this cripple caught, though, and sharpish. Word was that some top brass were coming to Manchester soon, for the Queen's visit, and an embarrassment like this could not – *would* not be endured.

The two sentries left the barracks, hurrying a short distance along Regent Road before swerving into a side passage. This led them to a black, unlit expanse of open land, the cobbles underfoot giving way to loose earth strewn with refuse. Very little could be seen of their surroundings. Ahead of them was a horizon of distant hills. To their left was the barn-like nave of St Bartholomew's, its yard crowded with pale gravestones.

''E only goes fer officers, right, Vern?' whispered Donlan nervously as they advanced, rifles at the ready. 'Shall we put one in't pipe, just in case, like?'

'Nay,' snapped Vernor. 'They want 'im breathin', ye numbskull. If ye catch 'im, give 'im a tap wi' yer butt.'

'Is it true that 'e's tried t'break into th'Colonel's 'ouse, t'get at Wray? T'finish 'im off?'

Vernor nodded quickly, but his answer was cut short by a series of shouts from inside the barracks, and the stamping of boots. A squad was being formed up to come and assist with the search.

''Ear that, cripple?' Vernor cried into the darkness. ''Ear that, you bleeder? We're comin' for ye! Ye'll regret triflin' wi' us!'

A ragged shape loped across the waste ground in the direction of the churchyard. The soldiers gave chase, weaving in amongst the tightly packed graves, holding their rifles upright in front of them. For a second they lost him; then both heard a scrabbling, rustling sound, and turned to see a figure in a badly torn coat scaling an ivy-covered wall with unlikely agility. Vernor started after him, gesturing for Donlan to head around the side and cut him off.

230

Donlan left the yard by a rusty gate, his eyes open wide, his heavy Enfield raised and ready to strike. The lane beyond was quite empty. He ran along it, checking every back alley he passed. There was no sign of their quarry. Vernor dropped into the lane with a curse and a shower of brick dust, twigs and ivy leaves. Together they hunted around for a minute or two longer, but it was no use. It was as if the cripple had taken flight from the top of the wall like a greasy, tattered owl.

The sentries looked at each other, knowing that they would now have to return and report their failure to the regiment. Wearily, they shouldered their rifles and started back towards the barracks. Before them, the spire of St Bartholomew's spiked up into a fire-tinted sky.

2

Kitson tried to keep away from it. He tried to keep the wide avenue of the nave between himself and the old master saloons, to confine his attention solely to the modern galleries where, in under an hour, he was to give his talk to the operatives of the Norton Foundry. He knew exactly where it was. The *Star*'s street philosopher had spent much of the past few weeks under the great glass roof of the Art Treasures Palace, detailing the immense collection, penning observations on the milling crowds, or nursing a port negus in the refreshment rooms. Every time he visited he attempted the same thing, and every time he failed. This occasion, despite the imminent arrival of Mrs James, her father and close to a thousand of his workers, would be no different.

Cursing himself, Kitson strode grimly across the strip of crimson carpet that ran down the centre of the nave. The Exhibition had been open for less than an hour, the few early morning visitors floating like motes of dust in the cavernous interior. On the opposite side of the transept, someone started to play a jaunty popular tune on the grand organ, the serried notes groaning through the building. The street philosopher passed quickly through the banks of display cases and into Saloon A, the room devoted to the Italian and Northern Renaissance.

And there it was, hanging on the line in the centre of the saloon – the *Pilate* from the Crimean villa. No matter how often he stood before it, Kitson always felt unprepared.

There was a fresh horror, a fresh dismay each time. As he looked at the painting, his chest tightened and a cold, damp shadow seemed to fall over the gallery. He could smell the musty kitchen once again, could hear the rainfall and feel Robert Styles crouched anxiously beside him; and he could see Captain Wray, cocking his revolver with his thumb.

Abruptly, Kitson turned from the *Pilate*, thrusting his hands into his pockets with such violence that a stitch gave out in the lining of his jacket. Facing him now, opposite the Italian wall which held the *Pilate*, was a dizzying expanse of early Netherlandish art; stiff-limbed, melodramatic *Crucifixions*; brightly clothed Virgins holding pot-bellied Christ-children, their little faces prematurely old; and minutely detailed portraits of gem-encrusted, fur-lined merchants. Kitson closed his eyes.

Away from the Exhibition, sitting at his desk or lying sleeplessly in bed, he had considered the *Pilate*'s presence at Manchester at exhaustive length. He had not expected ever to see the panel again. That Boyce had managed to get it out of the Crimea was amazing enough. Although Major-General Codrington had dismissed their claims, had Boyce been seen afterwards to have an old master painting in his possession, suspicions would certainly have been aroused; Kitson had even thought that the Colonel might have destroyed it in order to protect himself.

Now, however, Boyce seemed to be in the clear. The Tsar the panel had belonged to was dead, succeeded in 1855 by a son who was entirely unaware of its existence, if what the Crimean steward had said was true. Codrington and his staff – those of them who had survived the campaign – were hardly likely to remember the details of that brief, farcical hearing, given all that had come after it. And even if they did, the connection would now be impossible to prove. Since the war, Boyce was known to have bought a great many pictures; with the help of some forged papers, the *Pilate* could easily be claimed as one of these. Only Kitson and Cracknell knew its real source, and how it had been obtained – and what had a mighty lion like Boyce to fear from the likes of them?

The *Pilate's* presence in the Art Treasures Exhibition had not been hard to explain. After learning from Cracknell that Boyce was coming to Manchester, Kitson had asked around in Wovenden's – and discovered that the Brigadier-General, as he now was, was attending the Queen's state visit in two weeks' time. The *Pilate* was being hailed in some quarters as the sensation of the entire Exhibition, overshadowing even Henry Labouchere's Michelangelo, and its owner acclaimed as a connoisseur of the highest discernment and intellect. Bold and shameless as ever, Boyce was looking to win the praise of Queen Victoria herself with his blood-soaked plunder.

These deductions left Kitson completely furious, longing to see some kind of justice done. This, surely, had been Cracknell's intention when he had waylaid the street philosopher at the Polygon, but no attempt at contact had been made by his former colleague since then. For the first week, Kitson had expected him; for the second, his patience expiring, he had sought him out; and for the third he had grown convinced that Cracknell was no longer in Manchester at all. At that precise moment, in Saloon A of the Exhibition, Kitson wished that Cracknell would appear at his side so that he would have someone with whom to vent his seething fury – the only other person alive who would fully understand it.

Then, as always, he remembered Cracknell's own inexcusable actions, and the part he himself had played in them. This was not a man he could ever be allied with again, under any circumstances. If Cracknell was in the city somewhere, hatching his plots, Kitson was determined to remain uninvolved; especially if the stabbing of Wray was an indication of their nature.

He looked at his pocket-watch. Mrs James would be there in minutes.

After her spirited exchange with Cracknell in the Polygon, Kitson was half-afraid that she would end their friendship simply on the grounds that he was acquainted with such an obnoxious individual. But she had written to him only a few days later, initiating a frequent correspondence. Her letters were packed with thoughts and questions, so like her conversation that they made him smile as he read them. It was plain, though, that Cracknell's comments about her father were preying on her mind – as had been his intention. Several times, she asked Kitson directly whether he could throw any light on the so-called 'Tomahawk's' strange statements. He could not, of course, and no amount of inquiry in Wovenden's or anywhere else even hinted at an explanation. In writing his replies, he could only try to express the deep regard and affection that he felt for her, and set aside his fears that their connection was leading her into danger.

Mrs James had also communicated repeatedly how much she was looking forward to his lecture, and Kitson had resolved that it would be worthy of her anticipation. He had been completely prepared, a model of calm composure – before the Crimean panel had exerted its irresistible pull.

Without thinking, he turned back towards the *Pilate*. Eyes fixed upon it, upon that man with his impossible burden of blame, Kitson sat down slowly on an upholstered bench in the centre of the gallery. Forearms on his trembling knees, he pressed his sweating palms together as hard as he could.

After a long, gradual deceleration, the train jerked to a halt, causing its passengers to rock back and forth in their seats. There was a brief pause as they gathered their belongings, and then a vast throng of working people gushed out of the string of third-class carriages on to the covered platform of the special Art Treasures Exhibition station. A holiday atmosphere prevailed in amongst the drifting clouds of smoke and steam that billowed down from the engine. Clad in its Sunday best, the massive outing was alive with merry chatter, with gangs of children racing around its edges like swallows circling a steeple.

In the first-class carriage, Charles Norton got to his feet, the springs of the plush red upholstery creaking underneath him. 'This day will be remembered,' he announced, his voice heavy with portent, 'as the day when our Foundry, although successful already, set itself upon a still brighter path. Never before, I believe, have humble people been exposed to improving influences such as those contained in this grand building before us. The drunkenness, the indolence, the vice of our workforce will soon be but a distant, unsavoury recollection. They are, at this moment, but gnomes groping in the earthy darkness, guided by ignorance and instincts purely animal; but this thing, this great thing here, will open their eyes to the light. It will enable them speedily to take their proper rank in the great human family.'

The managers and wives assembled within the carriage applauded this declaration enthusiastically, some saying 'hear, hear' with sycophantic conviction. Jemima rolled her eyes. Her father had been rehearsing his little speech for days. It sounded to her as if he'd lifted the bulk of it from one of his Tory periodicals.

'I wonder what rank that would be,' whispered Bill, who was sitting beside her. 'That of idiot children, perhaps?'

Jemima glanced at her brother. Both were in high spirits. She was to see her friend Mr Kitson after three long weeks; and he simply enjoyed these company excursions, relishing the departure from the ordinary that they permitted.

Norton raised his hands, bidding his audience to fall quiet. 'All I ask, ladies and gentlemen, is that you make sure our men and women pass through the Exhibition's doors. I am quite convinced that once inside, the refining influence of the place, and the elevated glory of the paintings, will ensure their good conduct. You have all visited the Exhibition already, I presume?' There was a chorus of affirmatives. 'Well then, you'll be well equipped to answer any questions they might have. I believe it's all fairly straightforward, but it never pays to be too confident where the working man is concerned. Now, we dine at one. Our company here will meet in the first-class refreshment room – the rest of the Foundry in the lower-class extension. I shall be visiting the workers as they take their repast, to see how their experiences have touched them, and would gladly welcome any of you who might wish to accompany me.'

'So that will be all of them, then,' Bill observed archly. 'The governor is so seldom disappointed by his managers.'

Realising that her father was about to conclude his address, Jemima cleared her throat loudly.

Norton looked over at her, and for a second his insufferable patrician satisfaction faltered. 'Also, ladies and gentlemen,' he added, 'my daughter has arranged for a short lecture to be given in the modern galleries. The speaker is an authority on artistic matters, I'm told, and once worked in this capacity for the *London Courier* magazine. This will commence in one half-hour, and I urge you and however many operatives you can secure to attend.'

The reluctance with which this postscript was delivered brought a dry smile to Jemima's lips. After the ball at the Polygon, that same night in fact, Charles had summoned her to his study and ordered her not to have anything more to do with her Mr Kitson – or his friend Mr Cracknell.

Such tyrannical behaviour invariably provoked Jemima rather than cowed her, and an altercation had ensued. She had informed her father curtly that it was Mr Kitson she knew; and that Mr Cracknell was *not* his friend, he could be sure of that, and she would not be meeting that person again if she could possibly help it. At any rate, she'd continued, Mr Kitson could not be dropped as readily as he commanded, as he had been generous enough to agree to lecture the Foundry workers in the Art Treasures Exhibition at her request. Striking his desk with his fist, Charles had demanded that this address be cancelled right away.

Seldom one to tip-toe meekly around a potentially inflammatory subject, Jemima had barely paused before asking him if his objections were rooted in the Crimea. Had he encountered the newspapermen whilst they were working in the theatre of war for the *London Courier*? Did this have anything to do with the contract he had secured whilst staying in Balaclava?

Charles would not answer, stating wrathfully that none of this was her concern – that he was her father and she would obey him. She had retorted that she was not a daft girl in petticoats but a grown woman, and although forced to rely on him for food and shelter, she would not have him arbitrarily terminate her friendships without proper justification. The challenge had thus been made: either he explained his antipathy or the lecture would go ahead. She had heard nothing more.

Seeing that her father's speech was at an end, Jemima adjusted her bonnet, gathered her skirts and climbed from the train. The Norton workforce had spread along the lengthy platform as they waited for their master. A number had sat themselves upon benches, taken out packed lunches and a variety of bottles, and begun an impromptu picnic. Behind them, plastered on the outer wall of the Palace, was an over-lapping mass of lurid commercial posters, each bearing boasts and promises in elaborate script, with dense blocks of text beneath.

Charles Norton and his entourage of managers emerged from the first-class carriage. They put on their top hats as they stepped down, the spotless jet-black cylinders shining dully in the diffuse light.

'You people!' bellowed the white-whiskered proprietor, pointing at the picnickers as he strode up the platform. 'Throw that food away! There's to be no food taken inside the building, is that clear?'

Norton swept towards the corridor that led into the Exhibition, his offspring trailing a short distance behind him. Herded by the more junior members of the managerial staff, the workforce slowly followed, reluctantly abandoning their pies, sandwiches and bottles. Jemima watched as her father took up a position just inside the turnstiles, surveying the teeming mass of his employees as they formed into lines and were fed steadily into the Art Treasures Exhibition.

Then something odd happened. A tall, black-suited man, resembling a low-class undertaker, sidled up to him, tipping his stew-pan hat. They spoke briefly, Charles clearly wishing to dispense with their business as quickly as possible. The man withdrew to the shadows beneath the balcony, where three or four others, all similarly attired, were waiting for him. He relayed his instructions, making a series of efficient gestures with his right hand; and they all walked off purpose-fully in different directions.

The workers, once they were past the barriers, drifted into the vastness of the Palace, gaping at its lavish luxury. Slowly, they strolled towards the picture galleries and up to the transept, their conversations growing louder and livelier the further they were from the gaze of their master. The few visitors already in the Exhibition, seeing the Foundry's noisy approach, retreated to the first-class refreshment room, exchanging indignant looks as they went.

Bill returned from a book-vendor in the station corridor with two Exhibition catalogues. He handed one to his sister and then sloped away. Jemima studied the weighty volume for a few moments before tucking it under her arm, skirting the crowds of factory people and walking into the nave. The Foundry expedition was running early; Mr Kitson was not due to arrive for another ten minutes. She decided to take a turn through the old master galleries before going to their agreed meeting place in Saloon F. Several dozen of her father's workers were already wandering through the long, bright row of connected rooms, looking over the many hundreds of paintings they contained. They stared at grappling nudes and mythological beasts enacting alien, incomprehensible scenes; peered at grimy landscapes and discoloured portraits; shrugged before obscure allegories, and tales from the lives of the more esoteric saints. A large group of men and women stood before a cluster of fleshy Venetian pictures, pointing out certain anatomic endowments with lewd, echoing laughter. Seeing their employer's daughter approaching, they nudged each other and assumed a grinning, unconvincing decorum. But as she passed, their eyes returned to the naked, contorted forms on the walls, and they burst into hilarity once more.

Jemima went through to the far gallery, designated Saloon A, where the most ancient paintings were displayed. On her previous tour of the Exhibition, this was where she had spent the least time, being largely unfamiliar with the artists and schools it represented. As with all the old master galleries, the long, rectangular room had been arranged so that the northern paintings hung on one side, and the southern on the other – the idea being that a visitor could turn around at any moment and compare the productions of the two geographical regions. It was but sparsely populated. There was a single working family present, the husband and wife studying a mystical Botticelli *Nativity* in a state of sombre confusion

239

whilst their four children played hide-and-seek around the gallery seats.

And there, quite unexpectedly, was Mr Kitson, neatly shaven and well dressed, clad in a dark suit and hat with a pale grey waistcoat. He was standing, his arms crossed, engrossed in a large panel in the centre of the room. She felt a sudden, pure happiness. Jemima James and Thomas Kitson were together again, standing within the same walls, breathing the same air. Anything else could surely be brushed aside. She said his name, smiling broadly, and crossed the gallery.

The deep distraction with which he turned away from the panel, however, made her remember the many questions that remained unanswered. There was much she still didn't know – about him, and her father, and the disturbing interest that Mr Cracknell had in them both. This situation, she saw, could not reach an easy resolution.

Nonetheless, when Mr Kitson saw her, a genuine, slightly awkward delight suffused him, dispelling his anxiety. They spoke warmly for a few minutes, discussing the hanging scheme; he attempted to extract praise for the curators' achievements from her, having not forgotten her scepticism about the Exhibition on the day they met. She acknowledged that it was a remarkable feat of organisation, but said that the great cliff-faces of art towering over them on either side left her feeling overwhelmed rather than inspired. He chuckled, and went on to point out some of the more impressive loans that had been secured. Beneath his light-hearted conversation, though, lay something of the tender yet determined evasiveness that had characterised his letters. Jemima could not decide if he was trying to protect her somehow, or if that which he concealed was simply too painful for him to contemplate. She had read of the great difficulties encountered by those returning from the Russian campaign. Workhouses and asylums across the country had admitted scores of former soldiers who were utterly unable to resume ordinary lives – men reduced to vagrancy or madness by what they had experienced.

For he was certainly a veteran of the Crimea. After the

Polygon, she'd gone back to her pile of old *Couriers*. It had not taken long to find mention in an editorial of both a junior correspondent and an illustrator dispatched by the paper to the peninsula at the outset of the invasion, before its coverage came to focus on the controversial Mr Cracknell. The illustrator remained an enigma, but Jemima was convinced that the junior correspondent had been Mr Kitson. She tested this with some oblique references in their correspondence; to which he did not respond directly, of course, but neither did he deny what they implied.

Abruptly, Jemima realised that he was trying to hide something from her even then – that the locations of the paintings he talked about were being carefully chosen so that he could stand between her and the work he had been examining when she had entered the saloon. She immediately peered around him, noted the number on the frame and looked it up in her catalogue.

'What of this one?' she said, pointing out the entry with her finger. '*Pontius Pilate Giving Christ up for Crucifixion* by Raffaello Sanzio, from the collection of Brigadier-General Nathaniel Boyce?'

As she read the name of the owner, she understood something of the painting's significance. This was the officer who had been so censured by the *London Courier* during the Russian War – the villain of the Tomahawk's reports. Mr Kitson paled slightly at the mention of Boyce. Seeing that he had failed to distract her attention from the panel, he moved away, saying nothing, raising his face up towards the band of blue sky visible through the gallery's glass roof. Jemima looked at the *Pilate*. The subject was profoundly unsettling, certainly a league away from the sweetly pious works that had been positioned around it. Even a nearby depiction of the crucifixion itself by the same painter could not match its disturbing power.

'I have read of this work,' she murmured. 'It is attracting a good deal of attention, is it not?'

He made no reply. She realised that Mr Kitson, in his coverage of the Exhibition for the *Manchester Evening Star*, had not so much as mentioned its presence. Ever since that night on Mosley Street, Jemima had been an avid reader of the *Star's* street philosopher. In recent weeks, he had touched upon every aspect of the Exhibition, from the character of the crowds to the bill of fare available in the refreshment rooms. The collection itself had been described in detail, both in terms of individual exhibits and the rigorous educational principles on which they had been arranged. Raphael's *Pilate*, however, the painting Jemima had found Mr Kitson so transfixed by, the painting owned by Mr Cracknell's Crimean nemesis, had been omitted completely.

Also, rather more disconcertingly, despite the confident claims in the leading art journals that this panel had emerged from nowhere to appear in the Exhibition – almost as if Raphael had risen from the grave, executed one last commission and then dropped straight back in – Jemima found that it was distinctly familiar. The shape of the wringing hands, the tone of the purple toga, the terrible guilt in those haunted eyes: all were known to her. An impossible conviction gathered in her mind. She had seen Raphael's *Pilate* before.

Mr Kitson's voice cut through her confusion. 'Mrs James, I believe the hour of the lecture is approaching.'

He was holding a pocket-watch in his hand. As he replaced it in his waistcoat, he winced; the injury in his chest that she had noticed in the Polygon was clearly troubling him again. His main concern, though, was to remove them both from the presence of the *Pilate*.

'Do allow me to apologise for my strange mood,' he added with sudden earnestness. 'You caught me by surprise – that is all. Seeing you again, madam, is truly a tonic for the soul. You – you look very lovely, may I say.'

'Why, thank you, sir.' Jemima, caught off guard, blushed a little.

'And you know that I would stay alone with you all day if I possibly could. But we should not keep your father waiting.'

Jemima nodded, and cast a final bewildered look at the *Pilate*. She then slid her fingers into the crook of his arm and held on to him tightly as they walked together into the nave.

* * *

A party of Foundry men, thirty or so strong, emerged from the old master saloons. Bill lowered the catalogue he'd been pretending to read and studied them. Their intention was plain – they were leaving. He'd noticed that as the morning progressed, and their feet became sore, the novelty of the Palace had begun to wane for many of his father's employees, and its manifold, unfathomable glories had started to feel somewhat oppressive. Barely forty minutes in, and they were already streaming for the exits, not even held back by the prospect of their free lunch. Those who were going – and there were hundreds – were heading off past the collegial spires of the Blind Asylum, on to the Stretford New Road and back into the centre of the city.

The men he was watching were among this number. 'The stupidest exhibition that ever I saw!' declared one gruffly.

'There's nowt here but pictures,' another agreed. 'Let's off to the Belle Vue.'

This proposal appeared to meet with the approval of the group. They strode down the nave, shoving their way through the turnstiles and out through the main doors. Bill, still grinning at their remarks, caught the eye of a straggler, a sinewy youth with a downy beard and a wide, sensuous mouth. Both stood still for a moment, holding the connection; then, with deliberate slowness, they looked each other up and down. Lingering yet further behind his comrades, the boy turned right before the doors, going down towards the second-class refreshment room. A hit, thought Bill triumphantly as he started after him. A palpable hit.

As he strolled along the wide red carpet towards the turnstiles, however, he noticed a familiar figure lurking around a marble Magdalene on the northern side of the nave. It was the black-bearded, shabbily dressed Irishman – Richard Cracknell, the one-time Tomahawk of the *Courier*, who had introduced himself so forcibly at the Polygon.

Bill stopped dead. His immediate fear was that the fellow might have seen his mute exchange with the factory boy, and have realised what was transpiring. He could tell that the infamous war correspondent was the sort who might well decide to stir up a bit of trouble just for larks. But no,

Cracknell's attention was thankfully directed towards one of the modern saloons, where the exodus from the Exhibition seemed to have been halted, to some extent at least. Bill heard his father within, droning away through the partition wall; and then another voice took over, a voice altogether kinder on the ear. It was Jemima's friend Mr Kitson – his lecture was beginning.

Cracknell edged from behind the knotted stone tresses of his Magdalene and sauntered towards the saloon entrance. This brought him some yards closer to Bill; flashing him a reptilian smile, the Tomahawk tipped his dented topper and wished young Mr Norton a perfectly *splendid* morning.

3

As he began to speak, the last trace of Kitson's nervousness left him. Nothing, he thought, absolutely nothing restores presence of mind like having to address an audience.

Being reunited with Mrs James whilst standing before the *Pilate*, hearing her say Nathaniel Boyce's name and stare so intently at the panel he had stolen, had been severely disorientating. Kitson had been beset by an alarming sense that the two things he should be striving to keep apart were becoming inextricably tangled together. When he saw Charles Norton, however, standing in Saloon F with his managers flanking him like a royal bodyguard, and the loose crowd of perhaps two hundred and fifty working people assembled behind them, all this promptly vanished from his mind. Something awakened in him – an old assurance dating from his life as an art correspondent in the Metropolis, back when he would have been unable even to find the Crimean peninsula on a map.

Saloon F contained many of the Exhibition's most recent works, a number of which had been shown in the Royal Academy only the year before. Heeding Mrs James' comment about the overwhelming effect of the display, Kitson was careful to discuss one painting at a time. He explained the nuances of expression in Landseer's hounds; the meditation upon mortality in John Millais' scene of young girls burning leaves in the autumn twilight; the wealth of symbolic detail in Holman Hunt's representations of Shakespeare. And he threw himself into his task, summoning all his enthusiasm and fluency. Turning frequently towards his audience, he was encouraged by the signs of interest he found there. Some soon slunk away, of course, and others looked around vacantly – but a tight semicircle of people over a hundred strong was following his words with close attention.

Only once did he dare to glance at Mrs James, who stood beside her father. In her face he saw such pride and love that it made him stumble on his words; and he had to look away again before continuing.

Then he came to the *Chatterton*. He knew from the time he had already spent in the Exhibition that it was one of the most popular works on display. 'Here we see *The Death of Chatterton* by Mr Henry Wallis. It shows the young poet lying dead upon his bed, having poisoned himself in his garret after his work was rejected by a publisher. We see his dandy clothes,' Kitson pointed to the scarlet coat and turquoise britches, 'for which he was well known; the remains of his work, this shredded paper, which he destroyed in despair before committing his fatal act. Here is the vial of arsenic rolling on the floorboards, where it has fallen from his lifeless hand.' He lowered his head for a moment, an unexpected pulse of sadness beating through him. 'The – the poet is famous now, the subject of paintings and books, but he would have been much more so had he allowed himself to live. The picture tells us about waste, my friends, the waste of life, and of talent – how men are often their own worst foes.'

'Dear God,' cried a muffled voice close to the back, 'I reckon this poor cove's set to burst out crying!'

There were a few sniggers at this artless interruption; several at the front of the audience made shushing noises and looked around indignantly. Kitson was about to respond when he noticed a tall, distinctly sinister-looking man in a black suit settle next to Charles Norton like a great raven and whisper urgently in his ear.

Suddenly the labour-lord declared that the lecture was over, many thanks to Mr Kitson for his time, lunch would be commencing shortly if they would all start towards the second-class extension back towards the railway station. The crowd thinned, visibly split between disappointment at the premature end of their lecture and hungry anticipation of their meal.

Mrs James turned angrily to her father, demanding to know what was going on. He bade her be quiet and walked over to Kitson with barely contained menace.

'I don't know what your game is, you *dog*,' he fumed, 'how making clever lectures fits into whatever you two are planning, but I will be chumped by it no longer. I allowed you this chance for my daughter's sake, but no more!'

Kitson held Norton's bulging eye. 'Sir, I do not understand you. My only wish—'

Two black-suited men pushed through the remains of the audience, holding Cracknell between them. He was grinning as if he was having a marvellous time. It was him, Kitson realised, who had shouted out whilst he had been discoursing on the *Chatterton*.

'Thomas, what an informative talk! Quite fascinating! The contents of this gallery do pale beside that of Saloon A across the hall, though, wouldn't you say?'

The last lingering Foundry workers began to peer curiously at the loud, scruffy fellow being hauled before their employer. More black-suits appeared, shoving the operatives on their way and then standing guard at the gallery's entrances. The Foundry managers, at Norton's terse request, filed off obediently to the first-class refreshment rooms. Cracknell and Kitson were now alone with Charles Norton, Jemima James and half a dozen of Norton's black-suits.

'What is this?' Norton demanded, glaring from one to the other. 'What *is this*, damn you!'

'Father,' said Mrs James, looking at Kitson despairingly, 'you are mistaken. Mr Kitson has no connections with this person. He is not a part of whatever it is that you fear so much.'

'Jemima, leave us,' ordered Norton coldly. 'Go out to the nave, this instant.'

'I will *not*, not until I am certain—'

'Mr Norton, sir,' purred Cracknell with hideous, mocking

247

obsequiousness. 'An honour, truly, to stand before the Buckle King himself. And this structure of yours – well, it is beyond words. The finest of its kind since the Crystal Palace. Not a patch on that particular building, of course, but then no one really expected it to be, did they? Not in Manchester.'

'Shall we eject them, Mr Norton?' asked the black-suit who had whispered in the labour-lord's ear; he was plainly their leader.

'Tell me, though,' Cracknell continued, his voice rising a little as one of the men holding him twisted his arm further across his back, 'why on earth was such a festival for the eye, such a sumptuous visual feast, placed next door to a *blind asylum*? Are the Committee deliberately trying to incite distress amongst the unfortunate inmates?'

Norton drew himself up, obviously determined not to reward Cracknell's attempts at aggravation with any further loss of temper. 'You will no doubt be disappointed to learn that there were no deaths in the fire you started at the barracks, villain. All that was lost was a few outbuildings.' He turned to Kitson. 'And Major Wray lives on, despite your perverse conspiracy to finish him with your fake doctoring.'

Kitson grew exasperated. 'Again, sir, I do not understand your meaning. I am not involved in any conspiracy!'

'I will get nothing from either of you, I see.' Norton moved in a little closer. 'You're determined, I'll give you that much. But know this – any further attempt by either of you to interfere with my affairs or set my daughter against me will be met with a harsh penalty indeed.' He stepped back, nodding at the leader of the black-suits. 'Throw them out, Mr Twelves.'

To Mrs James' escalating protests, Mr Twelves took hold of Kitson's collar, twisting it hard, and began to drag him forcibly from the gallery.

The black-suits holding Cracknell attempted to do the same, but he dug his heels in. He had one more thing to say. 'All these men, Mr Norton, merely to guard against us two! Your silent partner must be arriving soon, I think! Have you set aside a guest apartment in Norton Hall, sir?'

Kitson, being marched out briskly to the nave, didn't catch

Norton's response. Twelves was a large man with evident experience at moving people who didn't wish to be moved; any resistance, Kitson soon discovered, was useless. One of the constables appointed to the Exhibition approached them as they neared the turnstiles. Twelves informed him that Kitson and Cracknell were just a couple of drunks who had been harassing the party of his employer, Charles Norton. Upon hearing Norton's name, the policeman immediately seemed to lose interest, turning on his heel and strolling off in the opposite direction.

Once they were through the main doors, Twelves propelled Kitson down the steps and released him. He was about to go back inside when he hesitated, seeming to reconsider something; then he hooked a fast blow into the side of the street philosopher's chest. Twelves had clearly detected Kitson's old injury and now he deliberately targeted it, his knuckles striking squarely against the ridged scar.

Kitson fell into the dust of the turning circle like a curtain cut from its pole. It felt as if his fragile ribs had been staved inward, their splintered ends rending tissue and pressing hard against the tender organs beneath. He struggled up on to his hands and knees, blue sparks squirming behind his eyes, and spat out a long, glutinous rope of spittle, shot through with a vivid strand of blood. A barking cough forced itself out of him, followed by another. Somewhere close by, he heard Cracknell laughing.

'Chest still bothering you, Thomas? That's what happens, my friend, when a wound is not allowed to heal properly!'

Kitson looked up dizzily, blinking away tears. Cracknell was sitting on the bottom step of the Exhibition, a freshly lit cigarette in his hand. His cuffs were frayed, his boots scuffed, his elbows patched and shiny; he looked every inch the impoverished gentleman. Behind him, inside the Palace's glass doors, two black-suits were watching them both carefully.

'Bloody well done with the widow, by the way. It would've been so easy for you to have overplayed your hand by now, but she's in a state of perfect readiness. I think she really trusts you, y'know.' He sucked on his cigarette. 'Absolutely perfect.'

Wrapping an arm tightly around his ribcage, Kitson managed to pull himself over to the step. An omnibus drew up before the façade, its passengers staring at him in alarm as they disembarked. He told himself to disregard these remarks about Mrs James, which were intended to anger him and thus put him at a disadvantage – a favoured tactic of Cracknell's. If he was to discover anything, he had to remain calm.

'You were waiting for a chance to catch me with Norton,' he said, hoarse with pain. 'To make him think that we are in league with one another. You want him to be suspicious of me.'

Cracknell only laughed again, slightly harder this time, and promised that all would be made clear.

'And the partner you mentioned – is it who I think?'

At this his former colleague gave a heavy sigh, and ground out his cigarette against the side of the step. 'It's in there, Thomas, in this oversized bloody greenhouse behind us – that blasted panel from the Crimea, for which good British soldiers were murdered.' He looked down at the crumpled butt between his feet. 'Even now, I still cannot think of it without the blood boiling in my veins. It shows how little he fears us, does it not, that he feels he can now parade the thing before the Queen herself without danger of exposure. He has kicked me down, kicked me down with his many hideous crimes, and now he pisses on me like a bloody great carthorse.'

Kitson summoned the last of his patience. 'Cracknell, what is it that you know about Charles Norton?'

This was not heard. Excitedly, Cracknell smacked a fist against his open palm. 'He imagines me helpless, but I am far, far from bloody helpless. My weapons of choice, as you well know, are the pen and the printing press, but these have been denied me – denied me by *him*, no less. So I am compelled to resort to other more imaginative means. And I need your assistance, old fellow. Your partnership. As things were – you know.'

There was a disconcerting resolve in his eyes. He is mad, Kitson thought. His spectacular fall from grace has left him deranged. The street philosopher's equanimity, already straining, began to give way. 'I will not help you. How can you even *ask*? I will not collude in your stabbings – or your fires.'

Cracknell studied Kitson for a moment, strangely satisfied by this unequivocal refusal. Then he patted him on the shoulder, sprang up from the step and trotted off towards the city. 'Until later then, Thomas!'

Kitson tried to go after him, but the stinging complaints of his chest prevented him even from rising to his feet. 'What of Norton, Cracknell?' he croaked. 'Answer me, damn you!'

4

Charles Norton walked up the grand staircase of the Union Club, his shoes sinking into the thick carpet. The large circular window on the landing offered its usual barren view of the flank of the next building along; but that morning the expanse of neat brickwork was bisected by a diagonal shaft of summer sunshine, divided equally into the brightest light and the blackest shade. The effect was quite dazzling, and as Norton rounded the corner and completed his ascent to the coffee room, a greenish, semi-circular after-image floated across his sight.

The coffee room of the Union was spacious, and decorated with a combination of stately oak panelling and ornate rococo plasterwork. There was even a modest fresco in an oval between the room's two chandeliers, depicting an allegory of Wisdom crowning Industry with laurels, enacted by blowsy ladies in flowing Grecian robes. Below this scene, high-backed leather chairs stood around low tables scattered with newspapers and periodicals. Infusing the room, as ever, were the rich, reassuring smells of fine tobacco and fresh coffee.

A cart clattered by outside, the sound uncommonly loud. Charles saw that the tops of the Union's tall front windows had been drawn down to admit what little breeze there was. He caught a whiff of roasting meat, and realised that they must be starting lunch. It was almost noon, and other members were beginning to arrive from their offices and warehouses. The room was filling with conversation about the state of play at the Exchange, the price of this or that, the new contracts that had been put up for tender – talk in which the proprietor of the Norton Foundry would usually have taken a keen interest. That day, however, was different.

Charles was slightly disappointed to find the Brigadier-General in civilian clothes. He had expected to see the searing scarlet of the infantry coatee before anything else; but this, he supposed, would have attracted unwanted attention. They had not met since the winter of 1855, but he recognised his associate straight away on account of that enormous moustache of his, so carefully pruned, the sharp tips now snowy white. The face behind, Norton noticed, was becoming jowled, and the features a little sunken. Nathaniel Boyce had aged.

The Brigadier-General had chosen a small corner alcove, tucked away from the main area of the coffee room. He greeted the labour-lord without enthusiasm, clearly regretting that circumstances had obliged them to see one another, and gestured towards the empty chair at the table with an immobile, gloved hand. As he lowered this hand, his right, it connected with the arm of his own chair with a dull crack – the sound of wood striking wood.

The third chair in the alcove, the one closest to its window, was occupied by a large young man of about twenty-two or -three, who was staring down into the street with open-mouthed, oafish fascination.

Norton regarded him uncertainly. 'I wasn't aware that anyone else would be present here this morning, Brigadier.'

Boyce clicked his tongue impatiently. 'Do not worry yourself, Norton. This is Captain Nunn, my ADC. You have nothing to fear from him.'

Nunn did not look around. Scarcely reassured, Norton squeezed into his seat. Both the soldiers were big men; there was only just enough room for the three of them, and Charles was obliged to sit sideways to keep his knees from brushing against Captain Nunn's.

'So who did it, Norton?' asked Boyce, sitting back. 'Who stabbed Archie Wray?'

Again, Norton glanced at Nunn. He still hadn't turned from the window. 'There is a rumour going about of an insane cripple – a man with terrible deformations and an implacable loathing of all soldiers. We are certain, however, that Richard Cracknell is involved somehow. He is in Manchester, making an annoyance of himself in his usual manner.'

Boyce narrowed his eyes; and then, to Charles' surprise, he smiled languidly. 'Do you know, I was wondering if my submission to your little Exhibition would flush him out. After I cut him down to size in the Crimea, the pathetic fool seems to have devoted his entire existence to wreaking some kind of vengeance. Quite tragic. Stabbing, though – that's a new one. Perhaps he has finally found his backbone.'

A china coffee-pot stood at the centre of the table, with an empty cup set before each of the officers. Thinking that he would very much like some coffee, Norton turned in his seat, looking for a waiter who might bring them another cup. 'He has an accomplice, also, this time. A fellow named Thomas Kitson.'

Boyce raised his eyebrows without much interest. 'Kitson . . . yes, I believe he was the *Courier*'s junior correspondent during the war. Very much second fiddle to our Mr Cracknell.'

There was a squeaking sound; Captain Nunn had pressed a fingertip against the window pane and was moving it across the glass as if following something down in the street.

Norton tried his best to ignore him. 'I'd assumed that their connection would be something of that nature. My own feeling is that they must be planning something together, for them both to be in the city at the time you have chosen to visit. This devil Kitson has already tried to strike at me through my daughter.' He lowered his voice. 'Do – do you wish us to do anything? I have men who will—'

'Colonel, I see him! I see him, Colonel!'

The words burst out of Nunn in a heavy spray of saliva. Norton started; the Captain was all but shouting. Boyce told him firmly to keep his voice down. The man gaped at his commander, his head lolling. The muscles in his long face were relaxed, like someone deep in sleep; his eyes were pale and soapy, entirely devoid of any reasoning intelligence.

254

'So-sorry, Colonel, but I *see him* – Captain Wray, sir, walk-walking in the street. Major Maynard, sir, is there, too, and Davy, sir, and Major Fairlie, and, and . . .'

'Really, Mr Nunn! Captain Wray, imagine that!' Boyce's tone was flat. 'Is Lord Raglan down there with them as well, perchance, or Major-General Codrington?'

The young officer turned back to window so quickly he almost put his head through it.

Boyce picked up his coffee cup with his left hand. 'The lad understands little and remembers less – and sometimes thinks he can see people who are not actually there. Our old comrades from the 99th Foot, in particular, make regular appearances in his daily life, Wray included.' He took a sip. 'One of several burdens placed upon me by my service in the Crimea.'

Norton nodded uneasily and then looked around again. Where were all the blessed waiters?

'And another, of course, is Richard Cracknell, the blunted Tomahawk. I fail to see how he could damage us, frankly. He'll probably just end up humiliating himself further.'

This seemed a little blasé to Norton. With gathering agitation, he told Boyce about the Polygon ball and the unpleasant events in the Art Treasures Exhibition two days before. Both incidents, he said emphatically, were intended to show how vulnerable they were; to demonstrate Cracknell and Kitson's ability to interfere, should they choose to do so.

Unmoved, Boyce set down his cup. 'Keep up your watch, then, by all means. Perhaps have a limb or two broken.' He lifted his inert hand into his lap, smiling again as he made some adjustment to it. 'How amusing, though, to think of him in the Exhibition, standing before my *Pilate*. How dreadfully that must rile him.'

This notion, and the malicious relish with which it was expressed, caused Norton's disquiet to grow yet further, and he was relieved indeed when Boyce changed the subject to business. The Brigadier-General revealed that he had found a replacement for Wray – probably on a permanent basis as it was deemed unlikely that the Major would make anything approaching a full recovery. Captain Rupert Morris, a distant cousin of Boyce's, was transferring to the 25th Manchesters before the end of June, and would thereafter be the Brigadier-General's man in the Cottonopolis, with whom Norton should conduct all his usual transactions.

Charles said that he understood, and then quickly ran through some of the Foundry's recent figures. Sales were healthy, he reported, due to a contract from Weller and Sons, the largest boot-maker in the North East. Boyce inquired about profits, and how much he could expect to see; and was well satisfied by what he was told.

Their business concluded, the Brigadier-General volunteered no further conversation. He looked absently around the room, drumming his fingers on his knee. Captain Nunn hadn't seen anyone else of note from his window, and was now talking to himself in a low monotone.

'How is it here?' Norton asked eventually. 'I'm told the Union has the finest rooms of any club in the city.'

Boyce frowned. 'Good God, I am not staying *here*, man.' The Union Club, Norton realised, with its industrialists and financiers, was well beneath a gentleman such as the Brigadier-General. 'No, I am going to the country for a few days. After that, I shall be lodging at the Albion Hotel on Piccadilly.'

'Are you sure you will not stay at Norton Hall? We would be more than happy to accommodate you.'

Norton felt acutely self-conscious as he asked this. A part of him had long cherished the hope that an acquaintance might be built between himself and his well-born associate – that he might yet manage to win the respect of this proud, difficult man. They had significant things in common, after all. Both had a keen interest in the fine arts, as his involvement in the Exhibition testified. And both knew the cold loneliness of the widower.

'No thank you, Norton,' Boyce replied with barely veiled distaste. 'The Albion Hotel will suffice. I will send word to you from there.'

A waiter, finally noticing Norton's presence, came over to his side. 'Can I bring you a cup, sir? The luncheon card?'

Embarrassed by his partner's rebuff, Norton rose to his feet. 'Nothing,' he muttered. 'I am leaving.'

5

Cracknell lay on his bed in the Model Lodging House, listening to the assortment of mechanics and junior clerks who also resided there maligning him through the thin partition walls. They complained about his airs; they moaned about how long he spent in the Model's bathtub; they wondered what exactly he did all day, since he didn't seem to have any manner of gainful employment. The Tomahawk sighed. Such a cruel descent mine has been, he thought. If only these blockheads knew who they maligned so freely! If only I could afford to be where I deserve!

Ten minutes later, with his usual sense of relief, he was heading across the Model's fly-blown hallway towards the front door, brushing at his old hat as if the touch of his hand might magically restore the faded fabric. Nodding to the ghoul behind the desk, he stepped out on to the London Road. Technically speaking, he was running late, his afternoon nap having raged a little out of control; but given the person he was meeting, he hardly thought it mattered.

God, how Cracknell hated Manchester. He'd hated it from his very first glimpse, through the window of his third-class carriage, blasted into its valley like a blackened, smoking crater. It is an abomination, he'd thought; an abomination to nature and to God. He hated the filth, of course, the clogging dirt, the indescribable stinks and the constant, pumping coal-smoke; the huge crowds of wretched, uniform humanity, surging through the lanes at their appointed hours, moving between mill, pub and slum-house; the low Irish, who were bloody everywhere, with their bare feet and starved, gormless faces, making him feel as if Cork had crawled over the sea to England to claim him back.

Most of all, though, Cracknell hated the immeasurable complacency of Manchester's elite, people like those at the Polygon – people like Charles bloody Norton – who sat atop this dismal ruin brazenly sucking out all the wealth. Their mendacious assertion was that their Exhibition, that paltry shed out at Old Trafford, had made their seething shit-sack of a city the new Athens, a glorious outpost of refinement and culture. To Cracknell, however, its purpose was self interest, plain and simple. These rich factory owners had mounted their art show because they were genuinely convinced that standing cotton-spinners and buckle-casters in front of a Hogarth, or a Raphael, or a Rubens, would make them more obedient – and therefore more productive on the factory floor. Before such greatness, their theory went, the working man would suddenly feel the natural order of things, abjure the bottle, and accept his place at the very bottom without complaint. It really was quite laughable, and made Cracknell think yet again that only a full-scale, palace-burning, head-chopping revolution would truly right this rotten country.

Standing for a moment before the plain frontage of the Model, Cracknell took a cigarette from his pocket. As he cocked his head to light it, he spotted the tail, loitering beneath the crude steel arches of the railway bridge. It was one of Mr Twelves' gang. Cracknell recognised him, in fact, from the fracas in the Exhibition: a stocky fellow, his face round and flattened like that of a pug dog. The Tomahawk tutted, blowing out smoke. This was rank provincial amateurism, to send a man to follow someone who knew him by sight. He was almost offended.

Cracknell walked along the London Road until it turned into Piccadilly, leading him past the Infirmary to the wide mouth of Market Street. This mighty thoroughfare glittered with gaudy shop-fronts, their lamps already burning against the soft summer evening. He started down it. As the working day drew to a close, Market Street was caught in a final throe of commercial activity. Carriages, tradesmen's drays and omnibuses all jostled together, ignoring the signs directing them to keep to their proper sides of the road. Cries of disputation rose above the creak of spokes and springs, the crack of whips and the tramping of iron horse-shoes. The pavements were similarly packed. Placid crowds drifted like livestock between shop windows, grazing on the displays; clerks and porters hurried for home or the public house.

The Tomahawk looked around. Not only was the pug-faced man still with him, but he had been joined by a friend. Two men could only mean that a beating was planned. Cracknell waited until he was in sight of the new Exchange building, looming up like the side of an enormous drum, and then crossed the road, pausing halfway over to scratch a carthorse's silky nose. Throwing away his cigarette, he weaved up swiftly through the dense, ramshackle lanes of Shude Hill until he came to Smithfield Market, rushing under its iron-and-glass roof. This was surely the perfect place to shake a tail.

Doubling back through the stalls, he pushed his way past pails filled with dried herring, piles of white cheeses and grubby, miscellaneous heaps of earthenware. He came to a large second-hand clothes stall on a corner plot, its wares hanging like shorn, dusty skins from an ornate series of wooden rails. The owner was busy with a customer. Seizing his chance, Cracknell slipped in amongst the multitude of suits, dresses, shawls and coats, concealing himself in the folds of old material. The clothes smelled strongly of stale sweat, the salty, human odour of a thousand different people. This was oddly comforting; Cracknell sighed, thinking he could happily remain there all evening, peeking out between the sleeves at the unknowing passers-by.

Then the pug-faced man in the black suit stalked into view, coming to a halt on the very corner on which Cracknell's clothes stall was situated. The Tomahawk noticed that he now had a small cudgel held up against the inside of his arm. These men, for all their bumbling ineptitude, certainly meant business.

It was a pretty straightforward manoeuvre – Cracknell

reached out, got an arm around the pug-faced man's neck and a hand on the cudgel, and pulled the rascal back into the clothes whilst keeping him off balance. The black-suit fought it, though, fought it hard.

'D'you know who you're serving?' Cracknell hissed when things were fully under his control. 'D'you have any idea what the bastard's involved in?'

The pug-faced man went still, saying nothing.

Cracknell tightened his grip. 'What, pray, are your instructions?'

This time he got a reply. 'Break yer legs.'

'That's *all*? Mr Norton's a bloody soft touch.'

'Aye, we feel the same.' The black-suit started to thrash his free arm around, trying to get hold of some part of his assailant, but couldn't make a purchase amidst the clothes.

Cracknell took the cudgel and twisted to one side, making the black-suit lose his footing. He grabbed at the clothes as he went down; there was tearing, something snapped loudly, and a great swathe of fabric dropped away, engulfing him completely. Skipping neatly out of the remains of the stall, Cracknell looked around for the other black-suit. He was nowhere to be seen. The stall-holder started shouting furiously at the pug-faced man, who floundered as if drowning in the heavy fall of clothes. Entirely unobserved, the Tomahawk left the market at the same point he had entered it and headed off to his meeting, tossing the cudgel in an alley on the way.

The Hare and Hounds on Albert Street was but a stone's throw from the Irwell, and the reek of the black river compelled Cracknell to hold his nose as he hurried through the mud and litter towards the tavern's soot-caked windows. He was most relieved to push against the peeling paint of the door and then step on to the straw inside, which at that point in the evening had only attained a moderate state of foulness.

The air in the wide, low-ceilinged room was miasmic with the sour smoke from clay pipes, farthing cheroots and hand-rolled cigarettes. Even so committed a tobacco-worshipper as Cracknell felt his eyes sting in protest at the polluted atmosphere. The clientele, newly released from their machines, were a lacklustre lot, staring at their beer-pots in a stunned, sullen silence. Their drinking was determined, he saw, done grimly to service a necessity rather than to provide a pleasure.

Even in the dull dinginess of the Hare and Hounds, though, locating his man was not difficult. Amidst the hushed exhaustion of the pub, his slurred singing gave him a certain prominence.

''*Ere upon Guard am I,*' rose up the familiar voice from somewhere at the back of the room, wobbling drunkenly around its East London vowels, '*Who – who dares to say that British pluck,*' here the singer stopped to emit a ragged belch, '. . . *is somewhat on the wane?*'

Cracknell dropped into the booth, the cheap carpentry protesting beneath the weight of his ample behind. He almost removed his hat, but then thought better of it. His man was a long way gone. It had plainly been an ale-for-breakfast day. Several empty pots sat on the table before him, surely only a small fraction of what he had imbibed. He was having some trouble remaining upright on his bench, and kept clutching at the table's edge with his good hand. By his side sat a young whore, about sixteen, bare-headed and streaked with dirt. Her skin was an unhealthy yellow colour, her hair a greasy black. Holy Christ, Cracknell thought, does the stupid fellow actually *want* a dose of the clap?

'Good day, Mr Cregg,' he said sardonically, 'I trust you are well?'

Cregg looked back at him with watery, unfocused eyes. Cracknell flinched at the sight of the ghastly, raking scars that covered one side of the man's face, the stump of the missing ear, and the pock-marked jaw and neck; the disfigurement was worse than he remembered.

Cregg, needless to say, didn't notice his reaction. '*That British valour never will be seen or known again?*' he staggered on, without acknowledging Cracknell's arrival. '*The Crimean page will yet be read, and 'onest cheek will glow . . .*' He stopped, confused and a little annoyed: he'd forgotten the words. ''*Onest cheek will glow . . .*'

Cracknell sighed, and turned his attention to the whore. 'What has he paid for? The whole fuck?'

"E give me sixpence.' She shrugged and looked away. 'Didnay tell what 'e wanted forrit.'

'So you thought you'd stop here, see if any more coins appeared, and then slope off when this poor sod collapsed in the gutter?' Cracknell sneered. 'That's your game, is it, lassie?'

Cregg's scored, sagging features lit up with simple triumph. *'When learning 'ow we nobly fought, and thrashed the stubborn foe!'* He drank deeply from his pot, brown rivulets of beer running down around the sides of the crude tin cup and over his unshaven chin.

'Begone,' Cracknell said bluntly to the whore. 'Now.' She opened her mouth to protest. 'Be thankful that I'm letting you keep the sixpence without extracting anything in return.'

The girl slunk away like a kicked cat, paused by another table on her way to the door, and was soon sitting herself down again.

Almost a minute passed before Cregg realised what had transpired. 'Oi, that was mine, you bastard! I 'ad plans there, so I did! Took me an age to find it!'

'It took you an age to find a rancid whore in Manchester? That I doubt, Mr Cregg. Now, gather yourself, if you can. We have much to discuss.' Cracknell scowled. 'Captain Wray, for example. And now this business at the barracks. D'ye not remember my instructions, man? You were to lie low until I sent you word. *Lie low*, Mr Cregg! D'ye want to end your stay in this miserable city with a Tyburn jig?'

None of this registered. 'Are you not 'aving a drink, Mister Crackers? Are you not? No? Well, I understand, chum, I really do. It's piss, the beer up 'ere. Bleedin' piss.'

Disregarding his supposed assistant's inebriation as best he could, Cracknell gave a brief, cautionary account of the incident in Smithfield Market, then began to talk of train times, hotel reservations and the subtle, ingenious co-ordinations he had devised for them to follow. Cregg was a less than receptive audience. After a few seconds of half-hearted pretence that he was paying attention, his head dipped down blearily towards the grain of the ale-splashed table, and he started to hum the tune of his song once again. Cracknell paused pointedly. Cregg misunderstood this as an invitation to repeat the song's newly remembered final line, even more volubly and boisterously than in his first rendition. Clenching his fists, the Tomahawk prepared a sharp comment to strike some sense into the hopeless buffoon before him; but sight of the fat tears that now crawled across Cregg's shredded cheek stopped this rebuke on his lips.

'Did we though, Mister Crackers? Did we?' There was an insistent longing in the man's voice. 'Did we *nobly fight*? What does that bleedin' well mean, anyways? What nobility is there in stabbin' or shootin' some poor bastard Russian, with as much of a clue as to why you're all there as you've got yourself? And what flamin' nobility is there in being damn well *dead*, Mister Crackers? Tell me that!'

Cracknell murmured something unconvincing about the unimpeachable integrity of the fighting soldier. It was not heard.

'And *thrashed the foe*! Thrashed 'im!' Cregg spat. 'Ha! And we wasn't thrashed right back? When I think of 'em, of all of 'em, and the things I seen and done, it makes me feel like *screamin'*, bleedin' well *screamin'* till me lungs come up right out of me chest.' He was starting to take deep, shuddering breaths, his battered face turning a terrible purple. 'When I think of the Major, who was 'onest as the sun and who *saved my bleedin' life*, lyin' there, 'is legs all buggered, and – and then what happened afterwards . . .'

Cregg collapsed forward on to the table, unable to continue. Cracknell leant over hesitantly and patted his shoulder, aware that they were starting to attract some proper attention. He softly reminded the weeping Cregg that the two of them were working towards balancing the scales right there and then and would avenge the wrongs that had been done to them. Cregg was quite inconsolable, though, his mutilated face buried in his arms, his body heaving as he sobbed. So this is where my money has gone, thought Cracknell with resignation, sitting back on his creaking bench. Down the throat of a man determined to drink himself into the madhouse. It is fortunate indeed that I have devised an alternative strategy.

With all the bad luck and injustice he had experienced up to this point, Cracknell still could not quite believe the gift that had been handed to him in the form of Thomas Kitson. He had been astonished to find his former junior in Manchester, scraping by as a street philosopher, a bloody penny-a-line man on some sad little local paper – and his amazement had only increased with each new discovery. The tentative affair with Jemima James, the razor-tongued widow; choleric old Norton, Boyce's willing tool, and his sodomite son; the general atmosphere of suspicion, of plotting, of intrigue; and now this, hired men in Norton's employ hunting him like a boar through the streets of the city. It was exquisite, almost too perfect. All he had to do was wait for the moment to grow ripe and then reach out to pluck it.

Cracknell looked dispassionately at Cregg, slumped snivelling in a puddle of ale. This was hardly a man to be relied upon during the days ahead. His mind was quite broken. The Tomahawk's choice was clear.

Before Sebastopol,
Crimean Peninsula
January 1855

1

The bundle of winter jackets that Madeleine carried was so large that she could barely keep hold of it. Her arms were stretched out in front of her, embracing her burden tightly, her interlocked fingers straining to contain the bulging roll of wool and leather. As she crossed the loose boundary between the French and British camps, stumbling on the rutted, frozen mud underfoot, one jacket began to slip from her grasp, beneath her left elbow. Cursing, she unclasped her hands and snatched at its sleeve; only for two, three, then four more to follow it on to the ground. With a small scream of rage, she threw down the rest.

The afternoon, like so many before it, had been spent making requests for supplies in the French camps. Madeleine was required to take centre stage during these expeditions, as Annabel's broken French and somewhat brusque, impatient bargaining style had proved less than effective at securing the sympathetic cooperation of Great Britain's Gallic allies. It was trying work, the French officers seeming to delight in a chance to deliver lengthy lectures on the shameful state of the British forces. How much more of their part of the line, she was asked repeatedly, would they cede to French control? How was it that the Turks – the *Turks*! – had managed to maintain a more effective fighting force? Did they realise that were it not for the deficiencies of Britain, Sebastopol would have fallen months ago, and they would all be at liberty to return home?

These officers also made it clear that they regarded her, a lady who had exchanged glorious France for miserable England, with some disdain. This could quickly be dismissed; a single pretty sob, or a plea made in the correct attitude of beautiful misery, had the prideful fools scrabbling on their knees, promising whatever they could in an effort to restore her spirits. But performing such expert manipulations quickly became wearying. At that moment, as she stood crossly beside the pile of discarded jackets in the winter twilight, Madeleine wanted only to return to her bed. She knew, however, that the tireless Annabel would have other plans for her, and that she would be on her feet until long after nightfall.

Madeleine hugged herself, clamping her aching hands in her armpits. Never before had she known such cold. It seemed to seep inside her, through her, chilling the marrow of her bones, frosting over her muscles and organs, making her groan and judder like an old railway carriage. She let out a shivering sigh as she stamped her feet against the iron earth.

At the head of the Worontzov road, quite close to where she had stopped, a heavy cart was being loaded with the sick and wounded. It was a French cart, with French drivers, but all the casualties were British, being taken down from the plateau to the port of Balaclava, some five miles distant – yet another demonstration, she realised, of the dependence about which she had heard so much that day. Civilian doctors and orderlies attended to the worst cases, lifting up stretchers and dressing injuries. One of these men had noticed her, and now stood staring. Cautiously, she returned his gaze. It was Richard's junior, Mr Kitson.

The Russian winter had gnawed away at the correspondent, as it had at everyone on the campaign. His heavy coat was missing a lapel, and a long tear across the shoulder had been but crudely fixed with ragged, uneven stitches. The beard that snaked out through his upturned collar was bunched into knotted, uncombed clumps. He had none of the defeated exhaustion that dogged the fighting men, however. After addressing the cart's driver in competent, efficient French, he came over to her, a thin smile on his face.

'Why, Mrs Boyce,' he said rather inscrutably, touching the bent brim of his cap. 'Imagine meeting you like this, *Madame.*'

Madeleine was uncertain how to respond. They had not so much as exchanged a word since the day she had landed. The impression she had gleaned from Richard's few remarks about his reporting team was that it no longer existed, properly speaking. His talk now was almost entirely of his own endeavours. Deciding nonetheless upon wary cordiality, she returned Mr Kitson's greeting.

He pointed towards the jackets. 'These are yours, I assume?'

Madeleine nodded. The wool, against the dark, frozen ground, was the colour of sour cream. '*Mouton* jackets, they are called – sheepskin, you see, with the wool left on?'

'Yes, I have seen the French wearing them. They will be most welcome among our own troops. We remain chronically ill-equipped on that front since the sinking of the *Prince* last November.' His voice grew strained. 'Forty thousand winter uniforms and boots, everything that is now needed the most, lost to the waters of Balaclava harbour.' Someone over in the cart moaned loudly, and called out an unintelligible word. Mr Kitson turned towards her. 'I must say that it warms my heart, *Madame*, to see you engaged so selflessly, and in such difficult conditions.'

Madeleine nodded again, hardly hearing this. She wanted desperately to ask him about Richard – if he happened to know where he was, despite the rift that had occurred between them. But this, she knew, would be far too brazen. 'You – you are helping with the injured, Mr Kitson?'

'I do what I can, Mrs Boyce, with the little knowledge I have managed to glean in the past few months,' he replied, rubbing his hands together. Madeleine noticed that his gloves, once grey, were almost entirely covered with bloodstains, their hues ranging from molasses to bleached orange. 'It was not my original role here, of course, but I find—'

He was interrupted by the arrival of Annabel, bearing a consignment of *Mouton* jackets almost twice as large as that which had overwhelmed Madeleine. After setting down this mighty load, and shooting a reproving look at her friend for delaying their mission of mercy, she proceeded to engage Mr Kitson in cheerful conversation. Madeleine had soon learned that Annabel saw people in a very simple manner, as worthy either of absolute approval or utter condemnation. It was as if the world appeared to her as it would on the Day of Judgement, when mankind would be divided neatly into the blessed and the damned. Mr Kitson, it seemed, had managed to win himself a place in the exalted ranks of the former.

Annabel declared that she had not spoken with him since before Christmas; had he managed to mark it in any way? He admitted that he had not. Annabel was forgiving, conceding that their current situation did not lend itself to pious celebration. She said that she had seen him on the docks, working as a medical orderly – binding wounds and administering medicines, filling in the endless forms, consoling the living and carrying the bodies of the dead. As she recounted this honourable list of duties, Annabel's face positively shone with admiration, whilst Mr Kitson murmured modest deflections of her praise.

Madeleine began to grow impatient. She wondered how she might intervene, and direct the conversation towards the *Courier* and its brave senior correspondent. Then, quite unexpectedly, Annabel did this for her.

'And what of your colleagues, sir?' she inquired, looking around. 'What of Mr Cracknell? He is not here with you, I take it?' Her tone now had a hard, critical note to it, indicating that the discussion had moved to one of the damned.

Mr Kitson shook his head. 'Mr Cracknell and I have not worked together for a number of weeks. I believe he is fully occupied with the composition of his *Courier* reports.'

Annabel pulled a grim, knowing face, and made an acid remark about Mr Cracknell's mounting fame.

It upset Madeleine to hear her lover talked about in this caustic manner. She wanted to leap to his defence, to say that they did not understand the nobility, the necessity of his labour – the labour that was increasingly keeping them apart. As her trials increased, so did her need for Richard. He was her consolation, her sole comfort in that hopeless, frozen land. She would finish a long, difficult day with Annabel and then wait at her window for his signal. More and more, though, it did not come. The explanation given was always the same: his latest report, the one that was going to finally bring justice to the British Army and demolish its unworthy commanders, her husband included. They had not managed to meet for over a week. An acute anxiety was building up inside her. She felt as if there was something urgent she had to say or do, or somewhere else she had to be; but she was petrified, unable to act.

'How about Mr Styles, your young illustrator?' Annabel asked next. 'Has he managed to bring that temper of his under control?'

Mr Kitson's expression darkened. 'I cannot say, madam, much to my chagrin. My own feeling was that he was becoming increasingly troubled, and should be recalled to England. I was overruled, however – quite comprehensively. The *Courier*'s editor simply did not believe that any man could suffer in war without having been struck by a bullet or run through with a bayonet.'

'Did this cause your break with Mr Cracknell, sir?'

'Not entirely. But it is true that my editor was not heeding me, my senior was not heeding me and Mr Styles himself certainly was not heeding me. I did start to wonder why I should supply the *Courier* with my views on the war when my views on the wellbeing of my colleagues were being so roundly ignored.' He paused. 'Do forgive me. I am sounding rather querulous.'

Annabel shrugged. 'Your position sounds perfectly just, Mr Kitson, in my opinion. And you have taken on good work indeed.'

There was a piercing whistle from the cartload of casualties.

'Speaking of which, I must be off,' he said apologetically, lifting his cap and exposing a nest of flattened, overgrown hair. 'Most pleasant to see you both. I hope we will meet again soon.'

Madeleine's eyes followed him as he swung himself up on to the cart, which had already started to trundle down the Worontzov road to Balaclava. Her despondency seemed to drench her, leaving her heart heavy and cold. She wanted to sit down; she wanted to be with Richard; she wanted to be *warm*.

'Come, my pet,' said Annabel with stout vigour, gathering up her *Mouton* jackets. 'We have to take these to the emplacements on Chapman's Hill. There are at least two more loads to be carried before tea.'

Madeleine stared down balefully at the formless woolly pile beside her, filled with a sudden hatred for Annabel and her endless, arduous tasks.

'*"Almighty God is able to make all grace abound to you,"*' her companion intoned, heaving her load up into the air, '*"so that you will abound in every good work."*'

2

Kitson left the Middle Ravine, the rocky, cannon-ball strewn corridor that formed the main route between the plateau and the siege-works, and paused beneath a lantern to give a quick account of his errand to an exhausted-looking watch captain. He had said no more than five words before he was waved on indifferently into the trenches of the first parallel.

It was almost ten o'clock. A bright moon hung overhead, framed by the two sides of the trench, casting a silver light over the icy, waterlogged path before him. Things seemed quiet that night, for the most part. There was the occasional patter of rifle fire from the French lines, off to the right, but the artillery pieces of both sides stood unfired. Kitson had never been this far forward – this close to Sebastopol, the object of the siege. The prevailing mood in the network of deep, fetid ditches that formed the mainstay of the British assault, however, was one of desolate apathy rather than resilience and determination. Those posted there were gaunt and bearded, their once-fine uniforms now little more than rags that, in many cases, failed even to cover their flesh sufficiently, let alone protect it from the cold. Kitson could feel icicles gathering in his own beard, yet he saw privates with nothing at all on their feet. The bitter temperature seemed to compel constant activity – these soldiers, however, were almost motionless apart from their shivering. Hunched or even prone in water several inches deep, most paid him no attention as he passed; but some looked up, following his progress with empty eyes, making him feel profoundly guilty for his own thick goatskin coat and seaman's boots.

Kitson focused upon his errand. It was a typically Crimean scenario, the kind that occurred dozens of times a week in Balaclava alone. He had been toiling on the docks as usual. The last of the previous night's sick had just been dispatched, either to the General Hospital just outside town or for transit to Scutari, when a clerk from the harbourmaster's office had appeared. Somewhat embarrassed, this man had announced that an officer from the Royal Engineers, a Major Nicholson, was required at the harbour early the next morning to assist with a civilian-led project of high importance. Nicholson was believed to be in the Forward Attack, overseeing the construction of the advance parallel, and no one could be found to go and fetch him. All the soldiers in Balaclava had just come down from the plateau, and flatly refused to trek back up to it again; and everybody else seemed suddenly to have pressing duties that prevented them from venturing from the town. They were his last hope.

Doctor Godwin, the surgeon supervising the docks, had turned wearily to Kitson and asked if he would consider undertaking this mission as a personal favour to him – it was very much in their interests to stay on the right side of the harbourmaster. Kitson had inquired about the nature of the project, but the clerk knew only that it was intended to relieve the trials of the fighting men. Resigning himself to another sleepless night, he had agreed.

After a few minutes the trench Kitson was following led him to a rifle pit. It was covered with what looked like horse skins and reinforced with sandbags and wooden pickets. Those who manned it were laid out, insensible, their guns by their sides; he had to repeat his greeting several times before eliciting a response. Groggily, the soldiers informed him that he was now in the third parallel, and that the officer he sought was somewhere up ahead. He moved back out into the trench, stepping around a large puddle and rounding a corner. Up in front of him now was one of the forward batteries, built into a large bank of stone and bolstered with deep earthworks, standing about ten feet above the parallel. A narrow rope ladder had been thrown down its side, leading to a ledge that had been carved into the main rampart. Kitson climbed the ladder and pulled himself on to it; and a second later was looking out over the siege of Sebastopol.

There was a white frost that night, setting a crisp shell over much of the landscape. The system of trenches looked like an ugly act of defacement, a series of jagged cuts into a long slope of smooth silver. Kitson could see the string of squat forts that asserted the Allied line, between which these trenches ran, and how they were matched, echoed almost, by the Russian positions around the outer suburbs of their city. Opposite the battery on which he stood, across three or four hundred yards of unclaimed ground, lay an expansive enemy fort, a crenulated block of reinforced earth that bristled with artillery. The night was so clear that one could even see the sentries who were patrolling along its crude ramparts. To its rear, in amongst acres of ruined buildings, the orange flickering points of hundreds of torches revealed vast teams of labourers enlarging and improving what was already there, and commencing new structures. As he surveyed all of this, Kitson thought that there could be no possibility of the British Army prevailing in a frontal assault on such a position – not in its current condition. Small wonder that they had arrived at such a dreadful stalemate.

Past the Russian defences lay the city itself. Its main streets were barricaded and filled with debris, but otherwise it seemed oddly normal. Few of its structures appeared in any way dilapidated or damaged. Their moonlit roofs formed an undulating mosaic of silver, pale blue and white, broken only by the bulbous minarets of Orthodox churches. Lights shone at windows and moved in the lanes below them; in greater numbers, perhaps, than one might expect to see in peacetime, but hardly enough to suggest a population in some terrible state of agitation or upheaval. The waters of the port itself were perfectly still, reflecting the disc of the moon, the very essence of tranquillity.

Kitson stepped down into the battery. It was long, holding in excess of twenty cannon. Much of it was swathed in darkness, but men could be seen shuffling in between the guns. He noticed a few of them, officers swaddled in the thick winter clothes denied to their men, exchanging a dour joke; and not for the first time since coming up to the plateau, he became worried that Cracknell might be among them, shaking hands, passing out cigarettes and gathering testimonies.

They had not spoken since well before Christmas. Kitson knew exactly how a reunion would go. There would be accusations and counter-accusations of increasing acrimony, culminating in him being harshly denounced as a deserter. He frequently saw people reading the *Courier* in Balaclava, and witnessed the savage arguments Cracknell's pieces provoked amongst both soldiers and civilians. They were now universally regarded as the work of one person only: the *Courier*'s man in the camps before Sebastopol. Kitson had come to believe that he had been quietly removed from the magazine's roster. He did not care enough even to confirm this. His experiences in Balaclava that winter had shown him that he could no longer react to the misery of others merely with the composition of a righteous paragraph.

The *Courier* reports themselves were difficult for him to read. It was disconcerting to see justifiable outrage at the misconduct of the war being mixed with Cracknell's biting vindictiveness towards those individuals he believed needed punishing – who often happened to be those who had also slighted or dismissed him. Boyce, of course, featured as regularly as Cracknell could work him in. To Kitson, this particular battle had been well and truly lost in the hut of Major-General Codrington. Cracknell fought on regardless, though, succeeding only in polarising opinion and winning the villain as many new supporters as detractors.

As he walked through along the battery, Kitson discovered to his considerable relief that the correspondent was not there after all. It was unsurprising, really; the front was huge, and filled with many thousands of men. The chances of them encountering one another were slight. He approached the artillery officers and inquired after Major Nicholson.

A minute later Kitson started into the advance parallel. It zig-zagged madly from the base of the forward battery towards the Russian fortifications, feeling out the line of the next parallel proper, running a good fifty feet beyond the main British position. Out here, as treating casualties in Balaclava had shown him all too clearly, the danger posed by sharpshooters was acute. He pressed himself against the side of the trench, in the hope that it would afford him some cover, and moved gingerly along it. The advance parallel was not as well worked as the others, nor as deep, its sides crumbling wetly to a floor no more than five feet below ground level. There were no soldiers at all in the length of the trench, and at first Kitson had thought it unmanned; but then he reached a rifle pit, its canvas cover peppered with musket-ball holes, and heard voices grumbling in its dark recesses.

He listened out for the sound of engineers at work – the clang of hammers, the scrape of shovels being pushed into earth – yet was greeted only by a stagnant hush. Carrying on along the parallel, he caught an unexpected noise beneath the squelching of his footsteps; a faint scratching that was both familiar and out of place. It was a pencil, moving rapidly across paper. This was not someone writing, though. The strokes were too long, too rhythmic. This was the sound of drawing.

Kitson edged along another few yards, around an acute corner; and there, sitting with his back against the trench wall, was Robert Styles. Swathed in the assemblage of the worn, ill-fitting garments that served so many as winter clothing, he was now heavily bearded, his cheeks hollow with malnourishment. His eyes were hidden in shadow beneath the brim of a fur-lined cap.

Styles was sketching away furiously in a small book, the open page angled to catch the moonlight. Before him, in a puddle, lay a dead, half-naked private, his knees drawn up to his chest in a final spasm. It was not clear whether this soldier's uniform had been incomplete when he died, or if parts of it had subsequently been scavenged by his comrades. His grey face was partly submerged in the puddle, which was freezing over, the ice reaching inside his open mouth;

his beard glittered with hundreds of frozen droplets. And his minié was under Styles' arm, the stock resting on the ground beside him, the barrel leaning against his shoulder.

Kitson stifled his unease. 'Styles? Are – are you all right, my friend?' he asked gently.

The illustrator did not answer, or even look up from his work. Slowly, Kitson sat down next to him; he noticed without surprise that the drawing was a detailed depiction of the expired soldier. The pencil began to move more frantically, scoring the paper with thick black lines, defacing what was already there. Kitson reached over and stopped Styles' bony hand, pressing it flat upon the page. The illustrator let out a groaning sigh and slumped forward as if cut down from the wall. They remained in silence for a moment. A tear patted softly against the drawing, followed by several more. Kitson put his arm around Styles' shoulders. The joints beneath his thin coat were sharp and hard. There is nothing left of him, Kitson thought; I am now the heavier man.

Suddenly, Styles coughed, gagging as if he was about to be sick; and then the stream of words began. 'I cannot stop thinking of it, Kitson, I cannot stop thinking about the cave. It will not let me be, I – I see it all day, then it haunts my bloody *dreams* as well. It will not let me be. I think of the rock in my hand, and – and that sound, and the way it *felt*, and dear God *it will not let me be.*'

The rasping panic in his voice made Kitson smart with guilt. The junior correspondent had left the *Courier* team two weeks after Inkerman, in the wake of the great storm that had sunk the *H.M.S. Prince* and so many of the other vessels moored in Balaclava harbour. In his desire to help the injured and to restore order to the decimated port, however, Kitson had entirely neglected a more immediate responsibility. It was true that they had disregarded him when he had first proposed that Styles be shipped back to England; the illustrator himself had stated quite unequivocally that he was fit for service and wished to remain in the Crimea. But he should not have been halted by that. He should have written to the boy's father. He should have convinced someone in the army, or one of the surgeons he became acquainted with in Balaclava, to make some kind of intervention – Mr O'Farrell be damned. There was no excusing his failure to do any of this. It was not too late, though, to start making amends.

Kitson rose to his haunches, looking along the trench. 'Where is Cracknell?' he asked tersely. 'Is he close by?'

It had long been his suspicion that the letter the senior correspondent had written to O'Farrell about Styles' condition had been inflected to make the whole business seem like the womanish hysteria of his over-sensitive junior rather than anything warranting genuine concern. Kitson found that he now actively wanted to see Cracknell again – to confront him about Styles.

The illustrator made no reaction to his question. 'The boots,' he muttered morosely, 'twitching like . . . like hen's feet. And I can hear that sound. I can hear it right now, as I speak. Dear Christ, all these blessed *bodies*, Kitson, I don't know how I can – how I will—'

Kitson looked at him. 'Robert, listen to me. I am deeply sorry that I left you, and must ask your forgiveness. But do not despair, my friend. We will get you home, I promise. As soon as I can arrange it.'

Styles fell quiet, tucking his drawing-book away in his coat pocket; then, without warning, he stamped on the icy puddle at the base of the trench, sending a long crack running between the dead private's blue lips. '*No*,' he said with hard, miserable resolve, wiping his tears away with his sleeve. 'No, I cannot leave. What is there in England for me? I have given up everything to come here, everything. Like you, Kitson. We are the same in this, are we not? Could *you* just go back?'

Kitson had tensed. 'No, but—'

'I must continue to work. I must see the truth of war. I must *capture it*, don't you see? I cannot leave.' Styles stamped on the puddle again. 'And what would he say if I left? He would say I am a weakling – a *coward*. I am *not*, Kitson. I did what was necessary in that – in that cave.' His hands began to shake, as if his anguish and his confusion were about to boil over once more; then he picked up the rifle that stood next to him and his fragile self-control was retained. 'I – I have shown my courage since, also, out here. In ways that he has not. That he *could not.*'

Kitson took a breath, looking up at the moon. Cracknell, he realised, was nowhere near the advance parallel that night; Styles was there alone. There was something about the way the illustrator held the rifle that alarmed him. He could not help but think that it was done with an ease brought about by usage. Styles had wielded a minié before. Had he not just claimed to have proved himself not only in the cave, when he smashed a rock into the skull of a boy-soldier, but also here in the advance parallel? It could not be avoided: Robert Styles, student of the Royal Academy, supposed illustrator for the *London Courier* magazine, had been fighting, and in all likelihood killing, alongside the enlisted men.

He decided to concentrate upon a modest goal. 'Robert, let us leave this trench, at least – go somewhere warm and find some supper. You must be—'

'And yet he mocks me still, whenever I see him. That bastard mocks *me*. That awful, rotten *bastard.*' With each word, he hit the ice at his feet with the butt of the minié. 'He thinks he can still lord it over me because of his grubby affair with Mrs Boyce. But how could I care about that now? I do not care. I have shown my courage out here. That *bastard* – I've shown my courage.'

Styles' speech degenerated into an embittered, vicious mumbling. He struck at the broken ice with greater force, a shard disturbing the stiffening neck of the dead soldier, making his head jerk hideously.

'Come, Robert,' said Kitson with a forceful joviality he most definitely did not feel, 'let us go back to the camps and have a tot of brandy. Haven't you had enough of this mud, my friend?'

A shot sounded nearby, disturbing the still night air like an anvil tipped into a millpond. Kitson and Styles both turned abruptly. It had been fired from somewhere on the advance parallel, towards the Russian lines. Two more followed a second afterwards.

'Who's firing?' demanded an officer's voice from the direction of the forward battery. 'Stand to, damn it, and name yourselves!'

'Hopkins, sir, and Reid, pit number three!'

'I see no attack! What the deuce are you shooting at, man?'

'It's Trodd, sir!' The soldier sounded amazed. ''E's gone over to the bloomin' Ruskis! Made a run for it!'

'Fire at will!' came the reply, louder now. 'Get that man! There are no bloody deserters in the 7th Fusiliers! Get him!'

The appearance of British soldiers, standing in their trenches or on the ramparts of the forward battery in order to take aim at their errant comrade, provoked a sudden explosion of musketry from the Russian fort. Kitson, crouched down with his hands over his head, saw to his horror that Styles was actually getting to his feet, looking out over the edge of the trench, cocking his rifle and bringing it up to his shoulder. Then, without hesitation, he fired, the sound stunningly loud; and missed, evidently, as he immediately tore open a cartridge, and unfastened the minié's packing rod, preparing to reload.

Instinctively, Kitson lunged over, pulling hard at the base of Styles' coat, causing the gunpowder to spill from the cartridge, down into the mud. The illustrator tried to kick his attacker away, only to have Kitson grip tightly on to his right leg. They staggered to one side, splashing through the shattered slush of the puddle, straying into a shallower section of the trench. Now out in the full glare of the moonlight, they were a clear target for the marksmen over in the Russian fort. Several musket-balls struck around them as the two men continued to struggle desperately with one another; then one sliced through Styles' thigh, twisting him to the ground.

Kitson took two steps back. Styles, teeth gritted, clutched at his leg. His fingers grew black with blood. 'Stay calm, Robert!' Kitson instructed firmly. 'Try to stay calm.' He walked forward, bending down to haul the injured illustrator to cover. A thought came to him, startlingly clear: *that will get him evacuated.*

The first musket-ball clipped Kitson's side, whipping through his clothing and catching the base of his rib-cage. He fell forward, landing on his knees in the freezing water. His hands went to his wound; his body was soft and horribly ragged to the touch. There was no pain, nor could he tell which parts of what he felt were ripped fabric, and which were ripped flesh.

Another ball hit his back, cracking the shoulder-blade as it ricocheted away and shoving him to the bottom of the trench. The pain started to come now, intoxicatingly, dizzyingly intense, beyond any expression. Kitson found that he could no longer move, that his legs were gone, and his arms lay useless. His eyelids dipped down, then snapped back open, then dipped down again; above, the white moon shone on blankly. Styles was pulling himself, grimacing, into the shadow of the trench wall. There was more shooting, but the sounds grew distant, floating over faintly from a remote, nightmarish land.

3

So much for the grand adventure! To the four winds with the noble patriotic enterprise! After the missed opportunities of the Alma, the terrible butchery of Inkerman, and the myriad agonies of a disastrous winter, this correspondent can state with absolute truth that there are now not ten officers in any division who would not be delighted at the chance of getting away from the Crimea.

Lord Raglan must carry much of the blame for this state of affairs. He, and those wretched men who follow his example, carry themselves about as if the disintegration of their army was, in truth, an awful bore, and not worthy of their attention; much less as if it was the direct result of their incompetence. Our old friend Colonel Boyce is, of course, prominent amongst this number. They have their warm houses, and their servants, and do not like to go out in bad weather (although they have valises packed with greatcoats, fur hats and numerous other items of sturdy winter clothing); whilst their men stand out in the snow, all but abandoned by our wretched Commissariat, trying to sew their boots back together with lengths of their own hair.

The word in the camps, amongst both officers and the common soldiers, is that Lord Raglan seems to take it precious easy. He is not often seen amongst the men of the line – and during those rare outings, the privates regard him with confusion, not having a clue who he is, whilst the officers run away in order to avoid having to salute him. Such is the feeling in the British Army as 1855 begins its grim progress!

Cracknell took a swig of coffee and a long pull on his

283

cigarette, flicking the ash over the side of the bed on to the floor; then he drew a line under the text, and beneath wrote *'Forward camp of the Light Division, 23rd January 1855'*. Yawning hugely, he reached under the covers to scratch his crotch. The very top of the tent was touched with sunlight. His pocket-watch read six o'clock: the day was beginning. He finished the cigarette and swung his legs out of the cot, lowering his feet into his boots, which stood open and waiting on the floor.

The tent was wickedly cold. Frost laced the stones of the ruined shed in which it was pitched. Among the many things claimed by the great storm of the previous November had been the *Courier* team's comfortable little hut. The winds had brought it down in a matter of minutes, exposing them to a screaming tornado of flying camp detritus. After gathering what they could catch of their fast-vanishing belongings, they had embarked upon an urgent search for shelter. It had led them to this dilapidated, roofless structure; soaked and shivering, they had crouched down gratefully in its filthy corners.

Once the storm had abated, Cracknell had slung a foraged standard-issue army tent over it, making what he considered to be a rather homely little place, with a sturdy stone perimeter that would offer some measure of protection from any further extremes of weather. Also, the foundations of the shed enabled them the luxury of private berths in what had once been livestock pens, each with a canvas curtain set across its entrance. But had he received any kind of thanks from his so-called colleagues for his ingenious labours? Of course he bloody well hadn't – and neither of the useless, ungrateful rascals had spent more than a handful of nights in it.

Cracknell walked from his bed-alcove into the central area of the tent, looking to the small charcoal stove on which he had brewed his coffee. It had gone out. He kicked the thing over with a violent exclamation, scattering soot across the earth floor. Wrapping his fur coat (a recent acquisition, not overly greasy) around him, and putting a wool cap upon his head, the senior correspondent searched about for something to eat. All he could find was a small piece of military-issue biscuit. In the middle of the tent was a crude writing desk fashioned from packing crates, its surface covered with his papers. Sitting at it, he nibbled on the rock-hard biscuit, took a soothing swallow of rum from his hip-flask, and surveyed the report he had just completed.

There were some fanciful sections, he had to admit; the occasional paragraph where a light patina of exaggeration, a laminose layer of drama, had been artfully applied. Throwing the biscuit into a corner and lighting another cigarette, he decided, as always, that this was unimportant. No names were involved, apart from those he sought to shame or disgrace. All kinds of people were talking, and saying all manner of things. And anyway, he thought with wry satisfaction, I have a reputation to encourage.

A couple of weeks earlier, O'Farrell had sent him a package from London. It had contained a long letter, the last few issues of the *Courier*, and a thick wad of cuttings from the rest of the British press. As Cracknell pored over them, he realised his reports from the front were proving somewhat incendiary – beyond anything he had previously heard about. The *Courier*'s circulation was soaring. Its offices were being deluged with letters of both the most expansive support and the severest censure. The impassioned debate inspired by the magazine's Crimean coverage, Cracknell learned with immense gratification, had spread to the very highest level. As Lord Aberdeen's government tottered before accusations of having mismanaged the war, radical members were quoting his words in Parliament (along with those of that weasel Russell of the *Times*) as part of their case against the Prime Minister and his Cabinet.

And these words were his, and his alone. Kitson had left him – had absconded to Balaclava to wander amongst the injured. This had been a harsh blow. He had always felt that it had been a mistake to send an art correspondent to cover a war, but with his guidance the fellow had been doing surprisingly well, easily surpassing his most optimistic expectations. Thomas Kitson had an undeniably powerful turn of phrase, and had seemed committed to his journalistic duty. He could not stay the course, though; he had let himself become distracted, and his vision muddied by inappropriate compassion. Ability is nothing, the senior correspondent reflected, without a strong, disciplined mind.

Which brought one to Mr Styles. His drawings were an ongoing disaster, an unending, unvaried procession of mutilated horses and mouldering soldiers, all of which were quite unfit for publication. O'Farrell had been adamant that he stay, however, that he be properly supervised and made to produce something more becoming a professional magazine illustrator – to get some recompense, basically, from the *Courier's* poor investment. Cracknell simply couldn't be bothered to explain to him why this was a waste of time. He had more than enough of his own business to attend to. As far as he knew, Styles was still around the camps, entertaining himself in his customarily grisly fashion. Sooner or later, he reasoned, O'Farrell would give up and recall him.

Abandoned by his subordinates, Cracknell had thus stepped out from the shadow of the team to stand alone in the limelight. O'Farrell had been doubtful at first, but had soon warmed to this state of affairs and set about creating himself a celebrity. The Tory papers, Cracknell saw, had voiced an overweening hostility towards the reports of the *Courier's* Crimean correspondent – a hostility which, as every true polemicist knew, could easily be turned to its target's advantage. A month-old article from *Blackwood's* had declared that this nameless personage *flings his censure about wildly and without reason, stabbing left and right like a Malay under the influence of opium, or a Red Indian on the warpath, with his bloodied tomahawk ever at the ready;* and O'Farrell, in his clumsy fashion, had pounced. The next issue of his magazine had carried Cracknell's report on the front page, as usual, but instead of being anonymous, it was attributed to 'the justly-stabbing Malay'; and the most recent piece was given to 'the honest Red Indian'. Both monikers had made Cracknell wince with embarrassment.

Sitting at the desk, he looked at his latest report thoughtfully, puffing on his cigarette, and then picked up his pen. At the bottom of the page he wrote, 'The Tomahawk of the *Courier'*.

Well pleased with his labours, Cracknell decided to venture out. The flaps of the tent were stiff with frost. He had to force them apart, as if he were pushing his way out of a cardboard box. The cold seemed to close around his face, making it ache most unpleasantly. He considered turning around and going back inside, back to bed. Then he reminded himself that there was no food in the tent, and hardly any liquor. He had to forage.

The morning sky was a deep, smooth blue. Sunlight was breaking slowly over the cliffs, turning the tents that covered the plateau from dull grey to shining white. Bearded men wrapped in russet rags moved about in amongst them, dazed and shivering. Surveying the camp as he trudged by, Cracknell felt a profound sense of wrongness. This was not how a military camp should appear at the outset of the day. It was so deathly quiet. There were no bugles sounding the reveille or calling men to their early parades; there was no drilling, no saluting, no shouting at the cack-handed soldier who fumbles with his rifle. There was no clanking of pots, no hissing of butter in pans, no smoke from fires rising up between the dense rows of canvas points. Indeed, the only smoke to be seen came from the chimneys of the cottages given to the senior officers. And very snug little holdings they look too, he thought, turning himself in their direction.

In his now confirmed role as the messiah of Crimean discontent, Cracknell knew that he would be unwelcome at pretty much all of those cosy farmhouses. His fame had inevitably spread in the army camps as much as it had back in England. It had made him a good many enemies. Cracknell didn't mind this in the least; he had always had enemies. The midnight shouts of abuse outside his tent, the threatening gestures and the efforts to impede his work all encouraged him. And he was openly celebrated, he found, amongst the aggrieved and the disillusioned. His arrival in a sympathetic hut or tent was often greeted with cheers, and he would be slapped on the back as he strolled about the camps – even as others swore in his face. There were officers among his friends, naturally, but few of these ranked above major, and none had been graced with lodgings of stone and mortar.

Cracknell carried on towards the farmhouses regardless. Up on the Heights at that time of day, they were the only places where food was to be obtained. Furthermore, there was one house among them with which he had a more than passing acquaintance.

Boyce had been fortunate indeed after the carnage of Inkerman. The *Courier*'s charges against him, and its ill-fated attempt to have him brought to justice, sank without trace – as did the incriminating painting that Wray had stolen from the villa. Cracknell tried to plant a few seeds of inquiry, seeds that would not lead Codrington back to him, but none took root. In fact, much to his disgust, tales had quickly circulated instead of Boyce's valiant conduct under a punishing fire; of his reckless but incredibly brave advance; of the inspiring manner with which he beat back the Russians, kept his companies together, and held his position against desperate odds until reinforced. Official recognition, however, had not been possible. The 99th Foot had lost more than one hundred and twenty private soldiers as a result of their commander's foolhardy tactics. But there was much approving talk nonetheless, despite Cracknell's best efforts to pre-empt or contradict it; and, before long, a rumour of a reward.

Sure enough, not five days later the undeserving blackguard was installed, along with Madeleine and his servants, in a solid, single-storey farmhouse on the southern edge of the Light Division's camp. This building had weathered the great storm with scarcely the loss of a roof-tile. It had tidy, commodious rooms in which fires were kept roaring for many hours of the day, and hot meals were regularly served; and low, wide windows that had, on occasion, permitted the rapid escape of a rather broad-bottomed Irishman.

Cracknell's intention as he walked towards Boyce's farmhouse was thus to enter through the yard, slide open one of these windows (he had one at the back in mind) and see what victuals lay within easy reach. Madeleine, he knew, would not be around. Miss Wade liked to get her out early. He did not mind this absence in the least. That morning,

Cracknell found that he could contemplate a spot of theft with crafty pleasure, but the thought of having to make the declarations of eternal, undying love that had become a condition of Madeleine's company (and the sole route into her undergarments) brought him only an oppressive sense of tedium.

A sentry was posted before the front door. Cracknell redirected himself slightly, affecting a casual demeanour. This soldier was a typically forlorn sight, his uniform in tatters, hugging his rifle close to him as if the wood might emit some warmth if it was squeezed hard enough. Seeing Cracknell, the mangy looking man unfolded his arms and started in his direction. The correspondent quickened his pace.

'Sir!' the soldier croaked. 'Stand for a moment, sir, will you? Just a word, sir!'

The voice was oddly familiar. Cracknell stopped and turned. 'How may I help you, soldier?'

'Pardon my interruptin', sir, but the Major told me all about you.' The soldier was talking quickly, plainly a little agitated. 'An' I've 'eard others a-talkin' since – 'bout 'ow you're an awful enemy to all them what've left us out 'ere to rot – an' to Boyce in partic'lar . . .'

Cracknell peered closely at the battered features, which were partly lost behind a patchy, colourless beard. 'My apologies, soldier, but have we met before?'

'D'you not remember, sir?' For a second, the man feigned offence. 'Ah well, s'pose there was plenty afoot that day. At the Alma, at the base of the 'ill, by the river. You crawled out of the waters like an 'arf-drowned cat. An' you told us that Boyce was dead.' There was accusation in his voice as he uttered this last statement, as if the correspondent, with this error, had somehow been responsible for preserving the Colonel's life. 'Dan Cregg's the name.'

Cracknell had no memory of this encounter. He could recollect the river and his little swim in it, and then Major Maynard leading the assault, but that was all. 'Ah yes, of course. Cregg. Yes, of course, of course. It gratifies me to see that you are still in one piece, man. Veterans of both the early engagements and this accursed winter are becoming rare indeed.'

Cregg chuckled sourly, which brought on a cough. 'Ha! Yes

sir, true enough, among the ranks at any rate. We're what y'might call a dyin' breed.' He coughed some more. Cracknell noticed that his right hand was swaddled in a thick mitten, whereas the other hand was bare. 'But then, can't say I've 'scaped entirely, sir.'

Cregg drew off his mitten with a pained grimace to reveal a mangled mess bound together with filthy bandages. As far as Cracknell could tell, only two functional fingers remained. Haltingly, the soldier then told the story of how he came to be injured, of Boyce's arrogant errors, and Maynard's senseless death. Standing in the sharp morning air, Cracknell grew steadily more interested. He gave Cregg a cigarette and encouraged him to enlarge upon what he was saying. Was he not tempted, the correspondent asked, to make more of the wound, and get himself shipped home? It looked rather serious, after all – could he even fire a rifle?

Cregg, however, was quite adamant. He was going to remain in the Crimea come what may. At first, Cracknell thought that in this unlikely looking mongrel of a man, he might have found a hero amongst the common soldiery, a noble warrior to hold up for the admiration of all England in the pages of the *Courier* – a moving counterpoint to the incompetence of those who commanded him. But as Cregg talked on, it became very clear that this was no popular champion. There was something unsavoury about him, Cracknell decided, a touch of the cut-throat, perhaps, of the criminal. He was hardly fit to be paraded before the crowd. And his motive for remaining at the front was not patriotism, nor was it a desire for decisive victory over their foe, nor even a loyalty to his brothers in arms; at least, not to those who still breathed. Cregg wanted to stay in the Crimea so that he could get his revenge on his regimental commander.

When he spoke again of Inkerman, his voice a low, nasal snarl, he positively shook with loathing. ''E took us out there, and then 'e 'id behind a rock. 'E 'id himself away, nice and safe, and left it all to the Major – as bleedin' usual. My mates was droppin' all around, and there wasn't nothing we could do. And then the Major . . .' Cregg looked at the ground. 'The . . . the Major was a decent cove.'

'I knew him,' declared Cracknell stoically, 'He was decent indeed. Honourable.'

The soldier met his eye. 'Aye, 'e was. I've never known 'is like. An' 'e was put through 'ell, sawn up and who knows what else – all 'cause of that cunt in there.' Cregg glared at the farmhouse door. 'That *cunt* – all 'e does now is sit about on 'is arse, complainin' about the lack of action. As if 'e'd know what to bleedin' do if action came! Prob'ly just get a whole bunch more of us killed. 'E shouldn't get the chance. And by the devil, even if it costs me neck, 'e won't get the bleedin' chance.' He stopped talking, and sucked furiously on his cigarette.

Cracknell studied Cregg's face, trying to work out if he would really take the action he threatened. It was a dull, angry red, the lower lip protruding, and trembling slightly. This man is in the grasp of all manner of powerful emotions, the correspondent thought, emotions which his confined, feeble mind cannot fully comprehend or manage. He talks of bold, savage deeds, but then many angry men talk of violent things that they dare not do. His assertions concerning Boyce's behaviour on the battlefield, though, were all too easy to believe. Such behaviour was typical of the man – unlike the heroic yarn of headstrong courage that had been spun by certain of Boyce's peers. Opponents this deserving, Cracknell thought with fierce, righteous purpose, are rare indeed. The correspondent took out his pocketbook, resolving that Cregg's account would form an electrifying addition to a future report from the Tomahawk of the *Courier*.

A sergeant-major approached the house. Throwing away his cigarette, Cregg slunk back to his post, and responded sullenly to the questions and instructions directed at him. Cracknell, scribbling busily, moved around to the side of the house, in the direction of its small yard. Pausing alongside a window, he leant his back against the cold wall.

He had laid down two lengthy paragraphs when an oil lamp was set on a table just inside the dirty window. He could hear voices. It was Boyce, a servant, and a couple of his officers. Cracknell stopped writing and listened.

'And this is really all that can be provided for us to break-fast upon?' Boyce was saying irritably to the servant. 'Bacon with eggs and beans? What do you think I am, man, a Yankee cowpoke? Are there no lambs' kidneys to be had on this entire peninsula?'

'General state of things is pretty wretched, sir, to be fair,' muttered someone in response.

Boyce sighed, as if he were the most put-upon fellow in all the Crimea. 'Very well, bacon with eggs and beans it is. Upon my honour, that it should come to this.'

Soon, the smell of frying bacon suffused the farmhouse, seeping through the window frame and up Cracknell's nostrils. His stomach began to growl so loudly that he moved a few feet along the wall for fear that the noise might give him away. He thought of Cregg, standing guard outside the front door, forced to endure the same torturous odour with nothing to look forward to but an ounce or two of hard biscuit and a piece of salted pork from an animal butchered before the campaign had even begun.

Cracknell reread the paragraph he had been writing. Its level of severity suddenly seemed desperately inadequate. He drew a line under it and began again, his features slowly lighting with a grin of acerbic glee. Just wait until the bastard reads this, he thought. It'll put him right off his blasted bacon.

The breakfasting officers started to talk about Balaclava, Boyce declaring that he was riding down to the port that afternoon. There were some civilians arriving, he claimed, old friends of his brother's whom he was keen to see. An officer – Major Pierce, poor Maynard's unworthy replacement – offered to accompany him. Boyce refused rather curtly, and promptly assigned Pierce a tedious regimental task that would keep him occupied for the rest of the day.

Cracknell realised that he had overheard something significant; Boyce, he could tell, was lying through his teeth. He stopped writing. Balaclava, he thought – now there's an idea.

4

Mr Kitson's skin was white as a fish-belly, and dreadfully clammy to the touch. Ever so gently, Annabel lifted him up on to his side, revealing a back sticky with congealing blood. There were two wounds, both to the upper abdomen, neither now bleeding with any persistence, praise God; but it was quite plain that he needed proper medical attention as soon as it could be secured for him.

She turned, looking for Madeleine. They had been walking along the Worontzov road, heading for the camps, when they had passed a French mule-train, bearing the night's sick and injured down to the harbour. This was hardly an uncommon sight, yet something had made Annabel stop; and then she saw them, Mr Kitson and Mr Styles, lashed to one of the wooden litters at the very rear of the column. She had raced over without explanation, and was now unsure if her companion had managed to keep track of her.

There she was, though, those slender shoulders hunched against the cold, making her way unhurriedly along the line. A large proportion of those on the litters were insensible. The rest moaned and shrieked with every bump on the road; some, delirious, let out burbles of maniacal laughter. Their clothes, such as they were, were blotched with blood, bile and excrement. The mules, smelling the blood and sensing the suffering, were braying in distress.

Madeleine was angling her head so that the rim of her bonnet blocked all but the road beneath her boots. Arriving at Annabel's side, her face wore an expression of confused, slightly petulant distaste. Then she noticed the men tied to the litter – the unconscious, pallid Mr Kitson, and his dishevelled colleague next to him, who clutched at a poorly bandaged thigh with his eyes squeezed shut, squirming around as if in the throes of a terrible dream. She gasped with shock, raising her hands to her face.

'Are – are they alone?' she demanded, staring frantically at the adjacent litters. Annabel looked back at her uncomprehendingly. 'Are they alone, Annabel? Tell me! Is Mr Cracknell here with them? Have you seen him?'

Now Annabel understood only too well. She frowned. 'No, dear, he's not here. Do not think of him – I'm sure he's perfectly fine, that one.' Standing up, she put a placatory hand upon Madeleine's arm. 'We must go back down to Balaclava with Mr Kitson, Madeleine. Otherwise . . .' Annabel looked around at the other men in the column. 'Otherwise I fear he will certainly perish along the way. Pass me the canteen, will you?'

Madeleine didn't hear her. 'No – I must find Richard. I must!' There was panic in her voice.

Annabel tightened her grip on her friend. 'Madeleine, you are coming with me to Balaclava,' she said strictly. 'You know that you can't simply wander off around the camps on your own. Please listen to me, my dear. You have not the first clue where that man might be.' Inwardly, Annabel cursed the smirking face, the swaggering confidence, the very blasted boots of Richard Cracknell.

As tears filmed Madeleine's eyes, Annabel moved forward and embraced her with firm tenderness. 'Listen to me, child. He is well. You must trust me on this. These men are not. We must help them if we can. We must do the Lord's will.'

Madeleine rested her head on her friend's shoulder, rubbing at her eyes. 'The Lord's will, yes,' she murmured. 'The Lord's will.'

With the permission of one of the French drivers, the women climbed up on to the two closest mules, joining the column as it advanced through a bleak, brutal landscape. The gullies between the colourless hills were choked with the decaying corpses of horses and oxen. Heavy clouds had smothered the early morning sun, and a putrid smell hung all about. Vultures cawed hideously to one another, their black and white wings beating at the still air. Even the accursed Cain, Annabel thought, would scarce deserve banishment to such a blighted territory. It seemed that few animals could easily survive there but those who sustained themselves on the flesh of the dead. There was no hay to be had anywhere; no one appeared to have considered what their horses would eat during that winter. Off to the east, Annabel could see two near-spectral creatures, looking truly apocalyptic in their emaciation, straining to drag a stout mortar along a ridge. That both lacked manes and tails, having had them chewed away by their starving fellows, only added to their ghastly, otherworldly appearance. She thanked God for the sturdy, omnivorous constitution of the mule she was riding, and gave the beast's rough, grimy hide a clapping pat.

As if in mockery of her gratitude, a few minutes later a mule towards the head of the column let out a scream as one of its hooves twisted in the frozen ruts of the track, breaking the leg. Two drivers held it down, intending to wait until the rest of the party had passed before ending the animal's pain. The men on its litter, knowing that they would be left with the dead mule, at the mercy of vultures and wild dogs, begged those trudging by them for help. None were able or willing to supply it. Annabel hardened herself, knowing she could not go to them, blocking her ears to their imprecations.

After the shot had rung out and the drivers returned to the column, she looked around at Mr Kitson. Her mind teemed with awful questions. Was choosing to save him above those poor wretches abandoned back there, or indeed above any number of others, somehow an offence to God? Was it the result of soulless, practical reasoning, bred by war and the constant presence of death? Was her ability to make such choices, such judgements, an indication of a grievous sinfulness at the very core of her being? She had no answers; but no regrets either.

Annabel kept up with the *Courier*. She had watched its once-welcome tendency to be controversial steadily develop into a determined, deliberate stirring up of scandal and outrage, regardless of verity and of benefit to no one but those who profited from its sale. How much, she often wished to ask those involved in its production, had actually changed since its programme of wild exposures had begun? How many lives had been saved? This, she felt, was something that Mr Kitson had realised too; and he had relinquished his duties to the *Courier*, to the irresponsible Mr Cracknell, in order to assuage the torments of his fellow man. This made him worthy of preservation, and she was prepared to answer to the Heavenly Father Himself for her decision to stay with him.

Mr Styles, however, was quite another matter. Had he not been injured and requiring assistance, she might well have thought twice about exposing Madeleine to his company again. Mr Kitson, she decided, was correct – this fellow should be sent home, and held somewhere secure until his fevered mind had repaired itself. He seemed to be lapsing into a delirium, muttering on and on about how Mr Kitson was to blame for his wound, with as much bitterness as if his colleague had fired the shot himself. Then, after gazing dumbly for a while at Madeleine, who tried to put as much distance between them as possible, he began to insist that he was perfectly all right, that he wished to get up off the litter and head over to the front lines, to see how the siege was faring that day. This was all said loudly and pointedly, as if intended to impress, but all it earned him was some less than polite requests from the occupants of other litters to keep his noise down.

At last, after several painful hours, they rounded a spur to see the whitewashed walls and terracotta slates of Balaclava. The town itself was little more than a few hundred humble fishing cottages clustered together in the shelter of a narrow inlet. Crowning the hills around it were the weather-worn remains of an ancient fortress long ago abandoned to ruin, its architects and purpose forgotten. Dozens of tall ships stood in the confines of the harbour like great gothic cathedrals of wood, iron and brass, their masts shooting up like spires, their cannon leering from the high decks like long rows of gargoyles. These shining giants of the British Navy were so large and so numerous that in places they all but covered the waters of the inlet. Indeed, some of them appeared to stand not in the sea but upon the land itself, entirely dwarfing the tight huddle of huts and shacks that fringed the quayside. The massive ships shared something of the silent serenity of the ancient cathedrals as well as their scale. They were nearly empty of life or movement; few had their gangplanks down, and traffic on these was sparse.

Balaclava, in contrast, seemed abuzz with activity. Crowds filled the main thoroughfares. Caravans of travellers struggled in from the surrounding landscape at a constant rate. And on the outskirts, teams of surveyors were taking measurements and making estimates for the planned railway line up to the camps. Construction was set to begin in early February. It would, everyone agreed, transform the war.

This view of the town, as Annabel well knew, was a cruel illusion. As one approached, it seemed a place of sanity, of cleanliness and plenty, of refuge after the madness of the front. It seemed, in short, like civilisation: the supply base where food, clothing and all manner of useful items could be bought, where pipes could be lit, stories exchanged, and rest deservedly taken.

But those expecting relief from hardship and death received a nasty surprise as they drew closer. The wretched merchants of the town, they quickly found, were not decent local people peddling their wares for honest prices, but opportunistic usurers from the surrounding lands – and Annabel's worst enemies, with whom she frequently did bloody battle. These fiends, entirely indifferent to the suffering of their fellow man, were prepared to sell goods of the very lowest quality for the very highest sums; and they had pitched their stalls, quite happily, in the midst of a plague.

Balaclava was the place where the disease-riddled Turkish Army sent its men to die. From the hills, where all looked so well, one could not see the ankle-deep effluence that ran through those crowded lanes, the scenes of desperate anguish that were being played out inside every dilapidated house and shed, and the rows of dead laid out in the streets once these scenes had reached their inevitable, unvarying conclusions. Every patch of waste ground had become a place of burial. Faces and limbs poked out accusingly from the fresh earth of shallow graves. Unspeakable smells wafted between the half-collapsed buildings, whilst the wailings of bereaved wives competed with the rapacious cries of the sutlers and hawkers.

The mule train forged steadily through all of this in the direction of the docks. Here, in the shadow of the majestic vessels that filled the bay, the chipped, uneven stones of the harbour were almost covered by messy stacks of bales and crates. A profusion of bold stamps, brands and labels indicated that they contained official supplies for the British expeditionary force, shipped out at the expense of Her Majesty's Government of Great Britain, for immediate distribution. Yet they had plainly been standing there for days, exposed to the snow, sleet and rain, devoid of any means of transportation and destined to rot where they had been left.

Annabel was used to such waste. Like the scenes they had just ridden past so calmly, it no longer provoked her. Climbing off the mule, she looked to her companion. Madeleine appeared distracted still, thinking no doubt of the undeserving Mr Cracknell. Mr Styles, also, had renewed his attentions towards her, and was trying to catch her eye with his usual doomed persistence. The sooner this is over, thought Annabel as she knelt to check on Mr Kitson, the better for us all.

A surgeon and a harbour official, both close to exhaustion but working hard to maintain their respective professional demeanours, approached the wounded men lain out on the cold stone. Before any treatment could be given, however, a heated argument began, the official waving a sheaf of forms in the physician's face. After wiping Mr Kitson's brow with the edge of her cloak, Annabel turned towards the bay. Amidst the merchantmen and gunboats floated a number of weather-beaten hospital ships – the means by which the wounded were conveyed to Scutari. Conditions on board these ships, she had heard, were truly wretched. It was said that a quarter of their patients died before they even left port. Annabel felt an absolute, crippling impotence. She could do nothing more for Mr Kitson. She had wanted to save him, yet had merely delivered him to a fate that was uncertain at best.

With a start, she realised that Madeleine was gone. The foolish girl had slipped back into the squalor of Balaclava. A young woman alone in this town was in serious danger; the heathen mussulman, as Annabel had been told on many occasions, had no respect whatsoever for the unveiled female. She stood, and was about to charge off down the nearest alley when the surgeon arrived at her side.

He looked at Styles and Kitson. 'Civilians,' he said in a tone of mild surprise, making a note on a form. 'What are they doing here?'

Without thinking, as she hurried away to begin her search, Annabel told him, 'They are from the *London Courier* magazine.'

At the edge of the harbour, she turned back briefly to take a last look at Mr Kitson, lying unconscious on the stones. The surgeon was unravelling his bloody coat to examine his injuries. Breathing a steadying sigh, she dismissed her fears and quietly intoned a dependable passage from the Psalms. *'Turn from evil and do good; then you will dwell in the land forever. For the Lord loves the just, and will not forsake his faithful ones.'*

'Heavens,' exclaimed the surgeon. 'Godwin! Have a look at this!'

Another surgeon came over, pacing along the line of ailing redcoats. 'Dear God,' he murmured. 'Thomas Kitson. I sent him up to the plateau last night, to fetch an engineer. We wondered what had become of the poor fellow. Must've fallen prey to a sniper down in the trenches.'

'Well, this wound is serious indeed. Broken ribs, a punctured lung . . .'

They looked at each other. Both knew that they weren't permitted to send civilian casualties to the General Hospital outside town. There was only one option.

299

'Excuse me, sirs – Doctor Godwin, Doctor Harris – might I be of some help?'

The surgeons turned towards the speaker, a mulatto woman of about fifty years of age, clad rather flamboyantly in a feathered hat, a thick green shawl and a striped dress. She was a good six inches shorter than the two men, but her brown eyes were fixed on them with sharp inquisitiveness.

'Mrs Seacole,' said Godwin. 'Are you settled aboard the *Medora*?'

He looked past her towards the abandoned munitions vessel moored on the far edge of the harbour that had been assigned to this redoubtable lady as her base of operations. All three of its masts had been sawn down for firewood; it was a sorry, broken thing. Godwin suspected that giving this old hulk to Mrs Seacole had been somebody's cruel idea of a joke.

The lady's eyes narrowed slightly. 'It is comfortable enough, thank you, but I think I shall try to find myself something a little more . . . permanent.' Her South Seas accent purred softly through the word. 'I heard you talking about this man here. Is he a friend of yours?'

Godwin sighed. 'An orderly, madam, and a most capable one. Injured during an errand I sent him on, by the looks of it.'

'And now he must be loaded on to a hospital ship. You are afraid he will perish before he reaches the hospital in Turkey – which he surely would, by my reckoning.' She reached into a large leather satchel on her shoulder and produced a roll of clean bandages. 'See to your soldiers, good sirs. I will take this man aboard the *Medora*. What is his name?'

'Thomas Kitson, Mrs Seacole, but there are forms I must complete, and—'

Ignoring him, she crouched down beside the stricken orderly and began binding his wound. 'There, Thomas,' she said gently. 'Mother will look after you.'

Doctor Godwin stopped talking. Like most at the harbour, he did not know exactly what to make of Mary Seacole. A mulatto nurse claiming to be an army widow, she had come out to the Crimea at her own expense and was utterly set upon helping the soldiery, for whom she seemed to have a boundless affection. The surgeon supposed she was simply a member of the strange carnival that sprang up along the fringes of every war; he was quite sure, though, that no harm could possibly come to Kitson in her care. He looked to Harris, who shrugged. The decision thus made, both turned towards the man laid out by Kitson's side. There were tears running down his face, and he was mumbling inaudibly to himself.

'Who's this other one?'

'Don't know the name. He's from the *London Courier*, apparently.'

Godwin studied the civilian's wound. The crude dressing was soaked, but the wound beneath was not desperately serious; the musket-ball had missed the bone by over an inch. He had lost a lot of blood, which had no doubt precipitated his present delirium, but not so much as to suggest that an artery had been punctured. There were many more grave cases arrayed along the dock; Harris was already losing interest, his attention claimed instead by a shuddering private a few places down the line. It occurred to Godwin that he could spare this fellow both the long voyage to Scutari and the disease-ridden hospital at its end.

'Well, as he has no military duties to perform, I see no reason why he shouldn't go back up to the plateau. All this needs,' he said loudly to the man, 'is regular bathing, fresh bindings and a long period of bed-rest. Do you hear? You write your reports from your cot, sir.'

The man seemed to nod, but did not stop his mumbling or focus his staring eyes.

Doctor Godwin started re-dressing the leg. He shouted for an orderly; one ran up a few seconds later. 'This man will be on the next cart back to the camps. Ensure that he is taken to the tent of the *London Courier* – someone will know where it is.'

5

The *H.M.S. Mallory* kept her distance from Sebastopol, steaming in a wide loop around the mouth of the inlet that held the besieged port. Her passengers, however, shared none of this cautiousness. They rushed over to the deck rail as soon as the enemy's base came into view, whipping out a great arsenal of telescopes and binoculars. Five tall ships had been scuppered in the harbour to form a barrier against hostile vessels. The waters of the Black Sea covered their hulls completely; hundreds of gulls could be seen perching upon the bare remains of their masts. To either side were large coastal batteries, studded with cannon. There was some thrilled chatter as artillery rumbled over on the plateau, sending up clear trails of smoke.

These passengers were, for the most part, that species of traveller referred to somewhat dismissively as *war tourists*: boys barely past adolescence visiting idolised elder brothers, unscrupulous would-be novelists and artists hoping for some exciting material, or simply wealthy loungers seeking diversion. The few professional men on board found themselves to be completely outnumbered. Charles Norton and his son-in-law Anthony James, not wishing to spend any longer cooped up in their cabin, were obliged to stand next to the roaring paddle-box in order to escape the crowd and review their notes.

They were making this hazardous journey for the sake of William Fairbairn's cherished project – a floating mill and bakery. Such a machine, he had told them with his usual enthusiasm, would be able to supply the entire British Army with fresh, wholesome bread, and would be entirely safe from contamination and disease. It sounded positively absurd to Charles, but he had humoured the old goat; a trip to a war-zone to indulge one of his whims would place him very firmly in the Norton Foundry's debt. James, however, had listened to him ramble on with genuine interest. And now, on the morning that they approached Balaclava, he was revealing the conclusions he had reached about the possible design of this unlikely contraption. It could be built on a base of two iron-screw steamers, he said in his intent, enthusiastic manner; a simple process of adaptation could produce an engine capable of grinding up to a thousand pounds of flour every hour. As they passed Sebastopol, rounding a steep headland, he began to go into further detail. Norton looked away, out to sea.

He had learned much about his son-in-law over the course of their two-week voyage. The man's brain never seemed to stop working. He was always sketching out plans, jotting down notes or poring over one of the scientific volumes he had lined along the sides of his valise; or he would be nodding in silent agreement as he read unsavoury radical journals such as the *Westminster Review* or the *London Courier*.

James was formidably ambitious, far more so than Norton had ever realised during the eighteen months or so that they had been acquainted. Charles had always considered him devilish clever – he had valued him for it, in fact, and been pleased that his daughter had married someone who could match her in this regard. On occasion, however, when they spoke, Norton was sure that he detected appraisal in James' eyes, as if the fellow was looking him over and making an unfavourable assessment. He sees a failure, Charles thought, a man of limited vision and accomplishments who has risen as high as he ever will; someone whose lack of ability has held back his own business and who, at the age of fifty-three, must still jump at the Fairbairns' every command. He compares himself against me and is determined to do better, damn him, both for himself and for my daughter.

Balaclava's bay was so crowded that the *Mallory* had to wait for over an hour before it could unload its passengers. Norton found that he was immensely tired and a little nauseous, and wished only to sit upon dry land; James, meanwhile, was noting down names of ships and making drawings of the hills around them. They were told that they had to disembark quickly as their vessel could only be at the quay for twenty minutes. It would then be taken to the rear of the bay, returning three days later to collect them and sail back to Liverpool.

The docks were jammed with people, military and civilian, drawn from a range of nationalities. It was far from the ordered British base Norton had hoped for. Army liaisons came forward to meet some of the war tourists; others obtained directions from officials and trailed off into the town in groups of two or three. Norton peered up the lanes after them, rapidly concluding that Balaclava was about as uninviting a place as he had ever encountered. It was positively medieval in aspect – were it not for the shabby uniforms one would not think one was in the middle of the nineteenth century at all. He resolved to remain as close to the sea as possible. Then he glanced down into the water and saw a decomposing camel bobbing in a stew of offal and splintered wood. The sight was so hideous and unexpected that he almost cried out.

His son-in-law, however, was unsurprised by their surroundings. 'It is quite as bad as has been reported, isn't it?' he said calmly, adjusting his pebble spectacles. 'If a firm was run like this, Charles, it would sink within a week.'

Norton, a hand over his mouth as he tried to hold in his last meal, did not answer.

James looked around. 'Where is our Royal Engineer?' he asked. 'Mr Fairbairn said that there would be one here to meet us.'

'I do not know,' Norton replied, lowering his hand impatiently. 'How the deuce *would* I know, Anthony? I'm sure he'll show himself in due course.'

James hefted his valise on to his shoulder. 'I could take this chance to climb around the side of the bay and begin the survey. Do you object?'

Norton indicated that he did not, thinking that Anthony James could jump off the blasted harbour for all he cared. He walked along the dock, keeping his eyes on the horizon and taking a cigar from his coat. As he lit it he could not help looking back at the camel. The animal had drifted a short distance out into the bay; he watched as it was caught in an undertow, its stiff legs breaking the surface and revolving grotesquely.

Forcing himself to turn away, he noticed that James had fallen into conversation with a disreputable-looking character with a wild black beard, evidently some kind of camp parasite or confidence man. They were shaking hands, getting along famously. Norton sighed, wondering if he should intervene; for all his energetic intelligence, James was a touch naïve and an easy mark indeed for an obvious ruffian like that. He decided not to. Perhaps such an experience would teach the fellow some humility.

Wandering further up the quay, puffing absently on his cigar, Norton passed the rows of injured. Rivulets of blood and urine were flowing across stones from where they lay, intermingling and running over the edge of the harbour into the sea. As he stepped between them, he heard a deep, authoritative voice up ahead. Looking up, he saw that it belonged to a senior regimental officer. This man stood several inches above the officials, civilian surgeons and Commissariat clerks who bustled around him. His undress uniform was startlingly clean and bright beneath a new-looking fawn surtout; upon his face was an immaculately maintained moustache of rather formidable proportions. To the dazed Norton, he seemed a figure of absolute proficiency – someone who could impose order even on such a rancid mess as Balaclava.

This officer was talking to the captain of the *H.M.S. Mallory*. Could this be their elusive contact in the Royal Engineers? After a brief discussion, the captain did point Norton out; but as the officer came over Norton realised that he was from the infantry. He asked Norton's business genially enough, though, and even nodded in apparent approval when the Fairbairns were mentioned. Introducing himself as Colonel Nathaniel Boyce, he said that he was in the town trying to use what personal influence he had to secure additional provisions for his men. The basic problem, he explained, was that Balaclava was just too far away from the main camps to serve as an effective supply base.

'But there is a railway being built, isn't there?' Norton inquired, rather flattered to have the undivided attention of a colonel. 'I'm sure I read something about it during my voyage.'

Boyce smiled thinly. 'There is indeed, sir. You engineers keep each other well informed. It is to go up the hill to Kadikioi, then on to the camps, eventually criss-crossing the whole plateau. I understand that the surveyors have been here for several weeks already and the Chief Engineer, a Mr Beatty, has just arrived.'

'You seem to know a good deal about this undertaking, Colonel Boyce.'

'How could I fail to take an interest, Mr Norton, when it will have such an effect on the lives of those under my command?' Boyce paused; when he spoke again, his voice was loaded to an almost imperceptible degree. 'Besides, I am on good terms with the Quartermaster-General's department. I receive regular bulletins on the progress of the railway. The Great Western Railway has supplied the tracks, and the contractor, Mr Peto, has supplied the sleepers and various other sundry parts – points and so on. I happen to know, however, that they only have enough spikes to last until Kadikioi. More will be required, many more, by the middle of March.'

Norton blinked, completely astonished by what the Colonel seemed to be inferring. 'Is – is that so, sir?'

Boyce met Norton's eye. 'Speed is the priority here, Mr Norton. The railway is not being constructed to British standards. Come, let me show you what they have done so far. We will have dinner afterwards, up on the plateau, where we can discuss this matter further. And you must stay at my farmhouse.' He looked over at the line of sick redcoats with a sudden, aristocratic coldness. 'There is disease here.'

Bidding the Colonel to wait for a minute only, Norton conducted a quick search for James. He was nowhere to be found, but Charles could not allow this great chance simply to slip away. After leaving word of his whereabouts with the captain of the *Mallory*, he started through Balaclava at Colonel Boyce's side. Anthony James was a resourceful man, he told himself; he would be fine.

'Ah, the saintly Madeleine!' called out her husband. 'Rescue many of my men today, did you, oh holy lady?' The officers around the table laughed. Boyce gave Lieutenant Nunn a sly, rather unpleasant wink, as if trying to make his adjutant complicit in his mockery.

Nunn moved uncomfortably in his chair. Mrs Boyce was, in his view, a remarkable woman, who deserved far more gentlemanly treatment than her husband bestowed on her. Nunn wasn't in love with her, of course. A good soldier did not allow himself to develop futile fascinations with his commander's wife, and he had let this opinion be known to those among his peers who had made such an open point of their devotion to her. He could not deny, however, that she was a rare beauty, and privately thought that the months she had spent attending on the campaign had only improved her appeal. It was as if the baubles of fashion had not enhanced her loveliness but obscured it, and now, as she stood in plain bonnet and skirts, her hair tied up simply, her beauty could shine with its full radiance. Displaying no emotion, he avoided his commander's gaze, ignored the mirth of his fellows, and shifted his position so that he was staring blankly at the fire.

Mrs Boyce removed her faded bonnet and cloak. Before she left the room, her eyes flickered over the Colonel, ably communicating all of the abhorrence she felt for him. They heard her chamber door slam behind her.

Boyce laughed, reaching for his wine. The Colonel was in uncommonly high spirits. They had a guest that night: in between Majors Fairlie and Pierce sat a grey-whiskered, bushy-browed chap of fifty or so, a civilian engineer, looking about him nervously like a mouse trapped in a nest of crimson-jacketed adders. This was unusual, to say the least. Boyce was not known for his hospitality, especially towards those who lacked both military rank and an old family name. Nunn was growing convinced that it had to be part of a mysterious scheme – part of what Major Maynard had hinted at on the day of Inkerman when he had challenged Boyce over Wray's disappearance from the battlefield. He had been unable to discover much more about this afterwards. There had been a closed hearing at the brigade headquarters involving the men from the *London Courier*, but nothing had come of it. Then Captain Wray had been invalided back to England at the end of November, even though he had seemed entirely healthy. Something had happened, and it was going on still, but the Lieutenant could not for the life of him work out what it was. No matter how unsettled his conscience, his wits were just too slow.

Boyce instructed the servants to bring some fresh bottles; Nunn felt a twitch of distaste at the sound of his voice. He suppressed it quickly. There was no proof of anything, he reminded himself. Colonel Boyce was his commanding officer. From his earliest days in the service, it had been impressed upon him that this relationship, and the absolute loyalty that went with it, was the bedrock of the British Army.

Major Pierce began to talk about the *London Courier*, explaining the situation to their guest in the crudest terms. Nunn despised Pierce. The Major was the worst kind of army bully, as vicious as Wray had been but fat and loud-mouthed with it. He was proposing that they mount a raiding party to go over to the correspondent's tent and 'do him in', as he put it. The Irishman was so widely hated, Pierce maintained, that the list of suspects would be hundreds strong. Nunn was quite sickened that this dishonourable notion could even enter the head of a major of Her Majesty's Infantry. Their civilian visitor was plainly a little taken aback as well.

Boyce seemed inclined towards tolerance, both of newspaper correspondents and violently minded majors. 'The *Courier*, Mr Norton, is nothing more than an organ of splenetic radicalism, to be avoided and distained by all people of intelligence. I feel that it is hardly shaming for me to be slandered in its pages – quite the contrary, in fact.'

He turned to Pierce. 'So for now, Major Pierce will bloody well let him be.'

There was a burst of well-oiled laughter from the company; Pierce protested that he had only spoken in jest. Lieutenant Nunn gripped the delicate hexagonal stem of his wine glass, pinching it until his thumb was white.

Looking around at the smiling, obedient faces, Boyce's eye snagged on his adjutant, sitting still and mute like a large, rather unambitious piece of statuary. As a parting shot, that insubordinate knave Maynard had contaminated this steadfast, dim-witted fellow with something of his own suspicious nature. Boyce had tried to reassure him, to steady him with routine, but to no avail. Although it was unlikely that he would ever deduce anything important, Nunn still knew a little too much for comfort. He remained a fighting soldier under Boyce's direct command, however. Perilous assaults would doubtlessly be made in the coming months, as the Allies resumed their efforts to take Sebastopol. Perhaps, at an appropriate moment, Lieutenant Nunn should be given a special front-line assignment.

'Excuse me, Colonel,' piped up their Mancunian guest, 'but I am right in thinking that your young wife is a nurse of some description?'

The plebeian fool was confused by my sarcasm when she came in, Boyce thought. 'She brings food and clothing up from the harbour, Mr Norton, in the company of another lady, a respectable Scottish spinster. They are held in great regard throughout the camp – and even by Lord Raglan himself. Do not be confused by my . . . frivolous manner towards her. Madeleine does valuable work, and she won't hear any talk of her returning home before the last sword is back in its scabbard.'

Boyce was determined that his wife should stay in the Crimea for as long as he was made to. He saw how she suffered, the daily hardships she endured, and it brought him a bitter satisfaction. She had wanted to be near her Irishman – well, she was near him. And may it bring them both all the damned happiness in the world.

Norton was clearly impressed. 'An admirable lady indeed.'

The Colonel nodded in acknowledgement. He was well pleased with this fellow. After many anxious weeks, a solution might finally have been found.

On the evening of Inkerman, after having his injured shoulder seen to, Boyce had gone to inform his accomplices of the success of their plan – only to learn that both had been killed in the morning's fighting whilst attempting to coordinate a British counter-barrage, driven from this world by a spray of Russian shell-splinters. He had been shocked, of course, and a little grieved to hear of the end of a pair of such fine fellows; but behind these muddled thoughts had sounded a clear note of triumph. It is mine, he had told himself, and mine alone.

Then that Irish pig had made his move. Boyce had been most angry with Wray. The Captain's orders had been to kill the two Russians, to prevent them from ever revealing who had removed the Tsar's treasure cache. However, Wray had somehow managed not only to shoot a British soldier as well, but also to be seen doing it by a pair of bloody *newspapermen*! They had nothing at all to substantiate their claims, thankfully, after Wray had quietly disposed of that second corporal whilst on night watch at the Left Attack. Major-General Codrington, a proper gentleman, had not stood for the Irishman's offensive posturing, and the *Courier* rogues had been soundly humiliated.

It had been a heavily qualified victory. Afterwards, to be safe, Boyce was forced to send Wray from the Crimea. And the painting itself, a rare and genuine Raphael for which the wealthiest Dukes and Lords in England would give half of all they owned, became a grave problem. Wray had at least thought to pack the *Pilate* away in an empty supply crate before bringing it into the camp; and there it remained two and a half months later, in a dark, dry corner of the farmhouse's apple cellar. But should the Major-General or any of his staff – or worse still, those scoundrels from the *Courier* – discover that he still had this masterpiece in his possession, the situation could become very black indeed.

Now, though, an escape route was surely opening. Boyce

had been monitoring the lists of civilians coming into Balaclava carefully, obtaining accounts of their proposed business on the peninsula from the harbourmaster. Charles Norton, a foundry man in the Crimea on behalf of another company, had stood out. This arrangement seemed to suggest that he was an inferior specimen, of the exact sort required; and sure enough, the fellow had just the right mix of greed and weakness. Norton was someone Boyce could work into a corner and keep there.

The Colonel stood, and suggested casually to his guest that they go outside to take the evening air before dinner was served. There was a moment of vaguely awkward silence as the Mancunian got to his feet and made his way over to the door; then the ever-vocal Pierce started off again, now lambasting the idleness of the Turks.

The yard at the back of the farmhouse was empty and extremely cold. Both men lit cigars. Norton's hand trembled, and not from the temperature – he was apprehensive.

Boyce adopted a steely, business-like tone. 'Here's the meat of it, Norton. Wyndham, the Quartermaster-General, is an old friend of my family. I am prepared to mention to him that I know of a foundry man from Manchester who will undercut the existing contract for railway spikes by half a penny per dozen – a foundry man who can keep up a regular supply of rapidly produced, low-grade components. He will be open to such an idea, I guarantee it. This is within your capabilities, is it not?'

Norton tried unsuccessfully to mask his excitement at what was being proposed. 'We are talking about a very big contract here, Colonel.'

Boyce puffed on his cigar. 'Enough to free you from the likes of the Fairbairns for good, I'd say – to raise your concern to the first rank of Manchester business. The kind of opportunity that is gifted only to a few. You will have to act quickly, though. The Quartermaster-General is not a particularly patient man, and speed of production is paramount. Can you do it?'

Norton was silent for a moment, as if running calculations in his head. Then he nodded. 'I can, sir.'

'I will want an interest, of course – a silent partnership. If this contract is fulfilled satisfactorily, there will be others. The army needs a great many cast-iron items, Mr Norton.'

Norton nodded once more, lost in his dreams of a golden future. At this moment, the Colonel thought, he'll agree to absolutely anything.

'And there is something else I would need you to do for me.' Boyce glanced across the yard towards the doors of the apple cellar. 'Something rather delicate.'

6

'You are a killer.'

Styles woke up, pulled abruptly from scrambled, blaring dreams of black caves and blood – of somebody talking urgently. He looked around in alarm for the person who had spoken. All was still and dark. The voice had sounded uncannily like his mother's; but she had been dead now for almost six years.

He tried to sit up, but his leg would not be moved. His mouth was dry and his head throbbed, but his thoughts were oddly clear. Slowly, he remembered certain events from the day just passed – the struggle in the trench, the sniper's shot, the impossibly long wait for assistance – but large sections remained lost to him. He could not say where he was, for instance, or how he had got there. The heavy blue murk was that of a tent in the middle of the night, yet he was enclosed in a narrow, dry-stone alcove. There was a smell of old boots and stale tobacco.

The close silence was broken by the sound of tent flaps being pushed hurriedly aside. Then he heard Cracknell's voice, no more than ten yards from where he lay.

'By Jove, it's dark as hell in here,' the senior correspondent grumbled. 'Where's my matches?'

There was a second's pause. Styles could hear breathing. A match was struck, and warm light filled the space outside his alcove. There was a thick canvas curtain between him and this light; but a half-inch gap at the curtain's side became a bright line through which he could clearly observe what was happening beyond.

Cracknell and Mrs Boyce stood by a desk, both wrapped up tightly in their winter clothing, their breath forming clouds in front of them. The senior correspondent threw a small sack of biscuit and a yellow slab of Dutch cheese on to the desk. As soon as his hands were free, Mrs Boyce was on him, kissing him all over his grimy face, pressing herself hard against him. Cracknell pushed her back firmly.

'Both were injured, you say?' he demanded.

She nodded, reluctantly delaying her attentions. 'Yes, both. We – we took them to the harbour. Mr Kitson is quite badly hurt, I think.'

'Good Lord,' Cracknell murmured in mild amazement, 'I must have been standing within a hundred yards of the poor devils. Ah well, Balaclava is an easy place indeed in which to miss people, especially if you're not looking for them. They'll be sent home now, at least. Neither one of them was cut out for war correspondence.'

Mrs Boyce began to cry. 'I was so frightened, Richard, that you might have been with them – might have been lying *dead* . . .'

He wrapped her up in the arms of his fur coat. 'Come now, Maddy,' he said, his manner softening, 'I was perfectly safe. I was here, in fact, asleep in my tent, whilst those young fools were out playing soldiers. You should not run off from Miss Wade, though. You could have been in a serious pickle if that dragoon hadn't found you and escorted you back up to the camps.'

She looked up at him with wide, disbelieving eyes. 'You – you saw us?'

Cracknell chuckled condescendingly. 'I did, on the outskirts of town. I was heading in the other way. I would've said something, Maddy, but I know the fellow. He'd have been over to tell your husband in a flash.' He paused. 'Besides, I had something to attend to.'

'How could you *see me*, Richard, and not even—'

'Madeleine, we must exercise a bit of care. Your husband is merely waiting for an excuse to strike at me. You know this. And I am here now, am I not? We have this tent quite to ourselves.'

She was easily won round. They kissed for a long time. Styles heard their lips gently sucking together. Before long, he could see that the fronts of both their coats were open, the sides overlapping, their bodies meeting in the space in between, their hands pulling at the clothes beneath. Their breathing became yet heavier. Mrs Boyce giggled, and said something about the cold; a moment later, Cracknell ducked away, igniting a small charcoal stove on the floor. He went back to her immediately, and Styles noticed the edge of her skirts rise up under the bottom of her coat. They then moved towards another alcove, close to the desk, and sunk into it.

The illustrator, staying silent in the shadows, found that he could watch all of this without any sense of consternation, jealousy or anger. He felt strangely removed, as if he were not a thinking, feeling person but merely an object, an inanimate witness. Reaching into the pocket of his coat, he took out his sketch-book and pencil.

'Richard,' she asked, from deep inside the alcove, 'what do I mean to you?'

There was a short pause as Cracknell fiddled with an obscure fastening. 'You mean more to me, my tender little Frenchie, than all the brandy in the world. Than all the cigars in the world.'

'What of the other women – of the other women you have known?'

'You are the finest by far. The most beautiful, the most exquisite – a rare treasure so precious that naught can equal it.' There was a faint, almost indiscernible note of weariness in Cracknell's voice as he said this. 'You would be my choice of all the women in creation.'

Styles could now see Mrs Boyce, half-naked, reclined on Cracknell's cot. Her shoulder, breast and thigh formed a rhythmic, curving pattern, which his pencil quickly traced out in the strip of candlelight that fell across the page of his sketch-book. Drawing her, even in this extraordinary, unseen state, seemed immediately familiar to him. It was as if his hand remembered the dozens of depictions it had made on the decks of the *Arthur* so many months before, and created a rapid, faithful likeness of a well-loved subject. The high, wide cheekbones, the skin over them lightly flushed with arousal; the large, dark eyes misted with love; the full lips curling with gratified amusement at Cracknell's sweeping declarations – all were captured in a flurry of economic strokes.

Cracknell, who was lying across from her, propped up on an elbow, was a very different prospect. His shoulder hid his face, and was round and pink like a side of bacon, heavily shaded with thick black hairs. Despite the privations of the campaign, something of a round belly could still be seen; and there, before Styles' dispassionate gaze, his member sprang into view, suddenly released from his trousers. It was an angry, tumescent red, like a raw root, strangely incongruous with the rest of the man, as if a swollen appendage from a quite different creature had been unaccountably attached to his burly frame. The pencil worked away busily.

Slowly, Mrs Boyce reached over and took it in her hand. 'What would you do, Richard, to be with me?'

'I – I would give up all that I am,' answered Cracknell with a slight tremor. 'I would turn in my post at the *Courier* in an instant, I would sell everything but the clothes on my back, I would sail any distance. Without you, dearest Maddy, life is but ashes.'

This speech finished, his hands vanished under what remained of her skirts. She moaned his name, pulling him towards her. There was a brief struggle, and a couple of oaths, and then her petticoats came away, revealing her nakedness. Cracknell cast the garments aside, and moved in over her, their feet, both still in their boots, scrabbling and bumping together as they positioned themselves.

'Will you ever leave me?' she gasped.

'Never.'

Styles turned over a page in his sketch-book and began another drawing.

7

Charles Norton made some enquiries, and then headed over briskly to a miserable-looking lodging house close to the quay. Once again, the stench of Balaclava was quite unbelievable; he put a handkerchief up to his face in a vain attempt to block it.

Someone called his name before he could enter. James was sitting on a wall at the side of the building. He was pale, his coat drawn tightly around him as he coughed into his hand. The lines at either side of his mouth were more pronounced, and the eyes behind his spectacles, although red with exhaustion, were strangely bright.

'What are you doing out here, Anthony?'

James coughed again, phlegm rattling in his throat. 'Believe me, Charles,' he whispered, 'it is preferable to being inside.'

Speaking quickly, Norton apologised for leaving him; and then, unable to contain his glee, said that he had brokered a deal the previous evening that would change everything for them. This awful war, Charles declared, was going to give them the chance they had prayed for. He took a sheaf of papers from his pocket and waved them in his son-in-law's face – urgent telegrams that had to be wired back to Manchester as soon as possible.

James, however, was not impressed. 'Who exactly have you been negotiating with, Charles?'

Norton shrugged defensively. 'An officer of infantry, that

is all. A man with an interest in the railway that is being built outside town. A man who has—'

'Colonel Nathaniel Boyce of the 99th Foot. That's right, isn't it?'

Norton didn't deny it. He gave a brief account of the situation regarding the spikes, and Boyce's long association with the Quartermaster-General – which would ensure the success of a bid from the Norton Foundry.

'For someone of high birth, the Colonel has a rare appreciation of business matters.' Norton paused carefully. 'He has already obtained a crate of the spikes currently in use, in fact, for us to examine back at the Foundry, and perhaps utilise as models. His men will be bringing it down from the plateau later today, to be loaded aboard the *Mallory*.'

James shook his head. 'So you have been neglecting the worthy task Mr Fairbairn assigned us to hatch alliances with corrupt soldiers – men prepared to exploit personal connections in order to bypass the normal conditions of contractual competition. Did it not occur to you, Charles, that abuses of privilege such as this might be a part of what has gone so terribly wrong out here?'

I am being judged once more, Norton thought, irritation souring his mood. 'I will attend to our errand for Fairbairn in due course, Anthony. Do you not understand what is being proposed here? Do you not understand what is being laid before us?'

But James would not listen. 'I have been speaking with people also, Charles. Yesterday afternoon I met Richard Cracknell, the Crimean correspondent from the *London Courier*. He shared a number of disturbing confidences with me.'

Norton snorted, remembering the officers' conversation in the farmhouse. 'Ah yes, the Irishman from the *Courier*. I have heard all about *him*.'

His son-in-law coughed again, and removed his spectacles so that he could wipe his eyes. 'No, Charles, I seriously doubt that you have. Mr Cracknell had come down to the harbour specifically to warn travellers such as ourselves about Boyce. He said that the Colonel has been trying to recruit men from outside the military for several weeks, to serve his own crooked ends.' He tried to put the spectacles back on his face, and only just managed it without poking himself in the eye. Norton realised that for all his vociferousness, James was desperately weak. 'Your Colonel is guilty of heinous crimes indeed. At Inkerman, he led his regiment to an entirely avoidable disaster through his own incompetence: this is a matter of military record. But he has also engaged in looting, Charles, and has had men killed, his *own men*, to cover up his robberies.' He started to cough. 'There is – is a – a *painting* . . .'

James was prevented from talking any further by a severe cramp, which seized his midriff and bent him over almost double. His spectacles dropped from his nose, chinking against the stones below.

For a moment, Norton stood very still, absorbing what he had heard. James knew about the painting in the crate – knew more than he did, in fact, about the murderous means by which his new partner had supposedly obtained it. His estimation of the deal itself was startlingly accurate as well, tearing away the comfortable net of self-delusion Norton had spun around himself. The truth of Boyce's venture could no longer be denied. It was corrupt – criminal, even.

He looked steadily at James' shivering, shuddering back, and suddenly he knew that his son-in-law was dying; one night in the festering filth of Balaclava was all it had taken for disease to claim him. None of Anthony James' immense ambition or ability would ever amount to anything. His daughter would be made a widow at twenty-eight. And he, Charles Norton, would take the opportunity Colonel Boyce had offered and make himself one of the foremost labour-lords of Manchester.

'A painting? In this place?' He furrowed his brow with good-humoured scepticism. 'What utter nonsense. That Irishman is an unhinged troublemaker, nothing more.' He became solicitous. 'You are weary, Anthony; weary and, I fear, a little credulous. Have you had any sleep, or anything to eat? I'm afraid that you might have caught something here, my lad – you need to go to bed. Come, we will find you a clean room. There must be one somewhere. On board one of these ships, if nowhere else.' Norton crouched down and picked up the spectacles. They were smeared with black mud and the left lens was smashed. He gave them back to James, who now had a hand pressed blearily against his brow. 'What would my Jemima say if I brought her husband home an invalid?'

Manchester
June 1857

1

Cregg had been waiting with Stewart on London Road for the better part of the afternoon. They passed a pint of gin between them, trying to keep their eyes on the modest doorway of the Model Lodging House.

This, Cregg knew, was his last chance. He'd seen enough coves go under to know well enough what was happening to him; he just didn't seem to be able to muster the energy to bring a halt to it. His acts against the army, against that bleeder Wray, hadn't brought him any real satisfaction or relief. Some days it even seemed like they had made things worse. His hand, his leg and his face all ached to high buggery, sometimes getting so bad that his insides twisted up and his eyes grew unreliable. There was one answer to all this and one answer only: the bottle.

His recollections of his time in Manchester were accordingly sparse – half-memories of dingy pot-houses and gin palaces, of dark alleys and rank, undrained courts, of squalid two-room houses and crumbling basements, all nestled in the shadows of pounding mills. There had been vomiting, a good deal of vomiting; some joyless fornication with a toothless whore not a day under fifty; and numerous clumsy attempts to position himself on floorboards already covered with coughing bodies.

At some point he had acquired Stewart, a pallid, sly looking Irishman. Cregg was dogged by the sense that Stewart was after something beyond simple companionship. He was a steady drinker, though, and didn't yet seem to be tiring of his new friend's lengthy Crimean stories, tearful eulogies to the Crimean dead, and Crimean songs, sung over and over with sodden earnestness. He said he was an ironmonger by trade, with a specialisation in making spanners – yet he had plainly practised little but self-obliteration for some time.

One morning, quite recently – three or four days ago, he thought – Cregg had woken at dawn in a turd-filled gutter with his mouth full of straw. This in itself was hardly unusual, but as he had sat up and tried to get his bearings, he found that he was also smarting with lost purpose. Before him was a public house called the Hare and Hounds. He could dimly recall entering it for an important meeting with his employer. Whether this had transpired or not he couldn't rightly say. Drink had close-shaved all remembrance of the day from his mind, leaving it utterly bald. He knew, though, in that brief moment of semi-sobriety, that he had duties in the Cottonopolis. He had come there for a reason. There was a proper scheme in place, a scheme for revenge. The nature of this scheme, however, and his role in it, were lost to him completely.

Shaking the worst of the filth from his greatcoat, Cregg had decided that he must see Mr Cracknell, offer his sincerest apologies, and make his best effort to get himself back on track. A few shreds of information clung to his bruised brain, like the scraps of an over-pasted bill left sticking to a wall after an attempt to tear it down. Cregg still knew where Mr Cracknell had based himself; and he swore that once he had drunk his shaking limbs back under his control, and soothed the beast that raged inside his skull, he would go there straight away.

And so there he was – a little late maybe, and not exactly clean, but chock-full of the best will in the world. The un-expected length of their wait was taking its toll, though. A soft impact on Cregg's upper arm told him that Stewart had gone to sleep, and was leaning against his sleeve. The crip-pled veteran lifted up their gin bottle. Only a quarter-inch of the dirty spirit remained. Bringing the bottle close to his disfigured face, he sloshed this liquid from side to side, momentarily transfixed by the tiny bubbles popping at its edges. Then, through the warped glass, he spotted the man he sought, swinging a cane as he walked briskly towards the Model. Dropping the bottle in the gutter, and leaving Stewart to topple on to the pavement, Cregg rushed over to intercept him. Cap in his hand, he made a boozy but heartfelt plea for forgiveness.

Mr Cracknell stopped with some reluctance. 'I cannot use you, Cregg,' was his impatient response. 'You were drunk in the Hare and Hounds, drunk as a bloody lord.' He leant in closer, sniffing, his nose wrinkling slightly. 'And by Jove, you're pretty bloody drunk now. How exactly I am supposed to lay complex plans, and make careful arrangements, with a man who can't stay dry for long enough to bloody well hear 'em? Answer me that!' The correspondent set off again. Six strides took him almost to the door of the lodging house.

Cregg, contrite and servile, scurried along at his side. 'I'll make amends, sir, promise I will. You know me will is strong, sir. What's the scheme, sir? What would you 'ave me do?'

Mr Cracknell turned around, quickly moving in close again, his voice sharp with spite. 'Your will may be strong, Cregg, but your mind is weak indeed. There is no place in my scheme for the weak-minded.'

A familiar feeling crept into Cregg. The situation was sliding beyond his control. Nothing he could say or do now would stop Mr Cracknell from dropping him. It was like all the other positions he'd lost, all the magistrates he'd stood before, all the demotions, humiliations and punishments he'd received in his wretched life. Bitter rage welled up inside him. 'So 'ow am I to get me vengeance, then?' *You fat paddy bastard*, he almost added. ''Ow am I to get Boyce, if you won't 'ave me?'

'Well, the Brigadier appears to be out of town at the minute,' Mr Cracknell replied, stepping up to the door of the Model, 'but my sources tell me that he is due at the Albion Hotel in a couple of days. You left your bayonet in Captain Wray, I understand, but I'll warrant that a fellow like you will have no trouble securing himself another weapon. Why don't you simply go over there and kill him?

325

Stick him one in the gut, perhaps? There, is that a scheme you can take in? You would certainly have your vengeance then, Cregg! Now, begone!'

Mr Cracknell opened the door and walked through grandly, as if the Model Lodging House was the swankiest address in all Manchester. It slammed behind him.

2

'Hello,' said Bill Norton, spying the soot-scarred back of a city cab through a tangle of wisteria. 'What's a growler doing here at this hour?'

His father glanced up from his half-eaten kipper. Promptly dropping his fork on to his plate, he cast aside his napkin and rose from the breakfast table. 'A business associate,' he explained curtly, walking around the back of Bill's chair. 'I will return shortly.'

Bill and Jemima looked at each other. The morning sun shone brightly through the breakfast room's large window, casting slanting shapes across the table between them. It was early still, but these blocks of light already shimmered with rising heat.

'Strange time of day for a Foundry call,' Bill mused. 'And since when did the governor's associates ride around in growlers? Every man-jack of them has at least one private carriage.'

Jemima lowered her eyes. 'You are right. It is strange.' She moved her coffee cup around in its saucer. 'Almost as strange as the readiness with which he agreed to let me go to the Belle Vue this evening.'

It had been a risky proposition – even Bill had seen this. The upsets of the company visit were less than two weeks old. Their father had forbidden Jemima from seeing Mr Kitson again, in the severest terms. And now all of a sudden she was requesting permission to accompany her brother and his friend Alfred Keane to the Belle Vue, Manchester's largest pleasure garden – a place she had not visited, and shown no desire to visit, since before her marriage. It would hardly have been a great piece of deduction for their father to realise that Mr Kitson had been contacted and would be meeting her there.

But Jemima had been determined to try. She said that she had to see Mr Kitson as a matter of urgency. This was not merely lover's hyperbole. Since the company visit she had been stuck fast in a quiet, bitter anger, which was far more significant than the impatient ire that formed a daily part of her character. It was an anger of rumination, and of ominous conclusions; Bill had thought about asking its precise cause, but swiftly decided that he didn't really want to know. Best to leave it to Mr Kitson.

'I take it that you are suspicious of his leniency.'

Jemima stared at him in disbelief. 'William, are you *not*?'

'Come now, Jem, what sinister motive could there possibly be? The governor has no inkling of our, ah,' here Bill paused, blushing a little, 'of our true pursuits once we are clear of these walls. Perhaps he simply wants peace.'

'I would put nothing past Father, and neither should you.' She got up. 'We must remain very much on our guard.'

Bill sighed, pushing away the remains of his plate of buttered toast. 'Very well, Jemima. As you say.'

He followed his sister out in to the velvet gloom of the hall. There was a faint smell of dried lavender and wood polish. The door to their father's study was firmly closed. Jemima went towards the wide staircase, heading up to her rooms. After a second's reflection, the heir to the Norton Foundry turned on his heel and strode down towards the hall's opposite end with sudden purpose. The sonorous tick-tocking of a dark grandfather clock seemed to echo his steps as he walked past.

Bill swept into a reception room, his silk dressing gown billowing around him, intending to throw open its patio doors, go out on to the lawn and feel the morning sun on his face. He shed his shoes and stockings before leaving the house. The grass was still damp with the last droplets of dew, but had a wonderful warmth and softness, sinking under his bare white toes like a quilt. For a moment, as the sun's rays hit him, his entire world dissolved in fiery brightness. Shading his eyes with his hand, he looked down to the willow lake at the lawn's end. His favourite gardener was at work among the bulrushes, already in his shirt-sleeves, his bronzed arms rippling as he dragged some driftwood to the shore.

He was filled with anticipation, excitement almost, about the evening ahead. Things had not been going so well of late for Freddie Keane and himself. Bill reckoned that their fathers had been plotting together; concerted moves were certainly being made to press both young men into their respective family firms. This was an anathema to Bill, but he was far better equipped to fight against it than his friend. Keane simply did not have the strength of spirit to weather such assaults and was allowing them to preoccupy him utterly. He was unable to think or talk of anything but his father's business plans. Although his knowledge of the details was scant, he remembered enough of what had been said to be able to predict the end of his life, properly speaking, and the commencement of an unbearable waking death.

But Bill was not inclined to worry about this. A good deal more than Keane's pouts were required to spoil the prospect of the Belle Vue on a summer's evening. They had not been there in some months. It was an easy place to move in, and an easy place indeed to meet like-minded acquaintances. After nightfall, away from the pavilion and the dancing boards, there were a great many secluded corners where sport could be had without fear of interruption.

Bill found that he looked forward to the more conventional pleasures of the place as well; to the rare sights, the drinks, and the dancing. Keane would be distracted, for a few hours at least, and Jemima would forget her anger and her misgivings completely once she was reunited with her street philosopher. Bill was quite certain of this. This little trip was exactly what was needed for all three of them.

He looked back at Norton Hall. Its western side was a slab of blue shadow, the dark windows seeming to contain a vast quantity of filthy water, as if the house was nothing but an enormous brick rain tank. Bill imagined smashing one on the ground floor, releasing a bursting cascade out on to the lawn, and watching the level drop in all the windows around it. This notion was in his mind so strongly he actually had to stop himself from stooping down and plucking a stone from a path that bordered the grass.

As he was gazing at this window, a sallow face floated to its surface – a square face, with a narrow mouth and round, black eyes. It was one of his father's hired men, the leader in fact; Bill recognised him from the company outing to the Exhibition. For a long moment, they contemplated one another. Then the hired man turned away.

'He beat you, Mr Twelves. Evaded you; gave you the slip. That's the rub, is it not?'

Twelves adjusted his hold on his stew-pan hat. His expressionless manner did not leave him, but Norton could tell that he was profoundly annoyed. The man's natural arrogance had been undermined by unequivocal failure. Charles found that he was rather enjoying himself, but was glad that the solid mass of his desk was between him and the black-suited investigator.

'God knows, it was a simple enough task. One would think that a man with your reputation would be able to do such a thing with ease.'

Twelves fixed him with a dispassionate stare. 'My employees let me down, Mr Norton. Ye know what that's like. I saw yours in the Exhibition, streaming out of those halls like the Jews after Moses, with nary a thought for the coin it'd cost you.'

Charles shifted uncomfortably in his chair. He did not like to think of the Foundry visit, and it pained him to recollect that this unsavoury fellow had witnessed it all.

'Most of 'em what go 'ave been reacting the same way, if it's any consolation. Pearls before swine, Mr Norton.' Twelves' mouth twitched into the very slightest of sneers. 'Down my way, they complain that working people can't afford to attend the Exhibition. But they can afford the

American Circus at Ordsall, for the same money. I don't see any going thirsty either, if ye follow my meaning.'

Norton sat forward. Twelves was managing to turn their discourse away from his own shortcomings. 'You have not been able to find him since, have you?'

The investigator remained outwardly unperturbed. 'Ishmaels like Richard Cracknell are usually pretty good at hiding themselves away. He'll appear again soon enough.'

'That may be so, but a chance has appeared for you to redeem yourself before then.' Norton cleared his throat. 'My daughter came to me this morning requesting that she be allowed to go to the Belle Vue Gardens tonight. In the company of my son and his friend Alfred Keane.'

'So the son is involved as well as the daughter.'

The brute was striking back at him now, striking back with an expert touch. 'It would seem so.'

Without altering his tone or his features in the slightest, Twelves managed to radiate malicious satisfaction. 'That is awful, Mr Norton. Both your offspring, your own flesh, as perfidious as Caesar Borgia. My sympathies.'

Norton tried to ignore him. 'My daughter obviously intends to meet with Kitson in the gardens somewhere. I think we can safely assume that Cracknell will be present as well. They will be attempting to draw her into their despicable schemes once more.'

Twelves' eyes were wandering coldly over the bookshelves behind Charles's desk. 'And what d'ye want us to do?'

The labour-lord put a hand to his brow. 'Watch them congregate. Ascertain the extent of my son's involvement. Wait until they are all together.' He spoke slowly and deliberately, choosing his words with care. 'Then you are to act. I want you to do to Cracknell what you were supposed to last time.'

Twelves had taken out his notebook. 'Only that? Surely more is warranted now, Mr Norton?' He plainly wanted revenge on the man who had embarrassed him.

Charles looked out at the dense, layered canopy of a cedar of Lebanon, and the gravel driveway that snaked beneath it. 'Do what I ask, Mr Twelves, and nothing more. Incapacitate him. That is all that is necessary.'

The investigator was not pleased. He wrote something down. 'And what of the other one – the street philosopher? The same?'

Briefly, Norton thought of that day in the Exhibition – of the protests of Kitson and his daughter, and the obvious regard she held him in. All of it had seemed genuine. He was certain, however, that it was merely another manipulation, part of the grand scheme that these two demons were orchestrating against him. He nodded. 'Afterwards, I want you to bring both my children back here. I will talk to them immediately.'

Norton smoothed his whiskers, setting his mouth in a hard line. This had to be done. The depths of their treachery had to be exposed once and for all. And it would cause such shame, such utter disgrace to be brought upon the pair of them that he would henceforth be entirely justified in exerting the full force of his will. His son would make a bonfire of his dandy clothes, and enter the Foundry before the month was out; and his daughter, swathed in ignominy yet again, would be sent away from Manchester for good. No other option remained. Jemima had an aged spinster aunt in Newcastle, her late mother's elder sister, who was famous for both the dull confines of her life and the bilious spirits which she inflicted on all who entered them. If the girl is so determined to be objectionable, he thought, let her kneel at the feet of an authority. She will soon learn something of the true boundaries that can be thrown around difficult women.

'You must succeed, Mr Twelves. My partner returns to town tomorrow, and I do not want him troubled by these degenerates.'

The investigator tucked away his book. 'I will take charge personally, Mr Norton. All will go smoothly.'

'Very well.' Norton stood, straightening his jacket. 'It is high time we ended this foolishness once and for all.'

3

The clap-board admissions hut was painted an unpromising shade of light blue, and covered with tawdry posters advertising the attractions of the gardens beyond, from stunning fireworks displays to evenings of Highland dancing. A battered old crone manned the turnstile, grumbling wordlessly at those who passed her. The Tomahawk slapped his sixpence on the plate with a grin, and pushed through into the Belle Vue. It was already seven o'clock. Things had to be got underway.

Reading the *Evening Star* in his cubicle at the Model, Cracknell had gained the distinct sense that Kitson was deliberately trying to aggravate him – to force a confrontation. *A disagreeable side-effect of our Exhibition,* one recent passage had read, *is the sudden rush to Manchester of so many faded celebrities – the spent, forgotten figures of yesteryear. They strut through the galleries at Old Trafford and stroll around the town like so many dull, dusty peacocks, stripped long ago of their best feathers. Their only goal is to be noticed by someone, anyone; it is their great hope, their ardent prayer, their single cherished aspiration. All people of sense and discernment, however, are utterly repelled by the reek of desperation that hangs about them. Their day has passed, their moment has fled – they are no longer of any special worth. Why are these poor wraiths the only ones to whom this perception is denied?*

Cracknell had not known whether to laugh with derision or pity at this feeble abuse. Well, Thomas, he'd thought, casting down the paper with some violence, your wish for a further encounter will soon be granted.

Free of Cregg, Cracknell was really soaring. Once again, he was discovering that he worked best alone. Finding out about this assignation in the Belle Vue, for instance, had been simplicity itself. Among other things, the past month's surveillance had yielded the tavern in which Norton's coachman took his refreshment whilst his master was busy in the Exchange. Wandering in casually, the Tomahawk had engaged the fellow in conversation and bought him a jar or two of ale. He'd proved talkative indeed, as men who sit with horses all day often did; before long Cracknell had extracted a full programme of the Norton family's social engagements for the next fortnight, including the excursion to the pleasure garden that same evening. It was the talk of the servants' parlour, the coachman had imparted with a beery snigger. They were saying that Mrs James had finally realised she was mortal like everyone else, and had to hunt herself down a new husband before it was too late. Cracknell had laughed heartily, certain that he had learned the location of the widow Jemima's next meeting with the street philosopher.

The plan should be kept fairly fluid at this stage, he decided. One of the wonderful things about being a lone operator was the flexibility; minute-by-minute adjustments could be made with ease. First of all, he would locate Kitson and the widow. Twelves and his band of black-suited fools were sure to be nearby. It was then just a matter of working out how best to direct events. A couple of things had to happen. Mrs James had to be told the full extent of her father's crimes – the wicked foundations on which his recent fortune had been constructed. And Twelves had to catch the three of them together, Kitson, Mrs James and the Tomahawk, deep in a conspiratorial-seeming conversation. As a result, Norton would be completely convinced that his daughter was betraying him; and when he came to confront her over it, he would discover that she knew exactly what kind of a man he really was. This was not adequate punishment for Charles Norton, not by a long distance, but it was a damn good start.

It was with mixed feelings, however, that Cracknell walked into the Belle Vue. He had never been a particular admirer of pleasure gardens. They had a prevailing air of safety, of enclosure, from which his very soul recoiled. The Chateau des Fleurs in Paris and the Crermorne in Chelsea both bored him witless. His expectation was that the Manchester version would be an inferior, decidedly grimy copy of these – like every other thing in the damned town.

First sight of the place seemed to confirm this. Tree-lined promenades encircled expansive flowerbeds and gently sloping lawns, dotted with refreshment huts of all descriptions, iron-and-glass greenhouses and aviaries, crude rockeries, pale plasterwork statues and poorly trimmed topiary. At the centre of the gardens was a long oblong lake with a single-jet fountain at either end. Everywhere were gangs of locals, pitched out on the grass with lavish picnics, engaged in noisy games of quoits and small-cricket, gaping and poking at creatures in cages, and splashing around the grey lake in brightly painted rowing boats. The majority were comparatively genteel, in dress if not demeanour; members of Manchester's commercial class, Cracknell concluded, the families of shop-owners, warehouse managers and the like. He had a keen distaste for such people. In his experience, they lacked the attractions of both the bloated, reckless rich and the pleasure-hungry poor, and tended to place prudish barriers of morality and piety in the path of real fun.

He started off into the gardens, swinging his cane, heading down through drifting fronds of willow towards the lakeside. Yellowed bird mess caked the stones beneath his shoes. The splashing of the fountains mingled with the piercing shrieks of children, racing wildly across the lawns. On the other side of the lake, a score of musicians were leaving a large oriental-style pavilion and filing across the open-air dancing boards before it. As Cracknell watched, they took their places on a raised orchestra stand, frosted with ornamental metalwork. Rich single notes and rapid flurried scales drifted across the Belle Vue as they prepared to play, slowly drawing an audience from the surrounding verdure.

'Now where would they be?' he wondered aloud, touching

a flame to the end of a cigarette. 'Where are you, Thomas, you faint-hearted goose?'

Cracknell knew that it was unlikely that Kitson and his lady of the furnaces would be lingering anywhere too public. Keeping his eyes peeled all the while, the Tomahawk thus embarked on a whistle-stop tour of the Belle Vue's zoological exhibits. He studied shabby, disgruntled eagles crouched on boulder-piles with chains fastened around their ankles, like so many feathery convicts. He stopped briefly at a paddock containing some decidedly obstreperous llamas, chortling to himself as they spat at some overcurious children. He spent ten minutes in the monkey house, watching the dolorous beasts within swing listlessly from one side of their gloomy cage to the other. Kitson, however, was nowhere to be seen. Abandoning the animal enclosures, he took a stroll through a couple of the larger greenhouses. Forced to remove his top hat in the sweltering climate, he gazed blankly at a few tubs of leafy, sprouting things, surveyed the decidedly Kitson-less crowd, and made for the exit.

The sun, now starting to set, was largely obscured behind the miasma of smoke and dirt that rose continuously from the city beyond the Belle Vue's walls. The shadows of the gardens had grown so long that they had begun to join, reaching out to one another across paths and lawns as if conspiring to end the day. A team of gas-men was hard at work across the lake, igniting the spherical glass lamps that were mounted on fluted iron pillars around the dancing boards. The orchestra stand was already lit up like a vast Chinese lantern, its reflection shimmering brightly on the water. Several dozen couples moved gently around the boards before it, to the parping strains of a popular tune Cracknell could not identify.

Seeing that evening was setting in, he steamed away towards the rear wall of the gardens, his cigarette puffing like a miniature funnel. Only one more corner of the grounds had to be explored before he could devote his attention to the pavilion and the dancing boards. It had yet to receive the attentions of the gas-men, and was growing a little murky, but there was still ample light by which to see and safely perambulate – and spot those who needed to be spotted. This last remaining area was dominated by a sizeable maze, fashioned from thick privet a good deal taller than Cracknell himself. A fingerpost informed him that at its centre lay the hermit's cave. Sounds of celebration were drifting over from the lake, but all before him seemed still and silent. Flicking away his cigarette, he entered.

It took him but a couple of minutes to fathom the layout of the maze. 'Hardly Daedalian,' he murmured with sly satisfaction. 'No match for the Tomahawk.'

Taking care to stay quiet, he was about to reach the cave at its heart when he heard voices close by, in the outer paths of the maze itself. His first thought was that it must be gasmen, come to light a lamp or two above the hedges. But then they drew closer, and he realised that they were nothing of the sort.

'Honestly, Freddie,' said one, 'you can be such a flat sister at times. These boys are extremely keen to meet you. They're from Bailey's place. Porters from the look of them, but well dressed – and rather muscular, I must say. And thoroughly capable and inventive chaps, by all accounts.'

'By their own account, you mean,' said his companion ill-temperedly. 'You will have to excuse me, Bill, if the thought of squiring some counter-jumpers you've found lurking in the blasted hermit's cave at the blasted Belle Vue Gardens does not have me pissing my britches with glee. Our entire future, if you remember, is cast in deathly shadow.'

A devious grin spread across Cracknell's face. It was none other than William Norton, accompanied by his close friend and partner in unnatural vice, Alfred Keane. During his time in the Cottonopolis, Cracknell had heard a good deal about this pair's doings. They were more famous than they realised among Manchester's lower orders. He withdrew to a dead end, and settled down to listen.

'That may or may not be the case,' Bill replied, 'but if it is, if your very worst predictions should come to pass – God forbid – then should we not be doing this sort of thing as often as we can? Whilst we still have the liberty?'

'Ugh, so relentlessly *optimistic*!' Keane groaned. 'God ain't forbidding anything, William, don't you see that yet?'

'You take my point, though, Freddie?' Bill insisted. '*Carpe diem* and all that?'

They were moving past him. Cracknell fell in a safe distance behind. Over the top of the hedges, in the direction of their voices, a blue and a black top hat could be seen in the gathering darkness, bobbing slowly away towards the cave.

'This debate is entirely pointless,' Keane declared coldly. 'I am here, am I not? Does that not indicate a sufficient measure of willingness, despite what I might say?' He sighed in a long-suffering manner. 'Will your sister not suspect, though – her or that string-bean beau of hers?'

Bill laughed disbelievingly. 'By my soul, is that *envy* in your voice, Freddie? Are you actually *jealous* of the favour our Mr Kitson has found with the delectable Jemima James?'

'Don't be absurd,' snapped Keane, so harshly that it made the denial a little unconvincing. 'Your sister may keep whatever company she chooses. I care not a fig.'

'Very well,' Bill answered slyly. 'I must say, though, that I can understand her interest. There's something about him – not immediately apparent, perhaps, but it's there. A kindness, one might call it, about the eyes . . .'

'But they will not suspect?' interrupted Keane tetchily. 'About our unexplained departure and long absence? That Kitson fellow is on the *Star*, if you recall – a damned *street philosopher*.'

'Oh come, Freddie,' Bill chuckled. 'We left them by the pavilion, with a bottle of Moët and a good view of the boards. They won't even notice that we've gone.' The pair had reached the middle of the maze. 'Now, cease your fretting. Our new friends are just ahead.'

Their footsteps retreated into the distance. The Tomahawk felt like breaking into a jig. This was a singular piece of luck. A solid, hard-hitting scheme for the evening had dropped into his lap all but fully formed. Before leaving for the pavilion, however, he crept towards the centre of the maze, sticking to its darkest corners. Beyond the system of hedges was a small courtyard. The blue top hat, recently discarded, rolled around on its cracked stone slabs. Rising up behind was a low artificial hill, into which had been dug a shallow cave. As he peered inside, Cracknell's wily smirk grew wider.

4

The conductor, clad in immaculate dinner dress, towered over the blazing hub of the dancing boards. Facing the dancers from his place on the orchestra stand, he waved his baton in a sequence of extravagant flourishes, as if marshalling them as well as the musicians. With one commanding sweep, he dismissed those gentlefolk in need of rest or refreshment; and with another, he summoned a fresh contingent from their tables, arranging them neatly upon the floor. The orchestra behind him struck up another waltz. A handful of working people, recently arrived from the mills, their faces washed of grime at the Hyde Road pump, stood at the edge of the boards as if considering joining the dance. An imperious glare from the conductor made them promptly decide that they could use some more ale first, and perhaps a slice of pie.

Surrounding the dancing boards and the pavilion were over a hundred circular tables, each with a small candle flickering in its centre. Waiters glided expertly between them, taking orders and delivering trays laden with bottles and plates. A mixed clientele sat at these tables, but all were alive with chatter, and engaged in careful scrutiny of those around them. Well-to-do parents fed their dazed offspring iced biscuits and Eccles cakes whilst they waited for the fireworks to start, smiling cheerfully but alert for the approach of any manner of miscreant. Parties of top-hatted men laughed uproariously, calling for more champagne, constantly on the lookout for female companionship of any character. Swells and jades, resplendent in borrowed finery, sipped cadged drinks and scanned for marks. And the factory operatives, massing on the lawns in between the dancing boards and the Belle Vue's outer wall, watched the waltz as if it was the gardens' most spectacular exhibit, whistling and whooping at their favourite couples. Scorning the waiters, these parties sent their younger members on missions for bottles of beer, unwrapped parcels of provisions, and settled down to enjoy their evening.

Thomas Kitson and Jemima James went over to a table at the fringes of the crowd, away from the noise of the dancing. Kitson's eyes were raking through the merriment all around them, trying to locate black-suited men.

Mrs James had written to him two days after the company visit. The letter had stated her continued confidence in their friendship, in simple, forceful language – words he had read many times over in his attic on Princess Street – and it had requested this meeting. This had surprised him. He had assumed that the best course for them to follow after the clash in Saloon F was to wait until after the Queen's visit, and Cracknell's departure from Manchester, before cautiously renewing their correspondence. The risk to them both at this time was surely great, yet he could not refuse her; and he had known that there must be a very good reason for her to make this reckless proposition.

She appeared not to have slept properly for some time, and was animated with anxiety. As soon as they sat, she began to talk; her voice, usually so elegant and even, slipped on her words like shoes rushing in panic over wet cobblestones. Her eyes remained fixed on the rust-spotted table-top.

'Mr Kitson, when we stood before Raphael's *Pilate* in the Exhibition, I was struck by a sense that I knew the painting somehow. In the – the furore that followed I had no opportunity to consider this further, but once I was at home it began to trouble me, very deeply.' She paused for a single second. 'I managed to recall where I had seen it before.'

A waiter set the bottle of champagne Bill Norton had

ordered in the centre of the table, and placed a glass before each of them. Kitson leant forward a little, studying Mrs James closely. She seemed near to tears..

'It was in the March of 1855. My father had just returned from the Crimea and informed me of my husband's death. Anthony was a gifted man, a – a brilliant man. His loss was difficult indeed for me to bear. We had only been married a year.' She swallowed, and took a deep breath. 'I was deep in grief, and could not rest. My doctor gave me a sleeping draught, a strong concoction of his own devising. I slept soundly, and felt asleep even whilst I was awake. I was in my father's old house in Lower Broughton – they would not let me stay in my marital house alone. Very early one morning, I came downstairs. Dear God, I had forgotten this entirely before that day in the Exhibition. I'm not sure that I knew exactly where I was.' Mrs James raised a hand to her face, pressing her fingertips against her brow. She closed her eyes. 'It was there, in the drawing room. That panel.'

Kitson stared at her. 'The *Pilate*? Are you sure?'

She frowned. 'Almost. It is difficult . . . I remember standing transfixed; and crouching on the floor, after a while. It seemed so unreal. I was found by the chambermaid and put back to bed with another dose of my sleeping draught. Some days later, I mentioned it to my father. He was dismissive, saying that it was just something he had picked up in Italy on his return journey with the intention of making a profit on a quick resale. I was a little taken aback that he had made such a detour whilst bearing news of my husband's death, but otherwise thought no more of it. The painting itself had already gone.' She lowered her hand and looked up at him. 'This is the connection, though, is it not? This is why Cracknell so despises my father?'

Kitson sat back heavily in his chair and glanced out at the looping line of bright orange dots that ran around the edge of the lake. So this was how the panel had been removed from the Crimea. Some kind of a pact had been made between Norton and Boyce. Kitson had devoted much of the previous week to hunting down Cracknell, in order to discover both what he knew and what he was planning, but without success. Now his former senior's antipathy towards Charles Norton had been at least partly explained.

He turned back to Mrs James. Despite the declarations of her letter, there was an uncomfortable tension building between them. She clearly could not help thinking that he had been concealing things from her. Kitson saw that only the truth would dispel this mistrust. So, as the waltz over on the dancing boards became a polka and then a foxtrot, he told of how he had come to be in the Crimea under Cracknell's leadership; and how the events on the morning of Inkerman had brought them to the villa that held the *Pilate*.

'It was from this secluded place that Boyce's men stole it,' he concluded. 'And afterwards, it seemed to vanish completely.'

Mrs James was growing more upset. 'My father's contracts,' she broke in. 'The spikes for the Crimean railway, and the first few batches of buckles. He obtained them through Brigadier Boyce, didn't he? In exchange for shipping his plunder back to Britain?'

'It seems likely.' Kitson hesitated, momentarily unsure of how much to reveal, but quickly deciding that she deserved to know everything. He looked at her steadily and spoke as gently as he could. 'There is more, I'm afraid. Men were killed – murdered at Boyce's behest to cover up his looting. Cracknell and I tried to draw the army's attention to this. We were not heeded.'

She stared back at him in absolute horror. 'But – but my father does not know of these killings, surely? Why would Boyce have told him of them?'

Kitson did not answer. It was his guess that Norton had either been aware of the murders from the start and been prepared to overlook them for his own benefit, or had been informed as soon as he was committed to the arrangement, in order to make him an accessory and thus ensure both his silence and his further cooperation.

Mrs James sat stunned, gazing blankly at the bottle of champagne that stood untouched before them. 'So Richard Cracknell is actually in the right,' she murmured. 'His provocations are wholly justified.'

A great disturbance erupted over by the side of the dancing boards as a table was thrown over and a good deal of glass broken. There were angry shouts and a high-pitched scream; the orchestra faltered, and then shuddered to a halt. All dancing stopped, and many of those at the far-flung tables rose from their seats, craning their necks and standing on their chairs to try to see what was causing the commotion.

Kitson got up. A bloody fight was underway; he could see someone lying on the floor, clutching at his neck, and several others locked in a pitched battle. His assistance was needed. He looked at Mrs James. She remained lost in her troubled reflections.

'I will return,' he said to her. 'As soon as I can.'

She nodded absently; and he started towards the boards, shouldering his way through the gaping crowds.

Although contending with his bad leg, which was now throbbing something rotten, Cregg still managed to stagger out in front, throwing aside a couple of tables and leading Stewart off into one of the gardens' largest unlit areas. They sustained their weaving pace for a few hundred yards, and then collapsed into a rhododendron bush.

'What did ye have to go and do that for, eh?' panted Stewart from amongst the leaves. 'I was enjoying meself, so I was!'

'Cunt was botherin' me,' growled Cregg. 'Did you not see wot 'e did to me leg? Did you not, Stewart?'

'That's our Dan,' his companion sniggered. 'A reg'lar blessing t' the people of Manchester. A friend t' all, aren't ye, Dan?' He laughed on, until Cregg signalled a wish for silence by punching him in the stomach.

After his rejection on Mosley Street, Cregg had drunk himself under for the best part of a week. He had emerged with a solid determination to destroy both Boyce and the bastard Cracknell, who had brought him this far only to abandon him. His liquor-crazed imagination assured him that by watching the *Courier* man as he went about his business, he could easily learn of the details of this precious scheme. It could then be cunningly adjusted so that it both did for

Boyce and blew up in the cocksure correspondent's face – leaving Cregg, the victor, to walk away wearing his satisfaction like a golden crown.

But the bottle impeded Cregg's efforts even to follow Cracknell, let alone outwit him. Catching sight of the newspaper man that afternoon, therefore, as he hailed a cab on Oxford Street, had been something of a turn-up – even more so because Stewart had clearly heard him instruct the driver to take him to the Belle Vue. Once there, however, after walking out to Ardwick and scrambling over a quiet stretch of wall, they had been completely unable to find him. They wandered around the grounds and greenhouses for a gloomy half-hour. Then Stewart, whose purse was somehow full again, suggested that they take refreshment over by the dancing boards. Some cotton-spinner had jostled Cregg, knocking his bad leg, and refused to meet his eye when apologising – and now they were hiding in a rhododendron bush. Bleedin' typical, thought Cregg as he crouched in the damp soil. Lost bleedin' everything but me knack for drawing trouble.

Pulling the brim of his cap low over his eyes, he peered out in the direction from which they had fled. A mob of working people, headed by a crusher with his stick at the ready, was advancing towards them, fanning out through the darkened gardens and muttering in a distinctly menacing manner.

'Stewart!' His companion had dozed off. 'Stewart, come on!'

Cregg didn't wait, but clambered out of the bush and charged off into the night. Someone spotted him, and the cry went up. Stewart, yelling in confusion, rolled from the rhododendron on to the surrounding lawn. He tried to get to his feet, but liquor overwhelmed him and he fell over backwards. Cregg, reaching a stand of trees, looked back. The mob was on Stewart, kicking viciously in the righteous belief that they had got their man. The policeman attempted to restrain them, but his shouts, and even blows from his stick, were being completely ignored. Cregg smiled grimly and headed for the gate.

*　*　*

345

Kitson finished binding the neck of a fallen factory operative. He felt oddly calm, and entirely lucid. After requesting dressings from the onlookers, he had been supplied with a dainty muslin shawl by the operative's weeping sweetheart; blood was already starting to blot through the pale blue fabric. The man shifted, trying to lift his arm, his eyes rolling in panic. Kitson instructed him to be still.

Nothing was happening to him. No awful visions were descending – no dismal delusions taking hold. Glancing up at the dense circle of faces craning in above, which displayed a mixture of concern, horror and morbid fascination, he listened hard, yet could detect no sounds besides the excited chattering of the crowd. Blinking, he returned his attention to the injured man. The operative's heavy, fearful features, his downy beard, all remained resolutely the same, secure from transformation. The circumstances were very like those in Tamper's Yard, where he had unwittingly saved Wray – on the day he had met Mrs James. A wounded man was stretched out before him. Blood coated his hands and was smeared liberally across the boards on which he knelt. Yet this time his perceptions were entirely unaltered.

Kitson stood, shards of glass crunching beneath his boots. Two policemen had arrived at the scene from the direction of Hyde Road; the constables were pushing apart the remaining combatants and helping those with more minor injuries to their feet. Wiping his hands on his jacket, Kitson informed them that the operative, although gravely injured, was out of immediate danger. It was clear enough what had transpired: someone had smashed a beer bottle over the victim's head, and then driven the broken end into his neck. One of the constables began canvassing witnesses for a description of the assailant. He was huge, some said, a giant with tattooed forearms like a sailor. Nay, he was little, countered others, weasly and dirty, a runt of a man. He only had one eye; he had no thumbs; he had a cudgel, or was it a dagger? His hair was uncommonly long; it was short; he wore a top-hat, a pill-box, a bowler. The only thing that united this profusion of accounts was the enthusiasm with which they were delivered.

Then one voice, loud and certain, rose over the clamour. "'E were a southerner – London type. A cripple. His chum, the paddy, called 'im Cregg.'

Kitson recognised the name straight away. Furthermore, he remembered where he had heard it – in the siege-works around Sebastopol. And this Cregg was described as a cripple, like Wray's attacker and the arsonist of the 25th Manchesters. A palpable sense of threat closed around him – Cregg's appearance in Manchester could not be a coincidence. He turned towards the table where he had left Mrs James. She had gone.

A party assembled behind one of the constables, and started out into the gardens with the intention of flushing out the attacker and bringing him to justice. Kitson walked rapidly to the edge of the dancing boards, the people parting before him with the particular deference reserved for healers. He stepped up on to a chair to give himself a better view across the lake. And there, over on its opposite bank, was Mrs James, moving hurriedly between pools of gaslight. A familiar, well-built figure was by her side, dressed in a top hat and dark coat. He had a cane gripped in one hand, and Jemima's forearm in the other. She glanced back, her pale face bathed in orange light; even at that distance, Kitson could see her alarm.

Mr Twelves watched coolly from the pavilion as Kitson of the *Star* plunged from his chair and sprinted off into the night. Twelves had, of course, noticed the abduction of Mrs James by Richard Cracknell. This was unforeseen; the assumption had been that the two men were working together. Nevertheless, they had to be followed. It was time to act.

Making a final entry in his notebook, the investigator gathered his men with a series of curt whistles and gestures. He held them in place for thirty seconds; and then commenced the pursuit.

347

5

'So heroic, ain't he,' Cracknell snorted. 'Stepping forward when he is needed most. So bloody *admirable*.'

They had cleared the lake, leaving the illuminated path and starting out across a lawn. Cracknell was moving fast, all but dragging Jemima along with him. Her exclamations of disbelieving protest were ignored, and her attempts to break his grasp entirely ineffective. It had all happened very quickly. She had been looking down towards the crowds on the dancing boards when a large hand had fastened around her arm and pulled her away as powerfully as if she had been attached to a locomotive. Cracknell had identified himself almost immediately, wishing her good evening before launching into a sarcastic speech about Mr Kitson's medical exertions.

'Yes, our Thomas is a regular Messiah!' Despite the speed at which they were moving, Cracknell seemed able to maintain an almost uninterrupted stream of words. 'I'll wager he's out amongst the many lepers of the Cottonopolis whenever he gets the chance, assuaging all manner of misery. Why, I wouldn't even be much surprised if his very touch healed!'

Jemima lifted her hand to protect her face and bonnet as they went under a tree, passing through a screen of twigs. 'Mr Cracknell, I—'

'It is the ideal place for such activity, I suppose,' her abductor went on. 'After all, the one thing this city has in abundance is its slums. Such filth, such abject despair! I thought I'd seen the worst this world had to offer out in the Crimea, Mrs James, but oh no! This city of yours has been a real bloody education.'

'What is your purpose?' Jemima managed to say. She tried again to shake herself free; he drew her closer to him and quickened his pace yet further. 'Where are you taking me?'

Cracknell behaved as if she had not spoken, pressing on towards the outer boundary of the Belle Vue. Soon they were amongst the animal cages, which now stood still and empty, the beasts having been locked away for the night. He paused by one, looking back towards the lake. Jemima peered over his thick shoulder. Mr Kitson could just be seen, a tiny figure on the gas-lit path, making after them. She did not have the breath to call out to him. Cracknell set off again. It was clear that some manner of snare was being set.

'Mr Cracknell, if you will not tell me why—'

'And I must say that your pleasure garden is not very impressive either, Mrs James,' Cracknell continued, in the same disapproving tone. 'Now I am no frequenter of the Crermorne, but at least there one can expect to see such things as French actresses dressed as the maiden Europa, making daring balloon ascents on the back of white oxen. Yet what wonders does this miserable place have to offer?' He gestured contemptuously at the cages. 'Parrots, monkeys and rowing boats!'

They reached the maze. Jemima, recovering a little from her forced dash across the gardens, realised that they were going to enter. She wracked her memory. All that was inside was a hermit's cave. Why on earth would he want to take her there? Cracknell stopped talking for a moment, a pensive finger raised, clearly trying to recall the path through.

She decided to try a different tack. 'My father is in league with Boyce, isn't he? He smuggled that panel back to England in exchange for contracts with the army.'

He looked at her, his face in shadow. 'So you have worked out that much, have you? I'm impressed, Mrs James, truly I am.' There was amusement in his voice. 'It is a strange pairing, your father and Boyce – like watching a dog trying

349

to play with a cat. But then, avarice glues together many uneasy alliances, don't it?'

Jemima didn't know what to say. She felt bitterly, savagely ashamed.

Cracknell started into the maze, pulling her to his side. 'I met your husband, you know, on the quay at Balaclava. He struck me as a decent, trustworthy sort, so I told him a few things about Boyce – who was nosing around in search of a greedy fool to exploit. Unfortunately, whilst we were talking, he found your father.' Although retaining its energy, his voice had dropped to little more than a whisper. They turned left, paced down an avenue, and then turned right. 'A few days later, I discovered that he had fallen victim to cholera on his very first night, whilst your father was making himself comfortable in Boyce's rather well-appointed farmhouse. One might argue, Mrs James, that Charles Norton abandoned your Anthony to the plagues of Balaclava, and that this neglect contributed to his death.'

This was one revelation too many for Jemima. In her blacker moments, she had wondered why it had been the younger, healthier man who had succumbed, if both were residing in the same place, whilst her father escaped completely. Even in the most violent throes of her grief, however, she had always been able to reason with herself, to state firmly that her suspicions were absurd and irrational, that there was a random element to contagion that could not be predicted or prevented. Now Richard Cracknell, who had been there and had spoken with Anthony mere days before he had died, was suggesting otherwise. She tried to draw in a breath; her body juddered painfully, and hot tears blurred her sight.

They emerged before the cave. Cracknell, all his hurry gone, released her arm. 'Your father richly deserves his punishment,' he whispered, before moving away towards the cave mouth.

Gasping, Jemima wiped her burning eyes on a corner of her shawl. Ahead, in the darkness, she could just discern the semi-clad bodies, and their rhythmic, urgent movements; she could hear groans, and the tight slaps of connecting flesh.

Cracknell was now leaning against the entrance to the cave, his hands in his pockets, waiting patiently. On the stones between them lay her brother's blue hat.

Jemima knew at once that Bill was in the cave. Was it to be blackmail? Was Cracknell going to hold this over her brother, over *her*, and thus direct them in any manner he pleased?

Somewhere behind her, Mr Kitson's boots thudded on the dirt floor of the maze. He did not share Cracknell's familiarity with the layout, however, and changed course several times, his feet skidding in the dust. He emerged, breathless, coming to an abrupt halt. His gaze went first to Jemima, his relief at finding her safe immediately fading at the sight of the anguish on her face. Then he looked at Cracknell, his brow creasing with fury.

Several of those inside the cave had heard the street philosopher's approach. There was a low hiss of warning, and seconds later three young working men ran out, refastening their clothing. They were plainly accustomed to such rapid flight, and kept their heads down to avoid recognition as they slipped around the back of the cave.

With a start, Jemima realised that a group of her father's hired men, the black-suits from Saloon F, had emerged silently from the maze. At their head was the square-faced giant who had dragged Mr Kitson out of the Exhibition – Mr Twelves. His features were impassive, and his heavy hands crossed in front of him.

'Hold them,' he ordered.

But before his men could act, there was a series of popping sounds from the direction of the lake, followed by a drawn-out whistle, decreasing steadily in pitch as if something was soaring up into the sky and then beginning a slow descent. Jemima looked towards this noise; there was a flash up in the night sky. The evening's fireworks display had begun early, in an effort to restore something of a festive atmosphere after the incident on the dancing boards. A blue rocket burst above the elm trees that fringed the maze, filling the small courtyard before the cave with coloured light. As the cloud of bright blue embers drifted

351

to earth, this light moved with them, causing the shadows to shift and lengthen. For a moment, a long blue finger extended into the depths of the hermit's cave, pointing out those who remained within.

Bill was pressed into one of the deepest corners, up close against another man. Both were naked below the waist, their trousers around their ankles. They had been too involved in their coupling to pay attention to their fleeing fellows. The blue light made them pause, however, and they glanced around in furtive alarm. Bill's eyes went straight to those of Mr Twelves, locking in recognition.

The group that Cracknell had assembled around the artificial cave exploded like a shell, flinging its parts throughout the Belle Vue Gardens. Disengaging himself and frantically pulling up his trousers, Bill Norton shot from the cave. Knocking Twelves aside, he crashed off into the maze, forcing his way through the bushes. His friend Keane was close behind. More men ran out from the shadows; Norton's black-suits gave chase, forgetting their mission, throwing punches and shouting obscenities as they did so. Kitson looked around quickly for Cracknell, but he was gone, his work complete.

Mrs James had immediately started after Bill Norton and Keane, calling out her brother's name, but had no hope of matching their speed in her crinoline. Kitson caught up with her in a small grove close to the greenhouses. Suddenly seeing the futility of her pursuit, she came to a halt.

'We are ruined,' she said flatly. 'Those men will tell everyone, the entire city. You heard their curses, didn't you, Mr Kitson – their disgust? It will be a terrible scandal.' She sunk to the ground, the crinoline's whalebone hoops jutting up awkwardly beneath the velvet of her dress.

'All is not lost, Mrs James. I will help you however I can.'

There was a loud crackle from the direction of the lake, followed by a rasping fizz; through a screen of branches, Kitson saw the luminescent reds and golds of the fireworks display glittering across the glass roofs of the greenhouses.

Mrs James gave no sign of having heard him. She held her face in her hands. 'Oh, poor Bill! All because of my father and his wicked secrets!' A sob shook her shoulders. 'And my husband – dear God, my *husband*. The old wretch did not tell me any of it, *damn him*.' She lowered her hands; tears were shining on her palms. 'What is your connection with all this?' she asked, without turning towards him. 'Did *you* meet Anthony out there as well?'

Kitson hesitated. 'I don't understand.'

'It appears that Richard Cracknell met my husband in Balaclava and told him all about that accursed *Pilate*. Were you not there too, Mr Kitson? And are you his accomplice still, in fact? Was not all of this, including our friendship, just a part of your plan to strike my father down?'

He went to her side, kneeling as quickly as his sore ribs would allow, and took her damp hands in his. 'It was not, I swear it,' he said firmly. 'I did not meet your husband or your father in the Crimea. I am your *friend*. I knew nothing of Cracknell's intentions this evening, and would have done anything to halt him. We parted on the very worst terms. Some – some truly dreadful things were done. It was my avowed intention never to see him again.'

At this, her eyes finally looked back into his; he knew immediately that she believed him. 'But why? What happened?'

Kitson released her hands. The night seemed to grow darker, and the sounds of the fireworks more sharp and violent; but already, before even uttering a word, he tasted an overwhelming relief, as if a pent-up confession was finally beginning. Sitting down beside her, he took off his hat and dropped it into the grass.

'I will tell you.'

Before Sebastopol,
Crimean Peninsula
June 1855

1

Looping his arm under the Russian's knees, Cregg braced himself and tugged hard. Nothing happened – the man remained firmly lodged beneath the gun carriage. He tugged again, groaning with the effort, his boots skidding in the dirt. The Russian's heavily patched trousers started to come down, exposing the sharp fins of his hips and a dark line of pubic hair, but still he did not move. Cregg cursed wearily, and let the lifeless legs drop back down to the ground.

To his left, over in the main body of the captured fort, the rest of the working party was busy reversing the parapet, toiling without pause in the early morning light. Gabions and fascines were being piled up to reinforce the new offensive wall, and fresh embrasures knocked through, so that the enemy's cannon could be turned about and brought to bear upon their own city. This working party was about a hundred strong, assembled from the reserve regiments. It had come down through the trenches of the Right Attack with a team of stretcher-bearers, shortly before dawn. The fruits of this latest British victory had been laid out before its reluctant members: an all but demolished position, strewn with loose rocks, torn sandbags and the broken bodies of dead and wounded men. Huddled in amongst the wreckage were the exhausted survivors of the original storming force, their attention fixed on the open ground before their hard-won prize in readiness for a Russian counter-assault.

Throughout the march to this fort, christened 'the Quarries' as it had been built within the pits of a long-abandoned open-seam mine, Cregg had griped and sworn without restraint. He had thus been selected by the sergeant in charge of his detail to remove Russian corpses from an auxiliary battery. This particular emplacement had plainly seen some savage combat, with fewer than a dozen able-bodied redcoats remaining inside. Some of them watched vacantly as their felled comrades were borne away, and Private Cregg began the grim business of clearing out the Russians.

Army procedure was simply to tip the corpses out on to the field of battle, for the enemy to collect under cover of the next truce declared for this purpose. Moving them was hard, nasty work. Although very thin, the dead men were still heavy, like bundles of lead piping wrapped up in sackcloth. They had to be dragged up high banks of earth and stone and then rolled over – which involved a dangerous moment of exposure to the ever-vigilant enemy snipers. Some were still alive, having escaped the bayoneting normally dispensed to Russian wounded left behind after their army had withdrawn. They clawed at Cregg's arms, begging and pleading in their garbled-sounding language. He did not respond, and tried his best not to look in their eyes as he heaved them down after the rest. Experience had taught him that this was the easiest way.

The Ruski under the gun carriage was one of the last. Gingerly rubbing his mutilated hand, Cregg wondered how the cove had got himself into this mortal scrape. It looked as if he'd been lying injured on the ground, and someone had deliberately run the cannon, a nine-pound naval gun, over the top of him. Cregg looked around. A private from the 88th was nearby, his rifle in his hands, crouched in a dark corner. He was peering out carefully through the remains of a wooden rifle screen in the direction of Sebastopol.

''Ere, cock,' Cregg grunted, 'lend us an 'and, would'ja? This poxy bugger won't budge.'

Without a word, the soldier stood his rifle against the wall of the battery and came over to help. Taking hold of the gun carriage in a manner that suggested he'd moved it before, he waited for Cregg to adopt a similar pose on its opposite side; and then, on the count of three, they lugged the cannon backwards. There was a crunching sound from beneath it, and the Russian's legs twisted to the side.

'Much obliged.' Cregg caught an accidental glimpse of the dead man's face. It was contorted with terror, the open mouth exposing a mess of scurvy-blackened gums. 'Tough fight, was it?'

The private looked at the floor, scratching his chin. 'Aye, worst we've 'ad for many a month,' he answered. Cregg saw that this was a fellow veteran, with the numbness that marked their type – the sort who could talk of slaughter as a farmer might discuss the rains. 'We took it easy enough, but the bastards kept at us all night, tryin' to win it back.'

Cregg went around the cannon and looked out through the splintered screen next to which his companion had been hunched. Before it lay scores of slain Russians, ten times the number he had removed from the battery. 'Blimey,' he said softly. 'So I see, pal. So I see.'

The other soldier moved to his side. 'This is just the start of it. Word is that the brass wants us to press at the Redan next.' He looked away, a bleak resentment creeping into his voice. 'This is just the bleedin' start of it.'

Cregg squinted over the bodies towards this formidable fortress. The Redan was the last line of defence before Sebastopol itself. That early in the day, and at a couple of hundred yards' distance, it appeared as little more than a blue block on the horizon, but its proportions were obvious. Cregg whistled through his teeth. 'That's a bleedin' whopper, ain't it, an' no mistake! I wouldn't want to be first out in front o' that bugger!' He leant back, pulled out a charred clay pipe, and then nodded towards a hole in the side of the battery. 'Fancy a smoke?'

His companion had edged back to his corner. He shook his head. 'I daren't,' he mumbled uncomfortably. 'Sarge'll have me knackers.' Picking up his minié, he gestured at the Russian with its stock. 'What about 'im?'

Cregg let out a dark laugh. 'Chum, that cunt ain't going *nowhere.*' After quickly checking for his own NCO, who was off in another part of the Quarries, he nodded a curt, faintly scornful farewell to his more obedient comrade, and then slipped out.

To the side of the fort was a long, scarred slope running down to the Middle Ravine, traversed by a single advance trench. Finding a narrow stone ledge that was well sheltered from the enemy line, Cregg made himself as comfortable as possible. He had tried to shield his hand that morning, but some jarring had been unavoidable. As a result, it now felt as if it had been dipped in hot tar. Wincing, he examined it. His remaining fingers, pink as sugar mice, stuck out uselessly from the stained, grubby wad of bandages. He could barely move them at all.

The arrival of a sweltering summer, when there was no longer any excuse for gloves or mittens, had made it harder to conceal his disability from officers. He was managing, though, just about, tugging his sleeve down and so forth – and with the present shortages of experienced troops, nobody was looking too closely. He was a touch concerned that no real healing seemed to be going on beneath his clumsy bindings, but he was at least getting good at gulping down the pain.

As he put a match in the pipe's bowl, Cregg heard screams echoing off the sides of the Middle Ravine. Sucking coarse smoke down into his lungs, he saw that this wide gully, the main artery of the Allied siege, was crowded with wounded from both the French and British armies. The Frogs had been engaged in a parallel action further along the line, and had also succeeded, taking the fort of the Mamelon Vert; and from the look of things, it had been a costly victory indeed. Hospital tents had been set up in the ravine, to which the injured were being carried in their dozens. Through an open flap, in flickering candlelight, Cregg caught sight of a man in his shirt sleeves vigorously working a hand-saw as if breaking up logs. Then he stepped back, his arms red, and an orderly lifted an entire leg from the table before him, taking it outside and adding it carelessly to a large, pale pile of amputated limbs.

With a start, Cregg realised that there was someone close to where he sat, out on the slope. His first thought was that

it might be a Russian scout, creeping around as they sometimes did, looking for an officer to take a pot-shot at. But
no – this was a civvie, clad in a long, tattered coat and a
black cap. He was hunched over some paper, taking frequent
looks down at the hospital tents in the Middle Ravine. He's
drawing them, Cregg thought. Rumours had been going
around the camps for some time about an artist who lived
in a cave on the French side of the ravine. They said he was
soft in the head, and that the Frogs treated him like a pet,
giving him food and firewood. Cregg was sceptical; there
were many hundreds of bored men up on the plateau, talking
all manner of nonsense. Seeing this chap now, though,
brought back a distant memory of Inkerman Ridge – of
hunting for a wandering artist with Major Maynard.

From somewhere in front of the Quarries, several muskets
were discharged, and British voices shouted in alarm.
Abruptly, the artist stopped what he was doing and rose
unsteadily to his feet, picking up a folder and limping off in
the direction of these shots. After only a few yards, he stumbled on the uneven ground, causing a sheaf of papers to slip
out the back of his folder. He didn't notice; Cregg called out
to him, but he was moving too fast, lost in a mad hurry to
get to the site of the shooting. A moment later, he'd vanished
around the edge of the slope.

'Rum cove,' Cregg murmured, dragging on his pipe, his
eyes wandering back to the spilled sheets of paper.
Impulsively, staying as low as he could, he edged over to
where they lay. Seeing that they were sketches, he scooped
them up and retreated to his ledge. Most were horrible –
bodies, skulls and suchlike. Cregg leafed through them
quickly, his face wrinkled with uncomprehending distaste.
Then he arrived at the saucy stuff.

The soldier was staggered by his sheer good fortune. On
these pages were none other than fat Mr Tomahawk and
pretty Mrs Colonel, fucking like wild beasts, rendered so life-
like they could almost have been panting away in front of
him. He blinked in astonishment, hardly able to believe it.

Ever since Inkerman, he'd been alert for opportunities to
get Boyce, to get him good and proper for what he'd done.

But he quickly realised that unless he was prepared to die himself, the Colonel was beyond his reach – and now that it came to it, Cregg was not entirely sure that he was quite ready to give up his life for the sake of revenge. So he'd been confined to glowering from the line as Boyce paced imperiously before them, imagining a bayonet stabbing into that rotten carcass, or a bullet cracking open that horrible head, but remaining powerless to strike against the bastard who had killed Major Maynard – who had the blood of so many of his pals all over his stinking toff hands.

Now, though, things were different. These pictures, with their mix of quim and scandal, would draw men from throughout the camps. Boyce would become the butt of a wicked joke that Dan Cregg would spread through the whole bloody army. This wasn't quite the satisfaction that he desired; but it would do very nicely for the time being.

An enraged bellow came from the fortifications behind him. 'Cregg, you blasted cur, where the devil are you?'

It was his sergeant. He'd been nabbed once again, and would certainly be flogged for shirking his duties. Yet even this could not put a dent in his good spirits. Wearing a tight, malicious grin, he tucked the drawings safely inside his tunic and went back into the battery.

2

As usual, the atmosphere in the British Hotel was thick with tobacco smoke and the masculine hum of military conversation. Merriment and laughter, however, so often found in the hotel, were in short supply that night. Every soldier gathered there had the subdued, anxious manner that always prevailed in the ranks on the eve of a great attack. They clustered around the fireplace, sat at tables and perched upon the barrels and crates that stood about, nervously discussing what few details were known. The majority had just been retired from the forward positions, and would not be fighting that day; but every one of them had friends, cousins or brothers in the assaulting divisions.

Slowly, Kitson knelt by one of the crude wooden columns that stood along the length of the hotel's main saloon, and wrung out a bloody flannel into a basin of water. In the past few hours, he had treated a long procession of cuts, sprains and dislocations, the results of soldiers being knocked down by exploding shells, or clipped by shrapnel. Such injuries, he had learned, indicated that the early stages of a major action were underway, with the heavy guns exchanging fire as a prelude to a large-scale infantry engagement. On this occasion, it had seemed that the initiative belonged to the Allies. The previous afternoon, they had bombarded Sebastopol with an unprecedented ferocity. Veils of fine grey dust had been shaken from the hotel's rafters. Nothing, Kitson had thought, could possibly survive such a concerted barrage. Sebastopol and everyone in it had surely been flattened.

Yet much of the talk he was hearing that night cast doubt upon this estimation. A party clad in the dark blue jackets and overalls of the Artillery Division were seated around one of the hotel's largest tables, swigging hot port from tin mugs and devouring generous slabs of Mrs Seacole's seed-cake. They had been working the thirteen-pound mortars throughout the bombardment, and had been so deafened by this task that they were virtually shouting at one another in their efforts to communicate. From their bellowed exchanges, Kitson and numerous others discovered that the order to cease firing had come too soon; that the mortars were not doing the damage expected of them; and that, most importantly of all, the advance of the infantry had been delayed for so long that any advantage the bombardment might have gained them was already lost.

'They'll have *rebuilt the bloody walls!*' yelled one despondently, a greasy hand cupped over his ear in a futile attempt to amplify his comrades' responses. 'Only *earthworks*, ain't they? He works damn fast, does the Russian! *Damn fast!*'

It took the emergence of the matron of the British Hotel, the benevolent ruler of this peaceful, cosy realm, through a door behind the long counter to lift the gloom that afflicted her clientele that night. Mrs Seacole was dressed for riding, a long cape covering her striped dress, and a capacious saddle-bag bursting with provisions slung over her shoulder. Upon her head was a wide-brimmed hat that sported a huge blue feather. Kitson realised that she was intending to embark on one of her mercy missions up to the plateau. Since they had left the *Medora*, she had undertaken these trips with greater frequency. She often proclaimed that she would not languish in the comfort of the hotel whilst the soldiers, her dear, brave sons, lay injured and needy at the front. Kitson, wary of whom he might encounter, had thus far declined to accompany her.

This stout, middle-aged mulatto lady was greeted with almost reverential warmth by the men assembled in the main saloon. They raised their cups, letting out weary cheers and banging fists on tabletops; a number called out 'Good evening to you, Mother Seacole' with earnest courtesy. She beamed back at them, returning their hearty salutations, her teeth shining white against a complexion the colour of strong tea. With every eye upon her, she walked around the counter's end, heading over to a table of regulars. In seconds they were all laughing uproariously, whilst the rest of the hotel's occupants looked on with envy. Kitson watched as she patted the cheek of one of her younger patrons, making a tender remark that made him blush scarlet and his comrades heave with fresh amusement.

This was her way, and it was effective indeed. The ease with which she mixed with the fighting men, and the great and honest affection she showed them, brought them true respite from their burdens. Kitson's admiration for her, for her open-hearted humanity, knew no limit. Her approach to the treatment of the wounded was expert, and very different from the clinical barbarity of so many of the male, Anglo-Saxon surgeons he had worked with at Balaclava harbour. This place, the British Hotel, was another source of wonderment. Mrs Seacole had summoned the building out of nowhere whilst Kitson still lay crippled in a hammock aboard the *Medora*. It had an improvised quality, the beams little more than stripped tree trunks, the counter fashioned from a portion of a ship's hull, still with barnacles attached; but these disparate, unlikely parts, seemingly knitted together by the sheer force of Mrs Seacole's will, formed a haven for those trapped in the Crimea.

Although she had taught him much during their time together, Kitson did not delude himself. He did not possess Mrs Seacole's unparalleled ability to soothe her patients' minds as well as their bodily afflictions, and would always remain her strange, nameless assistant. But he had thought of another way to repay the vast debt he owed her. Upon their return to England at the conclusion of the war, he had resolved to pen a grand account of this lady's Crimean endeavours, detailing her achievements and thus sealing her fame. Public appetite for a tale of such genuine heroism would surely be huge. Mary Seacole would become a celebrated, emulated person, known to all, loved by all – as she so richly deserved to be.

The main door creaked open behind Kitson, pulling him from these pleasant reflections. He turned, expecting another exhausted soldier to stagger in. Instead, he saw Miss Annabel Wade. She looked thinner, and was in a state of some anxiety, quickly taking in the smoky room. Kitson knew at once that he was the object of her search, but found that he was distinctly reluctant to approach her. He stood, his basin in his hands, waiting to be discovered.

Locating him, Miss Wade hurried to his side with evident relief. 'Mr Kitson, thank the Lord. I had heard that you were a part of this . . . concern.' She cast an uncertain glance around the hotel. 'I only pray that I am not too late. Sir, you must come back to the camps with me, right away.'

Kitson felt as if he had been caught – apprehended. He had assumed that no one who knew him from before his injury was aware that he was at the British Hotel. It was most disturbing to discover otherwise. He set down the basin.

Miss Wade drew a breath. 'It is Mr Styles. He is in the Crimea still.'

Kitson's mind went blank; his limbs were tingling, bursting with an energy so intense and powerful it somehow prohibited any movement. He managed to shake his head. 'Impossible.'

'I'm afraid not. He has been seen.'

'He was wounded, though, shortly before I was.' Kitson crossed his arms, trying hard to gather his recollections. 'Miss Wade, I was told that you accompanied us both down to Balaclava harbour that morning, and that we were due to be transported out on the *Charity*. I checked the patient logs as soon as I was able. There were a number of unnamed civilians aboard her when she sailed. Was not Styles among them?'

Miss Wade said that he was not, and recounted how, after staying out of sight for many weeks, the illustrator had recently started to appear again, his garb and bearing even more desperate than previously, wandering around the margins of the camp like a vengeful apparition. Some reports had placed him close to the Boyces' farmhouse, she said, and she feared for Mrs Boyce's safety, given Mr Styles' persistent, unnatural attachment to that young lady.

'He is known to come out during the larger actions. Some saw him during the taking of the Quarries.' Miss Wade shivered. 'They say he is armed.'

Kitson frowned, his shock turning to anger. 'I will not attempt to deceive you, Miss Wade. If Robert Styles' mind remains as clouded as it was a few months ago, then he is dangerous indeed.'

'But you are his one friend here, Mr Kitson, are you not? At the time of your injury, I gained the distinct impression that you had been attempting to restrain Mr Styles in his violent excesses. Can you not try to do the same now?'

Kitson did not answer. 'What of Cracknell?'

Miss Wade snorted sarcastically. 'Come, Mr Kitson, you know that gentleman far better than I. He vanished from the camps long ago. Those scabrous reports of his were beginning to make things difficult for him, I think – as were his wicked interferences in the Boyce household. No, he has been absent from all our lives for quite some time, thanks be to God.'

Before Kitson could say any more, a loud laugh close to his elbow told him that Mrs Seacole was approaching. A moment later she was with them, looking Miss Wade over with keen, friendly curiosity.

'And who is this upstanding lady, Thomas?' Her voice was deep and smooth, with a lilting Caribbean cadence.

Kitson made the introduction, briefly explaining the nature of Miss Wade's work.

Mrs Seacole nodded cannily. 'Yes, I have seen you round about, Miss Wade, doing good things up on the plateau, with the prettiest young creature by your side. Holding the men *transfixed*, she was!'

Miss Wade, although clearly on her guard, could not help but smile at this comment. 'My companion, Mrs Madeleine Boyce.'

'A fine beauty indeed, that one.' Mrs Seacole gave a contented sigh. 'Well, this is an honour for us, isn't it,

Thomas? We don't often get ladies in the British Hotel, and certainly not those from the proud Caledonian tribes. I am of Scottish ancestry myself, Miss Wade. Now, can I get you some refreshment, my dear? A pot of half-and-half, perhaps? Or a tot of shrub?'

Miss Wade was regarding her host doubtfully. 'Thank you, Mrs Seacole, but I—'

'How about a marrow pudding, then? Fresh up from the harbour this very afternoon! Are the marrow puddings not good, Toby?' she asked a nearby corporal with crumbs in his beard.

'Prime, Mother, prime,' he replied appreciatively. 'You're a rare treasure, truly ye are.' Miss Wade, however, could not be tempted.

Kitson, silent throughout this exchange, accepted his fate. He saw that he must do what his visitor asked of him. 'Mrs Seacole,' he broke in, 'I believe that I shall accompany you to the plateau this morning.'

Mrs Seacole gave every sign of being pleasantly surprised by this decision; a moment later, though, she was asking him concernedly whether his poor chest was up to it. Turning to Miss Wade, she told the tale of how she had removed Thomas Kitson, the wounded orderly, from the quay at Balaclava and taken him to her base of operations aboard the *Medora*. There, she had nursed him back to health; and when she had taken up proprietorship of the British Hotel three months later, her orderly had chosen to go with her.

'And now, having barely left this building in six long weeks, you wish to come up to the line,' she pronounced heavily, her eyes on Kitson's chest. 'You must promise me that you will be careful, Thomas. That is still a grave wound indeed – you must let Nature do her work. We simply cannot have some passing excitement undoing all the progress that has been made.'

'Certainly not, Mrs Seacole. I understand completely.' Although the bleeding had stopped and he could move around normally with little discomfort, Kitson was all too aware of his continued fragility. He was coming to realise that his ribs would never regain the strength they had before that night in the advance parallel.

'I'm sure that young Master Cowan can hold the fort in our absence, wherever he's got to. I suppose it is only right, Thomas, that you wish to help those most in need of it. He is quite adept, Miss Wade, with a mustard poultice and a length of lint!' She adjusted her riding cape. 'But there is another reason for this sudden change of heart, Thomas, is there not. Don't deny it, my love, I can tell.'

Miss Wade was plainly impatient to be off, thinking only of getting back to the camps, back to Madeleine Boyce. Her fears regarding Styles were very real.

'An old obligation, Mrs Seacole,' Kitson said. 'To a friend. It should not take long.' He had no idea if this were true. Who could say what might await him back at the camps?

'Someone you wish to save from destruction, I take it.' Mrs Seacole's jollity left her. Devoid of her usual happy animation, she seemed to age before him, the lines on her round face deepening in the soft oil-light of the hotel. 'Very well, Thomas. I have been talking to my sons this past day. They firmly believe that the Russians will be ready for them when the dawn attack is sounded. I fear that we are on the brink of a great disaster, my dears; one that we are quite powerless to prevent. The coming day will be a truly terrible one for all.'

But then, quite suddenly, she recovered her habitual cheer, bidding the room an expansive farewell, telling the soldiers to take their ease and stay as long as they wished. In return, she received a robust chorus of good wishes, as well as stern instructions to keep herself safe, and leave getting shot at by the Ivans to those who were paid to put up with it. Adjusting her plumed hat and her saddle-bag, she opened the hotel's door and strode out into the darkness, towards where the horses were tethered. Miss Wade was less than a step behind. Kitson pulled his jacket from the back of a chair and followed, closing the door after him.

3

The railway wagon reached the steepest part of the ascent to the camps. As the team of horses pulling it began to strain, the navvies walking beside the tracks started up a chant. They kept time with steady monotony, their low intonations punctuated by the crack of the driver's whip. Cracknell, perched atop a pile of ammunition crates in the back of this crude, heavy cart, told himself to be patient: even without an engine, this was still the fastest route to the front. He listened to the creaking of the rope harnesses, and hoped that the fellow manning the brake had his wits about him, lest something gave way and they found themselves rolling back down towards Balaclava.

Behind the wagon, several dozen sailors were trudging across the sleepers, kept uncharacteristically quiet by the prospect of the morning ahead. These blue-jackets were to serve as storming parties, supporting the great mass of infantry; the scaling ladders they would carry into the assault hung from the wagon's sides. Every man there had been assigned this duty after losing a lottery aboard his vessel, and one could tell this from just a single glance at their grim faces. Shooting down ladder-bearers was the obvious way to hinder an attack on a fortified position – as the Russians would surely be aware.

The skeletal remains of innumerable broken vehicles and cargo containers were heaped along the sides of the road, dimly visible in the gathering dawn. Lights from the supply base at Kadikioi shone up ahead, catching from time to time on the eyes of feral dogs watching their progress from the cover of the surrounding meadows. The scent of wild flowers drifted over the wagon, carried on a breeze that brushed gently through the long grass. On the left, rising up to a sharp, dark line against the softening sky, was the Black Sea.

To the relief of all, the wagon finally made it on to the plateau. The railway track curved in towards the huts and barns of Kadikioi, and then ran straight on to the forward camps. Seeing the many hundreds of white tents, spread across the blue-grey fields like points of light on a rippling lake, brought cheer to the Tomahawk's heart. He was positively itching for action. Balaclava, although greatly recovered from its ghastly winter, remained somewhat dull for a man accustomed to the front line. The most thrilling it got was the occasional afternoon's horse racing staged by the cavalry at the nearby village of Karani. Much to his disgust, he had managed to miss the assaults of the previous week due to a bout of diarrhoea brought on by some suspect seafood. A decisive victory had been won at the Quarries. The significance of the operation was ably attested to by the numbers of injured brought down to the quay. Watching this bleak procession from his window, Cracknell had vowed that when the next column was made, he would be there.

The railway cart, by now a familiar sight, was largely ignored as it trundled by the endless tents and parading soldiers. A few blasts of artillery were heard – the rear batteries, Cracknell reckoned, grabbing the chance for a bit of early morning practice before the day's labour got underway. He turned to where the plateau dipped down towards Sebastopol. From such a distance, the besieged port city and its fortifications looked like an ugly, disfiguring knot in the smooth grain of the landscape.

Half an hour later, the wagon reached the final stretch of track. The driver slowed it as much as he could; then the navvies strode around, swiftly untethering the horses and leading them away whilst the cart was still in motion. Cracknell climbed down, staggering a little as he dropped to the ground. Behind him, the wagon hit the buffer at the track's end with a loud clang. Men from the Quartermaster-General's department were upon it immediately, distributing its cargo amongst their regimental counterparts. Cracknell spotted none other than the Quartermaster-General himself, directing the proceedings. A decidedly reptilian creature, responsible for much suffering in the Tomahawk's book, he was also known to have an old family connection with Boyce. This man was the source, unwitting or otherwise, of whatever bait had been used to reel in Charles Norton – Cracknell was sure of it. And when this war had finally worn itself out, he had vowed that he would discover the details. He would use his prominence, his reputation, to expose them all.

Cracknell made for the old *Courier* tent, intending to retrieve the field glass he had left locked in his sea-chest. He wasn't entirely sure what he would find. Shortly before he'd left the plateau, this worthy structure had been subjected to several attacks from those angered by his reports. It had been partly collapsed, the canvas slashed with an officer's sword; and he could smell that someone, several people in fact, had relieved themselves on the top of his desk. He had already decided to leave for Balaclava, but these incidents only increased his determination to do so. The animosity of these people would only grow more intense, after all; the Tomahawk of the *Courier* was not about to soften either his views or their expression. How the hell could he? Lord Aberdeen's disastrous government had fallen, it was true, but who had replaced him? Yet another aged aristocrat, Lord Palmerston this time, a man over seventy years old with poor hearing, poor eyesight and a famously belligerent temper. Cracknell's feeling about 'Pam', as he was known, had been bad from the start; and sure enough, the bullying villain had since shown that he was set on continuing the war until some manner of British victory was achieved, regardless of the cost. He wanted Sebastopol, in short, and was pressuring Raglan to deliver it. This was the reason the army was to be thrown at the Great Redan that morning. Cracknell knew in his bones that this rather literal tactic would lead only to calamity. All he could do, though, as ever, was observe what transpired and report it back to his readers.

Approaching the tent, he was surprised to see clear signs of habitation. Was it soldiers – renegade Turks perhaps? Or Tartar peasants? The Tomahawk adopted a fearless, commanding expression, pushed open the flaps and strode inside.

Robert Styles was sitting in the middle of the dirt floor, lit ghoulishly by the embers of a dying fire. A winding vine of smoke curled up and out through a ragged hole that had been sawn out of the tent's roof. Cracknell's writing desk had been pushed roughly to one side. Heaped upon it was a mass of drawings, some heavily worked up, others a mere handful of pencil strokes. They had been made on any available scraps of paper, over maps, newspapers and even pages of his own handwritten notes, left behind when he had gone to Balaclava. Their subject, of course, was the underbelly of the campaign: death, disease, emaciation and madness, rendered with horrible precision. Cracknell grimaced with distaste. They were like visions of the bloody Apocalypse.

All the other furniture, the stools, stoves and sea-chests, had been crammed unceremoniously into what had once been bed alcoves. There was no useable bedding in sight. It was clear from Styles' appearance that he was sleeping on the ground like a man of the line. He was dressed in a stained green jacket that must once have belonged to a private from the Rifle Brigade. A black forage cap lay by his side, and an old greatcoat was draped around his shoulders. Mud crusted his clothes, and one of his legs was dark with dried blood. His beard was unkempt, matted and colourless, and he was painfully thin, his sun-tanned skin stretched tight over his bones. He was drawing, his wasted hand darting across the paper.

The senior correspondent stood in stunned silence. He remembered that he'd never quite got round to ascertaining that Styles had left the Crimea. His assumption had been that the illustrator was shipped out after being wounded that January – not unreasonable, he felt, considering that Madeleine and her friend had laid him out on the quay at

Balaclava. That the boy had vanished soon afterwards was deeply unfortunate, but hardly uncommon. Cracknell had asked O'Farrell to pass on his condolences to the family.

Kitson, on the other hand, he'd known about. Balaclava's churning rumour-mill soon reported that his one-time junior was at work in Mrs Seacole's British Hotel. This was a lamentable dereliction of duty – a desertion, in fact. It was also completely predictable. The art correspondent, unable to cope with the turmoil of battle, had removed himself to a safe distance, playing nurse to ease his guilty conscience. Contemptible, but there it was. This, though – this felt as if he'd arrived home from a lengthy trip abroad to discover that the forgotten fern in his window, which should have died quietly, had actually grown to a supernatural size, engulfing his entire house.

'Mr Styles, what the devil are you doing here?' Cracknell said abruptly, in a loud voice that held both humour and a note of confrontation.

The illustrator stopped work and looked up at him. He did not speak, or offer any expression, either of welcome or dislike, at the return of the Tomahawk. But Cracknell fancied that he could see something stir in those sunken eyes. A touch unnerved, the correspondent decided to use a more openly amicable approach. He went down on his haunches, and threw the butt of the cigarette he'd been smoking on the fire. It was fuelled, he now saw, with the stocks of dismantled Russian muskets, some of which were patterned with elaborate carvings.

'How's the leg?' he asked with gruff warmth, forcing himself to look at Styles. His complexion had the texture of old cloth, with earth rubbed into its very fibre; Cracknell caught a whiff of old clothes and decaying gums. 'A bit better, I hope? Upon my life, you're as sun-browned as a bloody blue-jacket! Quite some change, young sir; quite some change.'

Styles did not reply. He went back to his sketch.

Casting his mind back to his last days on the plateau, Cracknell recalled the occasional sense that someone was moving around just outside, hovering on the edge of the tent's stone foundations. At the time, he had imagined it was some vengeful soldier trying to put the fear into him. Now he was beginning to think differently. 'When did you move yourself in here?'

Still Styles said nothing.

Cracknell raised an eyebrow, and took a bundle of cigarettes from his pocket. 'Well, I have been lodging in Balaclava these past few months – on *Courier* business, y'understand.'

The *London Courier*, in truth, had been a secondary reason for the Tomahawk's relocation. Rather more prominent had been the issue of Madeleine Boyce and her husband. In the weeks after that memorable night in the *Courier* tent, they had grown rash, meeting in the Boyces' farmhouse with greater regularity. There had been a series of abominably close shaves, Cracknell managing to leave literally *a single second* before the cuckold made his entrance. He was perfectly happy to beat a rapid retreat every once in a while – he found it stimulating, in fact. Such situations, however, had been getting a little too frequent for comfort. He had started to feel that Madeleine was deliberately courting them. There was a marked carelessness in her treatment of their arrangements. 'Now, Maddy, you're quite certain that Nathaniel is on duty for the entire morning?' he might ask. 'Oh yes,' she would reply airily; and then they would be interrupted, often whilst in full flight, by the sound of a booted foot upon the stoop.

She was becoming unbalanced. Her demands for declarations of his fidelity and unwavering passion grew yet more frequent and more desperate; and his responses, delivered as convincingly as ever, plainly no longer satisfied her. It was the awful tension of the siege, Cracknell had theorised. It was preying on her reason, leading her to desire, even to prompt, dramatic conclusions. But whatever the explanation, it was all growing somewhat perilous, for both of them. He had decided that it would be best if he removed himself from the camps, and from the Boyces, for an indefinite period of time. Madeleine had not taken this at all well, of course. Cracknell had managed to calm her only with elaborate plans of the escape they would make together when he returned for her later in the campaign. They would go to southern Spain, he promised, to the orange-groves of Andalusia. There would be a pretty, sun-kissed villa with a view of the ocean, many thousands of miles beyond the reach of Nathaniel Boyce; there would be children, a family, a future filled with love and happiness. Eventually, tearfully, she had agreed to let him go.

Cracknell offered the bundle of cigarettes to Styles. Unexpectedly, the illustrator accepted, pulling out three of the crooked paper tubes. Two went in the pocket of his green jacket, the other in his mouth; he lit it, not sharing the match with Cracknell. 'Have you been to Balaclava lately, Styles?' There was no response. Cracknell lit his own cigarette. 'You would find it much improved, my friend. Place is almost English in aspect, these days. Provisions of all sorts are in plentiful supply – including, quite unbelievably, winter clothing for the troops. Winter clothes, in June! They all say that they're expecting their summer dress by Christmas. It would be amusing, would it not, if this idiocy had not consigned so many to their graves.'

Styles stayed quiet. Cigarette dangling from his lips, he started applying shade to a form which, even viewing it upside down, Cracknell could tell was a cadaver of some kind.

'The Turks are gone as well, thank Christ. There are a number of shops now, a restaurant, a telegraph office – which is very useful for us, as you might imagine. I even saw a bloody *photographer* last month, taking views of the harbour. Fenton's his name – they say he's been up in the camps as well. Some competition for you artists there, eh, Styles!' The illustrator did not react. Cracknell took the cigarette from between his lips and moved closer to the fire, sitting himself on the floor. 'And would you credit it,' he went on slyly, 'I've also discovered a few whores at work amongst the cottages. Doing a brisk trade, of course. Why, I had to make my appointments days – nay, *weeks* in advance!'

This joking revelation had been intended to foster a bit of manly bonhomie between them, and perhaps elicit a knowing chuckle from his grimy companion – after all, he was a young man, was he not? The travails of the romping gent, in Cracknell's judgement, were of universal amusement to the male of the species, and especially to its hot-blooded youth. In this, however, as in so much else, Robert Styles was a disappointment to his sex. He breathed out a great cloud of smoke, those eyes now glinting with an unmistakable malevolence. He seemed to be gathering up his energy. Cracknell realised that Styles was preparing himself to speak, something he clearly hadn't done in some time.

'Why are you back?' he demanded, his voice a hoarse snarl.

Cracknell, slightly thrown by the violence of this utterance, paused for a moment. He sucked on his cigarette. Well done, Mr Styles, he thought, I was very nearly worried for a moment there. Very nearly.

'There is to be a great attack this morning,' he replied, hardening his manner. 'Did you not hear the early parades? They are to storm the Great Redan. It will be an advance over two hundred yards of open ground, straight at a solid wall of Russian cannon. The French are doing the same further down the line, against the equally redoubtable Malakhoff Tower. A lunatic plan, if you ask me, devised by desperate, unimaginative generals who are entirely out of ideas.' Cracknell laughed mirthlessly as he studied the end of his cigarette. 'But, Styles, strangely enough, they *didn't* think to ask me.'

Looking over at the strange figure before him, the senior correspondent suddenly decided that the best course of action was to re-assert their professional relationship – to knock the dust off the contract that gave him authority over the boy, and impose a much-needed sense of hierarchy on Styles' disordered mind.

'It is my duty to witness this piece of folly for the readers of the *Courier*,' Cracknell stated firmly, pulling out his dented silver hip-flask. 'And, I might add, yours also. Your bond to O'Farrell still holds, lad. I see that your muse has not deserted you. Let's see if we can coax a publishable scene out of that obstinate pencil of yours, shall we? A view of the Redan from the forward trenches, perhaps?' He pointed a stern, stubby finger in Styles' expressionless face. 'Just be certain to follow my lead, d'ye hear? And keep a tight hold of your nerve – you'll sure as hell have need of it.'

The illustrator stopped drawing, threw his half-smoked cigarette aside and got up. Carelessly, he added his latest piece of work to the drift of papers atop the desk.

Cracknell gave the flask a shake; it was empty. With mild irritation, he realised that he had forgotten to fill it before leaving Balaclava. He set it down by the fire and consulted a scratched brass watch. 'I have someone to see before heading for the front – an old pal from the 57th who says he has information for me. I suggest we meet before the Quarries in, say, half an hour.' He hesitated, and then said with heavy emphasis, 'Can you manage that?'

Styles gave the very slightest of nods. His aggression had left him as quickly as it had appeared. Beneath the dirt, Cracknell fancied, the illustrator now had an almost juvenile aspect; he began gathering up his equipment with schoolboy haste. This was going rather well, despite all their past differences. The Tomahawk was finding that the notion of having a subordinate at his side once again was oddly appealing.

Cracknell flicked some ash from his cigarette and then took another pull. 'You realise, I take it, that Kitson has gone. He has abandoned to *Courier*, abandoned *us*, to work over at that glorified pot-house on the Balaclava road.'

Styles, rummaging through a heap of tarnished military equipment piled in the tent's far corner, did not answer. Kitson's fate was clearly of little interest to him.

The senior correspondent rose to his feet with a groan. 'This hardly matters, of course. We two are the *Courier* team now, Mr Styles. You and I, valorous and unstoppable!' He almost reached out to grip Styles' bony shoulder, but thought better of it. He glanced down at his companion's bloodied trouser leg. 'You *are* fit for this, aren't you?'

Styles straightened up and moved out of the corner towards the tent flaps. Cracknell started when he saw the pistol; a second later, he recognised it as his own neglected revolver. The illustrator must have broken into his sea-chest and found it there. He'd quite forgotten that he owned the damned thing. The gun, liberally smeared with black grease, seemed enormous in Styles' bony hand. He span the chamber with apparent expertise, wiped the pistol on the arm of his jacket and then pushed it into his belt.

For an instant, Cracknell found himself looking straight into the boy's yellowed eye. It brimmed with bitter contempt.

'I will be at the Quarries,' Styles muttered as he left the tent.

4

Boyce held the worn, much-handled sheet of paper between finger and thumb, turning it over slowly in the candlelight. Nunn's nervous, simple face stared back at him from the other side of the tent. Twisting the left point of his moustache, Boyce made himself study the drawing on the sheet a second time. The Colonel knew his art. He had learned it at his father's side, in the family picture gallery, and had toured Italy as a young man in order to see for himself the very best that mankind had produced. Such knowledge, he had been raised to believe, was among the qualifications of a gentleman. He could tell, as he examined the lines and shading, that this image was too realistic, too painstaking in its observation of incidental details to be a production of prurient fantasy. It had to be admitted also that it was the work of a man of true talent. The likenesses were quite remarkable.

Boyce found that he was immensely tired. The vitalising excitement that had filled him only a few minutes earlier, as he stood watching the columns of the 99th start for the Quarries, had drained away completely. Sitting there in the shabby tent, he had to stifle a yawn. He was far too fatigued for anger. His mind was dull, indifferent, empty. He rubbed his itching eyes with a leather-gloved knuckle.

'There are more?' he asked eventually.

By way of reply, Nunn passed over four or five other sheets, all in a similar condition to the first. The sketches upon them were of the same subject, broadly speaking, and were equally graphic in their treatment; but they showed later moments in the act, different arrangements and practices. Boyce winced to look upon them, knowing that these were scenes with which he was now burdened for the remainder of his days.

'And you found them upon whom, exactly?'

'Private Cregg, Colonel. From Third Company.'

'Cregg . . . the name's familiar. Is he regularly punished?'

'Yes, Colonel. I believe we have flogged him eight times now, over the course of the campaign.'

Sighing heavily, Boyce dropped the sketches into a loose pile. As he rose from his chair, flexing his stiff knee-high boots, he caught sight of himself in a looking glass propped up in a dark corner of the tent. It was not a pleasing prospect. He was dressed in the current uniform decreed for officers on trench duty, which he considered to be quite absurd. Over a plain shell jacket, he was obliged to wear a ridiculous short tweed coat, lined with cheap, moth-eaten fur, and on his head he sported one of those abominably seedy forage caps. The moustache did manage, as ever, to lend him some gravity; but still, over all, he felt he had the appearance of First Ruffian in some strolling players' sensational tragedy. He turned away sharply.

Boyce had meant to take action a good deal earlier. Some months back, he'd almost caught them together – he'd been certain of it. The gossip-mongers, catching wind of this incident, had grown busy once again. The Colonel had felt their mocking eyes upon him, and heard their wicked tongues clacking in his wake. The weight of provocation quickly became unbearable. He had resolved to give that fiend from the *Courier* a good horse-whipping, to demonstrate to the blackguard that he was up against a man of honour, who would go to some lengths to preserve it. But the cunning fat fox he hunted had somehow got scent of the hounds, and fled to some burrow or other; and, sensing traps, had also begun to keep well away from the henhouse. Before long, it was clear that the affair had cooled. Madeleine became yet more uncommunicative, if that were possible, retreating to her room as soon as she returned from her morning expeditions with Miss Wade.

The Colonel's occasional efforts to wring information out of her yielded nothing. Her spirit had been sapped utterly. She cared not how hard she was struck, and endured whatever brutal attentions he felt inclined to force upon her without protest – indeed, without any visible response. At times, when they convened in his farmhouse, the officers of the 99th could hear her sobs through the walls. The pressures of the campaign, Boyce told them; the sights of war are bound to take an inevitable toll on the female mind.

He had been satisfied, in the short term at least. She was suffering, that much was plain – which was all well and good as far as he was concerned. Let it be some small castigation, he'd thought harshly, for the filth she has flung against my name. And when this is all over, when we have won this damned war and returned to England, some changes will be made, changes that young Madeleine will not find to her liking.

Yet now, many weeks later, this had been brought before him, as if from nowhere. It was taking some time for the full consequences to impress themselves upon Boyce's weary mind. Weathering rumour and his own suspicions was one thing. But this – sketches taken from the hands of a private soldier, after they had been seen by God only knows how many others – was quite another. He looked down at the image on the top of the pile. Madeleine was straddling her lover with her back to the artist. The Irishman's scrotum could be seen, dark and shrivelled beneath the smooth white curves of her buttocks, nestled between his thick, hairy thighs. Both, Boyce noticed, were wearing boots, and the discarded clothing around them seemed appropriate for the depths of winter. These drawings were some months old.

'And he was showing these around? To other private soldiers?'

Nunn swallowed hard. 'He was, Colonel.'

'Were there officers present?'

Nunn hesitated, blinking, opening his mouth to speak and then shutting it again.

'Mr Nunn,' said Boyce, now with menace in his voice, 'answer me, damn you. Were there men of rank present?'

Nunn stood as if at attention, his square chin in the air. 'Yes, Colonel.'

Boyce lowered his head. 'What division?'

'The Light, sir. And the Fourth, if I'm not mistaken – the 18th Regiment of Foot.'

Boyce fell silent for a long time. It was over. They would all talk, of course they would. His disgrace, his dishonour would spread through the army faster than the blasted cholera. No high post for him; no, his career was effectively finished. No one would be able even to look him in the eye without having to suppress a laugh. Such was the fate of the betrayed husband, the cuckold – he became a laughing stock for all.

'This is a brave thing you have done here, Mr Nunn,' he said at last, 'bringing these to me. You are a brave man.'

'Thank you, Colonel.'

'You are wasted as an adjutant, I see that now. A soldier of your mettle belongs on the open field, leading the troops, not fretting over the safety of his superiors.'

'My only wish is to serve the Queen, Colonel, in whatever post is deemed right for me. It is an honour—'

'Of course, of course.' Boyce cleared his throat. 'I've decided to relieve you of your responsibility to me, Mr Nunn, and reassign you to the first line. You will go from here and take your rightful place in the Forlorn Hope.'

Nunn blinked again. This, as Boyce knew well, was the stuff of his youthful dreams. Tales of the Forlorn Hope – those noble, heroic souls responsible for the triumphant sieges of the Peninsular War – were in large part responsible for the boy's early decision to embark upon a life of soldiering. 'Sir, I—'

'Think of it, man!' Boyce boomed over him. The moustache quivered slightly, as if electrified. 'This is the final obstacle before us. This fort is Russia itself. When it crumbles, the Bear will crumble soon after. We must be bold, and advance. And I'm permitting you to be at the front of that advance – to win a victory to rival that achieved by the Iron Duke at the fortresses of Badajoz, or Ciudad, or San Sebastian. The frontal assault, Mr Nunn, as a part of the Forlorn Hope! There is nothing more gallant, nothing in all of soldiering. Were it not for the responsibilities of command I would be there alongside you. I envy you, sir. I envy you this great chance for glory.'

The Lieutenant, poor fool, was almost choked with pride. 'Colonel, I can only hope that I prove worthy of the faith you have placed in me.'

Boyce nodded. 'Go forward, then, into the trenches, and report to Colonel Yea of the 34th. Know that the 99th will be directly behind you. Good luck, Mr Nunn. We will shake hands atop the Redan.'

Nunn saluted and turned on his heel, making to leave. 'One more thing,' Boyce added, stopping the Lieutenant in his tracks. 'This man Cregg. A thoroughgoing rapscallion?'

Nunn pulled himself back to attention, and nodded. 'Of the very lowest kind, Colonel, despite his long service.'

Boyce picked up the drawings, rolling them into a tight tube. 'Would such a man, in your opinion, benefit from the same opportunity I have given to you?'

'From a place in the Forlorn Hope? It would certainly do him no harm, Colonel,' replied Nunn guilelessly.

'See to it. That will be all, Mr Nunn.'

A quarter of an hour later, Boyce emerged from the tent, the sketches safely inside his shell jacket. Lieutenant-Colonel Fairlie and Major Pierce were sitting nearby, dressed for battle. Fairlie was puffing idly on a cherry-wood pipe, leaning back on his fold-down chair with his highly polished boots up on the low crate that rested between them. He was studying a map of the Russian fortifications by the light of a small oil lamp, his neat grey beard and furrowed brow giving him a donnish air. There was no outward sign of nerves about him, but then Joseph Fairlie was famously cool-headed. This made him an effective officer, whose undeniable achievements during the taking of the Quarries had obliged Boyce to elevate him to his present rank. The loutish Pierce was more obviously apprehensive. He was hunched forward in his seat, his blond, straw-like hair poking out from beneath his cap, forcing himself to read a newspaper. The thin, tightly printed pages shivered slightly in his grasp. Both men stood as he approached.

'Where was young Nunn off to, sir?' asked Pierce. 'Seemed in a dreadful hurry.'

'He came to me asking to join the Forlorn Hope,' Boyce replied. 'I saw no reason not to grant him this request.'

'Bloody hell,' murmured Fairlie, clearly impressed, 'rather him than me.'

Boyce looked down at Pierce's paper. It was the *London Courier*. After a report in February had included a particularly scathing – and widely-read – description of a freezing, half-starved sentry of the 99th standing guard outside a farmhouse whilst his officers feasted and laughed within, he had prohibited his officers from so much as picking up a copy of the despicable publication.

Pierce followed his gaze. 'Apologies, Colonel,' he said, diffident and a little shamefaced. 'Just trying to keep up with the snake – see which way he slithers and all that.'

'And?'

The Major cleared his throat. 'Oh, he's all incensed about some trip up the coast that was mounted a few weeks ago,' he replied. 'A joint force was assembled to take a Russian supply port – place called Kerch. The Turks destroyed a museum, apparently, and went on a bit of a rampage, abusing the locals and so forth. French had to shoot a few of 'em before they'd desist.'

Fairlie tamped down his pipe-bowl with his thumb. 'Hardly surprising.'

Boyce snatched the copy of the *Courier* from Pierce's hands and quickly located the column headed 'Crimean Dispatches from the Famous Tomahawk of the *Courier*'. His eyes flitted over the account of the action at the supply port – heavily biased drivel, as usual – slowing only as they reached the closing paragraphs.

So the operation at Kerch was a success, but one has to ask how it could have been otherwise. It was an unopposed landing – yet even so innocent people died needlessly due to the callous oversight of those in command. There was failure, then, even in victory; but this correspondent finds himself saddened by the inescapable reflection that our forces have failed in almost everything they have attempted. The explanation for this lies in their leaders, who have been appointed with no reference to merit, and been allowed to remain in their posts even after horrific displays of ineptitude.

Our commander-in-chief missed the opportunity of taking Sebastopol when it lay virtually undefended; and, like so many of his officers, he sat complacently in a nice warm farmhouse whilst a savage winter devoured his army. But he is the son of a lord, and is well connected on both sides of the Commons, so he remains in his post. Our Quartermaster-General, to select another, has good interest at the Horse Guards, and several noble friends besides, and so receives and retains an appointment for which no one believes him qualified. There are countless other examples in the Cavalry, the Infantry, the Transport Service; one simply has to choose a department and corruption's taint can be found.

One thing, however, must be understood: all abuses of privilege out here in the Crimea are but fruit of a rotten tree. Back in England, a man is made war minister because he is a duke; another becomes a war secretary because he is that duke's cousin. Our government and army are parcelled out as if they were aristocratic estates – rather than great public trusts to be employed for the benefit of the people.

The Colonel could read no more. He screwed up the paper and cast it to the ground. Even though it did not specifically address him, Boyce could see the oblique references plainly enough – the warm farmhouse, the charge of corruption against the Quartermaster-General. 'Fruit of a rotten tree indeed,' he spat. 'Damn that fellow!'

Pierce nodded. 'Treasonous dog should be hanged, post-haste. I've been saying so for months.'

Fairlie puffed on his pipe, a contemplative look on his face. 'Is there not truth to some of it, though? What he says about that old rascal Pam, for instance?'

Boyce glared at him. 'There most certainly is *not*, Lieutenant-Colonel! Lord Palmerston deserves the support of every patriotic Englishman. This . . . this *filth* should be countered. It should be bloody well *stopped*. The blackguard has gone too far.'

'Quite,' Pierce agreed loyally. 'Someone should publish the details of how *he* conducts himself. See how his precious reputation looks then.'

The determination to act was setting hard in Boyce's mind. 'Does anyone know where he is?'

His officers glanced at each other. 'Balaclava's our best guess,' said Pierce. 'He didn't show at the Quarries for some reason, but today's action might draw him out.'

Boyce looked around at the hundreds hurrying through the camp of the Light Division to their appointed posts. He straightened his jacket; the sketches rustled slightly against his chest.

'Go to the men,' he ordered. 'I will join you shortly. There is something that requires my attention.'

5

Madeleine could not sleep. Pulling her sheets around her, she had moved to the chair by the window, and was watching the columns of soldiers trudging along the murky road outside the farmhouse. This movement of troops had been going on for some time now; she knew that the Guardsmen that were then filing past were part of the reserve force. Those unfortunate enough to be at the front of the attack would already be in place. She prayed ardently that the sun would stay down, that the day would not arrive, that the great assault would not begin, that hundreds of those men who had marched past her window would not soon be sent out to meet horrible deaths. But the light of the coming morning could just be made out, colouring the clear sky along the very edge of the horizon.

Annabel would be at the door of the Boyces' farmhouse at five o'clock, ready to head towards the battlefield. Madeleine was dreading the purposeful knocks that would summon her forth to the hospital tents of the Middle Ravine. Since the supply lines had improved, and the provision of food and clothing to the soldiers had ceased to be such a serious issue, her indefatigable companion had decided that it was best that they redirect their energies towards providing medical assistance. Madeleine had grown accustomed to dishing out soup, or woollen hats, or cheese; but she was certainly not accustomed to nursing writhing, sweating, bleeding men, some torn open or missing limbs, who forced out their last words in terrifying, frenzied barks, and grabbed at her with all their strength. It was too much for her to bear. She often had to excuse herself and return to her bed. Weeping between the cold sheets, she would imagine Richard being brought to her in the Ravine, his innards unwinding bloodily into her arms, and there being nothing that she could do to save him.

It was the uncertainty that particularly tormented her. The weeks since he had departed were slowly mounting up into months. No word was sent as to his new location. Desolation crept into Madeleine; a dark part of her began to believe that he would never return, that she was stranded with no hope of release. Her last sight of him had been from this very window. It had been early morning. Nathaniel, returning from the trenches, had just slammed the front door behind him. Richard had been racing from the farmyard, as he had done so many times before, half-dressed with his arms full of clothing, leaving a trail of frosty breath behind him in the chill February air. What had happened to him after this, after he had vanished behind the yard's dry-stone wall, she could not say.

He was still the *Courier*'s Crimean correspondent, of course. Nathaniel would not allow the journal in the house, but on her wanderings with Annabel she occasionally came across a copy. Annabel, reading it, would shake her head, and say a few curt words about the recklessness and arrogance of this 'Tomahawk's' style. Madeleine would at first give ardent thanks that he was still alive, that he did not lie in a mass grave somewhere. A moment later she would succumb to misery as her morose confusion at his absence deepened yet further. Seeing her distress, Annabel would pat her arm with rough sympathy and tell her that the scapegrace was supremely unworthy of her affections. This did not help.

It was an impossible mystery. Madeleine had no option but to go on, avoiding her husband and his tortures as best she could, moping along beside Annabel, longing for Richard. Since his disappearance, she found that many aspects of the war that she had previously been able to endure had become quite overwhelming. Every stuttering of rifle fire, every stray shot from the Russian artillery, made her want to cry aloud with despair as she imagined, with startling clarity, bullets cutting into her lover's body, and the ground exploding under him – casting him into a ditch, where he would perish in agony, her name upon his lips.

Madeleine's surprise, therefore, when Richard Cracknell suddenly came into view, trotting alongside the column of Guardsmen, was so great that she felt as if it might stop her heart where she sat. She blinked and stared, her mouth falling open.

He looked well, very different from the half-starved, mud-splattered, mortally injured hero of her desolate fancy; he looked prosperous, in fact, well dressed in a new overcoat, peaked cap and boots, and even a little plumper than he had been in the Spring. Wherever he had been, he had taken good care of himself. Madeleine leapt joyfully to her feet, the bed-sheets falling around her. He was coming back. They were going to Spain at last, as he had promised. At any moment, he would leave the column and head towards the farmhouse door, towards a blissful reunion after a lengthy, dismal separation. She clutched her hands before her breast, tense with anticipation.

But he kept on going. She watched the striding figure in absolute disbelief. He was not coming to meet her, to take her in his arms and rescue her from this place. He was going on to the front, to risk his life needlessly once again, for the sake of his magazine.

Madeleine went cold, her hands falling slowly to her sides. Thoughts she had never dared even to entertain dropped into her mind with the awful, leaden certainty of truth. Richard had deliberately chosen to stay away for all this time. He had most probably been nearby, lying low, avoiding her. He had cut her loose without a word – discarded her as one might leave an unwanted newspaper on the seat of an omnibus.

She was not aware of having left the farmhouse or crossing the yard. The next sensation she registered was the coarse weave of Richard's new coat between her fingertips as she took hold of its sleeve and pulled him off to the side of the road. Together, they lurched down a gentle slope. She dragged him behind a ruined outhouse. Some of the Guardsmen, seeing this, let out lewd whistles.

They did not kiss, or embrace, or even touch. She released his sleeve as soon as she could. Richard did not seem particularly surprised at her sudden appearance. For a moment, his face was expressionless; then he smiled, and reached out a hand towards her.

She dodged it as if it were a bayonet. 'Where have you been?' she asked coldly.

'Look at you, Maddy,' he murmured softly. 'Out here in your petticoats.'

Madeleine ignored this. She repeated her question. Three feet of empty space gaped between them. The sound of tramping boots drifted over from the road.

Richard let out a condescending sigh, as if her behaviour was somehow irrational. 'Over in Balaclava, that's all. Writing my reports.'

She glared at him in astonishment, feeling her tenuous composure slipping away. 'Writing your reports,' she echoed flatly. 'What about me, Richard? What about our *love*?'

He seemed to be considering reaching out for her again; but the violent anger gathering in her eyes deterred him. 'Maddy, it was growing dangerous for both of us. You must admit this. Your husband was poised to act. There was talk—'

'*Talk*?' she spluttered incredulously. 'You said – you said you would risk anything to be with me – that you *loved me*. You said it many times, Richard. What is Nathaniel, next to that? *Il n'est rien – rien de tout!*'

'Calm yourself, for God's sake.' He glanced over his shoulder. 'I – I would have come for you, when the time was right. Taken you to Andalusia. I still will.' And then, after a pause, he smiled at her again, an expression clearly intended to convey rueful longing. 'I missed you, Maddy. By God, how I bloody missed you.'

Glowering, Madeleine looked back at him, studying his face. It had changed; something was deeply, deeply wrong.

Her Richard was gone. This person before her was a char-latan, an impostor, playing his part with a terrible lack of conviction.

'You are *lying*,' she said, her voice trembling with fury and anguish. 'You are a liar, a wretched liar. How could you leave me in this place for so long, without a word? Have you no notion of what I have endured in these past months?'

'Maddy, come now . . .'

The first sob almost doubled her up; she thought she might be sick, so tight and hard was the convulsion. 'I have been deserted,' she managed to cry, gulping for air, 'oh, I have been cast aside!'

Her defences down, Richard managed to take hold of her. 'Maddy, my girl,' he said firmly. 'You have grown over-excited. Go back to the cottage, this instant. I must continue on to the front now, but I will come to you after the battle. We can discuss this then.'

She writhed with all her strength, trying to free herself from his arms. 'I do not believe you! You are a *liar*!' Realising that she could not escape, she clutched his coat tightly, sinking her nails into the fabric. 'I stayed out here for you,' she hissed, their faces close. 'Out here in *hell*. I risked my life. Did this mean nothing to you *at all*?'

Overbalancing in this desperate clinch, they staggered to one side. Madeleine's bare foot caught on a root; she stumbled, losing her grip and collapsing to the ground.

Richard managed to remain upright. His cheeks were flushed. 'Return to the cottage, Madeleine,' he instructed tersely. 'We will talk later.'

Then he turned back in the direction of the advancing columns, rounding the corner of the outhouse, leaving her sight for ever.

For a while, she lay where she had fallen, in a pool of splayed petticoats, looking up at the fading stars, feeling the tears dry on her face. Then she rose and walked back numbly to the farmhouse, drawing curious stares from the trickle of soldiers that still moved along the road to the front. She passed the glowing window where, only ten minutes earlier, she had sat dreaming fretfully of the chance of being reunited with her lost love; not knowing then that he was not lost at all but false, false to his very core.

Nathaniel was standing by the hearth in his trench uniform. He held some worn sheets of paper in his hands.

6

Kitson opened the flap of the *Courier* tent and peered inside. It was empty, but the smoking wood-pile at its centre and a strong odour of fresh sweat suggested that it had recently been occupied. He entered carefully.

Miss Wade followed a moment later, her lips pursed and her fists clenched, as if ready to help with the restraining of a writhing madman – ready to bind him with stout rope and have him hauled off to Bedlam. She was visibly disappointed to discover that such assistance was not necessary. Kitson quickly checked the shadowy corners of the tent, soon moving back into the light of the guttering fire.

'Heavens above, would you look at this place!' the Scotswoman muttered. 'If ever proof of derangement were needed, Mr Kitson, this clammy den would certainly suffice.'

Kitson walked to the desk and surveyed the drawings that covered it. 'Styles has certainly been busy,' he said quietly. 'It would seem that he has—' He stopped dead. There was an old hip-flask at the edge of the smouldering fire-pit, standing in the dust like a tiny gravestone. 'Cracknell was here. This night.'

Miss Wade shook her head. 'No, that scoundrel's been gone for almost as long as yourself, sir – as I told you. He's still writing his grand-standing nonsense for the *Courier*, but he's departed from the front.'

Kitson looked at her. 'I'm afraid I must disagree, Miss Wade. He has returned, for this great assault I suspect. And despite everything, it would appear that he's come to claim Styles as a companion for his mission.' This scenario, although terrible to consider, was the only one he could entertain. 'They must be stopped. I have to find them.'

Kitson's hard conviction was causing Miss Wade to doubt herself. He could tell that her thoughts were turning to Madeleine Boyce – to the new threat that the return of Cracknell posed to her young friend. 'I shall go to the Boyces' farmhouse,' she declared, starting for the tent flaps. 'This very minute.'

As Kitson made to follow, a ferocious din started up outside, from the direction of Sebastopol – an enormous clamour of voices backed with the crackle of musketry. Emerging into the crisp dawn air, he saw Mrs Seacole standing in her stirrups, her blue feather bobbing as she strained to make herself as tall as possible in order to see over the surrounding tent-tops. The next second, there was a sequence of loud blasts, issuing from the Allied lines. The battle was starting, but they all knew at once that the plan had gone seriously awry.

'Good Lord, my dears,' proclaimed Mrs Seacole, 'I do believe that the Russians are attacking *us*.'

There were no lights at any of the farmhouse's windows. Annabel reached into her bag of supplies and drew out the clasp-knife she had secured there some weeks earlier for the purpose of protection. It occurred to her that Cracknell might be inside with Madeleine right now, leading her into further sin, subjecting her to his foul usage. She lifted her knife, thinking that maybe, if this was indeed the case, she would permit herself to cut him a little for the good of his soul.

The front door was ajar. She eased it open with her palm, the hinges squealing as it swung back to reveal a scene of disorder. Several chairs had been smashed, and the parlour table knocked on to its side. Annabel caught her breath.

It had to be Styles. Mr Kitson was wrong – he was not at the front at all. He must have forced his way in, and embarked on an orgy of destruction. Perhaps Madeleine had chased him off, and then gone for help; or perhaps she lay hidden and trembling beneath a bed, whilst the madman stalked the house searching for her with evil mischief in mind. Annabel gripped her blade, asking God for courage.

'Madeleine?' she called out, her voice strong and clear. 'Madeleine? It's me. Don't be alarmed. It's just Annabel.'

No one answered. Annabel edged forward through the gloomy room, knife first, her feet dragging through fragments of chair and pieces of broken crockery, expecting at any moment that a stooped form would lunge at her from the shadows, a savage cry on its foaming, poisonous lips. She cursed the choices she had made. Why had she gone to the British Hotel? Why had she wasted so much time listening to that strange Mrs Seacole witter on? Madeleine had needed help – and where had she been?

'Styles,' she said, putting some steel into her tone, 'Styles, if you're in here, you show yourself right this minute. Styles, you demon, if you've hurt her...'

Outside, in the distance, the sounds of battle were escalating, but the small farmhouse seemed quiet and empty. Annabel advanced into its narrow hall. *In God I trust,* she mouthed silently, her heart thumping; *I will not be afraid. What can man do to me?* Only one door was open, the doorway seeming bright in the surrounding darkness. It was the door to Madeleine's bedroom.

Through the bedroom window, as she approached, Annabel could see a deep blue sky, still tinted by night, flashing with shell-fire and signal rockets. The room itself was neat and orderly, at least compared with the parlour. Indeed, the only possible sign of any discord was the stripped bed, its sheets piled loosely on a chair by the window. Annabel almost relaxed, her knife lowering a little.

Then she saw the foot.

It was naked, waxy white and quite lifeless, sticking out from underneath a brown woollen blanket, just past the end of the bedstead. Annabel's clasp-knife clattered to the floorboards as she rushed, staggering, into the room. Dark stains dappled the blanket; Annabel felt the dragging weight of wet cloth as she tore it back. Madeleine lay on the floor, her arms folded neatly in her lap. She was staring blankly towards the window. Blood saturated her petticoats, and pooled over the boards around her. Into it were pressed several sheets of sketching paper, entirely soaked and crumbling apart, whatever had once been drawn upon them obliterated.

Annabel dropped down into the blood, slipping in it a little as she lifted Madeleine up, trying vainly to support her lolling head, and whispering her name frantically; then, after only a couple of seconds, her desperate hope suddenly disappeared, and she abandoned her friend to death. A ragged, sobbing sigh burst out of her lips. She hugged Madeleine with all her strength, the dead girl's arms poking out stiffly from her tight embrace.

A moment later, Annabel looked around her with savage fury, half-expecting the murderer still to be in the room, hiding behind the door or lurking over by the wash-stand. No one was there. She was quite alone. Her anger faltered; she tried to make herself search for some definite indication of who had done this – to study Madeleine's wounds and the area where she lay. But her dear young friend, cradled in her arms, was so terribly cold. She could not think.

Bowing her head, Annabel attempted to pray, to beg Almighty God for strength and understanding. This too, however, was utterly beyond her. There was no consolation to be had on that bloody bedroom floor. Her Madeleine, her beautiful, precious Madeleine, was lost.

7

Boyce's arrival in the crowded rifle pit drew a throaty, impatient growl from the senior officers assembled within. They had been waiting for him for nearly fifteen minutes: the meeting of a general and eleven other colonels, poised to lead a major action that could bring the enemy to its knees, kept in suspension solely by his tardiness. At the centre of the pit, dressed in a dark blue frock-coat rather than the tweeds worn by his subordinates, stood General Sir John Campbell. He looked pasty and drawn; rumour had it that the terrible tension of commanding the impending attack was rapidly bringing his health to ruin.

'Mr Boyce!' he snapped. 'What is the meaning of this?'

By the General's side was Colonel Yea of the 34th, appointed as second-in-command, who was as florid as Campbell was pale. He scowled through his monocle. 'Bad form, Boyce. Damned bad form.' There was a rumble of concurrence from his fellows. 'The French are *fighting*, y'know, whilst we linger here! The Bear has launched an attack against the Mamelon!'

Boyce ignored everyone in the pit but Campbell. He came to attention. 'My apologies, General, but I have just discovered that my wife has been killed. That is the cause of my regrettable lateness.'

The disposition of the pit towards him changed immediately. Campbell was aghast. '*Killed*, man? But how?'

'A Russian, sir.' Boyce was careful to keep his voice

398

sorrowful, but calm. 'Dressed in civilian clothes – a spy, perhaps, or a deserter thinking to steal a few items from my house to fund his flight to the mainland. My wife appears to have disturbed him. He shot her with a pistol.'

The dismay of those around him was palpable. 'Did you catch this villain?' one of the colonels asked.

Boyce nodded. 'A couple of privates from my regiment pursued him out into open country, at the rear of the plateau. They managed to bring him down with their miniés.' He paused. 'But nothing could be done for my poor Madeleine.'

There was a brief silence. 'My dear fellow,' mumbled Campbell. He looked at the ground uncertainly for a moment before coming to a resolution. 'You must be relieved of your command,' he said firmly. 'Who is your lieutenant-colonel? You must be relieved, Boyce, straight away. I insist.' The colonels, now filled with pity and a little guilt for their impatience, made a range of sympathetic sounds, signalling their agreement.

Boyce, still at attention, looked into Campbell's bloodshot eyes. 'General, I humbly request that you permit me to fight this engagement. My place, sir, is here. It is where my dear wife would wish me. What use has war for a man in mourning? Far better that I serve my Queen and country, and face those who took my Madeleine from me.'

The assemblage of officers and adjutants, their attitude to Boyce now quite reversed, murmured admiringly. 'Jolly good show,' someone pronounced; 'A fine display,' declared another.

Campbell nodded understandingly. 'Very well, old chap, very well,' he said, laying a hand briefly on Boyce's shoulder. 'Now, I'm afraid we must proceed.'

The old General turned slightly, and raised his voice, addressing the group. They were told that Lord Raglan had every confidence that the French would repulse the Russians from the fort of the Mamelon, and then go on to take the Malakhoff Tower as planned. Once it was theirs, the attacking brigade of the Fourth Division, led by Campbell himself, would approach the Great Redan from the left; and that of the Light, under Colonel Yea, would approach it from the right.

Campbell looked around the men in the rifle pit. 'Go to your men and await the signal – two rockets, to be fired together. But be aware that when the Tricolour flies above the Malakhoff Tower, we attack. May Heaven watch over us, gentlemen. God save the Queen.'

'God save the Queen,' repeated the officers, coming to attention before moving off into the trenches with their aides.

Boyce stood still as his peers strode past him, uttering awkward words of condolence. Madeleine's voice still rang in his head, screaming at him as he pursued her around their little farmhouse. She had shown him contempt and anger before, countless times, spitting names at him in her mother tongue, glaring at him defiantly after he'd quieted her with his fists; but all the ordeals of their wretched marriage had been as nothing compared with the searing hatred that had poured out of her then. She had reacted to the drawings as if they were the product of his turpitude rather than her own, as if the stigma of her repulsive wrong-doing was somehow reflected off her, like bright sunlight off a polished silver tray, dazzling the accuser instead of the accused.

Her immediate wish, naturally enough he supposed, had been to seize them, and tear them to pieces. This could not be allowed. He had decided that the sketches were to form the centrepiece of a divorce case so devastating it would see her all but driven out naked into the wilderness. She dived across the room; he moved to avoid her; furniture was upset before them both. Realising the futility of her pursuit, she started to throw plates, cups, pans, even chairs. Tiring of this after a minute or two, he strode towards her purposefully – prompting her to flee into her room, shrieking as she went.

The first flies of the day were stirring in the trenches. Boyce waved some of them away with his hand, trying to remember what action he had thought he was going to take as he followed her. The memory seemed somehow dislocated from him, as if it were something he had seen someone else do, or perhaps read about somewhere. She had slammed the door behind her and attempted to shut him out, but she was no match for him in a contest of strength. He forced his way in, gripped hold of her quite savagely, and asked if she was aware, if she had *any conception* in that empty, frivolous head of hers, of the irreparable damage she had done to him? Of the deadly blows her shameful conduct had cast against his name, his reputation, his honour?

Even as he walked through the British works, with the sounds of mortal struggle drifting over from the Mamelon, the recollection of the laugh Madeleine gave in response to this question made Boyce shudder. It had been so bitter, so caustic and scornful that it made him let go of her and take a step back. The drawings slipped from his grasp, scattering on to the floor around her. She was no longer interested in them, however. Crouching in the candlelight like a vicious animal, she started to speak, in a strange, rapid voice, of how openly she had defied him; of how she had assisted her lover with the concoction of his venomous reports for the *Courier*; of how she had been in his arms only minutes before, exchanging words of eternal love; of how he was going to be watching the attack that very morning, alert for errors.

His hand had gone to his gun. Had he been hoping that this would be enough, that this alone might check her, and make her fall silent? Or had he been intending to draw it, to use it, even then? He could not say; but she watched him closely, and did not pause even for a second. In fact, if anything, her revelations became frantic, her accent growing thicker, the words emerging so quickly that they were packed tightly together into blocks dictated only by her gasping breaths. She was not so incomprehensible, though, that he could not tell that she was saying things that had no place on the lips of a woman. It was filthy talk of *fucks*, *quims* and *pricks*; disgusting disclosures about the extent of their depravity, their heedless disregard of the risk of discovery; foul boasts of how many times they had fornicated in his bed, in amongst his sheets, or on top of his trunks, sprawled out lustfully over his uniforms.

The first two shots were fired simply to put an end to her and her devilish utterances. She had been thrown down immediately. He remembered the sight of the singed holes punched in her petticoats, and the welling blackness beneath. She was not dead then, though. Her hands, flung out as she had landed, started to find their way slowly towards her wounds, scrabbling through the drawings which lay beneath her. Her eyes were open very wide, her mouth gaping. The expression on her face, he recalled clearly, was not one of shock, or agony, or terror, but of a strange relief.

Boyce had realised that she was trying to speak. But he'd heard enough. His face impassive, he levelled the pistol a second time and fired the remaining four bullets in quick succession. Gun smoke filled the small, airless room, making him cough. Slowly, Boyce reloaded the revolver, putting the spent percussion caps back into his ammunition pouch. He went over to the window, extinguished the candle that stood on the sill and peered outside. The yard was empty, as was the road beyond it. Turning back, he bent down to place Madeleine's outstretched arms in her lap, and then covered her with a blanket taken from the pile on her chair, thinking to create an impression of propriety, of official awareness, should anyone come across the body before he returned. He left the house soon after.

It was justified. Boyce knew that it was justified. What man of honour could have done otherwise before such provocation? He resolved not to dwell upon it. He had other matters to look to now – other enemies to repay. What was it she had said? *'He will be there, you hopeless fool – he will be there, watching you with a righteous eye! And when men die because of your stupidity, he will ensure once again that the whole of England knows of it!'*

Boyce entered the advance works around the Quarries. The trenches and pits were filled with the soldiers of the Light Division's assaulting brigade. Fairlie and Pierce were up ahead, conferring with some captains and subalterns from the 99th. It was starting to grow light. Boyce was confident that his prey was nearby, and would soon make himself apparent. He selected a suitable vantage point and settled down to wait.

8

Private Cregg sat in the advance works just beyond the Quarries with the larger part of the assaulting brigade – men from six regiments, all awaiting the order to move. Over the top, after two hundred yards of almost entirely open ground, lay the Great Redan, its guns firing across diagonally at the French forts.

The day was not seven hours old, yet for Cregg it had already delivered a couple of most unwelcome orders. First of all, he had found that the 99th's battalion had been assigned to the attacking rather than to the reserve brigade. Then, as if that wasn't bad enough, Lieutenant Nunn, the same booby who'd swiped his drawings, had taken him out of his company, and directed him up to the very front of the attack – to the line they called the Forlorn Hope. Hardly a name to lift a cove's spirits, he'd grumbled as he climbed to his feet.

The cause for this miserable twist of fortune, Cregg knew, had to be the drawings. For a short while it had been perfect. Dozens upon dozens had seen them, and spread the word to all their pals. Then Nunn had stuck his nose in and it had been a quick slide down from there. Boyce had been told right away, you could bet on that. This posting to the Forlorn Hope reeked of him. Dan Cregg was a dead man. The drawings would be burnt, and the joke forgotten. As ever, the Colonel had won, and the private soldier had lost – lost the lot.

And to top it all, his hand was giving him serious trouble. The two remaining fingers had grown yet more stiff and inflexible, rewarding his tentative efforts to move them with sharp shocks of pain. He had no idea how he was supposed to fight in this condition. Even holding a rifle was proving a stern challenge. The ache was spreading, as it often did, from his arm, up the muscles of his shoulders and neck, to the base of his head. His dejection became laced with impatience. Oh come on, he thought, it's all but light, let's just get it bleedin' over with. The idea of an end, right then, was not entirely without appeal.

'Sharpshooter!' someone shouted.

Bullets struck the rim of the trench, about fifteen yards from where Cregg sat; then, in a cloud of sandy dust, a man tumbled down amongst the redcoats sheltering there. It was one of theirs, making a dash overland to the advance parallel to avoid a lengthy trudge through the trenches. Was it a messenger, bearing news of a reprieve? A change of plan?

No such luck. The dust settled to reveal a wiry, clean-shaven civvie, dressed in a colourless coat that was flecked with dried blood. Cregg squinted – there was something faintly familiar about him. The soldiers of the 33rd, amongst whom he'd landed, were helping him up, brushing his coat and handing him his hat. Glad for any manner of distraction, Cregg picked up his minié and crawled along towards him, over the boots of his comrades.

'Oi, cock!' he yelled over the roar of the Russian guns. 'Oi, look 'ere, pal!'

The man was spluttering, spitting out dirt and feeling his ribs as if checking a wound. He looked up at Cregg, his face pale with pain.

'Now, I know that I knows you,' Cregg carried on, pointing at him with his good hand, 'but I can't say where from. You any wiser?'

The man coughed; there were spots of blood on his lips and teeth. 'I believe I bound your hand once,' he managed to shout, 'down at the British Hotel.'

Cregg snapped his fingers. 'That's it – the British 'Otel! Back before that nigger bitch 'ad me threw out.' The soldier considered this new arrival with sceptical wonder. 'What you doin' 'ere, cock? Takin' a leaf out of Mother bleedin' Seacole's book, are we, and a-comin' up to work among the fightin' men as they fall?'

He didn't respond to this. 'My name is Thomas Kitson,' he stated, as loudly as he could. 'I'm looking for someone – Richard Cracknell, the newspaperman.'

Cregg grinned. 'Oh yes, I know that gent. We are good pals, me and Mister Cracknell.' He gave this Mr Kitson a mysterious wink.

The fellow paused uncomprehendingly for a second. 'There is another man,' he went on, 'another civilian. An illustrator. Younger. Have you either of them? Please, it is of the greatest importance.'

Cregg thought of the drawings, and how he had found them. Those damn things had caused him quite enough trouble already. He was saying nothing. So he shook his head. 'If they're anywhere, I'd say that-a-way, back at the Quarries. You've come too far forward, pal.'

Without another word, Mr Kitson started back along the trench, keeping low.

'Remember me to Mister Cracknell, if you find 'im!' Cregg bawled at his back. 'Dan Cregg of the 99th!'

'They've done it!' cried Cracknell, squinting through his field glass. 'God save 'em all, they've done it! The Mamelon is safe! *Vive la France!*'

The redcoats crowding the trench around him gave a muted cheer. Cracknell lifted the glass again, poking it carefully through a crenulation of pickets towards the smooth hill occupied by the fort of the Mamelon. This ugly structure, built around a hill from a loose collection of sandbags and low stone parapets, was sparking with cannon-fire. It was surrounded by a thick covering of the slain and the wounded, the majority of them Russian. Loose, panicked columns of enemy soldiers were streaming away from the position towards their own line. A large French force was commencing a counter-attack, companies of scarlet-trousered Zoaves charging around the sides of the hill, heading towards

405

the unclaimed territory that separated them from the Russian defences.

Cracknell excitedly swivelled his glass in the direction of this no-man's land. Looming up over it, through a thin film of early morning mist, was the French target – the Malakhoff Tower. The tower itself was circular and about five or six storeys high. It had been ruined some time ago, one of its sides having almost completely collapsed, but it had served as the focus for one of the largest concentrations of earthworks and artillery on the Russian line. As the correspondent watched, its guns began to fire on the advancing Zoaves.

'By my soul,' he muttered, 'I should really be writing this down.' He opened his pocketbook and licked the tip of his pencil.

The Tomahawk had been hard at work for almost a minute when someone stood before him, blocking his light. He knew at once who it was. 'Why, Thomas Kitson,' he exclaimed sarcastically, without looking up. 'It's been months. How the hell are you?'

'Where is Styles, Cracknell?'

He sighed; such a predictable question. Closing his book contemptuously, he gave Kitson his full attention. His former junior had a new, almost clerical formality about him, due largely to his beard having gone; only a pair of modest sideburns had been retained. The fellow was also leaning slightly, like a building with a couple of rows of bricks knocked out of one side. One of those long arms was against his midriff – the location, Cracknell guessed, of his injury.

'Shouldn't you be back at the British Hotel, Kitson?' he sneered. 'Swabbing wounds and washing the feet of the crippled soldiers?'

Kitson grasped hold of his shoulder. 'Tell me where he is.'

'What the devil is it to you?' He pushed Kitson away. 'You forfeited your contract months ago, my friend! The affairs of the *Courier* are no longer your concern!'

The guns of the Malakhoff were growing louder, and the bursts of explosive noise began to have a bruising, ringing impact upon the ears. Occasional, distant shouts of *'Vive l'Empereur!'*

drifted out from the battle, along with the wails of the wounded. Kitson shoved past him, heading on towards the right side of the Quarries, powered by an evidently over-whelming determination to hunt Styles down. Cracknell realised that, like him, Kitson must have only very recently learned that their illustrator was still on the peninsula. He knew that Kitson had an abiding sense of responsibility for the boy, stemming from a rather self-important notion that he had somehow inspired Styles to put himself forward for service in the Crimea.

At any rate, Cracknell had no solid information as to the illustrator's whereabouts, even had he been inclined to share it. Styles had failed to appear at their designated meeting place. Given his continued enthusiasm for the blackest parts of war, Cracknell's supposition was that he'd gone further forward than had been agreed. The Tomahawk of the *Courier*, for all his famous bravery, had decided down in the trenches that he would hang back a little for this one. Above, the brightening sky was as clear as glass. It was going to be a fine day. Climbing out before a large Russian fort in such conditions was little short of suicide. A massacre was surely on the cards; but, as he watched Kitson walk away through the siege-works, the senior correspondent knew that he could hardly now permit himself to remain to the rear of both his feckless juniors. Pocketbook still in his hand, he gave chase.

A few yards apart, the two former comrades turned a corner and crossed through a large rifle pit, which had been reduced to little more than a deep crater by recent artillery bombardment. It was crammed with soldiers from the assaulting brigade, preparing themselves for action. They had a bleak alertness about them that was very different from the stoic demeanour of the Guardsmen Cracknell had passed in the reserves. As he tucked away his notebook and fumbled with a cigarette, however, the correspondent realised that a number of those crouched down in the shadows were also regarding him rather strangely.

The Tomahawk of the *Courier* was well used to bearing the scrutiny of both officers and the common soldiery. He was, after all, a face of the campaign, a readily recognisable character. The looks he was receiving that morning, however, were different somehow. Usually he inspired either admiration or scorn, and although both of these sentiments were present, they were tempered with something else, something unaccountable; something that was fiendishly close to mockery. Cracknell could not imagine what he might have done to deserve this change. Was it his lengthy absence from the front, perhaps?

Halfway across the pit, the facings on these soldiers' jackets went from white and green to yellow, and their disposition towards him grew noticeably more hostile. Cracknell looked at the numeral on their caps. It was as he suspected; they had moved in amongst the battalion of the 99th. Whilst the majority of the rank-and-file were illiterate, they had no doubt been filled with lies about the Tomahawk and his work by officers loyal to their Colonel, his frequent target. The soldiers began to hiss and mutter, and stick out their boots to trip him. Someone spat, and a milky gobbet of phlegm landed on the shoulder of his blue coat. Kitson had vanished.

Major Pierce came into view. Spotting Cracknell, his swine-like features lit with malicious pleasure. 'Well look here!' he cried. 'This, men, this here is the bugger who called *us*, the brave comrades of Her Majesty's Army, the fruit of a rotten tree! He called us rotten, my lads, *rotten* – in the bloody papers as well!'

Intrepidly, Cracknell stood his ground, doing his best to correct the Major's scurrilous distortion of his words – to point out to the idiot soldiers that he was on their bloody side, and that their officers were about to order them to their deaths for no useful purpose. But it was no use. They started kicking and punching, spitting on him again, pulling at his clothes, tearing away both his field glass and his pocketbook – all the while shouting '*rotten yerself!*' As he was beaten down, Cracknell found himself almost laughing at the absurdity of it. After all that had happened, could it really be his fate to be killed by a mob of *British soldiers*?

Then, with eerie suddenness, they all backed away, falling quiet as they did so. Cracknell lowered his arms and peered upwards. Before him was none other than Colonel Boyce, his moustache erect and furious. The correspondent wiped some blood from his lip and opened his mouth to speak. Boyce grabbed hold of him, heaving him to his feet and throwing him back against the wickerwork gabions of the trench wall with a brutality that took him quite by surprise.

'What are you doing out here, villain?' Boyce growled. 'I thought you had learned your lesson about such interference!'

'That was but a brief sabbatical,' Cracknell replied quickly, trying to appear conspicuously unbowed by his opponent's savagery. 'Wouldn't miss this one for the world. Frontal attack on an enormous fort, without the benefit of a bombardment? Lord Raglan certainly is confident, I'll say that much for him.'

'That son of a lord, you mean? The fruit of your rotten tree?' The Colonel reddened with rage. 'By God, you will pay for your calumnies!'

'Where is the *Pilate* then, Boyce?' the Tomahawk retorted. 'Did Norton get it home safely? What did you have to offer him in the end?'

The leather of Boyce's gloves squeaked as he screwed up the correspondent's lapels and forced him back into the gabions; they began to crack open with the pressure, releasing a stream of gritty soil on to Cracknell's face.

Boyce was close against him now. 'I have killed her,' he whispered coldly.

Cracknell squirmed, rubbing the dirt from his eyes. 'What?'

'I have killed her,' Boyce repeated, 'and I swear to God that before this morning is out I will kill you as well.'

Then the Colonel released him, stepping away and rejoining his men, watching for his reaction. Cracknell pulled himself back upright, shaking the earth from his coat, staring back at Boyce in complete mystification. Slowly, he realised what he had been told: Madeleine had been murdered by her husband. That such a thing could happen had never so much as entered his mind. It seemed impossible. With disturbing vividness, he remembered how she had struggled in his arms not an hour before; he could almost feel the warmth and strength of her slender young limbs, fighting with a vigour that had made him smile a little even as she'd cursed him.

Cracknell could think of nothing whatsoever to say. Then, all at once, he knew that he had to get as far from Boyce as he possibly could. He shouldered his way roughly through the redcoats towards the opposite side of the pit.

'Let the fool go,' the Colonel ordered disdainfully, somewhere behind him. 'He is nothing to us.'

9

Two signal rockets raced upwards side by side, the white plumes climbing fast through the soft peach of the morning sky. The eleven colonels, in their different parts of the line, watched them disbelievingly. This was without doubt the signal for the attack, but the black and green triangle of the Russian flag could clearly be seen flying above the Malakhoff Tower. Its guns still fired on the French, and large numbers of infantry still clashed around it, rushing back and forth between the Russian earthworks, scrambling to form firing lines and battling bloodily in the trenches. The basic condition for their assault had not been met – yet there, hanging above them like a pair of great comets, was the plain instruction to proceed nonetheless.

Every one of the colonels knew, however, that it was not their place to question the decisions of the High Command. They swallowed hard, finishing off their interrupted prayers and drawing pistols and swords. Some took out their service whistles, and sounded shrill notes over the bellowing of the guns. Others simply started up the shout.

The men of the line stood, wiping their sweaty faces, waiting for that final torturous second, knowing for certain that their time had arrived, that the dreaded order had been given; and then, urged on by their sergeants, they pitched forward. The crumbling, sun-baked trenches quickly robbed the attack of its order, and the soldiers of the Forlorn Hope emerged in twos and threes, scrabbling out of the disintegrating works,

411

floundering desperately as they tried to rise to their feet and ready their miniés. In place of ordered ranks of redcoats, thousands strong, marching unstoppably onwards, were a few hundred confused and dusty men, wandering about in the last pools of low mist, looking for fellows and officers still stuck in the earth behind them.

Lieutenant Nunn drew himself up and considered the Great Redan. It was a formidable sight, the sloping 'v' of its façade sitting beside the ruined suburbs of Sebastopol like the crude visor from some gigantic medieval jousting helmet. It appeared to be entirely unscathed by the previous day's bombardment, the cruel point of its salient sharp and intact, the smooth earth of its sides interrupted only by the square holes of gun emplacements. The ramparts were high and heavily manned. It seemed, from the open ground before the Quarries, to be utterly unassailable.

Striding through the shapeless mass of soldiers, Nunn shouted for a sergeant to bring the companies into line. Before anything could be done, however, a row of bright points flashed along the front of the Redan as a number of its guns fired together; and much of the ragged Forlorn Hope was wiped clean away. Back at the trenches, scores were struck before they even had a chance to stand upright, collapsing amidst splintered pickets or being flung backwards on to those assembling behind them. Dazed by the noise, Nunn found himself to be surrounded by the wounded and dismembered. A moment later, as their initial shock turned to blind panic, these men started to howl piteously – their cries drowned out almost immediately by another round of cannon-fire from the Redan.

Nunn walked further forward, repeating his order as loudly as he could. No one heeded him; the only NCOs he encountered were dead. To his great relief, he came across a captain from the 7th Fusiliers, a short man with a downy moustache.

'What should we do, sir?' Nunn cried.

The captain's lips moved and one of his arms waved about emphatically, but Nunn couldn't hear a thing. His ears were filled with a thick, thunderous sound, as if he were standing beneath a mighty waterfall. Then the captain stopped speaking with a sudden jerk, his face changing, his gesticulating arm falling down. He had been struck heavily in the lower midriff, and was losing blood by the pint. Eyes rolling back, the officer slumped to the earth.

Through the storm of shrapnel, grape and rifle fire, Nunn saw that a large group from the Light had managed to get out all at once in front of the Quarries, and were assembling about twenty yards from the British line. The last vestiges of the Division's first wave, its Forlorn Hope, were falling in with them. A proper forming-up was proving impossible, however, as the troubled mass of men shifted constantly, none of them wanting to be left exposed at the front or sides. They were like a shoal of crimson fishes being menaced by unseen sharks. Every moment, these rapid, invisible predators would swoop in from the mingled clouds of smoke, mist and dust to claim a few more of their number.

Without thinking, Nunn sprinted over, a ricochet whining by his boot. Colonel Yea, his monocle in place, strode up to them, stepping over bodies, yelling for order, for a disciplined retreat to the trenches. 'Bugler!' he screamed, looking around him. 'This will never do! Where's the bloody bugler to call them back? *Bugler*, damn it!'

Quickly seeing that there was no option but to advance, the brave Colonel paced before the group, directing them to form up, gesturing to the fort ahead, his ruddy face composed, his jaw jutting out defiantly. Nunn understood immediately that it was to be a rush for the batteries, a splendid, dauntless charge; but Yea had not covered more than ten yards with his loping, long-legged gait before he was caught in a tight stream of grapeshot, which whipped his mangled body around in a grotesque twirl before letting it fall before those he led.

All resolution left the men at this sight. Some came to an uncertain halt, and were hit themselves in the seconds that followed. Others headed back over the killing ground towards the trenches, deciding to take their chances against the Russian cannon-fire, or dashed for what shelter there was nearby, ducking down into low hollows, hiding themselves

413

behind rocks, banks of earth and even the bodies of their comrades.

As Nunn was making for a wide, shallow crater, he noticed a figure hunched behind a pile of split sandbags. The fellow was dressed in a green jacket but was plainly no rifleman; he was filthy, stick thin and wearing a ragged assembly of other clothing that did not belong in any military uniform. He had a revolver, which he lifted above the sandbags and fired, without aiming, towards the Redan. All six bullets were let off in less than ten seconds, the pistol leaping around crazily at the end of this shooter's spindly arm. Amazed, Nunn shouted at him to get back, but could not even hear his own voice.

A cloud of dust passed over him, blocking his view of this person; instead, on his other side, he saw some privates from the 99th, the scoundrel Cregg and a couple of others, scurrying to the British line. He called them over, and ordered them to fall in behind him. Suddenly he could see the man in the green jacket again. He had been joined by two more civilians. One was trying to get his attention, but was being ignored as far as Nunn could tell. The other was Richard Cracknell, the lusty blackguard from Cregg's odious drawings – the rank perverter of the inestimably fine Madeleine Boyce. The Lieutenant started angrily towards him.

The shell-blast was massive and very close. It sent shrapnel ripping into the sandbags and knocked the approaching group of soldiers to the ground in a bloody haze. The large form of their officer landed heavily at Kitson's feet. The explosion had blown the forage cap clean off his head, along with a good deal of his hair. He was quite still, one of his eyes half-open. Kitson glanced at the others. Two of the three privates were unquestionably dead; the third was covered in blood and thrashing around, his mouth forming agonised, unheard obscenities. Those who shouted, as Kitson had been told many times on the quay at Balaclava, could usually be left until last. He went to the officer, a young lieutenant. Moving around behind the stricken man's shoulders, Kitson lifted the man's head gently, and set it in his lap. He could feel the fracture in the skull – two sections of bone sitting at slightly different levels, with a sharp, indented line running between them. Taking a thick roll of Mrs Seacole's bandages from his pocket, he set to work.

In the corner of his vision, Kitson noticed that Styles was chancing a look over at the Russian lines. The illustrator had met him with a confused expression, at once defiant and irritated and deeply, profoundly frightened. There had also been the smallest trace of relief, Kitson thought, at seeing him again; but his refusal to go back to safety had been absolute. Styles was set on seeing this mission of his through to its conclusion, whatever that might prove to be. Left in the Crimea, his delusions had clearly grown ever more acute. Had Cracknell known he was still there, or had he simply failed to notice it? Either way, it was a shameful piece of neglect.

He glanced at his former senior. Cracknell sat hunched down behind the sandbags with his arms crossed tightly in front of him, staring at the ground. No pocketbook was balanced on his knee; no cigarette was stuck in his mouth. Kitson had noticed this distraction back in the advance parallel, when Cracknell had caught up with him in the seconds before the attack had begun. Something had happened to him in the minutes since their reunion. Before he could ask what it was, though, they had seen Styles limping out after the first line and set off after him. Cracknell had been as eager as Kitson to start this pursuit. His wish, however, had plainly been to get out of the British works rather than to rescue the errant illustrator.

The cannon-fire intensified yet further as the guns of the Quarries started to bombard the Redan, in an effort to bring some relief to the British infantry caught before it. Kitson peered over at the Russian fort; round shot was thudding into the sloping walls with ineffectual puffs of dust, completely absorbed by the loose earth.

Once the lieutenant's head was securely bound, Kitson moved on to the surviving private, pulling him into the paltry shelter offered by the sandbags. Whilst he was doing this, he felt a biting contraction in his chest. It was the third time this had happened since he had left Mrs Seacole at the Quarries, brought on by the exertions of his ill-advised rush towards the fighting. He had done exactly what she had told him he must avoid, and was already discovering the cost. Something had been torn, and was deteriorating further with every step he took; he had made a cursory examination back in the trenches, and discovered fresh damage beneath the skin. His chance for a straightforward recovery was lost.

There was no time to lament this now. The private, thankfully, had lapsed into unconsciousness. Kitson realised that it was the soldier he had encountered in the advance works – the man with the injured hand who had claimed to know Cracknell. One entire side of his body had been blasted with hot shrapnel, tearing apart his worn uniform. His right leg was pulped, more or less, and bleeding heavily. A fragment had struck against the side of his face, stripping away much of the flesh. Readying his bandages, Kitson quickly bound the leg and then checked the private's side; although a little scorched, it was largely undamaged. He turned to the man's face.

A lone bugle sounded in amongst the gunfire, and for a moment Kitson felt weary hope; but then he heard that it was sounding an attack rather than a retreat. Turning towards the Allied lines, he saw that in defiance of all reason and tactical sense, the men of the Light and Fourth Divisions were still coming, with scaling parties now rushing out alongside them. It was a futile endeavour. The tall ladders, and the sailors who carried them, would be scattered to pieces by the relentless fall of grapeshot long before they could pose any threat to the Redan.

Kitson looked to Cracknell. The correspondent grimaced and shook his head. This action was rapidly becoming a catastrophic failure.

Then, at the same instant, both men realised that Styles had gone.

Boyce left the picketed end of his trench surrounded by two companies of his men, ensuring that he was well shielded from the hail of shot and shell that immediately fell upon them. Around a third of the soldiers were hit; their Colonel looked back towards the trench to see a great cowering mass of the 99th still there, hesitating fearfully. Pierce was at their head. Boyce waved his sword crossly, ordering him on to the field. The Major forced himself forward, starting up a shout. He was halfway to Boyce's position when his torso was caught by a cannon-ball, and split open like an orange burst mercilessly beneath a descending boot heel. The ball also killed one of the soldiers behind him and took the leg of another; the rest, soaked in bloody viscera, turned and ran back to the trench.

There were more reports from the Redan. Like the Forlorn Hope before them, the 99th broke apart, running in every direction. After a short dash, Boyce found himself in a dried-out ditch no more than three feet deep. Through the choking dust, he could see that a dozen of his men were already in there, and a couple of his officers. One of them was Lieutenant-Colonel Fairlie, who crawled over to his side. He had been injured in the upper arm, and was shouting something about the scaling parties. The Redan, their target, still seemed an enormous distance away. Boyce extended his field glass and looked across the battlefield. It was covered with the fallen, their numbers increasing by the second. None of the other battalions were making any more progress than they were.

Then he saw him, Cracknell of the *Courier*, scuttling away to the left, past a group of skirmishers from the Rifle Brigade who, miniés raised, were trying to pick off Russian artillery spotters up on the battlements of the Redan. This was it: his chance to put the revolting toad down for good.

'I must go to the left side of the attack,' he said to Fairlie, 'and find Sir John. We must reconsider our plan.'

'Agreed, Colonel,' Fairlie replied, 'but please, send a sub-altern. Lieutenant Fox is here, and I'm sure—' A shell exploded nearby; a private slumped backwards, his skull shattered. Fairlie was immediately on his feet, yelling orders and pointing with his sword. 'Over there, quickly! They are targeting this position – we must move ourselves!'

Boyce checked his revolver and started after the Irishman.

10

Hopping over corpses and craters, the Tomahawk suddenly came to his senses. He had allowed this situation to run out of control.

Up ahead, Styles was moving diagonally before the Redan under the cover of a thick screen of smoke. They were leaving the main attack. The level ground before the great fort was turning into a gentle slope, furrowed in a manner suggesting that it might once have been cultivated land. He knew where they were heading; they would soon come to the remains of a graveyard, fringed by some ruined suburbs. They had kept moving thus far, and that was sensible enough – but now their best, nay, their *only* hope for survival was to keep their heads down and wait for nightfall or the declaration of a truce for the burial of the dead. He put on a spurt of speed, passing Kitson almost immediately, thinking that he would throw the illustrator over his shoulder and carry him to shelter if he had to.

As he drew level with Styles, he saw the shattered pieces of headstones, leaning this way and that; and past them, a street of collapsed buildings, pounded down almost to their foundations, that once had been part of the outer reaches of Sebastopol. Grey-coated Russians slipped through these ruins, retreating into their earthworks before a company of British skirmishers. Like them, this company had managed to creep past the largest guns, and were now attempting to launch an attack on one of the Redan's supporting batteries.

Cracknell grasped Styles' arm. 'Woah there, Mr Styles!'

The illustrator tried to shake him off. 'I am not afraid, damn you!' he cried, his face twisted with fury. 'I am no coward!'

The effect was actually rather startling, like being snapped at by a rabid dog; Cracknell almost let go. Then a bullet whined past them, coming from the opposite direction to the Redan. The correspondent turned to see Boyce back on the rutted slope, taking careful aim with his revolver, attempting to fulfil the threat he had made in that rifle pit. All but lifting Styles from the ground, Cracknell ran with him towards the nearest dark doorway.

It led to what must once have been the parlour of a comfortable townhouse, now missing its upper storeys and all of its doors. The remaining windows were all firmly shuttered. Entering this room was like ducking into a coastal cave to escape a tempestuous sea-storm. Although still immensely loud, the pounding of the guns was muffled enough to allow some ease of communication, and after the turbid atmosphere outside, the air seemed clear and cool. The room's decorations were still largely intact – an odd contrast indeed with the carnage and devastation of the battlefield. The walls were covered with a pine-green paper, and a dusty spherical lamp hung overhead. Several robust pieces of furniture, fashioned from dark wood and plainly too weighty for impromptu removal, were arranged across the polished stone floor. Breathing hard, Cracknell released Styles, pushing him forward. The illustrator stumbled, the pistol clattering on to the flagstones.

'To hell with you, Cracknell,' he spat, sobbing now. 'I am no *coward*, d'you hear me?'

Cracknell looked to the doorway; Kitson walked through, panting, holding his injured chest. He pointed back incredulously towards the battle. 'So Boyce is actually trying to *kill you* now?'

The Tomahawk rubbed his sweaty brow against his sleeve. 'He most certainly is. Something has happened. My work, perhaps – or something more.' He lowered his head. 'He says he has already killed his wife.'

Kitson's dismay was evident but he managed to suppress it. Cracknell could not help but admire this. What a team we might have made, he thought, had the fellow only retained his focus. Their eyes met; they were thinking the same thing. Boyce would be there any moment.

'We should go,' Kitson said. 'Now.'

Cracknell nodded. 'There is a ravine on the other side of the cemetery that we could head for, if we—'

A shell exploded close to the house, on the opposite side to the doorway. Debris rattled against the shutters. English voices with thick Yorkshire accents could be heard shouting out to each other, something about drawing the Russian fire. It was obvious what was happening – the enemy was manoeuvring their heavy guns so that they could destroy the ruins, and the British soldiers taking cover within them.

Cracknell noticed that Styles was down on the floor. He had reclaimed the revolver and was reloading it frantically. The boy had clearly overheard his revelation about Madeleine. Cracknell's first thought was that he was preparing the pistol as a protective measure, to repel Boyce; then Styles glared at him with such abhorrence that he could not fail to see the truth. The bullets being loaded into that gun were meant for him.

There was a gigantic crash outside, and a falling spar knocked in a shutter on the far side of the room. The Russians had finished bringing their heavy guns about; the bombardment of the ruined suburbs had begun. Black smoke rolled in through the broken window and the doorway, quickly filling the parlour.

Boyce, as he entered, could see bodies moving about in the gloom, across a bright crack on the room's far side, and down on its pale stone floor. He knew that others from the magazine's reporting team were in there also, and had decided that they should rightly meet the same fate as their odious leader.

This was the moment. Richard Cracknell was trapped before him. A pistol was ready in his hand – the very same weapon used not three hours earlier to kill the woman with whom the villain had conspired to topple him. There was a gratifying appropriateness to this. The Colonel's finger curled around the trigger.

Before he could shoot, however, another gun flared in the murk. The door-frame splintered, and something seemed to catch against him, knocking him back out of the house. Boyce tried to level his pistol, to return fire into the smoke-filled parlour; but realised he couldn't move, or indeed feel his right arm below the elbow. He looked down at it. The bullet had entered the forearm, about four inches above the wrist, breaking a bone and pushing it out through muscle, skin and uniform. A gory mess was dribbling out of the bottom of his sleeve, over his glove and the revolver held within it, and dripping down into the dust.

Boyce gasped hard, flattening himself against an outside wall, raising his watering eyes to the sky. The strength leaked from his body. He slid towards the ground. Transfer the revolver to your other hand, he instructed himself. Go back in there and bring this to its rightful conclusion. The Irish cur and his lackeys are your bitterest enemies. They know far too much. *Bring this to an end.*

But he could not. The pain was simply too great. Boyce struggled to his feet and shook the pistol from his useless hand. His moustache flapping loose, the Colonel clenched his teeth and started towards the nearby skirmishers.

It took Kitson a few seconds to realise that Boyce had gone. Taking his hands from over his head, he looked about cautiously. Styles was frozen in a thin blade of sunlight, still pointing the revolver at the empty doorway. Cracknell was half-hidden beneath a sturdy table across the room, where he had dived after the first balls had struck the outside of the parlour.

Kitson's only thought was flight. The Russian artillery could bring down their shelter at any moment, and Boyce was surely set to return. They had to leave right away. He assessed the bashed-in shutter. There was space enough for them to clamber through. This was an escape route.

He gestured to Styles. 'Quickly, this way!'

421

The illustrator did not react. Instead, he turned the pistol towards Cracknell, fumbling a little as he drew back the hammer. Seeing his intention, Kitson rushed forward, grabbing at both Styles' hands and the greasy gun they held. It leapt in their unsteady, conflicted grasp, the report smothered entirely by the bombardment. A fist-sized hole was blown in the top of the table Cracknell was sheltering under. Styles bent his arm, twisting away, curling himself up; they fell to one side, the revolver becoming lost between them.

'Styles,' Kitson shouted, 'please, my friend—'

He felt the pistol's mechanism move under his fingers, and the abrupt jolt as it fired. Styles lurched violently. Kitson released the gun and backed away; and the illustrator flopped over on to his back.

The bullet had gone in at the base of Styles' throat, just above the collarbone. Kitson had but an instant to note the location before it became swamped in blood. He took out his bandages, pressing the entire roll hard against the wound, but it was no use. He could not staunch the flow.

Styles looked up at him, blinking rapidly. He dropped the revolver and took hold of Kitson's sleeve. His blue eyes were bright in his grimy, ashen face. All his confusion and misery had departed; Kitson caught a painful glimpse of the enthusiastic, innocent young artist he had met on the beach at Eupatoria only nine months previously. He was saying something, visibly straining for volume. Still pressing vainly on the bullet hole, Kitson moved in as close as he could, until the illustrator's beard scratched against his ear.

Styles' voice was choked, the words wavering on his grey lips. 'My – my work, Thomas . . .'

'Be still, Robert,' Kitson instructed. 'Do not move. All will be well.'

'My work, see that it . . .'

This was all he could manage. His eyes went dull and the hand slid back to his side.

Kitson sat back numbly and stared at it all, at the man he had killed, at the blood that soaked his clothes and ran away thickly between the stones of the floor, surrounding them both with a dark lattice of lengthening lines. The smell of it seemed to reach down through his mouth and nostrils to his innermost being, coating him, staining him indelibly with its sticky, nauseating warmth. He threw down the bandages in despair and looked across the parlour. Cracknell was on his hands and knees beneath the table, an oddly incongruous, comical pose. He was regarding Kitson and Styles fixedly, his expression unreadable.

There was a single moment of silence and stillness; and then round-shot tore into the squat structure around them, punching through it as if it were made from cardboard. Supporting beams gave out, releasing an avalanche of bricks; walls collapsed; cornerstones cracked and shattered. Then another ball hit, and the ruined townhouse fell in on itself.

Manchester
June 1857

1

Charles Norton walked up the steps of the Exchange with his managers arrayed around him. They strode between the building's massy columns, through its grand doors and on towards the main Exchange room, at the steady pace of businessmen with deals to make. Usually, it brought the proprietor of the Norton Foundry enormous satisfaction to enter this cavernous chamber in such a manner. As he stepped on to the floor, the long rows of fluted pillars stretching away on either side of him and the great glass dome gleaming up above, he would feel like a senator in ancient Rome, or a lord taking his place in some exalted feudal hall. Today, however, was different.

The vast crowd gathered there was quiet to the point of taciturnity. This was quite normal; there was never any vacant gossiping or laughter in the Exchange. The room echoed with hushed murmuring as laconic phrases passed back and forth, accompanied by winks, nods and a range of other coded gestures. This was the sound of Manchester's best minds doing the business that had made their city so prosperous. These men were Norton's brothers-in-industry, his own kind – but today he was deeply wary of them. Gathering his nerve, he kept walking until he stood in the very centre of the room, in the disc of weak sunlight that was projected down through the dome.

Slowly, the Exchange noticed Norton's arrival, and a change of feeling swept through the crowd. Every eye turned towards him. Could this be a show of respect, he wondered with momentary hope; could his fears be entirely without foundation?

He soon saw that this was not the case. The looks directed at him were positively unpleasant – snide smirks and leers, and even the occasional glare of censure, as if he was complicit in some terrible crime. Agents and exchange clerks started to mutter behind their hands and pocketbooks, the bolder and more malicious among them pronouncing certain words with a purposeful loudness, intending that he should hear. *Sodomite*, they hissed; *bugger-boy*.

After a few minutes of this, the Foundry managers excused themselves uncomfortably and left the building. Charles knew straight away against whom these foul accusations were being levelled. Full of helpless, indignant anger, he resolved to face these scoundrels down, to show them that as well as being obscene and ungodly, what they claimed was groundless slander. But it soon became clear that no matter how much resilience he displayed, no one would do business with the Norton Foundry that day. Backs were turned and noses were lifted; even William Fairbairn, whose acclaimed floating mill and bakery could not have been realised without his assistance, would not even speak to him. In the space of two short days, it seemed, he had become an outcast. Enraged, bewildered and humiliated, he departed to a mounting chorus of low jeers.

Out in St Anne's Square, Charles fired a curt 'home' at the coachman before throwing himself into his carriage. As it rolled off, he took the shining top hat from his head and dashed it to the floor. Sitting back, trying to regain his calm, he sifted through the events of the past thirty-six hours once again.

Mr Twelves had failed to appear on Saturday night, either with Bill and Jemima or without. The coach-and-four had returned bearing but a single passenger: his daughter, in a state of intense anger. Something had plainly taken place that evening, but she would not reveal what it was, no matter how voluble and furious his demands. She would not even look him in the eye, in fact, and had swept upstairs to her rooms with barely a word. Forcing himself to be patient, he had retired vowing to hold his peace and see what the following day would bring. Bill spending a night away from Norton Hall was hardly unusual, after all. There could be any number of explanations for this turn of events.

Then, the very first thing on Sunday morning, before Charles had even dressed for church, a note had arrived from Mr Twelves terminating their contract with immediate effect. Charles had not known what to make of this. Twelves was not a man easily upset. As he had gone about the observances of the Sabbath, Charles had grown increasingly convinced that he had been outfoxed somehow. Terrible suspicions began to gather in his mind. What might the fiend Cracknell and that damned street philosopher have told his disloyal children? He had prepared himself for a tempestuous confrontation. Neither, however, had appeared; Bill did not return from the city. Jemima did not so much as open her door, refusing even to admit her maid. Charles had dined alone, and went to bed severely disquieted.

He could never have dreamed, however, that the new day would bring such a staggering development. It was beyond his ability even to contemplate. There simply *could not* be any truth in it. Charles Norton stared numbly at his boots, his head nodding with the motion of the carriage.

The next he knew, they were pulling up in front of Norton Hall. Stepping on to the gravel, he noticed that the front door had not been opened to admit him. He walked over slowly; still it remained firmly, obstinately shut.

'Where the deuce is that butler?' he muttered under his breath, rapping on the stained glass panel set into the door with the end of his cane.

Eventually, the door was opened by a stammering, scarlet-cheeked parlour-maid, who revealed that the butler had resigned his post and left for the city. Charles, doing his best to hide his dismay, soon discovered that a number of the other servants had also abandoned his household. And what was more, Jemima had still not emerged from her chambers. He decided that this had gone on for quite long enough. Storming upstairs, he hammered on her door, demanding to be admitted. When this did not elicit a response, he strode back to the landing rail and took a deep breath. Then he charged shoulder first.

The lock was a delicate one, designed for the purposes of privacy rather than to serve as a barrier against determined assailants, and it broke with a loud crack. The sitting-room door flew inwards, depositing Charles Norton on the carpet. Jemima considered her father coldly from behind her writing desk. They got to their feet at the same time, one with rather more poise than the other.

'Jemima, explain yourself!' he shouted as soon as he was upright again – quite neglecting, in his fury, to straighten his skewed necktie. 'Tell me what happened at the Belle Vue, this instant!'

'Surely you know,' she replied. 'Have your black-suited men not reported back to you?'

He pointed at her. 'Don't you *cheek me*, my girl, or I swear—'

'You tried to trap us. You tried to trap your own children.'

Charles rolled his eyes at this. 'I had to, don't you see? Where is your brother?'

Jemima glared at him. She had been determined to preserve her self-control should this encounter occur, but it was slipping away nonetheless. 'He will have left the country by now. I don't know his destination. Your spies uncovered a little more than they were expecting.' She recalled the scrawled note left on the seat of the coach-and-four, waiting for her when she came to depart the Belle Vue. *Don't know what we'll do*, it had said. *Damn him for this! My life in Manchester is quite finished! Keane says America, and I'm inclined to agree. Leave too, Jem, for God's sake! Leave while you are still able!*

Her father was aghast at this revelation, but he quickly recovered his sense of moral superiority. 'They were a necessary evil. You were consorting with my enemies, Jemima!'

'You mean with those who actually know the truth about you, about your marvellous success out in the Crimea – your railway spikes, your wretched buckles!'

Charles crossed his hands in front of him and looked at

her severely; he had already guessed that these matters were involved. 'You speak of things that are beyond your capacity to understand. I'll thank you, however, not to take the word of strangers over that of your own father. We are bound by blood, and I will not have you—'

'Tell me that you did not know of the murders,' Jemima broke in with forceful impatience. 'Tell me that you did not know what your friend Nathaniel Boyce had done to acquire that panel when you agreed to smuggle it back.'

This caught him unawares. He stared out of the window, brow furrowed, refusing to answer.

'Very well then, Father, tell me that you did not leave Anthony in Balaclava whilst you were off making your deals. The risks of that place were well known. You were responsible for him – he was there to assist you. But you went up to the plateau with your murderous friend and you left him. Is that not so?'

Charles was silent for another tense half-minute, his face turning brick red; then he burst into speech. 'How could I have possibly known, Jemima? How do you expect me to have—'

He stopped, suddenly running out of words. His attempt at righteous, indignant wrath was undercut entirely by the guilt in his voice. Turning away from his daughter with a heated exclamation, he marched from the room and thundered down the stairs.

Jemima sat again, putting a hand to her aching forehead. Wiping away an unexpected tear, she glanced at the valise that sat packed and ready in her bedroom, and then up at the clock on the wall. There were still several hours to go.

2

Boyce made a quick survey of the cobbled stable-yard at the rear of the Albion Hotel. Most of those employed there were engaged in the preparation of a large, imperial blue barouche for an afternoon drive; rather optimistically, in Boyce's view, as the heavy clouds gathering overhead held a clear threat of rain. Striding swiftly past this vehicle, he headed for the stall closest to the gate – the meeting place proposed in the anonymous note left for him that morning at the Albion's front desk. Seeing him pass, a fat-faced fool he supposed must be the head groom called out an impertinent salutation, whilst doffing a cheap-looking cap. Boyce ignored him.

The stall contained a single, aged grey. There were no stable-hands within earshot. Boyce stood stiffly beside it, taking a cigar from his coatee to create the appearance of a gentleman soldier who had merely stepped outside for a quiet, solitary smoke. He did not have long. There was a call he had to make, for the sake of form; and then he was due to dine with a group of prominent noblemen, all keen collectors of Raphael, in town for the Queen's visit to the Art Treasures Exhibition.

'Are you there?' He hissed this through gritted teeth, looking straight ahead rather than into the stall, so that anyone watching from a distance would not be able to tell that he was addressing someone.

'That I am, sir,' replied a voice from inside. 'May I come out, d'ye think? I don't know what they've been feeding this poor beast, but by God, even Hercules himself would balk at sweeping up this stinking mess.'

'You stay where you bloody well are. I will *not* risk anyone seeing us together, do you understand?' Boyce fingered the unlit cigar. Since the loss of his hand, lighting the damn things was something of a challenge. At that moment, he could not chance an error, a spillage of matches perhaps, that would inevitably prompt some idiot to rush over and proffer his assistance.

A soft chuckle came from the stall. 'No need for such a tone, *Brigadier.*' The speaker moved forward from the shadows, placing a large hand on the old grey's neck. Boyce glanced over to make an assessment. He was a typical example of his kind: badly dressed and groomed, tall but with a swaggering, stooping posture that marked him out as an irredeemable degenerate. The faintest touch of a smirk lingered on his square, low-born face. It was plain that this wretched fellow considered himself something of a buck. 'I am a professional, afore all else. No one will see me.' There was a portentous pause. 'Twelves is my name.'

'I don't give a damn what your name is, knave. What was the meaning of that note? Explain yourself, this instant.'

Twelves seemed to be deriving some insolent amusement from Boyce's assertive manner. 'My meaning is simple. I have information on your enemies. My men and I have been watching them these past few weeks, and we could be useful to ye. Useful indeed.'

'So you discovered my . . . acquaintance with Norton.'

Twelves looked away. 'Not too difficult, Brigadier, if I may say.'

Boyce thought for a moment. The situation was becoming ever more pressing. The Queen would be in Manchester the very next day. It was unbelievable that Norton had failed to deal with this. The man was a fool, and they'd both paid a heavy price for his ineffectiveness. Their connection would have to be severed. The scandal of Norton's sodomite offspring was certain to ruin the Foundry. Boyce was confident that none of this disgrace would ever touch him personally; Norton could not reveal anything about their deal, about the *Pilate*, without incriminating himself as well. But it was a vexatious blow all the same.

'What do you know?' Boyce asked.

'Thomas Kitson's address, for starters. A tenement on Princess Street, not a quarter-mile from this very spot. We've kept a close watch on it. I don't doubt that there will soon be contact between 'im and Mr Cracknell.' Twelves cleared his throat. 'If ye were to provide the necessary payment, we'd be happy to follow 'em, see what they're up to. Or we could—'

'Kill them,' Boyce instructed. 'Kill them both, tonight. This has to end. I need not remind you that Richard Cracknell has proved tiresomely resourceful. There will be no more mishaps or unwelcome surprises.'

'Ye have my word on that.' The investigator scowled. 'It would be hard to imagine another interruption as abhorrent as the unnatural filth my men and I witnessed in the Belle Vue.' He shook his head. 'Can't have any link with such deviancy in my line of work. Does untold damage to a man's reputation – and reputation, Brigadier, is all. Shall I assume that ye are also out of whatever arrangement ye might have had with that wretched family, sir?'

Such upright decency, Boyce thought, from a paid assassin. 'There was no arrangement. Remember that. We were merely acquaintances.'

The slightest of smiles returned to Twelves' unsavoury features. 'Very well.'

Boyce replaced the unlit cigar in his coatee and brushed the cuff covering his wooden hand. 'I will leave your imbursement here at the Albion, with notice that it is for a local apothecary. It will be a generous sum for the work. Should you be caught, I will of course deny all knowledge and leave you to your fate.' He turned his head a fraction, meeting the hired man's eye. 'Be sure that you tell them at whose behest it is done. And make Cracknell suffer. I wish him to suffer.'

'He will, sir, never fear. They both will.' There was now a note of something very like admiration in Twelves' voice. 'May I say, Brigadier, that it is always a pleasure to serve a

434

gent who knows 'is mind. I can truly respect that. No *qualms*. One thing ye encounter a fair amount in this trade, sir, is qualms. Norton had 'em in spades. Cause no end of bother.'

Boyce frowned, his tolerance for this meeting at an end. 'I do not ask for your damned *respect*,' he snapped. 'Just do as I order.'

He swivelled on his heel and walked back towards the hotel.

Cregg reached into his pocket for the bottle. It was crudely cast from brown glass and had no label. He could not remember purchasing it, or what it contained. There were only a couple of swallows left, at any rate – reckoning that he'd need the steel, he popped the cork and drained it in one. The liquid caused an involuntary twitch, and then a deep shiver. He smacked his lips together, flipping the empty bottle around so that he held the neck, and then brought it round abruptly against the wall beside him.

With reverential care, Cregg lifted up the broken end. The jagged edges glittered in the gaslight that seeped into the alley from the square beyond. You can keep your rifles and your bayonets, he thought – give me a good sharp bit of glass any day of the bleedin' week. He stole to the alley's mouth, and took a careful look at the open ground beyond.

Piccadilly was heaving with crowds. Teams of labourers and carpenters were busy preparing the decorations to mark the Queen's procession through the city the following day. Multi-coloured poles were being erected along the length of the main promenades, and capacious wooden balconies were going up in front of almost every building. Beneath the flat orange light of the gas lamps, wagons loaded with flags and banners were being emptied, their contents hung everywhere that could possibly accommodate them. Around this industry, large numbers had gathered simply to watch and chatter. Many of these spectators had umbrellas under their arms and glanced up frequently at the sky, which had grown increasingly stormy as the afternoon's light faded.

All of this stood in his favour, Cregg decided. The combination of crowds, colourful banners and rainy gloom meant that he'd be able to get across the square without drawing any undue attention to himself. Then he could get his satisfaction, and melt away like the darkness at dawn. He had a notion that whilst the crushers were busy mopping up at the hotel, he could do a spot of robbing on the London Road or thereabouts with a good chance of success, drumming up some ready funds to get him on the next train back to the Metropolis, and away from this arse-hole of a city for good. The plan seemed so simple, so damn sound, that he cursed himself for not settling on it sooner.

He studied the entrance to the Albion Hotel. It was lit up brightly against the evening. He'd have to keep a close look-out, and pick his moment carefully.

Leaning down to check the makeshift sackcloth dressings he'd applied to his leg, Cregg felt suddenly unsteady, his head light. He wondered how many days it had been since he'd eaten anything. His eyes seemed to be losing their focus. He blinked, and the orbs of gaslight that lined the promenade each produced a twin, a perfect double that slowly drifted back over until the two images aligned and became one once more. He knocked the back of his skull against the bricks behind him three times, took a few deep breaths and then peered out at Piccadilly again.

The Royal Infirmary stood opposite the alley, rising up imposingly in the centre of the square. Cregg's dizzy stare roamed from the columns of the portico, up to the dome and then settled on the main body of the building beneath. A lamp had just been placed in a window on the first floor. Beside it, a nurse was leaning down to help a man with a heavily bandaged head to sit up in his bed, so that he could see something of the preparations underway outside. The nurse was solicitous and gentle, even taking hold of the man's arm to help him to the sill. Cregg wiped his watering eyes and gulped, unwanted remembrance of his own time in hospital coming to him with ugly clarity.

After falling before the Redan, Cregg had been out for the best part of four days. He had awoken from this black slumber to find himself bound and bleeding in the hospital at Scutari. His bed was in the cellars, away from all daylight, where the low stone arches echoed dully with screams and whimpers, and the ragged sound of weak men vomiting. The nurses were but distant, pale figures, drifting like phantoms through the corridors.

Confined to this grim dungeon, Cregg grew confused. The agony from his wounds was constant, gnawing, utterly unbearable. The face, at first, was particularly bad. He was beset day and night by fat Turkish flies, which tried to crawl in amongst the bandages and lay their eggs in his tattered cheek. He could not sleep, and in the tomb-like darkness a voice in his head started to mutter nasty things. It reminded him repeatedly who was to blame for his ordeal – who had mashed him up, killed his pals, and deserved to bleedin' well die himself. And it did not stop once he was back in old England either; only liquor, he soon learned, an earnest devotion to hard liquor, could quiet its jabbering.

Some whistles from across the square pulled him back to the present. A small crowd had gathered around the entrance to the Albion. The porters were attempting to keep them back as a fancy carriage was waved up to the door. Inside the hotel, he saw the briefest flash of a red sleeve. It was time for him to act.

Cregg started out across Piccadilly, the bottle sliding a little in his clammy palm. He stepped over a pile of pale flower garlands, which were about to be strung up between the gaily-coloured poles. The first drops of rain fell upon his ruined features as he hurried on.

He passed by the glossy horses, all champing at their bits, and the coachman, who was pulling up his collar against the breaking storm. He'd go for the neck. There'd be no quarter for the bastard then – he'd be certain to breathe his last on the cobbles of Manchester. And what a well deserved end it would be.

There he was, stepping out of the hotel: Colonel Boyce. Now trussed up as a general or some such, but still the same old bleedin' Boyce, pretty much unchanged in Cregg's eyes. See how he steps towards his carriage, the crippled veteran fumed, so full of his own worth, and his power over the rest of us! And those moustaches, those bleedin' moustaches, so sharp and huge! Boyce had presided as Cregg had dangled half-naked and bloody from a cartwheel, his head lolling, weathering the lash; Boyce had cowered beneath those rocks at Inkerman, whilst Major Maynard was lost to the Russian guns; Boyce had jutted into view at a dozen skirmishes afterwards, directing decent men to their doom whilst staying safely in the rear. And Cregg was willing to bet the shirt off his back that it was Boyce who had ordered him to the Forlorn Hope for the first assault on the Great Redan.

For a long second, Cregg was so overwhelmed by the sight of his intended victim that he stood transfixed, almost fearful, like a rabbit before a stoat; then his hatred, his resolution flowed back into him. He shoved aside the handful of people who stood between them, the broken bottle ready in his hand.

'It might – could—' Nunn began. He stopped, shaking his head in frustration. Boyce paused just before the door, regarding him with some impatience. 'It seems to, to—'

'Come on, Mr Nunn,' said the Brigadier-General. 'Out with it, man.'

'R-rain, Briga-Brigadier,' Nunn mumbled. 'It seems to be about to . . . about to—' He stopped, wiping away the excess of spittle that had gathered around his lips with a handkerchief kept in the sleeve of his dress-coat expressly for this purpose.

'Rain?' Boyce looked out of the nearest window, over the heads of the crowd. 'So it has arrived at last. Honestly, this wretched city. Tell the porters to bring an umbrella, would you?' Nunn started to amble uncertainly across the lobby. 'Actually, Mr Nunn, stay where you are. I'll see to it.'

They called him an idiot, but this was not true.

For a long time after his return from the war – a year, they told him – Nunn had not been able to remember anything. His parents, his sisters, his oldest friends, all had come before him, and had managed to elicit no response whatsoever. Francis Nunn, First Lieutenant of the Paulton Rangers, seemed to have lost his mind to a piece of Russian shrapnel.

Then, quite unexpectedly, his father received a letter from none other than his former commander; and within a week, Brigadier-General Boyce had arrived at the Bath sanatorium in which Nunn had been sequestered. The effect of this distinguished visitor's presence upon him was pronounced and immediate. He had struggled to stand the moment Boyce first entered the room, and soon began to speak, to answer simple questions – far more than he had done since his return from the war. The Brigadier-General had stayed for several days, spending long hours alone with him, discussing their time in the Crimea together. These conversations had proved a stern mental test for the depleted young officer. Boyce had been keen indeed to learn what he could or could not recall.

A few months afterwards, Nunn had received the appointment. He found himself dressed up in a uniform once again, and dispatched to the Brigadier-General's headquarters. He was, he slowly came to understand, an aide-de-camp, and a captain. His duties seemed to consist of little more than following Boyce around, opening doors for him, standing behind his chair, and sitting in his carriage. Nunn experienced some unease at this strange new life, but was unable to identify its cause. He felt as if his brain was wrapped up in stifling gauze, as if every word he tried to utter was a fiendish puzzle he simply could not solve; as if even the very simplest of actions was a double-time march up a steep hill with a full field pack strapped to his back.

The Brigadier-General returned with an umbrella. 'I do hope this latest downpour won't delay us any further,' he said briskly, handing the leathery contraption to Nunn. 'Colonel Bennett told me that poor Wray is usually asleep by seven. I wouldn't want to have to make the journey out to Bennett's place again on another occasion.' The Brigadier-General looked at his aide-de-camp. 'You remember Wray, Mr Nunn, don't you? You have spoken of him before.'

Nunn blinked, trying his hardest to think. Nothing came to him.

The Brigadier-General sighed. 'No matter, Mr Nunn. Do not trouble yourself.' He gestured towards the carriage outside.

Summoning all his powers of concentration, Nunn opened up the umbrella, stepping through the Albion's double doors as he did so. There was only a narrow stretch of open ground between the doors and the carriage. The wide umbrella almost covered it completely. He held it up in the air with a reasonable approximation of smartness, and Brigadier-General Boyce emerged into the wet Manchester evening.

Nunn's reactions were not what they once had been – far from it. But he noticed the man in the torn coat moving quickly around the carriage's rear wheels, and he saw the lights of the Albion glint upon something sharp in his hand. Instinctively, he swept the umbrella from over the Brigadier-General's head and pushed it hard into this man's path. The attacker tried to keep coming, snarling loudly, going for Boyce now like a mad mastiff. A broken bottle speared through the fabric of the umbrella as its metal spokes bent and collapsed. Nunn felt the glass cut into his upper arm. Still pushing with the umbrella, he proceeded to beat the man down with his other hand, balled into a hard fist.

Nunn's long convalescence had not diminished his physical strength, and soon the attacker was lying defeated in the gutter. Nunn then forced the hand holding the bottle to the ground, treading on it firmly, shattering the weapon. The attacker cried out as the fresh shards were pressed into his palm, and reached around with his other hand to claw at Nunn's boot. With a start, Nunn saw that it lacked a number of fingers. He leant down and peeled back the remains of the umbrella.

Up until then, everything had happened too rapidly for the crowd to follow, but as the torn flaps revealed a hideously disfigured face, contorted with crazed energy, they recoiled with a gasp. Nunn found that there was something extremely familiar about this face. He stood very still, studying it carefully, spectral recollections drifting slowly over him.

''Allo, Lef'tenant Nunn!' said the attacker boisterously, in an East London accent. His defiant grin exposed further the extent of his mutilation. 'Cat got your tongue, 'as it, cock? What you doin' still trailin' around be'ind that cunt in there? Eh?'

Nunn turned. The Brigadier-General was seated in his carriage, not even bothering to look out of the window to discover what was transpiring in the street behind him.

'I'll get you yet, Boyce!' bellowed the attacker, suddenly furious. 'I'll get you! You bastard!'

Two constables arrived at a run, one urging Nunn to step back whilst the other struck his stick against the attacker's jaw, and then across his shoulders.

'Shut your noise, ye hear?' said the policeman harshly to the disfigured man sprawled at his feet. 'Or d'ye want more?'

The man spat out a bloody tooth with a sneer. 'You ain't got nothing that I ain't tasted before, Peeler.'

The stick rose and fell. More policemen arrived, and made their own enthusiastic contributions to the felon's subjugation. The constable at Nunn's side apologised to him for the inconvenience. He nodded absently, and climbed into the carriage.

The vehicle's springs creaked under Nunn's weight. He sat down opposite Boyce, lost in perplexity. His commander was busy attending to his moustache with his remaining hand, the left, helped by the small grooming kit that was kept on board the coach at all times for this purpose.

'Who was that ruffian, then?' inquired Boyce incuriously. 'Some drunkard, I suppose?'

Nunn stared out at the dome of the Infirmary, which wore a gleaming patina of rainwater, and the drenched labourers in the square below, toiling on despite the deluge. 'C-Cregg. I think. A private . . .'

Boyce looked up keenly, closing the mirror. 'Yes, I remember the name. It cannot have been him, though. He was killed before the Redan on the same day that you and I received our injuries.'

Nunn put a hand to his brow. His head was throbbing. 'There's something else, Brigadier. Something about dr-drawings.' He sighed in exasperation, and felt hot tears welling in his eyes. 'Wicked drawings. And there's more besides, b-but I can't recall what it – what I . . .'

Boyce paused, as if considering this, and then shook his head with grave certainty. 'No, Mr Nunn, my apologies, but

441

I can recall nothing about any drawings, wicked or otherwise. That is but a product of your beleaguered mind, I fear, as is your encounter with this long-dead infantryman. I would advise you to let such treacherous thoughts go, so that they can trouble you no longer.' He studied Nunn's arm, as if noticing the cuts on it for the first time. 'Some of those are rather deep. Come, we must go back inside and have them properly dressed.'

3

As one who watches Manchester with a dedicated eye, your humble correspondent cannot help but observe that much is currently being said around the provinces of our busy city on the subject of disgrace. Gossip of an exceptionally scurrilous sort is shuttling back and forth across every shop counter on Deansgate; it is drifting in whispers around the august warehouse-palaces of Portland Street and the reading rooms of the Athenaeum; it is being shouted lustily over the playing fields of Peel Park. Every word of it, needless to say, concerns a pair of young gentlemen from two of our foremost families. It is being reported with ludicrous confidence that these men are holed up in the cellars of one of their fathers' premises, a corrupted cabal at their disposal, laughing at us all; and elsewhere others swear that they have been seen climbing together on to a train at Bank Top, loudly proclaiming their intention to escape to the Far East, where they will be able to indulge their aberrant appetites in absolute freedom. The term 'disgrace', of course, is frequently and vehemently applied.

We do not seek to comment on the gentlemen's alleged crimes, or to speculate as to their whereabouts. We do, however, find ourselves thinking that this term, with all it implies, is lamentably excessive. Should it not rightly be reserved for those who have committed acts of grievous harm – for those who have wronged their fellow man, or betrayed a sacred trust? These two souls have injured nothing but our sense of propriety, a fluid notion indeed in a city such as ours. All we ask for is some consideration of the complexities involved in this sad matter. Language, when so misused, when so hysterically twisted, stands in danger of losing its meaning completely.

Kitson reread this, his final paragraphs of street philosophy, and folded up the piece of paper on which it had been written. He knew full well that Thorne would not print the piece. The *Star*'s role was to fan the flames of scandal, not to attempt to dampen them. But he bound the report up anyway, along with his letter of explanation, and pushed both under the door of the magazine's office. A gust of wind ran up the straight back of Corporation Street, carrying a cold spattering of rain. Kitson started back down towards the traffic of the warehouse district, heading for his attic, his mind taken up entirely with what he was about to do.

As he reached King Street, he was pulled from his thoughts by a sudden commotion a short distance up the pavement. A team of constables, about eight strong, had emerged from an alleyway, carrying a writhing man between them. They were heading for the classicised bulk of the new Town Hall – built, like so many of Manchester's more recent public buildings, on the Athenian model – which also housed the 'A' division of the city police in its basement. This was most probably an uncooperative felon being taken down to the cells. Their captive could be heard cursing with all his might, demonstrating an insane passion which, along with his ragged, grimy clothes, indicated that his was a life of drunken vagrancy. He was not a Manchester man; there was a cockney twang to his obscenities. Kitson watched this fractious party with mild interest. Then the vagrant started to shout about the Crimea.

'Shelled, I was! Bleedin' shelled, by those bastard Russians! *Shelled*! Look at me legs, me face! All 'cos o' that toff cunt back there! What you protectin' 'im for?'

'Stop your cursing, villain,' ordered one of the constables as he attempted to grab hold of this indigent veteran's thrashing legs, 'or I shall make blessed short work of ye!'

At once, Kitson felt certain that this man was known to him. Ignoring the quickening rainfall, he walked over to get a better look. That distinctive pattern of injuries, with severe wounds to the face, hand and leg, coupled with the crowing, indignant whine of a voice, left no room for doubt. The scarred man being borne unceremoniously towards the station was the private he had treated as the Redan's guns had roared all about; the same one he had met in the advance parallel in the last minutes before the assault, who had insisted that he knew Cracknell. Kitson also remembered that he had heard his name, a single syllable he couldn't quite recollect, in the Belle Vue Gardens only two days previously, when a witness had identified him as the perpetrator of that brutal attack upon the factory operative.

The felon was hauled inside, still screaming; and a dark form lodged in the corner of Kitson's eye as abruptly and painfully as a speck of grit. He turned slowly to see a short, swarthy man in a worn black suit, writing something in a notebook. This man was standing some twenty yards from him, on the corner of Cross Street – the most straightforward path back to Princess Street and Kitson's tenement.

He cursed under his breath, deciding immediately to head towards Piccadilly and then double back down Fountain Street. Setting off at speed, he ran straight into a loud checked waistcoat, well filled by the person inside it. A thick arm wrapped around his shoulders and steered him into an alleyway.

'They are watching your domicile as well, my friend,' Cracknell imparted calmly, 'They want us both, and not for a spot of earnest remonstration.'

Kitson ducked under his arm and leant heavily against the alley wall. He'd known that this encounter was inevitable. Cracknell was not yet finished in Manchester.

'I think it's time we had a proper jaw, don't you? All we've managed so far have been snatched moments – the briefest of meetings under some rather unfortunate circumstances. You must agree that we owe one another a civil conversation, at least. We should drink a glass to our fallen friends. To James Maynard.' Cracknell paused, eyeing Kitson slyly. 'To Robert Styles.'

Kitson did not allow himself to react to this. It was surely significant that after several weeks of determined evasion,

Cracknell was suddenly so keen for them to talk. Perhaps, he thought, this was at last a chance to draw some answers out of him. He looked around, refusing to meet his former senior's questioning gaze. The black-suit at Cross Street appeared not to have seen them. 'The police have your henchman.'

Cracknell shook his head with a rueful laugh. 'Oh no, my association with Mr Cregg ended a good while ago. He developed a worrying taste for stabbing people, as you might well remember. I heard that he's just tried to do in a certain Brigadier-General, in fact, over on Piccadilly, outside the Albion Hotel – that's where they caught him.'

So Boyce was in Manchester. The second stage of Cracknell's revenge was imminent.

'No, that business at the Belle Vue – the distraction he caused – was purest serendipity. Good fortune has shone upon this little undertaking of mine. I am not a pious man, Thomas, but as I said to you at the Polygon, there is a higher agency at work here. Justice is being done.'

'You're just cutting that crippled soldier loose, then, without a backward glance? Leaving him to the Manchester police?'

Cracknell merely grinned, then tapped Kitson's shoulder with the cane he was carrying. 'I have a place in mind. Will you accompany me?'

Kitson nodded reluctantly, thinking that if nothing else Cracknell probably represented his best chance of evading Twelves and his minions.

They walked the length of the alley at some speed, soon coming to Market Street. Carts trundled past, bearing cargoes of banners, flags and poles, their wheels churning in deepening puddles. Kitson grimaced as cold raindrops splashed against his shoulders. Cracknell, however, was swinging his cane with complete nonchalance, entirely indifferent to the muddy rainwater that was saturating the cuffs of his ill-fitting trousers. He led them a short distance towards Piccadilly before weaving across the road and starting up the gentle hill on the other side.

Smithfield Market appeared between the buildings ahead

of them. The iron-and-glass pavilion was lit against the premature darkness brought by the weather, and a great crowd was taking shelter beneath it. A group of mill-girls were screaming as they pushed each other out under the jets of water that cascaded from the market's overflowing gutters.

Cracknell turned, craning his neck, peering back down the hill. 'They're following,' he said. 'Come, Thomas, this way.'

Kitson looked back also, and could see nothing but shops shutting up and people rushing to escape the downpour. Cracknell, meanwhile, had disappeared down a narrow lane across from the market. Kitson hurried after him.

The rainfall seemed to slacken off almost completely, reduced to the odd stray drip. Looking up, Kitson saw that this was not due to the passing of the storm, but to a multitude of decrepit balconies, strings of forgotten washing, and the lean of the subsiding tenements, all of which were blocking the water's path to the ground below. The only illumination came from the occasional candle flickering forlornly on a window ledge. Infants played in the gutter, their tiny hands full of slopping sludge. The stench of faeces and urine mingled thickly in the air with the sweet reek of decay.

They turned, and turned again; Kitson grew uncomfortable. Despite a number of months' residence in Manchester, he had seldom ventured so far into its darker regions. But Cracknell seemed perfectly at ease in the stinking alleys, the dilapidation and misery causing him no apparent concern. He was walking fast. Kitson was having to exert himself simply to keep up. Old memories returned to him, memories of trailing behind the senior correspondent as he pursued his pleasure amongst the dusty stones of Constantinople; and later as he chased the army across the battlefields of the Alma Valley and Inkerman Ridge. There it was, that same broad back, confidently leading the way, utterly convinced of its own imperviousness.

'Ancoats,' Cracknell declared, waving his cane around, 'in all its tumbledown fury. Never mind that bloody Exhibition,

447

this district is Manchester's most notable achievement – although I think we can bet that on the morrow, the Royal nose will not be brought within a half-mile of its many distinctive smells. They say that Ancoats is to Manchester what Manchester is to England: the fundament of the fundament. D'you know, Thomas, I honestly think that the simple fact of this place, and the way the working people must live within it, is justification enough for the destruction of their masters, whatever else the grasping bastards might have done.'

'Well, you have certainly destroyed Charles Norton,' Kitson replied curtly. 'You have destroyed his entire family.'

Cracknell chuckled. 'Oho! Is that *pique* I hear there? If you are referring to your widow, Kitson, do please recall that I warned you quite explicitly that there would be trouble in that quarter. And I make no apologies for being a little ruthless. A cat in gloves, my dear fellow, catches no mice.'

'She knew nothing of her father's business. Neither did her brother, for that matter.'

'But pain, Thomas, is purgative, and that family needed a bit of bloody purgation, did it not? Your widow has her charms, I'm sure, but she watched her father's rise without questioning it for a moment. She took up her rooms in his mansion, and bought herself great wardrobes full of fine clothes, without a single second's hesitation.'

Kitson formed tight fists inside his pockets, digging his nails into his palms. 'She had just lost her *husband*, damn you. She was hardly—' He stopped himself. There was absolutely no point continuing with this argument.

A dozen filthy faces were regarding them silently from a nearby cellar. After waiting with a sarcastic smile to see if Kitson had any more to say, Cracknell started off again. They came to an area of open ground – a small yard before the steep rise of a gigantic mill. Impassive brick walls stretched upwards, hard and featureless after the diseased jumble of the alleyways. Running along their tops, at least thirty feet above the ground, were the windows, thousands of small panes arranged in lines inside a leaden grid. The dirty glass glimmered weakly, offering only the very slightest suggestion of gas lighting within. A great droning, crashing noise issued from this austere building, drowning out the splashing and trickling of the rain. It ran on and on, a continuous three-second cycle of disastrous, unbearable sound, clattering away incessantly. This, the tireless rhythm of the power looms, was difficult enough to endure out in the yard; the effect on those confined inside, Kitson thought, must be of another order altogether. The two men crossed the cobbles hurriedly, eager to be away.

Cracknell led them on towards the Oldham Road, Ancoats' great thoroughfare and the site of some of the city's largest factories. Chimneys towered above the lanes, pumping out smoke that seemed to vanish shortly after it had left them. Kitson put a hand up to his face; there was wet, sooty dirt sliding across his cheek, driven on to it from the atmosphere by the pouring rain.

'Cracknell, where the hell are we going?'

'Somewhere close. You'll like it, Thomas, I promise.'

A long row of pawn shops and pestilent-looking boarding houses brought them to a large junction lit by a single sputtering lime-light. Cracknell stopped under a tavern sign, checking the streets for black-suits. The symbols upon this sign had mostly been obscured by dirt, but Kitson could just make out a heraldic shield, some feathers, and a crude scroll on which had been painted *The Trafford Arms*. He recognised the name. It was a popular inn and concert-room, whose custom consisted entirely of the operatives from the mills found all around it. They stepped inside.

The sounds of a lazy jig, played on fiddle, drum and flute, drifted through a large room with a balcony and a low stage. It had been built in what could loosely be described as the Tudor style, with the uneven wooden beams left exposed, and it was packed to the rafters with working people of both sexes, each with a jar of ale in their hand. Many had pipes or cheroots also, and tobacco smoke filled the Trafford Arms as water fills a bucket. Animated conversations were underway, the music almost lost amidst the raised voices and bursts of laughter. It was warm; Kitson was suddenly aware of the cold drips that were running down his back and legs.

Cracknell skirted the long tables and took up a place in the middle of the bar, leaning against it like a regular. His faded gentleman's garb, and especially his garish waistcoat, were conspicuous indeed amongst the drab caps, fustian jackets and plain cotton frocks of the rest of the Trafford's clientele. He was behaving, also, with a notable swagger. The first thing he did was buy drinks for all those around him, filling the barmaid's cupped hands with coppers. This magnanimous gesture was met with a decidedly ambiguous murmur and a couple of grudging nods of acknowledgement. Cracknell, entirely unconcerned by this response, handed Kitson a glass of spirit, knocking back one himself in a single swallow. This liquid, gin he supposed, had the appearance of old dishwater and smelled like burned rubber. Kitson drank it anyway.

Beer was next, a jar of dark porter. After making a healthy start on his, Cracknell lit a cigarette and scanned the Trafford's balcony. He saluted a bald-headed man in a red neckerchief who sat gravely at the balcony's edge with a company of roughs gathered around him. This fellow, Cracknell explained, was the Trafford's landlord, a Mr Bairstowe – who, he'd discovered, had once clashed unpleasantly with Mr Twelves and his underlings, and would not now permit them inside his establishment. The Trafford was a haven; a place where they could catch their breath and consider their next move.

Putting a hand on the coarse, unpolished bar, Kitson took in the tavern, working out the best escape route and thinking about how long he would need to get back to Princess Street. Something was going on, he was sure of it; this all felt rehearsed. Cracknell had another reason for bringing him here. I will wait for half an hour, he thought, let him have his civil conversation, and then I will leave.

The Tomahawk looked at Kitson and grinned. His former junior was practically a visual definition of unease – ideal for his purposes. They stood out like goats in a sheep pen, and were drawing a good deal of attention. He puffed on his cigarette and took a cool swig of porter. It was time to get back to the business of the evening.

'No,' he announced after a few seconds' silence, 'there was rot in the Norton family, and it needed to be gouged out. The railway, Thomas, the bloody *railway*! So many times I rode it, marvelling at its effectiveness, little suspecting that the very nails holding it together were the product of greed and wickedness! I had no notion of this whatsoever until I returned to England in the winter of fifty-five. Such a boon to the troops – and yet being exploited by Boyce for his own gain!'

'So you have brought down his accomplice,' Kitson said, reaching stiffly for his jar. 'Boyce will have been damaged also. He must have an interest in Norton's business.'

'Undoubtedly, although I could find no trace of a formal connection between them. The Brigadier has protected himself with exceptional effectiveness, I must say. I haven't even been able to discover where the brute has been living since he was invalided home from the war. But now I will finally get my vengeance. And by Christ, there's a lot to avenge.' Cracknell paused. 'He took her from me, Thomas – *stole* her from me.'

'You are referring to the late Mrs Boyce, I assume.'

'Such a beautiful, spirited creature, cruelly cut down by that *demon*.' The Tomahawk drew himself up. 'I cannot accuse him directly, of course. The murder was covered up very nicely, blamed on a rogue Russian – Boyce produced a couple of witnesses from his regiment, as well as the body of the supposed killer. Neither can I get at him, in the Metropolis or elsewhere. The obstacles are simply too great.' He fixed Kitson with a direct, resolute stare. 'Up here, though – up here there is a real chance. And I must take it. I must do whatever I can to obtain justice for my poor Madeleine.'

Kitson banged his glass down impatiently on the bar. 'Oh, come now, Cracknell!' he exclaimed irritably. 'You seem to forget that I was *there*. You would have me believe that you have come here as a vengeful lover – but I spoke to Annabel

Wade on the day Madeleine Boyce died. You had deserted her, taken flight to escape the wrath of her husband and pen your vitriolic reports in safety. You had not seen her for *months*. Your affair was over.'

Cracknell dropped his cigarette butt on the ground, crushing it beneath his boot, somewhat wrong-footed by Kitson's hard certainty. 'She was killed, Kitson, because of her connection with me,' he said quietly, 'because of her love for me. You cannot deny this.'

'Perhaps so, but it was a love you did not return. You knew the manner of man Boyce was. Did you not think, even *once*, of the danger you were placing her in with all that Tomahawk nonsense?' Kitson made a disgusted sound. 'This grand act of yours does not work on me, Cracknell. Stop pretending that you are in Manchester to avenge Mrs Boyce. You are here for yourself.'

A comic singer, wearing a drooping ruff and a pair of outsized pantaloons, ambled on to the stage of the Trafford Arms. His appearance was greeted by applause and raucous cheers from the audience, with a good number of those seated rising to their feet. Several even climbed up on top of benches and tables.

Drawing in an exaggerated breath, his arms open wide, the singer launched into an account of young Billy Taylor, pressed to sea. It was clearly a regular tune at the Trafford, as within the space of a bar or two the entire crowd, except the two newspapermen, were belting out its lines into the smoky air with considerable gusto. '*Soon 'is true love followed after,*' they sang, '*Under name o' Richard Carr; and 'er lily-white 'ands she rubbed all over, wi' nasty pitch and tar!*'

Cracknell finished his porter. A disconcertingly genuine anger had started to itch away inside him. He raised his hand, beckoning over a plain-featured, wide-hipped barmaid in a dirty apron. After ordering more beer, he turned back to Kitson.

'I'll admit that I have other reasons for hating him,' he retorted sharply, raising his voice to be heard over the singing. 'You must know what he did to me.' It hurt Cracknell even to think of this matter; but, simultaneously, he found that he wanted desperately to drag it out into the open once more, to bask again in the toxic injustice of it all.

'I have heard that letters were written to the *Times*,' Kitson said carefully.

Immediately, Cracknell reached into his jacket and pulled out the clipping. It was heavily worn, and falling apart where it had been folded; he could have recited it by heart if requested. He laid it on the bar in front of Kitson.

The presence of certain civilian war correspondents, it read, *has been a nagging irritation to all fighting on this campaign. One man in particular, an employee of the* London Courier *magazine, has made an active annoyance of himself from the day the expeditionary force set sail from England. He has cast his abuse about widely, selecting targets from the most senior generals through to the stalwart men of the line, doing considerable damage to morale. Recently, he named all British soldiery in the Crimea 'fruit of a rotten tree'; here I use his own despicable expression.*

During the first assault on the Redan, his interferences became rather more direct, and have prompted me to write this letter in the hope that it might lead to some form of punitive action being taken against him. I witnessed him running amidst the men of the Light Division at the height of the attack, shouting seditious slogans, undermining the confidence of the soldiers and interrupting their advance. In my opinion as an officer, this absurd behaviour contributed directly to the failure of the assault and the deaths and injuries of a number of soldiers; indeed, my own wound, which has caused me to be sent home, was inflicted as I attempted to correct his disturbances.

I implore those with direct authority on this person to consider this incident and summon him away from the Crimea as soon as possible; and I entreat the ministers of our government to impose some manner of formal restriction upon civilians who seek to enter a theatre of war, so that the disastrous, inappropriate bravado of the Courier's *man cannot be repeated.*

It was signed *A commander of Infantry, July 1855*.

Kitson finished reading it. He made no visible reaction. 'And this led to your being recalled by O'Farrell?'

Cracknell nodded. Whilst the trials of 'Richard Carr' were loudly detailed all around them – including her less than successful attempts to splice the main-brace, and then sneak to her Billy's hammock once the moon was high above the waves – the Tomahawk told of his fall. He had actually managed to persevere until the final three-day bombardment of Sebastopol in early September, and the miserable failure of the second British assault on the Great Redan: their final humiliation, in which Sir William Codrington, the *Courier*'s old pal, had played a prominent, inglorious role. When the Russians had withdrawn from their fortifications the following morning, after the successful French occupation of the Malakhoff Tower, Cracknell had been among the first to venture past the enemy defences and into the burning town. This had brought him no satisfaction or triumph, however. The Redan, that impregnable bastion, had been but a miserable mess of scorched earth, splintered timber, dead Russians and camp litter; and Sebastopol itself a ruin only, knocked to pieces by shot and then set on fire. It had seemed a paltry thing, an empty accomplishment that was neither victory nor defeat, completely unworthy of the many thousands of lives it had cost.

Furthermore, the publication of Boyce's letter in the *Times* had made it almost impossible for him to operate. No soldier or sailor of any rank would tolerate his presence, even for a second. He was cursed and spat at wherever he went. Every one of his friends seemed either to be dead or to have been invalided home. And perhaps most crucially, the *Courier*'s circulation had begun to drop. Before long, O'Farrell had grown nervous and he was summoned back to England. Not a word of his had appeared in the *London Courier* since.

'All of which leads me to this place, Thomas, to a grubby tavern in Ancoats, standing before you with my clothes torn and stained and my last few pennies jangling forlornly in my pockets.' Cracknell felt like laughing aloud at this ludicrous state of affairs, if only to mask the black despair that was gathering inside him. 'I sell to anyone who will consider me. The *Dublin University Magazine* ran a piece last winter. But I'm the Tomahawk of the bloody *Courier*, aren't I – the disgraced relic of an ignoble war that everyone wants to forget. I am friendless, Kitson, entirely friendless, thanks to Nathaniel bloody Boyce.'

Cracknell took a deep, soothing drink from the fresh jar of porter that had been set before him. It was good, he told himself, that his blood was up; it would make the attainment of his object that evening all the easier. He could not help but think, however, that their conversation was starting to veer off course. Kitson, bless him, had somehow managed to get the Tomahawk struggling like a kitten in a rain-barrel to justify himself – when he was in fact the wronged party, the innocent victim. He knew that he must change the tide of their discourse, and dislodge this sanctimonious street philosopher from the seat of judgement on which he was becoming so damnably comfortable. It was time, in short, to launch an attack of his own.

He looked Kitson over. The fellow's clothes were clean enough and in decent repair, but they looked to be second hand; there was no watch-chain either, and his boots were old. 'I must say, though, Thomas, that you yourself are hardly the picture of journalistic success. How on earth did *you* end up here?'

Kitson realised that he was now leaning against the bar. For the first time in days, his chest had stopped hurting. His cheeks were flaming; no longer did the wet jacket feel so cold against his back. In fact, was it even still wet? He had already been in the tavern longer than he'd intended. Cracknell's story had held him, if only because of his sheer amazement at the man's capacity for self-delusion; but he would take his leave soon.

After draining his beer-jar, Kitson gave a terse account of how he had fled the Crimea the very afternoon of that first attack on the Redan. Totally deaf, half-mad with guilt, and still caked with a thick mixture of blood and dust, he had simply walked aboard the first steamer bound for Constantinople, without sending word to anyone. Back in England, after a period recuperating at a cousin's house in Highgate, he had tried for a time to find work in the hospitals and infirmaries of London. The sight of death, however, and the feel of warm blood on his hands and clothes, quickly proved to be more than he could bear. Eventually, on the advice of a friend from his days in art correspondence, he had come to Manchester and introduced himself to Edward Thorne of the *Manchester Evening Star*.

'Street philosophy was the only employment Thorne could offer,' Kitson explained wearily. 'This didn't concern me in the least. I didn't care what I did. I only wanted to be away from everything, from everyone, thinking that I could repair myself if I was only left alone. I—' The porter was going to his head. He was talking more than he meant to, saying things certainly not suited to his former senior's ears.

Cracknell's expression was unsympathetic. 'But then this bloody great art exhibition came along and upset all your plans, eh? Enough to attract old colleagues you probably thought you'd shaken off for good, and old enemies you'd quite forgotten, all brought together in your sooty refuge! Well, my commiserations, Kitson, truly.'

Another song began, this time a Lancashire clog hornpipe. Some space was cleared, and led by the comic dancer up on the stage, the revellers clomped about in their wooden shoes with whooping enthusiasm. Arms were linked, skirts gathered up, and caps thrown in the air.

'Tell me,' Cracknell asked loudly as he lit a cigarette, 'did you consider my plight at all when you fled so promptly from that ruined house? When you *abandoned me*, Thomas? I was trapped in there for hours, y'know. I had to claw my way out through several tons of masonry, and then creep back to the British line under the cover of darkness – all the while thinking that I was about to get shot in the back by a Ruski sniper.'

Kitson drank from his second jar. Cracknell was goading him, and he would not rise to it. His only thought back in that collapsed parlour had been to leave, to hide himself away. Before heading for the cemetery, though, he'd noticed that the table the correspondent had been sheltering under was still intact, despite being largely buried under a fall of bricks. He had not gone to help. Cracknell, he'd felt, deserved to be left.

'I knew that you would manage to save yourself somehow.'

'It was your final dereliction of the *Courier*, I suppose – leaving your erstwhile mentor for dead.' Cracknell paused thoughtfully, smoke spilling from his lips. 'Do you know, I often reflected whilst in the Crimea that your desertion was in fact a singular piece of good fortune. It allowed me to find my true level. You did not understand our mission, and you were certainly never committed to it. As soon as things got a little difficult, you simply melted away.'

Grinding his teeth, Kitson took hold of the iron bar-rail with both hands. He would not relent and give Cracknell what he so plainly wanted.

'You're more of an *observer*, Thomas, aren't you? You will not act to bring about change – you will not take a bloody stand. I mean, look at you now. A bloody street philosopher, a purveyor of gossip, of empty-headed prattle! After all I tried to teach you about the duty of the correspondent to truth, to matters of import!' He stopped to drink, wiping his mouth reproachfully on his sleeve. 'I admired you, at first. There was wit in your pen, and vigour, and serious intelligence too – but you lacked the strength of will to hold them together. You possessed every gift except the one needful – the pearls without the string.'

The voluble bombast in Cracknell's voice was enough to cause something of a disruption. A number of those dancing eyed him with open dislike.

Kitson hunched his shoulders and lowered his head; it was no use. He could not leave this unanswered. 'You mean I lacked your capacity for selfish indifference,' he snapped.

Cracknell curled his lip. He had won. 'You are referring to Madeleine Boyce again, I take it.'

'And Robert Styles.'

Cracknell laughed – he actually *laughed* at this mention of their illustrator's name. 'How could I forget? A fellow with a similar weakness to your own, Thomas, if you don't mind me saying, but with the very opposite inclination – a mind prone to an excess of brutality and morbidity rather than sentimentality.'

'*Sentimentality?*' Kitson turned towards him. 'I helped many on the docks. In the British Hotel.'

457

'A drop in the bloody ocean,' Cracknell replied coldly. 'A single line of one of my articles did more for the cause of the common soldier than an entire year of mopping up gore for Mother Seacole. But then, how can I expect you to understand this? Both you and Styles were utterly unable to grasp the simple, potent role of the war correspondent.'

'Keep it down, can't ye?' growled a voice nearby. Up on the stage, the singer slid neatly from the hornpipe into a comic ballad, greeted with a universal bellow of approval. '*A friar came to a maid when she went to bed,*' he began, warbling earnestly up at the balcony, '*Desiring to have her maidenhead . . .*' The crowd erupted into salacious whistling.

'Like you do, you mean,' Kitson cried, 'with your pointless, protracted feuds,' He snatched the *Times* clipping from the bar and held it in Cracknell's face. 'How, pray, was your crusade against Boyce part of any effort to relay matters of import – to bring about this change you boast of?'

Cracknell said something about how Boyce, apart from his various terrible crimes, was a symbol of the turpitude of that war; a symbol of both undeserving privilege and callous incompetence.

Kitson ignored him. 'For you to talk so freely about the neglect of duty would be amusing in its hypocrisy if the consequences had not been so tragic. You were our *senior*. Robert Styles was broken by your taunts, by trying to keep pace with you, with what you insisted we all do. I told you he had to be sent home, many times, yet you did not do it. And it cost Styles his life.'

The song went on behind them, the singer raising his voice in an attempt to drown out the heated disputation at the bar. '*But she denied his desire, and told him she feared hell fire . . .*' The audience joined in; more faces turned towards the two newspapermen.

Cracknell took a sip of beer. 'You talk, Kitson,' he said levelly, 'as if *I* were the one who shot the boy.'

This remark, delivered so calmly, robbed Kitson of his breath, winding him as suddenly as if he had been slammed hard against the floor. A momentary vision flashed across his mind: of Styles' wasted limbs, twitching for the last time on the bloody tiles of the parlour, a fraction of a second before they were buried forever beneath a heavy fall of Russian masonry.

Kitson faltered, his gaze dipping down. 'That is something I must live with. I – I cannot forgive myself for my part in his death.' He looked back at Cracknell. 'And I cannot forgive you either. We failed him. He was our charge, our comrade, and we failed him appallingly.'

Cracknell rolled his eyes and finished off his porter. 'Oh for Christ's sake, listen to yourself! So damnably sensitive, so full of bloody drama! Drink up, man, before you collapse in a swoon.' He summoned the barmaid and requested more gin, sliding an extra sixpence in her apron as he did so with an air of lascivious benevolence. 'The sad truth of it,' he continued bluntly, 'is that Robert Styles wished to die. There was nothing either of us could have done to prevent it, short of binding the poor fellow in chains. Don't you remember all those ghastly drawings of his?'

Kitson flinched. He had in fact brought a small number of Styles' works back from the Crimea with him, taking them from the *Courier* tent on that last afternoon and tucking them inside his filthy jacket. His intention had been to try to honour the illustrator's dying wish; but, as he had expected, it had been impossible to engage the interest of any respectable publisher. The bundle of gruesome studies had lain untouched at the bottom of a wardrobe in his cousin's attic for nearly eighteen months.

'Death was his fascination,' Cracknell pronounced. 'A lunatic obsession. Styles wanted nothing more than to join the fallen soldiers he studied so assiduously. He wanted to die. If it had not been by your hand, Thomas, it would've soon been another's. Perhaps even his own.'

'*Tush, quoth the friar, thou needst not doubt,*' went on the ballad, accompanied by the scraping of the fiddle, '*If thou wert in hell I could sing thee out!*' The tavern exploded into uproarious mirth.

'You cannot honestly believe that.'

Cracknell merely raised an eyebrow as he polished off his second measure of gin.

Kitson glared at him. 'So you feel nothing – no shame, no remorse, not even the smallest sense of responsibility? Two young people died as a direct result of your neglectful behaviour. The Norton Foundry will surely close, bringing want and worry to its many hundreds of employees. William Norton has been forced to flee the country, and Jemima James has been reduced to almost certain penury. And yet you feel *nothing* – nothing but your righteous wrath about the evils of Nathaniel Boyce?'

Cracknell picked up Kitson's beer-jar and took a long draught; then he set it down, his moustache heavy with foam and his cheeks red as radishes. He paused for a few seconds, as if considering what his former junior had said. Then he grinned. 'Astute as ever, Thomas!'

Kitson strode away from the bar with livid energy. He had heard enough. It was time for him to leave.

'Wait, my friend, wait,' Cracknell begged with a boozy chortle, jogging after him and fastening a hand around his arm. 'What about Mr Twelves?'

'That is my concern, is it not? If they are even out there.'

'I cannot let you go outside. They will surely murder you.'

Kitson looked into Cracknell's rosy face, trying to find an explanation for this concern for his wellbeing, and saw at once that it was somehow part of the scheme – part of the reason he had waylaid Kitson on King Street, brought him to this place, plied him with drink, and tried so hard to provoke an altercation between them. He attempted to free himself, and they began to grapple; a table went over with a crash. People began to shout.

Men, the landlord's roughs, were soon prising them apart. Mr Bairstowe himself looked down from the balcony, and asked what the trouble was. He addressed Cracknell by name; they were plainly acquainted. This was the world in which his former colleague had hidden himself so effectively for all these weeks.

'Oh, nothing, Bairstowe old chap,' Cracknell replied breezily, 'just a difference of opinion. I will replace any drinks that were lost.'

Bairstowe snorted. 'As if ye could. Who's this with ye?'

'An old friend from my days on the *London Courier*. He's at the *Evening Star* now.'

Kitson shook off the man who was holding him. 'I am no friend of his,' he said fiercely; and then he walked out of the tavern into the rain.

4

The musicians started up again, and another song began. Bairstowe walked slowly down the balcony stairs, stopping by the door. Cracknell found himself being escorted over to him. The Trafford's proprietor crossed his arms. He had the flattened, broken nose of a retired pugilist, and was regarding the swaying Tomahawk with weary amusement.

'Time for ye to leave as well, I think, Mr Cracknell,' he said. 'Afore my other customers tear out that bushy beard of yours.'

Cracknell gave a throaty chuckle. 'My apologies, Bairstowe. You know how these things can go. What is the hour, if you please?'

'Aff past eight, near enough,' someone mumbled.

'Heavens, early still.' He chuckled again, and made a great show of stumbling into the man beside him. 'Yet I feel already that I should be heading to my bed.' The barmaid appeared and sullenly returned his cane, which had been left leaning against the bar. He bowed to her in gratitude.

'Aye,' agreed Bairstowe, nodding at a man to open the door, 'and not a moment too soon. Good night to thee, Mr Cracknell.'

Outside, Cracknell looked around for Twelves. There was no one at all in the rainy street. Perhaps Kitson had been right. He straightened his jacket, shrugging off his show of inebriation like a cloak and directing himself not towards London Road and the Model Lodging House, but somewhere else altogether.

Then he caught sight of them down a side alley, silhouetted

against a distant gas-light: four black-suits standing around their victim, who lay coughing at their feet. Immediately, he started back to the Trafford. Reaching the door, he wrenched it open.

'Mr Bairstowe!' he bellowed. 'There's something out here I believe you might be interested in!'

Kitson landed on his side and curled up on the wet cobble-stones. The stick had struck him in the stomach, close enough to his old wound to set off a great sparking bonfire behind his eyes, and lay him out, entirely helpless. He hadn't seen his assailant; he could tell, though, that more than one man stood around him.

'So this is the end,' said a nasal, inexpressive voice somewhere above him. It belonged to the man from the Belle Vue – Mr Twelves, the leader of the black-suits. 'This is it for ye, Mr Kitson, and no mistake. No gang of bugger-boys to rescue ye this time. Brigadier Boyce has ordered you dead.' He tapped a knotted cudgel against his leg. 'And it will 'appen.'

Before Twelves could act, however, someone barked his name with gruff aggression, the word ringing flatly off the close walls of the alley. It was the Trafford Arms landlord, Mr Bairstowe. Kitson could hear the sound of boots walking purposefully across the cobbles towards them.

'Twelves!' Bairstowe repeated. 'What did I bleedin' well say about your lot comin' round 'ere, eh? Weren't it clear enough for ye?'

There were thuds and grunts; feet scuffed and scrabbled against the stones. A black-suit fell close to where Kitson lay and had several savage kicks planted in his midriff. Kitson struggled up on to his elbows. Twelves tried to stop him, to beat him back down with his cudgel, but was dragged away by another man before he could lift it. The two of them exchanged a few jabbing blows and then toppled together into a deep, filth-choked gutter.

Kitson managed to rise to his knees. He peered down the alley. It was filled with brawling men, wrestling, punching and kicking at each other with vicious vigour. Both sides were obviously experienced at such backstreet combat, and it was brutal indeed. Kitson saw a man – he could not tell which group was which in the darkness – pitched head first against a cluster of lead drainage pipes that snaked down the alley's wall. There was an empty clang, and he slumped senseless to the ground. And there, on the opposite side of this desperate fight, was Cracknell, looking on excitedly, holding his cane like a sword as if ready to swipe at anyone who came near him.

Their eyes met through the ducking heads and flailing limbs. 'Run, Thomas!' Cracknell cried. 'Run, my friend!'

Kitson needed no further encouragement. Arriving on the wide Oldham Road at a brisk trot, clutching his side, he started down towards the centre of the city. He could not now return to his attic. Princess Street was a good half-mile away, and there could easily be more black-suits along the route. All that was there, in truth, were some old clothes and a negligible sum of money. Time was beginning to run rather short, also; the train was due to leave Bank Top in under an hour. He turned right at the bottom of Oldham Road on to Swan Street, splashing heedlessly through dirty puddles, wincing at the continued complaints of his chest.

It was now plain that an act had been staged in the Trafford Arms, in classic Cracknell fashion; an act that Kitson had fallen for completely. Cracknell had wanted to cause a disruption, and had manipulated him towards that end with every success. The reason for this he could not fathom. No details of his scheme against Boyce had actually been revealed. Neither had he tried to recruit his one-time colleague to his cause.

Cracknell had clearly believed everything that he had said, though. Kitson's attempts to challenge his wilful, self-serving distortions concerning Styles had not had any effect whatsoever. Rather than simply reawaken his anger, however, this realisation made Kitson recognise the inflections that he himself had given to their tale. After years of black confusion, he could now regard those events with a new clarity. He had contributed to the illustrator's death; but the blame was not his alone, far from it. And he, unlike Cracknell, felt deep remorse for what he had done. In this simple fact he could sense the possibility of redemption.

Up amongst the clustered roofs before him, a dirty locomotive chugged along a raised railway into the immense hulk of Victoria Station, a line of carriages trailing behind it. Kitson stopped briefly, catching his breath, following the engine with his eyes; then he hurried over to the station's long front, where a row of hackney cabs stood before its thick Doric columns. He selected one and climbed inside, directing the driver towards Cheetham Hill. The interior smelled of cheap perfume, cigars and wet leather. They started with a jolt, wheeling off towards the outskirts of the city. Sitting back on the cab's flattened cushions, he looked out at the storm and the soaked decorations that swung helplessly in its clutches. Few people were about, and traffic was at an absolute minimum. The empty, waterlogged streets shone like canals beneath the City Corporation's gas lamps.

Jemima stepped on to the landing of Norton Hall, her valise in her hand. She wore her plainest bonnet and a long, sturdy cloak, a costume calculated not to attract notice. Her fine clothes, all bought with Foundry money, remained in her wardrobe, and of every book and journal she had collected in her rooms, only one volume had a place in her valise: the London and North-Western Railway Almanac.

Many of the servants had departed Norton Hall, keen to escape any contaminating association with the scandal that had broken there. As Jemima crossed the stair, however, a footman strode along the hallway below to her father's study. She moved close to the wall, concealing herself in the gloom; no candles or lamps had yet been lit in the understaffed house.

The man opened the study door. Jemima could see her father sitting in the red glow of a guttering fire, an open watch in one hand and a full glass of liquor in the other. He looked immensely tired and careworn, clearly lost in embittered contemplation of the events that had reduced him with such devastating speed. Jemima knew that he had nurtured dreams of a great dynasty, stretching off into the mists of futurity, long after he himself was dead; dreams that would now surely come to nothing. She felt a stirring of pity, and an unexpected impulse to go to his side. Then he spoke, and she checked herself.

'Where the blazes have ye been?' he bawled at the servant, his voice rough with drink. 'I rang five minutes ago! *Five minutes ago*! What do I pay you for, to sit warming your idle feet by the scullery fire? You worthless dog!'

Her reasons for leaving, for never wanting to set eyes on Charles Norton again, returned to her forcefully. The grandfather clock chimed nine. She had to leave. The tirade in the study went on, out of all proportion with the perceived offence. Her father's enraged voice echoing around her, Jemima took her valise in her arms in order to avoid accidentally bumping it against anything in the dark, and crept along the hall. She extracted an umbrella from the stand. The front door opened a crack, just enough to allow the passage of a slim woman and all her worldly possessions; and Jemima James slipped away from Norton Hall entirely unobserved.

The rain was so heavy that it almost forced the umbrella from her grasp. She walked rapidly down the drive; the lamps of a hackney cab shone up ahead, waiting at the gate as they had agreed. As she neared it, she saw that its windows were misted up with Mr Kitson's breath. She climbed inside, dropping her umbrella to the floor and sitting with an exclamation of relief. Raindrops drummed upon the roof of the cab as it turned back towards the centre of Manchester. Mr Kitson sat across from her, deep in shadow; she could see, however, that he was smiling. Jemima was light-headed with exhilaration. It was underway. They would soon be free. She looked over at him, her partner in this bold action, and returned his smile.

'Thomas,' she said.

And then they were reaching out across the cab, embracing each other, kissing with a determined passion. His hands slid quickly beneath her cloak and across the sheen of her gown. Hers gripped on to his jacket, the damp material gathering under her fingers.

5

The six open carriages rolled up the Stretford New Road to peals of thunder, which all but drowned out the patriotic cheers of the bedraggled, threadbare crowd. Rain had plastered the proud plumes of the dragoon escort down against their helmets, turning them into slick black query-marks of sodden horse-hair. The personages within the carriages, from the Royal tutors in the first to the Queen and her Consort in the last, were largely concealed from the public eye beneath expansive umbrellas. A cold wind had started to blow, tugging at hats and coats, whipping up the fabric of the triumphal arch at the Old Trafford toll gate, exposing its skeletal wooden frame. The sopping soldiers of the 25th Regiment of Foot, turned out to line the final stage of the route, watched the passing of the Sovereign to whom they had sworn their allegiance with rather less reverence than they might have done on a clear day.

Up ahead was a notable assembly indeed, waiting inside the Exhibition building with a reasonable display of patience. There sat lords, dukes, earls and marquises, accompanied by graceful spouses, and clad in the finery of their station; influential Members of Parliament from the Government and the Opposition, including none other than Lord Palmerston himself, grumbling loudly about the cold; bishops and archdeacons, generals and colonels, every one in full uniform; and a varied multitude of people of fashion, of the arts, of industry and of science. A good number were far too important themselves to

467

be overly excited by the approach of the Queen – and those who were not did their very best to appear as if they were, and muffle their thrilled whispers.

The deafening drum-rolls of the skies, however, were causing agitation in some quarters. A circle of engineers and architects gathered around Sir Joseph Paxton, designer of the Crystal Palace, earnestly debating the risk of lightning striking, and perhaps even igniting, this iron-and-glass structure. Utter nonsense, declared Sir Joseph, smiling reassuringly at some alarmed ladies who sat nearby, the chance was negligibly small; for what, he asked, in a building containing so little wood in its upper regions, could a spark possibly catch against?

The first carriage arrived at the Exhibition, and soon the whole Royal procession was queued up before the façade. Footmen, rainwater running off the brims of their top hats, urged a rapid descent – as their Queen was left exposed to the downpour for every second that they dallied. Lords and ladies, princes and princesses were hurried from their vehicles and into the building with little ceremony, in order to make way for their Monarch.

Queen Victoria rose, stepped down and entered the Exhibition hall. As she was directed through to the reception room, where the Royal party was to reassemble before the ceremony, a massive orchestra stirred.

The sound of the rain on the glass roof, Boyce fancied, was like a vigorous round of applause, an untiring ovation for the Queen, and for men like himself, the heroes of her Empire. He was standing at a carefully selected point, under the balcony, close to the vestibule that led through to Saloon A, where his *Pilate* was on display. It had been suggested that he do so by Colonel Phipps, an admirer of his who was serving in the Royal entourage. It was understood that the Queen's tour of the collection was to be strictly private, but Phipps was certain that he could win Boyce a moment of the Sovereign's time whilst she stood before his painting, to tell his story and win him the honour of her attention and interest.

Since his arrival in Manchester, Boyce had been amazed by the speed with which the reputation of his *Pilate*, and of himself as its discoverer, had spread as a result of its inclusion in the Exhibition. The previous evening, at his dinner with the aristocratic Raphael enthusiasts, he had been informed repeatedly that he was the envy of the art-loving nation, a veritable prince amongst connoisseurs. The Queen and her Consort, they had assured him, being the wise patrons and collectors that they were, would certainly wish to meet the man who had discovered such a work.

And now it was about to happen. Boyce knew, of course, that this was about far more than painting and connoisseurship. It could well be the defining moment of his life – the moment when he came to the Queen's notice. It could lead to promotions, preferment and titles; and to introductions to eligible ladies of the highest rank. This one brief moment before the Monarch could, in short, mark the beginning of his ascent to the very summit of society.

The Queen made her entrance to rousing cheers and a rendition of the National Anthem. Boyce stood impassively through the tedium of the ceremonials that followed; through the interminable addresses where everybody stated their esteem for everybody and everything else; through the to-ing and fro-ing of the vulgar dignitaries of the factory city before the Royal group up on the dais; through the undeserved knighting of their fat shop-keeper of a mayor. What honour, he asked himself with growing impatience, could there possibly be in men of commerce?

The Brigadier-General had soon decided that he was best rid of any connection, however clandestine, with the sphere of business. It was supremely undignified for a man of quality. His severance from Norton, although somewhat inconvenient from a purely financial standpoint, could be seen in every other regard as a blessedly clean release.

Eventually, these ceremonials came to an end, and to the sound of more cheers the Queen and her court, attended on only by a few members of the Exhibition's Executive Committee, made a rapid retreat into the picture galleries. The orchestra struck up, and a buxom Italian lady stepped forward and started to sing a soaring, swooping solo. Boyce did not recognise the piece. He had not the least interest in music.

His hour was growing close. He studied his moustache, on which he had invested an additional measure of time that morning, in the muted reflection of a display case. It formed a perfectly symmetrical white 'W', glowing in the drab light of its surroundings. He straightened his dress-jacket. All was in order.

An equerry, one of Phipps' men, emerged from the vestibule and cleared his throat discreetly. Boyce nodded to Nunn, who stood by his side, his wounded arm in a sling, quite entranced by the singing. He thought it best to keep the boy close. Poor Nunn had a tendency to blurt out all manner of things, without warning – including fragmentary recollections from the Crimea that, if heard by the wrong ears, had the potential to cause his commander significant difficulties. This could be controlled; Boyce had learned that if sufficiently distracted, his aide-de-camp became as quiet and compliant as a well-trained hound. At that moment, the music in the hall was fulfilling this purpose admirably. Boyce peered into Nunn's eyes for a second, searching for even the tiniest flicker of awareness of the events that had brought them to this point. They were quite empty. The Brigadier-General left him gaping at the orchestra and went through.

The gloom in the picture galleries exceeded even that of the great hall. Rain beat against the glass above, and could be seen sluicing across the sloping panes in long loops, the sky beyond only a shade away from black. The glorious assemblage of works of the ancient masters was reduced in these conditions to a pattern of dull greys and browns. It was hard indeed to discern any detail. Even the subjects of most of them were rendered unclear. Boyce located his painting though, in the very centre of the display. He noticed with some alarm that it was cloaked in obscuring shadow. The Queen would barely be able to see it.

Before he had time to protest, however, the Royal party strolled into view. The Queen led, with Albert by her side, dominating the group entirely. Everything in the saloon, in

470

Boyce's eyes, seemed immediately to rearrange itself around her progress. She was short, and the body beneath her skirts was undeniably a little rounded. The face framed by her bonnet and bow was long-nosed, also, and rather amply cheeked; but she has a radiance, the Brigadier-General told himself, a regal radiance that cannot help but leave her loyal subjects utterly enchanted.

The Queen looked relieved that the Royal party was removed from the thousands in the great hall. Then, surveying the paintings with obvious dissatisfaction, she asked for a lamp to be brought so that they might be viewed properly. Mr Thomas Fairbairn, bewhiskered labour-lord and chairman of the Exhibition, informed her humbly that no illumination of any kind was permitted in the building, due to the risk of fire. Ignoble dog, Boyce thought harshly; that is your monarch you address with such casual flippancy! If it were down to me, I would have you dragged from the hall and flogged, flogged before all of your wretched peers!

The Queen's eyes, however, were shining with ironical amusement. 'We have many pictures of our own, Mr Fairbairn,' she said in her clear, authoritative voice. 'We believe that we can prevent these from catching fire. Besides,' she added with a glance up at the skylights, 'it is not as if there is no water to hand, is it?'

The courtiers and members of the Executive Committee, who had gathered in a crescent around her, made a polite patter of sycophantic laughter. Prince Albert smiled, stroking the plump hand the Queen had placed on his arm. Sweeping strains of music drifted in from the main hall beyond.

A lamp was brought. The yellow gas flame actually made the rest of the saloon seem darker, as if it was late in the evening rather than shortly after midday. Pictures were lit brightly as the lamp was carried by them, only to be plunged back into shadow once it had passed. It was handed to Sir George Grey, Secretary of State for the Home Department, who bowed to Victoria before asking where it might please her Majesty to begin her inspection of the paintings.

'Wait,' said the Queen sharply, noticing Boyce standing in the corner. 'Who is that soldier over there?' All good

471

humour had left her in an instant. The tone she used was not admiring, nor in any way amiable, nor even distant and imperious. It was hostile. Every head in the saloon turned towards the Brigadier-General, who had frozen stiff with apprehension. 'Did we not give the clearest instructions that no one beside our own party and certain members of the Executive Committee were to be present in the picture galleries this day? Did we not?'

Colonel Phipps rushed over. 'Please excuse the impertinence, your Majesty, but allow me to introduce an old comrade of mine, Brigadier-General Nathaniel Boyce.' The Prince Consort, to Boyce's immense relief and delight, made a noise that indicated recognition of his name. 'The Brigadier was gravely injured fighting in the Russian War, where he distinguished himself on a number of occasions.'

This was a wise revelation. The Queen's interest was engaged, and her antipathy disappeared entirely. Her eyes flickered over him again, playing, it seemed to Boyce, on the moustache with a gleam of unmistakable regard; and coming to rest, finally, on the immobile wooden hand.

Phipps nodded to him, signalling that he should approach. 'He is also the owner of the painting of *Pontius Pilate Washing His Hands* by Raphael, made so famous by its inclusion in this Exhibition.'

At this the Queen of England, sovereign of all the mighty Empire, looked at Boyce and smiled. 'Brigadier, please excuse our manner, but on occasions like these there are so very many people seeking to impinge on our time. It really cannot be said often enough how grateful we are for your bold service – and sacrifice – in the Crimea. And you have our warmest congratulations on your acquisition,' Victoria continued. 'A Roman Raphael – as we understand yours to be – is a rare prize indeed.' She turned to Prince Albert. 'Our husband prefers the sterner feel of the early Northern schools, but we are still won over absolutely by the eternal beauties of *Il Divino*. Come, you must tell us how you came to possess it.'

Boyce followed the Queen to the picture, inwardly rehearsing his tale of miraculous good fortune whilst rooting around in a Florentine curiosity shop, his chest swelling with pride, his head swimming with golden visions of his glorious future. To converse with the Queen! Greatness was surely in his reach.

The lamp was raised to the *Pilate*. There were a couple of shocked gasps and then a decidedly awkward silence. The rain beat on the glass roof; the enormous choir sung in the great hall. The sixteen-year-old Prince Edward, slouched on one of the saloon's seats, looked over to see what had captured the company's attention so completely. He let out a hard laugh.

Someone had set about the *Pilate* with thick brushes and house-paints, smearing over the delicate ancient hues with a coarse, oleaginous mess. The picture had been utterly ruined, that much was apparent straight away; but worse still was the malicious purpose that lay behind this desecration. Upon the bowl had been written '*the 99th Foot*', and the water within it coloured a lurid red – a red that dripped down from the rubbing hands. Pilate was washing off blood. One of these hands was now black, as if gloved, and was fastened to the forearm with several bulky straps. Across the top of the panel, in letters ten inches high, was printed 'THE FRUIT OF A ROTTEN TREE'. Emerging from Pilate's mouth was a crude speech-bubble containing the words, '*A painting bought with the blood of English soldiers – and cheap at the price!!!*' And there, on the noble Roman's face, white and glaring, was a resplendent rendition of the moustache, its points stretching outward across the canvas like the wings of an albatross.

How long did the silence continue after the Prince's laugh? Boyce was never able to recall. A minute, five, ten? Half an hour? No one in the saloon knew how to react. Those who were not staring at the defaced painting in faintly horrified confusion were looking to the Queen, intending to take their lead from her.

'Brigadier,' said Victoria at last, the ghost of a smile on her pale face, 'we do believe that they have captured your moustache to a tee.'

There was some low laughter at this, both from courtiers

and the Executive Committee. Albert shook his head indulgently at the cruelty of his wife's wit. Thomas Fairbairn had
crossed the room, and was engaged in urgent conference
with the chief steward.

Boyce stood as if nailed to the floor. Blinking rapidly, he
was beset with a powerful, distorting sense of everything
collapsing inwards, the glass above coming loose and falling
down in great plates, partition walls toppling, and iron girders
snapping like brittle bones. The orchestra in the main hall
seemed to be sliding into horrible, tuneless discord. He was
all too aware of who was responsible for this act. That blackguard Twelves had clearly failed in his task. It had been a
grave error on his part, he now saw, to assign such a delicate errand to that cocksure fool. And this was the cost.

The Brigadier-General's eyes darted to the Queen and her
party. Those around her were red-faced, making ineffectual
efforts to conceal their mirth. Victoria herself was regarding
him with curious amusement. This, he knew with dreadful
certainty, was how she would remember him for ever more:
as a dark, controversial joke, as one who had, for whatever
reason, earned himself a determined and rather eccentric
enemy. There would always be an indefinable question
hanging over him; there would always be a touch of the
ridiculous appended to his name.

The sound of the rainfall upon the Art Treasures Exhibition
had changed. Where once had been admiring applause, there
was now only thunderous laughter, the mocking laughter
of thousands, all of it directed at him.

6

The Tomahawk lit a cigarette beneath his borrowed umbrella, relishing the brief warmth of the match against his fingers. As he shook it out, he noticed a dark fleck on his thumb: a crescent of dried paint, still lodged under the nail. Grinning wickedly, he scraped out this tenacious mark with the end of the match.

He knew, of course, that he really should not be there, standing in amongst the sparse, soaking crowd that had washed up on the front steps of the Art Treasures Palace like debris after a shipwreck. He knew that he should have fled the city the previous night – made that late train for Liverpool as he'd been planning. But the desire to be present when the trap was sprung, to see its awful results for himself, had proved impossible to resist. He reckoned that he could easily slip away afterwards.

The scheme was going extremely well so far, he had to say. Kitson had exceeded expectations, rising volubly to meet every piece of carefully honed provocation and even joining him for a little tussle in the middle of the tavern. The action outside with Twelves had been an additional bonus; Cracknell had made sure that the investigator was getting a suitably sound thrashing from Bairstowe and his men before he left for the Art Treasures Palace. And the landlord had been grateful for the opportunity, he could tell. This was a fellow who could be relied upon to cover a chap's back should the crushers come to call.

All in all, the Tomahawk had been provided with a gratifyingly robust alibi. He had already drafted a lengthy letter, in fact, addressed to a hypothetical inspector of the Manchester police. *Regretfully, sir, it concluded diffidently, I cannot recall the exact hours of our sojourn in the Trafford Arms, as neither I nor my renowned friend from the* Evening Star *were quite ourselves. You can be sure, however, that Mr Bairstowe, the proprietor, and our fellow customers will remember our time there, and the lamentable condition in which we left. Indeed, I might venture to assert that we were certainly in no state to undertake the ambitious, infamous act that has so damaged the Brigadier-General.*

There was another rolling rumble of thunder overhead. Cracknell peered out from under his umbrella, taking in the imposing ironwork façade and the elaborate patterns it contained; then his eye wandered to the tall glass doors, which were locked firmly against any intruders. Through them, past a colourless reflection of himself and those around him, he could make out the colossal nave, packed with the beautiful and brilliant, yet still looking decidedly dreary in the tempestuous half-light. He had padded up this very same hall not twelve hours earlier, in rather different conditions, with a pair of paint-pots dangling from each hand, having forced his way into the special railway corridor and crept past the two dozy Peelers on duty by the main entrance. The work itself had been done by the flame of a tiny candle, its light carefully channelled by the heavy fold of his cloak.

Had he felt anything as he daubed the oily paint over the graceful forms, as he destroyed with his mortal hands an eternal work of art, created by one of the greatest geniuses ever to lay brush on canvas? Yes, he most certainly had. He had felt an enormous satisfaction, a mighty sense of justice being done. For what is art after all, he reasoned, but so many objects – objects that men will kill to possess? That painting was a symbol of Boyce, of all his murderous wickedness; and it was with a spirited pleasure that Cracknell had gone about its destruction. And as destructions went it was pretty damn creative. He had laughed softly as the subtle moderations of colour and masterful insights of expression of the long-dead Italian were obliterated by the crude, vengeful strokes of the very much still-living Irishman.

Suddenly, a minor fracas started up inside the Exhibition Hall, the splendidly dressed audience parting in attitudes of agitation, knocking over chairs in their haste to remove themselves from something's path. Then, to Cracknell's delight, Brigadier-General Nathaniel Boyce came into view, pushing aside lady and gentleman alike as he charged for the exit. Moving through the turnstile, he all but yanked the metal arm from its socket; and a moment later the doors exploded open, releasing the Brigadier-General out into the rain.

It had happened. Cracknell knew that victory was his. The blow had landed as squarely, as solidly as he could have hoped for. And now his defeated foe had been brought before him for an unexpected *coup-de-grace*. Boyce staggered to a halt, roughly unfastening the high, gold-encrusted collar of his dress uniform. He was breathing hard, and looked most unwell, very pale but with a startling shot of crimson in his cheeks. Well, so much the better.

Cracknell threw away his cigarette. 'Boyce,' he called out coolly. 'Over here.'

The officer turned. Upon seeing Cracknell, he let out an alarming howl, a primitive, almost bestial roar of rage, and dived towards him. Boyce's hair was awry, his ridiculous moustache in the process of collapse, and his eyes quite, quite mad.

The Tomahawk's intention had been to say 'For truth', or 'For Madeleine', or words to that effect – to let the old bastard know exactly why this thing had been done. Boyce's increasingly rapid progress in his direction made him hesitate, though; and when the Brigadier-General drew his dress sword in a manner suggesting that he fully intended to use it, Cracknell realised that he may have misjudged the situation somewhat.

Boyce and his magnificent uniform already had the attention of the crowd gathered there on the steps. The sight of his sword, flashing in the grey afternoon, elicited a spasm of alarm. Like a flock of startled geese the people retreated, leaving Cracknell exposed before the fuming Brigadier-General. He began to speak – just as Boyce lunged.

The sword was ceremonial, intended for grand parades rather than slaughter, but the Brigadier-General still managed to drive it a good few inches into his foe. Cracknell wavered for a moment, his lips moving wordlessly, and then dropped to his knees. With a grimace, Boyce planted a highly polished boot in the centre of the Tomahawk's collarbone and made to pull the sword out; but the awkward angle, and the sheer force with which the officer wrenched it towards him, caused the slender blade to snap suddenly. The two men flew apart. Cracknell hit the Exhibition steps with a heavy groan, his umbrella leaping from his hand and bouncing down to the turning circle.

The Brigadier-General quickly regained his balance, altered his hold on the sword's filigreed hilt and prepared to stab at his enemy with the broken end. Before he could do this, a large constable intervened, seizing his arm and commanding him to desist. Boyce tried to shake this man off, and the next instant half a dozen constables were on the Crimean hero, wrestling him to the ground.

Raindrops struck against Cracknell's face, filling his eyes, his mouth, running down through his black beard. Someone close by called for a doctor. He managed to lift his head, and received a blurred impression of a hard, straight protrusion with a jagged end, poking up just above his right nipple. Beneath it, under his cloak, a bright red blot was spreading steadily across the grubby white of his shirt.

And past this he could see Boyce, still struggling to get at him, yelling with helpless, choking fury as he was taken away. Although now faint with pain, the Tomahawk could not help but let out a shallow, coughing laugh.

'I – I am well,' he announced hoarsely, to no one in particular. 'Quite well . . .'

At Sea
July 1857

1

And so, the column concluded, *the Brigadier-General is now in custody of the Manchester police, charged with attempted murder – a man disgraced. The precise motive for the Brigadier-General's vicious assault remains unknown. His victim asserts that he was present as an independent citizen, there only to cheer his monarch. The Exhibition authorities have pleaded ignorance; its chairman, Mr Thomas Fairbairn, has said that the Brigadier-General had spoken briefly with the Queen and then excused himself from the building rather suddenly. The picture saloon in which this audience took place was closed to the public the morning after the incident, but has since reopened with the display slightly adjusted. It all seems to be an impenetrable mystery.*

In the wake of this brutal and unprovoked attack, however, we note that questions are being posed in certain quarters about the Brigadier-General's private affairs. These have focused upon his recent accumulation of wealth, and the suggestion that he benefited from inappropriate links with a certain Manchester foundry – one that prospered during the late war. The police seem reluctant to scrutinise this matter, but we understand that a number of informal investigations are already underway.

The victim, Richard Cracknell, the Tomahawk of the Courier, *lies injured in the Manchester Royal Infirmary; yet already he is writing again, and has promised this publication a full account of the attack, as well as his views on the rumours of further wrong-doing, for inclusion in our very next number.*

Kitson put down the paper. So there it was. Somehow,

Cracknell had prevailed. He looked around the state-room of the *H.M.S. Stromboli*. It was decorated in a sparse, functional style; a smattering of travellers sat eating sandwiches from paper parcels and leafing idly through books and magazines. Despite everything that had occurred, he felt the slight rekindling of an all but forgotten regard. A little disquieted by this, he rose to his feet, picking up the European railway almanac he had just purchased from the counter at the stateroom's aft end, and headed for the door to the deck. He left the copy of the *London Courier* lying on the table.

A group of chattering children hung from the rail of the *Stromboli* like washing on a line. They were staring at the coast that emerged steadily from the haze before the ship, pointing out details to one another as it drew nearer. Parents and governesses stood close behind, hands clutching their hats and bonnets to their heads, their shawls held tightly against the brisk sea wind. Squinting in the afternoon sunshine, Kitson could see a long strip of yellow beach, some low cliffs, and the rise of green fields beyond. Directly before the *Stromboli* was their destination, the port of Boulogne, a jumble of pale stone crowned with steeples. The bay was crowded with vessels, from fishing skiffs to large steam cruisers like the one he stood upon. Kitson rested against the rail and put his left hand upon it. The polished brass was cold to the touch. He looked down at his new plain silver ring, tapping it against the rail. It made a pleasingly sharp, reverberating sound.

Pooling their scant resources, Kitson and Jemima had managed to purchase two unostentatious wedding bands upon their arrival in London. They had taken them immediately to a small church in an alley close to Ludgate Circus, where the vicar was known to be sympathetic to those in need of a rapid betrothal, carried out with the minimum of questions asked. The wedding breakfast had taken place at a modest supper-room on the Strand, filled with barristers' clerks. The first hours of marriage had been spent wandering the streets and parks of the Metropolis, savouring the sweet sense of being alone together, many miles from those who might lay a claim on them; the wedding night had passed in a lodging house close to London Bridge station, chosen for its convenience for catching the first morning train to Dover. Neither of them had spoken much throughout this time. It was as if both were a little dazed by the audacity of their actions. They had eloped. They had taken this great step together. They were united by it.

The marine air, after the thick atmosphere of Manchester, seemed to be almost miraculously free from taint. Kitson could already feel the salutary effect upon his injured chest. The pain had yet to disappear, but it was becoming bearable. He put the European almanac under his arm, just as the children at the rail rushed back inside, affording him a clear view of his wife. She was standing as far forward as she could, gazing at the dark, glittering waters beyond the *Stromboli*'s bow; and at the huge open vault of sky above. The steam horn let out a blast, the note resonating through the deck-planks. Their vessel was starting to manoeuvre into the harbour, squat tug-boats paddling up to meet it. Slowly, the steamer rotated, the wind picking up and sweeping hard down the length of the deck. A corner of the almanac's cover bent open, the gust flicking swiftly through the thin pages within.

Jemima's bonnet came loose. With a cry, she turned and reached out, catching hold of it just before it was carried away into the sea. Seeing Kitson, she smiled, her auburn hair unfurling in the breeze; and he started down the deck towards her.

483

Author's Note

Although much of *The Street Philosopher* is based closely on actual events and a number of historical figures make brief appearances, both the main story and the principal characters are completely fictional. The 99th Foot (Paulton Rangers), in particular, is an invention, imagined as a typical line regiment in the Light Division of the British expeditionary army – albeit one with some rather untypical officers. There was a 99th regiment in the British army at this time, but it spent the duration of the Russian war in Australia guarding the penal colonies. Also, although the Art Treasures Exhibition included numerous works attributed to Raphael, a depiction of Pilate washing his hands was not among them. No such painting has ever existed, and Queen Victoria's tour of the Exhibition went off without incident.

Many sources were used in the writing of this book; all distortions and errors are, of course, my own. The Crimean sections owe an important debt to the *Times* reports of William Russell, with whom some of Cracknell's more admirable attitudes originate, and to the many published diaries, letters and personal accounts written by the soldiers and civilians who were involved in the war, notably those of Nathaniel Steevens, Frederick Dallas, Roger Fenton and George Lawson.

Among the modern texts used, special mention must be made of Matthew Lalumia's *Realism and Politics in Victorian*

Art of the Crimean War, which first interested me in the representation of warfare – visual and verbal – in the mid-nineteenth century press. A vital reference work was Alastair Massie's *A Most Desperate Undertaking: The British Army in the Crimea*, a catalogue of the 2004 exhibition at the National Army Museum in Chelsea. Also frequently consulted were volumes by Trevor Royle, Clive Ponting, J.B.R. Nicholson, A.J. Barker, Albert Seaton, Andrew Lambert and Stephen Badsey.

The massive amount of contemporary literature generated by the Art Treasures Exhibition served as the foundation for the Manchester sections. This included the lengthy coverage provided by the *Times*, the *Art Journal* and the *Illustrated London News*; the enormous catalogue; the *Art Treasures Examiner*, the official magazine of the Exhibition published throughout its run; and the plethora of unofficial, slightly domineering guidebooks with titles like *What to See and Where to See it*. Especially informative were *Cornish's Stranger's Guide through Manchester and Salford* and *The Visitor's Guide to Six Days in Manchester* – general guides to the city produced to coincide with the Exhibition which provided a detailed and fascinating counterpoint to the famously grim portrait of mid-nineteenth century Manchester found in Friedrich Engels' *The Condition of the Working Class in England*.

Two modern histories were particularly helpful: *The Public Culture of the Victorian Middle Class: Ritual and Authority in the English Industrial City 1840–1914* by Simon Gunn, which introduced me to the concept of street philosophy, and Martin Hewitt's exhaustive study *The Emergence of Stability in the Industrial City: Manchester 1832–67*.

Thanks are due to my agent, Euan Thorneycroft, without whom it simply wouldn't have happened, and all at AM Heath; my editor, Susan Watt, whose guidance and incisive comments were instrumental in shaping the novel, and the team at HarperCollins; Emma Logan and Lorna Plampin, who waded through the first draft and offered early encouragement; Katie Espiner and Joy Chamberlain, for help and criticism in the initial stages; James Middleton, for those articles on the Crimea; the staff of the British Library and National Art Library; my mother and brother, for their unwavering support; and SLH, the best, always.